T
DEVIL'S
HONOR

Cover design by Deke D. Wagner

Printed in United States of America

ISBN-9781791761561

3rd EDITION

For questions, comments & concerns address:
dekedean@gmail.com

Wagner, Deke D.
The Devil's Honor: a novel / Deke D. Wagner—3nd ed.

1. Germany, England—History—World War Two—Fiction. 2. U.S. Army Air Corps. 3. The O.S.S. 4. Luftwaffe 5. P.O.W. —Fiction.
Title-TDH666353

A Novelwerks Creation

Typeset in Times Roman

For Ethan,
for his interest in my writing
and everything winged and propeller-driven.

ACKNOWLEDGMENTS:

In acknowledging the help he has received in the writing of this novel the author expresses a debt he cannot adequately repay. In gratitude he can but name those people whom he has received encouragement and whose time and effort have been freely and graciously given. In the instance of my mother "Mutti" Almut Wagner-Wilson, Mack and Katrina Blauvelt, Edda Woolard and Mike Clagett. Absent their assistance, good advice and forbearance, this novel might have never been written.

"The greatest way to live with honor in this world is to be what we pretend to be." **— Socrates**

U.S. ARMY AIR CORPS
propaganda poster
(circa 1944)

THE DEVIL'S HONOR

A World War II Novel by
Deke D. Wagner

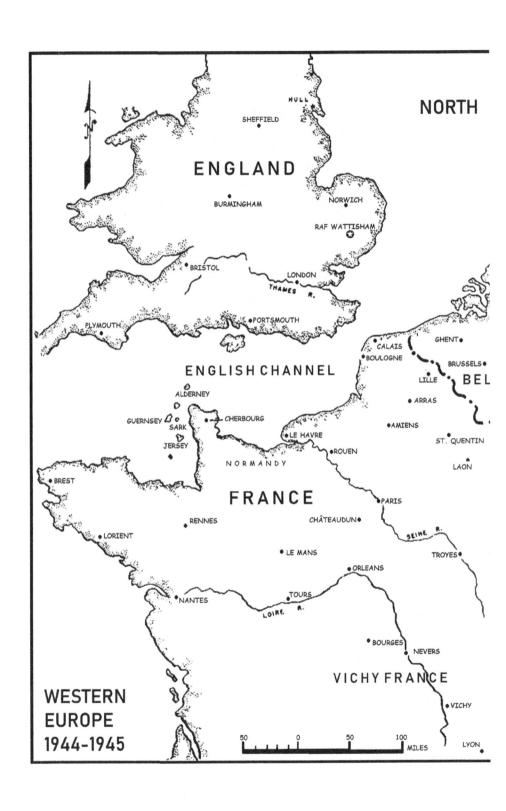

PART ONE

CHAPTER 1

THE CAMP ALARM WAS BLARING! Someone was trying to escape! The suddenly awakened Japanese guards leaped up from their sleeping mats, bleary-eyed and shaken, and put on their boots and pants. Others already on duty bolted into action beginning yet another exhaustive search, turning on extra searchlights, scanning the darkened prison compound with angry, slanted eyes, cocking their rifles and machine guns. They knew who was trying to escape. He'd been trying for the better part of a year now, and tonight seemed like the ideal time to try again. And if the guards caught him this time, they'd kill him for sure. They were infinitely tired of his repeated little games of cat-and-mouse.

"Fucking bastard!" cursed the lean, rugged-looking thirty-one-year-old with thinning blond hair. "That rotten son-of-a-bitch is at it again!" He kicked the ragged blanket from his legs and lurched up from his straw mat, stalking across the dirt floor of the wooden hut to a bamboo barred window. He looked out into the darkness and tried to see what was going on. Another man who'd been lying on the ground next to him got up and stood next to the glaring, blond-haired American officer, smiling, nodding.

"Right clever of him, I'd say, Captain Daley," said the man, a gaunt British Major with a tatty mustache and greasy battle dress fatigues. "And on Independence Day, no less. A jolly good show."

Daley sneered contemptuously. "Humph! That goddamn jerk knew the camp commander would be lenient today, letting the prisoners have their Red Cross parcels and extra rations for chow."

1

"Righto. And the guards got an extra ration of *sake,* too, I'm told." The gaunt Englishman stroked his whiskery chin. "Some of them are probably quite blotto by now, I'd imagine."

Daley scoffed. "And they'll be pissed as hell once they get their little yellow hands on him again. They'll beat the crap out of him for sure. Probably just kill him, chop his fucking head off. These Jap bastards don't fool around. They're really sick of his shit."

"Indeed." The gaunt Englishman nodded glumly. "What's this, his fifth or sixth attempt?"

"Seventh!"

"Ah." The English Major frowned. "Then you're quite right, old man. They'll kill him for sure this time."

"Yeah, for sure!"

Outside in the prison courtyard, Japanese guards scurried around in frantic gaits, running back and forth, shouting, cursing, yelling, ordering each other around. It had been determined now that the prisoner had escaped from the solitary confinement hut, a place where he'd recently spent a lot of time burrowing his way out from under a corroded corrugated metal panel. From there, he apparently crawled to the wall, the main partition of the camp, an eight-foot bamboo palisade, where he previously carved out a little hole just big enough to slip his lanky frame through. He must have worked on it for days on end before getting locked up in the confinement hut, yet one more time, this time for cussing out a camp guard. A bloody nose and a busted lip preceded that trip to solitary. But it was well worth it. It gave him time to work on the hut's corroded panel. An old teaspoon he'd stolen from the Japanese officer's mess a month before gave him the impetus to dig every time he got sent to solitary, usually for seventy-two-hour stretches. He worked on it only at night and when most of the guards were sleeping while the others stood around laxly, standing guard in one of the four twenty-foot watchtowers that framed the prison compound. It took him exactly twenty-nine days and nights, and ten trips to solitary to accomplish it, but accomplish it he did. However, the hole carved in the wall was just a nicely perpetrated ruse, a neat trick to throw off the Japs, get them thinking he'd slipped off into the night through that jagged little hole. He had no intention of leaving on foot.

And right now, as he skulked amidst the shadows, hiding, waiting, watching, he thought about Daley and the British Major. He just couldn't leave them behind, he had to help them escape. Why? He didn't rightly know. Daley had never been friendly to him—downright mean was a better term. The Major was indifferent towards him, an astutely smug British officer who thought more of a man's station than of the man himself. They were career army officers, so they didn't mince words or waste time on enlisted men, especially those who'd tried to bypass time-worn prescripts by lying and cheating their way to a commission. But all of that didn't matter anymore. They were Allied soldiers, and they deserved a chance at freedom just as he did. Besides, three men might have a better chance at escaping than just one. Well, that's what he told himself, anyway. That was another good reason for having them along.

"Jack, old boy," he said to himself with a hoarse laugh. "You got your halo on crooked. Yes-siree bob, you sure enough do!"

He hopped up and scampered across the courtyard, dodging a Jap squad of passing troops, their officer leading them with a drawn sword. Then he adroitly danced past a searchlight's probing beam and dashed over to the officer's cells, intent on freeing Daley and the Major. All around him, he could see and hear the effects of his glorious deed. The camp alarm was blaring and Jap guards were swarming all over the place. And not too far off he could hear the rumblings of truck engines as they were started up, the Japs intent on driving them out into the countryside to search for the escaped prisoner. And that was the very thing he'd hoped they do. Traversing the Japanese mainland on foot was not his idea of a well-planned escape. Driving a truck would be much better. You see, he had planned his escape quite well, and he knew what the Japs would do when they reckoned he'd slunk into the night through that little hole in the wall. Just like every escape attempt before, he had fled on foot only to be captured soon thereafter. Tonight was different. He had thrown them a big fat curve ball and they would be hard-pressed to figure it out right away. Now, he just had to get Daley and the Major free, then mosey over to the motor pool and get in one of those trucks and drive out of there. And he knew just where he was going to go afterward. He had worked out every detail.

After slowly working his way back to the officer's cell block by stealthy crawling on hands and knees, he found the cell Daley and the Major were being held in. He grinned impishly as he inserted the key into the lock and unlocked the door. He was met with disbelieving eyes and hanging jaws when he opened the door. They were stunned, to say the least. Shocked was a better way of putting it.

"Good heavens!" the Major gasped his faced etched in disbelief.

"What the hell?" Daley uttered staring at the ragged-looking man. "Thought you'd be long gone by now, Sergeant."

"Naw-sir, not by a long shot, Cap'n." The man, who really was a sergeant said, then quipped: "Stop calling me that, alright? I'm a Captain, just like you. Remember?"

"The hell you are!" Daley retorted glaring hotly. "You're a fucking Sergeant. Always have been and always will be."

"Gentlemen, gentlemen," said the Major urgently. "We don't have time for theatrics. We must vacate the premises immediately. The bloody Japos are lurking about!"

"Right," Jack agreed. "Let's get the heck outta here before they get wise, huh? Let's get over to the motor pool and steal us a truck."

"Steal a truck?"

"That's what I said."

"You're fucking crazy! We'll never make it."

"Sure we will. C'mon, let's hot-foot it."

Daley, the Major, and the man supposedly a Sergeant darted from the prison cell, then carefully made their way to the motor pool after locking it, hopefully giving the cell the illusion of still being occupied. The three men moved with heedful purpose as they sneaked by one Jap sentry after another, then watched as a Type-94 truck rumbled through the front gates loaded to the rails with armed guards. The bait had been taken! The Japs were convinced that Jack had escaped through that little hole. Now they were sure to scour the countryside in search of him. Little did they know that he and two other fellow inmates were lurking in the shadows nearby, slowly moving toward to the motor pool where another truck stood parked and idling. Soon, they'd be driving out of the prison themselves. And Jack led the way, determined as ever to escape this hellish place.

"Say, Sergeant," Daley asked as he cowered in the shadows amidst a searchlight's probing beam. "How the fuck did you get a key to our cell, huh?"

"Killed me a Jap, that's how." Jack glared at Daley. "I wish you'd stop calling me by that already. I'm a—"

"Hell no!" Daley snarled. "Not in this lifetime, you phony son-of-a-bitch. I know who you are and I'll never call you by that rank."

Jack smiled devilishly. "Son-of-a-bitch, aye? Well, this son-of-a-bitch just saved yer sorry ass. You better be appreciative."

"Never!"

"Oh, come off it you two," the English Major interceded. "You lads need to set aside your differences for now and concentrate on getting out of this bloody place."

"Shit!" Daley cursed.

"Yup, yer right, Major," Jack concurred. "We better focus on gettin' the heck outta of here. We can save the bickering fer later."

Daley huffed and shook his head, saying nothing.

"That's the spirit, lad." The Major then clapped Daley on his back. "Look here, Captain. We've got to pull together and get through this. Our finest hour is at hand; we need to get to one of those trucks and motor out of here whilst the blody Japos are still figuring things out."

"Whatever," Daley grumbled. "Let's move it. We don't have a lot of time. The Nips will be checking the other cells soon, and when they find out we're gone too, all hell is gonna break loose."

"You got that right, Cap'n," Jack said, rising from his crouch. "We gotta make our getaway, and real quick-like now."

With that said, Jack lurched forward towards the motor pool, a wry smile on his lips. He bounded ahead, running in a half-crouch skulking to one hiding place to another, until he was within a few yards from the motor pool, eyeing the idling three-and-half-ton truck, its Japanese driver milling about aimlessly. Jack figured he was waiting for the next squad of guards, waiting for his comrades to load up—so there was no time to waste. He turned to Daley and the Major once they caught up with him, both men crouching be-hind him, panting, sweating because the humid temperatures.

"Looky here, fellers," said Jack, "I'm gonna hop up and take out that Nip driver so we can commandeer the truck, okay?" He produced a glistening straight-razor from the pocket of his ragged khaki trousers, grinning devilishly.

"Jeez!" Daley remarked, a bit surprised. "Where in the hell did you get that thing, huh?"

"Never mind," Jack replied, snorting. "It'll do the trick, don't you worry. I'll sneak up and slit that Nip's throat, then we can hop into that truck and ride the hell out of here."

"And where do we go from here, Sergeant?" the Major wanted to know. "Do you have a destination in mind?"

"Sure, Major, I got a place in mind."

"Want to let us in on it?" Daley insisted.

"Nope. You'll find out soon enough."

That stated, Jack got up from his crouch and moved toward the Jap driver, brandishing the razor-knife like a fiendish murderer, hiding behind a stack of petrol drums, eyeing his quarry as if he were some sort of wild animal to be slaughtered. In Jack's mind, he *was* an animal, a sub-human creature that needed to be gutted for very good reasons—one reason being revenge. Jack hated the guards and one more dead one wouldn't hurt his chances for getting into Heaven because he knew he was bound for Hell and eternal damnation. There was no doubt about it in his warped mind; the Devil and all his angels were waiting for him, he knew it all too well. But when that day finally came that was the real question. So he averred to see it happen in the distant future, not now. Too much had to be done still and a few more people had to die. A sad state of affairs but that's how he felt about it.

He edged closer to the driver, squinting, holding his breath, moving lightly on his feet, his worn-out canvas shoes not betraying his cat-like movements. It was over in a second. He pounced on the driver, cutting his throat with one swift stroke, spilling the man's blood in a very precise way. The Jap collapsed to the ground gasping miserably, his windpipe cut, his struggles quickly silenced by the swiftness of death's bony hand. Jack laid the dead man out on the ground, then dragged him behind a stack of crates, leaving a trail of blood on the ground, a telltale sign of his grisly deed. It didn't matter, by the time the body was discovered, they'd be long gone and far beyond the camp's walls.

Daley watched all of this with a wary eye. He knew Jack was capable of such things. He'd seen him perform some bloody deeds before, not with a razor-knife, mind you, but with a high-performance fighter plane. That fellow had been the scourge of the Pacific for a little while gunning down one Japanese plane after another. To see him take down a Jap up close and personal, gutting him like a fish, was a bit unnerving, he had to admit.

"Nice work, Sergeant," he said grimacing inside, rising from his crouch. "Now let's mount up and get the hell out of here."

"Right-o," the Major agreed, snapping up the dead Jap's Model 99 rifle and cycling it for action. "Now that we've pinched this little pop gun, we can at least defend ourselves, aye?"

Jack nodded. "Yup. We'll need it alright, Major." He folded the razor-knife and stashed it in his pants pocket. He reached down and snatched the Jap's hat off and put it on. "I'll drive. If we play this right, we can cruise out of here with all the commotion going on."

"I'll ride shotgun," Daley insisted, moving to the passenger side of the truck's cab, jerking the door open. "You ride in back, Major. You'll have a good view of things back there with that rifle, just in case we're followed. Okay with that?"

"Sure, mate. Whatever you say," the Major replied evenly although he wasn't so sure about that; he was the senior officer, and he thought he ought to ride up front. Howbeit, he mounted the truck's tailgate, hefting himself into the canvas-covered truck bed, then took up a sitting position atop the floorboards, aiming the rifle out the back end of the truck. If someone happened to follow them they'd get a nasty surprise.

Jack revved the truck's engine a moment, then released the parking brake. "Here we go, amigos. Get ready for a wild ride."

"C'mon, let's get rolling already!" Daley rumbled.

The truck lurched forward as Jack gassed the accelerator, steering the three-and-a-half-ton truck like it was an over-sized sports car, rolling out of the empty motor pool towards the front gate. "Get down, Cap'n. Hide! The Japs will see those golden locks of yours a mile away."

Daley's mouth jerked open ready to spout another bitter obscenity, but he held it back. Jack was right, he hated to admit. His blond hair would surely draw some attention. He slunk down amid the floorboards and waited, watching Jack's every move. With that Japanese garrison hat on and with his naturally swarthy features and black hair, he certainly could pass for a Jap soldier. Well, at least at a distance and in the dark, that is.

7

Jack eased the truck onto the trackway and drove to the front gate. No one took special notice of it as it rumbled by, most assuming it was just another patrol being sent out to search for the escaped prisoner. In truth, most of the Japanese guards were too worried about what the camp commandant might do if the prisoner wasn't captured. His wrath was legendary; they knew a severe beating or even death could follow. And to die as a mere prison guard? That was not an honorable death. Many would prefer to commit *hara-kiri* instead of dying at the hands of an executioner. They had a fearful incentive that night: catch the wretched American prisoner or face death and disgrace.

Jack approached the gate. He pulled the Jap garrison cap tighter over his brow trying to conceal his face a little more. He gripped the steering wheel with tense hands and stared straight ahead. The gate guards hardly noticed the lanky American from Texas, thinking he was just another comrade, waving him onward with stiff hands, muttering in Japanese. Jack gassed the truck and drove on, driving out of the prison camp, heading for his proposed destination.

"Sayōnara!" Jack shouted in Japanese, waving. *"See you in Hell, my little slanted-eyed buddies."*

One of the gate guards waved back, nodding. All he heard was *"Sayōnara"* under the din of the noisy diesel engine. He didn't even get a good look at Jack's face. He didn't care. All he could think about was his sweet little geisha girl back in Yokohama and how she would ravage his privates all night long. He was due to get off duty in just an hour and he wanted to get as far from Camp Yomi as he possibly could. He knew the camp commandant would be downright furious if the American wasn't caught, meting out the harshest of punishments. But little did the guard know, three prisoners had escaped, not one.

"Where the hell are we going?" Daley asked, sitting upright in the passenger seat. "Got some special place in mind, Sergeant?"

Jack chuffed. "Dang it!" he cursed. "I told you I'm a Captain."

"Oh, no you're not—*Sergeant* Castillo," Daley reaffirmed snidely. "You're a no-good, lying, two-bit noncom from Texas, my two-faced friend. A first-class loser and a low-down dirty dog."

Jack sneered. "Alright, Cap'n. Have it your way. But when we get to where we're going, yer on yer own, see?"

"Yeah?"

"Yeah."

"And where *are* we going?"

"Yokohama Airbase."

"Yokohama Airbase?"

"Yup. They got some real fine airplanes there. Thought I'd fly one out and head south—back to civilization."

Daley laughed. "You are fucking crazy, pal. And just where do you think you'll fly to, hmm?"

"Saipan, to be exact."

"Saipan? That's at least... fifteen hundred miles from here."

"Fourteen hundred and forty-nine, to be exact."

"It might as well be two thousand, you jackass! You'll never make it without being shot down by Jap fighter patrols, or just plain run out of fuel over the sea."

"I gotta try. It's an officer's duty to escape."

"An officer? Huh! You ain't no officer, buddy. And besides, the only Jap planes that could make it are their bombers, and they require two pilots to fly them."

"And that's where you come in, right?"

"That's right!"

"Well, I hope there's some Betty bombers at that airbase."

"You're really out of your mind, you know that? That place will be thick with Japs. We won't get anywhere near any one of those planes before some Nip sharpshooter plugs us."

"Naw. You're wrong. That place will be deserted at this hour, just like an old west ghost town. The Nips don't fly too much at night, Cap'n. Especially their Zero squadrons."

"Yokohama Airbase is a fighter base?"

"Yee-up." Jack jerked a succinct nod. "Home of the 302nd A.G. They're equipped with the latest Zero fighter."

"And how the hell do you know that?"

"Work detail, Cap'n." Jack winked. "When the guards drove us out there to work on the runway not so long ago, I took notice, asked some questions, made some friends."

"You—made friends?" Daley scoffed. "You don't have any friends, Sergeant. Not in this country that's for damn sure."

"Found out all I needed to know, you see. The 302nd A.G. protects Tokyo from our B-29 bombers... not so good, I think. But they fly the A6M5, the fastest most heavily armed Zero to date. It can fly nearly two thousand miles on just one drop tank. More than enough fuel to reach the Mariana Islands. That's where our fleet is right now, you know."

"You'll never make it. Because you don't know the first god-damn thing about flying a Zero. You've got more guts than brains, Sergeant. I'll give you that much."

Jack bristled. "You call me Sergeant one more time, Cap'n, I promise, I'll make you regret it."

Daley chuckled. "Oh, yeah? Well, I look forward to it—"

"Easy, mates!" the voice of the British Major sounded from behind them. "What's going on, aye? Where are we headed?" He had crawled up to the truck cab's back window and tapped on it, getting their attention.

"Yokohama Airbase," Daley quipped.

"Bloody hell! Are you serious?" The Major was aghast.

"That's what the man said," Jack chimed in. "Steal us a Jap plane and fly the hell outta this dang country."

"That's insane. That place will be crawling with Japo sentries."

"Not at this hour, Major. Half the base will be asleep."

"And how do you propose getting past the sentries at the front gate, hmm, Sergeant?" Daley asked, arms folded over his chest, a mean look in his eyes. "That base has topnotch security, I'm sure."

"It does," Jack replied, glaring back at Daley. If he didn't have to keep his hands on the steering wheel and keep driving, he would've throttled that Captain, or better yet, cut his damn throat. He didn't like being called Sergeant. As far as he was concerned, he had earned the rank of Captain by shooting down 27 Jap planes and setting a record. But as fate would have it, he got shot down himself. He'd gotten too cocky in the end and it had cost him everything.

Jack evinced a sly grin and tugged on the brim of his hat.

"With this outfit and some fancy Jap gibberish, I'll finagle my way right past those Jap gate guards, wait and see, Cap'n."

Daley eyed Jack suspiciously, scowling, then noticed the regulation Japanese army shirt he was wearing, complete with ribbons, collar tabs and unit badges. He had on a complete Japanese army uniform sans the brown boots and belt an officer typically wore. He still had his ragged old canvas deck shoes on, though, a pair he'd acquired a year ago from Navy submariner who'd died of malaria.

"Where in the hell did you get that fucking getup?" Captain Daley wanted to know. He stared incredulously, wondering why he hadn't noticed it before.

"I told ya—killed me a Jap."

"You killed an... officer?"

"Yup. That son-of-a-bitch we called Hatchet Face."

"Hatchet Face" as Daley recalled, was so named because his face had the uncanny attributes of a hatchet—sharp and piercing. He was a mean, coldhearted S.O.B. and the prison camp's disciplinary officer. He routinely beat Jack and a few other prisoners with a stick resembling a Louisville slugger. Since many of the prisoners couldn't properly pronounce their Japanese tormentor's name (many times they didn't even know their real name) they gave them a nickname instead.

"Jesus Christ, man," Daley cursed softly. "If you get caught, they'll fucking murder you. Oh, you can count on that, brother. Killing a Jap officer?... You're as good as dead now."

"Probably so. That's why I'm flyin' outta here. I ain't got nothin' to lose but my life at this point. And that, according to you and the Japs, ain't worth a hill of beans."

"You got that right—"

"Knock it off, you two!" the Major interjected irritably, getting a bit exasperated by the two Americans' constant bickering. "We've got to pull together if we're going to survive this. The Sergeant has obviously worked this all out way ahead of us, Captain. Let's see it through, aye? Maybe we can get off this bloody island after all. What do you say?"

"Right, sure, whatever," Daley replied, scowling.

"Good show, Captain. Let's see how far we can go, what?"

"Yeah, lighten up, Daley. We just might pull this off."

Onward Jack drove, following the winding curves of the roadway, constantly checking his mirrors for pursuing vehicles. But he saw none, no one had followed him. The Japs weren't wise to his little ruse yet. That was good because if they suspected he was driving a truck and wearing a Japanese uniform, playing the role of a Nippon officer, he'd never make it past the front gate of Yokohama Air

Base. The airbase which was actually a naval air facility, wasn't too far from Camp Yomi. That's why work details were routinely sent over, usually to repair the runway after an American bombing attack. Jack spent many a day there filling in umpteen bomb craters, working a spade, pushing a wheelbarrow, and watching the 302nd Air Group perform their daily routine which were mainly training flights. Daley and the Major never spent a single day at the airbase, being exempted of manual labor because the group commander of the 302nd was a gentile naval officer, and he would not allow officers of any army or air force to do any sort of backbreaking work. Jack, on the other hand, was not exempted. However, when one of the Japanese fighter pilots, a young ensign and an ardent follower of the air war and current events discovered that Jack was indeed the infamous John J. Knight of the 5th Air Force, he immediately befriended him, and eventually, had Jack relieved of his onerous work details. The young ensign even introduced him to the other pilots, which Jack soon found out, were a squadron of upper-class naval officers from exceedingly good families.

The fighter pilots of the 302nd, Jack learned through some artful questioning, had all been strongly coerced by the military government of Japan to serve in a front line combat unit. Drafted was more like the truth. Only the group commander, a thirty-one-year-old man named Lt. Commander Wataru actually had any real combat experience, serving previously with the Tainan AG—Jack's old nemesis. He had been shot down and wounded by an expertly flown Marine Corsair and was duly sent home after a lengthy convalescence. He later took command of the 302nd. Wataru was also impressed with Jack's exploits and he took a liking to the erstwhile American ace, showing him around the facility, inviting him to eat in the squadron mess, explaining Japanese combat operations. He even allowed Jack the privilege of sitting in the cockpit of a Zero, and gave him a crash-course on its operating procedures!

After a nearly thirty minute drive, the three escaped prisoners arrived at Yokohama Air Base. And just like Jack predicted, the place was virtually deserted save the two sentries at the front gate. He rolled down the window and rattled off something in Japanese as one of the sentries approached the truck—impressing the hell out of Daley with his quick and authentic sounding phrasing, almost sounding like a real Japanese officer—then flashed an I.D. card of some kind. The guard nodded, bowed, then directed his comrade to open the gate and let the truck pass through. Daley, of course, was crouched down on the floorboard again, hiding, fearing his blond hair would give away the ruse. Once the truck drove through, he sat upright again.

"So what did you say to those two monkeys, huh?" Daley asked. "That was some fancy sounding lingo."

"I told them I had a special delivery for Commander Wataru."

Daley made a face. "Who the fuck is Commander Wataru?"

"A friend of mine."

"A friend of yours?"

"That's right. He's the group commander of the 302nd."

"What? How in the hell do you know that?"

"Spent a good bit of time around this place, Cap'n. Learned me a few things here and there. Since you were an officer, you didn't have to go on work details. I did. I made the most of it, you see?"

Daley didn't see, but he suddenly realized Jack had planned his escape thoroughly. While he'd sat around Camp Yomi languishing in his cell bemoaning his fate, enduring beatings, starving half to death, slowly deteriorating, this Texas upstart had been planning a big escape. The thought of escaping had never really occurred to Daley; he was convinced it was near to impossible to escape Camp Yomi, and even more impossible, the Home Islands of Japan. It was a hell of a long way to the nearest American base, which he had no idea where one might be; the Japs never told the prisoners anything about the war or how things were progressing. Daley didn't know that the tide had turned and Japan was losing badly. Only the frequent bombing raids by B-29 bombers hinted at such things. He suspected, though, the Japanese weren't doing well by the sudden reduction of food rations and the increasingly savage nature of the guards. They were getting more and more sadistic.

Jack drove the truck down the darkened roadway leading to the main hangers. Along the hangar apron and taxiway he saw a row of parked airplanes, Mitsubishi A6M5 Zeros, to be exact. There was also two of twin-engine Betty bombers parked nearby. He also saw the diminutive silhouettes of two Jap sentries patrolling the grounds of the operations hanger. Other than that, no one else was around.

He parked the truck next to the maintenance hanger and got out. Daley got out, too. The English Major hefted himself out of the truck bed, moaning grievously, having endured the whole trip in the back of that shuddering and shimming Japanese utility truck.

"Bloody hell, man," he grumbled wearily. "That was too much, I say. Next time, I'm riding up front, Captain—"

"Hesh up!" Jack insisted in a loud whisper. "Or them Nip guards will hear that Limey accent of yours."

"Too late," Daley said. "They're coming over here."

"Dang it!"

Indeed, they were. The Jap sentries had seen the truck parking, then heard the faint sounds of conversation, a conversation they didn't readily recognize. They strode over, their rifles slung over their shoulders. Jack snatched the rifle from the Major's hand and cycled the rifle's bolt.

"Alright now," he said. "Time to do some fancy acting, you two. Get your hands behind your backs and pretend like they're cuffed. I'm a Jap officer and you're my prisoners."

"Like hell I am!" Daley objected.

"Oh, come off it, Captain," the Major interjected. "Play along, for God's sake. Or we've had it."

Jack nodded, gesturing with the rifle. "C'mon, Daley. Snap to it, fella. It's Time to do some real fine academy award acting. Clark Gable's got nothing on you, bub."

Daley growled. He put his hands behind his back and kept them concealed from the approaching sentries. The Major did the same. Jack moved behind the two men and held the rifle waist high, pretending to keep them at bay by barking a couple of Jap expletives. His Japanese was remarkable, Daley had to admit. He had learned quite a bit from his Nippon captors. He even had the proper inflection down pat.

The sentries strode over, muttering casually, smoking cigarettes.

"Nani ga oki teru?" one of them asked, wanting to know what was going on, gazing at the three shadowy figures; the utility light mounted above the side door of the hangar only cast them in a dim pool of light.

"Nanimonai!" Jack replied evenly, saying *'nothing'* then jabbed the rifle into Daley's back, nudging him forward. *"I've got two pris-*

oners here for Commander Wataru. They're Allied aviators. He wants to interrogate them. So mind your own business, eh?"

As Jack stepped forward into the light, one of the sentries got a good look at his uniform. He instantly recognized the collar tabs of an Army 1st Lieutenant. He didn't recognize Jack's face, though, although he had seen him around the base a few times with Commander Wataru and some other pilots of the 302nd. The fact that an escaped American prisoner in a Japanese Army uniform was standing right in front of him did not dawn on his simple mind. He stiffened, him being just a lowly seaman. He bowed and apologized.

"Sorry, sir. Wasn't expecting anyone out here tonight."

The other sentry, a Seaman 1st Class, and just a bit smarter, wasn't so easily put off. He inquired: *"Why is an Army Lieutenant escorting American prisoners to a naval air facility? And at this hour? I don't think Commander Wataru is even awake right now. Something very fishy is going on here!"* He was staring right at Jack's canvas shoes.

Jack grimaced, he had not planned for this. Captain Daley and the Major stood by silently, hands behind their backs, wondering what was being said. The Major understood some of it but Daley didn't have the faintest idea what was being said. He had never bothered to learn any Japanese while at Camp Yomi because he truly despised the Japanese. He only knew a few curse words that was about it. And now he was beginning to chafe a bit at Jack's constant jabs and his clever Nippon repartee. He decided to take matters into his own hands.

"Fuck you, you Jap bastards!" he raged, lunging forward, grappling the Seaman 1st Class, tackling him, knocking him down.

The other guard whirled backward and unslung his rifle and tried to fire it. Jack dropped him where he stood with a point-blank shot. The rifle cracked, echoing loudly. The guard fell down dead.

"Now you've gone and done it, lad," the Major quipped worriedly. "The whole blinking base will be awake now!"

Meantime, Daley pummeled the Jap sentry, pounding him with his fists, sitting on top of him. The guard fought back and knocked Daley off, only to be shot dead where he lay. Jack's expert shooting had killed yet another Japanese sentry. Jack shook his head angrily.

"That was stupid, Daley," he snapped. "Real stupid!"

"Kiss my ass," Daley returned. "Somebody had to do something. Your act was falling apart pretty damn quick."

"I had everything under control, you jackass. I could've talked my way out of that—"

"Like hell you could!" Daley stripped the rifle from the dead Jap's hands and tossed it to the Major. "Here, you're going to need this." Then he picked up the other rifle and cycled a round into the chamber. "Better get ready for a fight, fellas. The Japs are on high alert now."

"Bullocks!" the Major imprecated bitterly.

And so they were. The sentries at the front gate had heard the shots and were racing up the tarmac in a Kurogane scout car. Elsewhere, lights were flicking on at the officer's barracks and commander's hut. Then the emergency siren began to wail shrilly. The whole air base was suddenly on alert. Soon, Japanese airmen and noncoms alike would be stalking around the base wondering what the commotion was all about.

Jack sighed irritably. "Aw, this ain't cuttin' it, man," he said to Daley. "You've gone and messed everything up."

Daley scoffed carelessly.

"What do we do now?" the Major asked with little confidence, cycling the rifle. "If we fight, we'll surely be massacred."

"Then we'll die fighting," Daley answered boldly.

Jack shook his head. "Horsefeathers! You two are on your own now. I'm hightailing it outta here. Like—right now."

With that said, Jack dashed off into the darkness, running toward the line of parked Zeroes. He was still intent on flying one out of there, and he knew he didn't have a moment to spare. He ran for the nearest Zero, the one he remembered was Commander Waratu's. He saw the drop tank slung underneath the center-line of the fuselage and knew it was ready for a morning flight. You see, Commander Waratu had told Jack he was going to fly a cross-country sortie to Osaka (another naval air station) the day after the 4th. So Jack knew the Zero had plenty of fuel.

Jack reached the Jap fighter in five seconds flat. He ditched the rifle and yanked the wheel chocks away, then swung himself up onto the wing and jerked the canopy open. He slid into the cockpit seat and put knowing hands upon the control column, then toggled the starter. The Zero belched to life. The tachometer pulsed with power, rising to 2800 rpm's as Jack revved the engine. The 1,130-horsepower radial throbbed powerfully. Jack permitted himself a little smile, thinking, laughing at the absurdity of the moment. Two years ago he had been fighting Zeroes, now he was going to fly one. Never in his young life did he think he'd ever get such a chance. It was a strange feeling, but he liked it. He reached up to close the canopy, the emergency siren just a faint sound in his mind—

"Oh, no you don't, pal!" he heard the gruff voice of Captain Daley rumbling in his ear. "You're not going anywhere—*Sergeant!*"

Daley was standing on the wing, the rifle pointed straight at Jack's head, a sneering grin on his lips. Jack just sat there a moment, grinning himself. Then he calmly reached down in the cockpit and whipped out a Nambu semi-automatic pistol... and blasted off a round into Daley's chest. As the bullet struck home, hitting Daley squarely above the heart, he gasped and fired too. The bullet grazed Jack's shoulder, then ricocheted into the control panel. Daley fell off the wing—shot dead.

"Sergeant, huh? I promised I'd make you regret that."

Jack revved the engine to full-power and taxied out for the runway, all the while, Japanese airmen and mechanics alike ran pell-mell for the scarpering Zero fighter, fully awake now, fully aware that someone was trying to steal it. The lanky Texan groaned painfully, feeling the effects of the gunshot. But he was smiling, thinking about Wataru, the Jap group commander. He'd always carried a sidearm in the cockpit in case he was ever shot down in flames. Wataru was no *kamikaze* or *Bushido* warrior nor did he wish to die in a burning plane. The Nambu pistol was there for a very special reason—to take his own life in the event of a fire. Why not just bailout or use a parachute? Jack had asked him that day. Live to fight another day? Wataru smiled and simply told him:

"That is not the honorable Japanese way, my friend."

Jack lowered the flaps and turned onto the runway. Off to his left, he saw a Jap scout car coming towards him, little flashes of light flaring hotly. Those little flashes were gunshots. But the bullets came nowhere near the Zero, the hours of darkness effecting their aim. Jack held the brakes and revved the engine to full power. When the shuddering and shaking inside the cockpit increased until every nut and bolt seemed to jerk loose, Jack released the brake and the Zero lurched forward, increasing speed with every second. The dim white lines of the runway merged together into one continuous blurred line until they dropped away beneath him. The shuddering ceased, and he was airborne.

Jack had to search a moment for the landing gear lever, vaguely remembering where it was. He found it and eased the lever back and heard a heavy clank beneath the plane as both wheels came up and locked into position. He climbed 500 feet, circled around, then headed south. He had done it; he had escaped! A year of careful planning had finally paid off. He was free and flying high again. Now he could plan his revenge on those who had forsaken him, seek out those who had tried to derail his career. Killing Captain Daley was a good start. But first, he had to make it back to American territory. And before that, he had to get away from Japan. Not an easy task. But he was up for it. He nodded, grinning blissfully. "Here I come, Rose."

Down below, the British Major stood and watched as the faded-green Zero soared away, climbing steadily across the sky, his arms held high as he was swiftly surrounded by angry Japanese sentries, their rifles aimed at him. And the Major was grinning. "Good show, Captain John J. Knight," he rejoiced. "A jolly good show, indeed."

CHAPTER 2

COLONEL DAVID M. MCKAVITT guided his P-51 Mustang on a parallel course with the B-24 Liberator formation, leading the 479th Fighter Group over the territory known as the Third Reich. The 479th was escorting bombers of the 91st Bombardment Group on yet another long-range bombing mission into Germany. McKavitt had taken full command of the Group a week before D-Day, after a long hiatus from combat flying. After winning the Medal of Honor for downing 28 Japanese planes in the Pacific Theater, he went on a lengthy war bond tour across the United States visiting nearly every major city in America. It was also a publicity tour, hailing him as a national hero and the all-conquering American ace. And all of that got very old, very fast. He desperately wanted to get back into action again.

But the Air Corps General Staff wouldn't allow it, saying they couldn't risk losing such a highly decorated officer to air combat, or worse, to German flak-fire. So, he resigned himself to the enviable task of being a national hero for a time, making personal appearances, making speeches, having his picture taken, living the life of a celebrity. And when rumors of an Allied invasion of France became a reality, McKavitt begged the General Staff to transfer him to a front line squadron. His request was curtly denied. Only after petitioning General George C. Marshall, an old friend of his father's, was he transferred to the 479th FG. The 479th had been activated in October 1943 at Grand Central Air Terminal, near Long Beach, California. Equipped with the P-38 Lightning, his old mount, he helped train the group for combat and also served as a west coast air defense organizer for the IV Fighter Command of the 4th Air Force.

Stationed at Santa Maria Army Air Field in California, McKavitt spent the better part of his days flying training missions and trying to convince the Army Air Corps to send the 479th overseas to Europe. He eventually persuaded them even though the defense of the west coast initially took priority. Nonetheless, it was decided to deploy the 479th FG to England for heavy bomber escort duty. The Group was shortly reassigned to RAF Wattisham, England in May 1944, and assigned to the 65th Fighter Wing, VIII Fighter Command of the 8th Air Force.

The 479th FG consisted of three squadrons, the 434th, the 435th, and the 436th. The aircraft of the group had no cowl markings, unlike other 8th Air Force fighter groups. The P-38's were marked only with colored tail rudders. The initial inventory of the P-38 Lightnings, many of which were hand-me-downs from other groups, were painted in olive-drab camouflage, sporting geometric symbols on the tailfins to identify the squadrons; white for camouflaged aircraft, and black for unpainted (natural metal finish).

The 479th FG escorted heavy bombers during operations against targets in France, Holland, and Germany, and often strafed targets of opportunity, flew fighter-bomber, counter-air, and area-patrol missions. But the 479th was primarily tasked with escort duty, shepherding the heavy B-17 and B-24 bombers across the English Channel deep into enemy territory; they also flew the occasional fighter sweep. All this until the long-awaited Normandy invasion of June 6th, 1944. During the invasion, the 479th patrolled the beachhead. They strafed and dive-bombed German troops, bridges, locomotives, railway cars, barges, vehicles, airfields, gun emplacements, flak towers, ammunition dumps, power stations, and radar sites, all whilst on escort or fighter-bomber missions. As the Allied armies drove across France during the summer and fall of 1944, the 479th flew far-ranging area patrols to support the breakthrough at St. Lô and the airborne invasion of Holland.

Later, the 479th received a Distinguished Unit Citation for the destruction of numerous aircraft on the ground in France during August and September, and for a huge dogfight over Münster. Then it converted to the P-51 Mustang between September 10th and October 1st. Now the conversion was complete. Yet McKavitt sighed bitterly, he had not scored one kill during that entire time—not one!

"Five minutes to initial point," McKavitt heard the B-24's group commander sounding in his headphones. *"On target and on time."*

McKavitt glanced at his cockpit clock and verified the time with his wristwatch. Then he glanced at the fuel gauge and noted the amount; just enough to get back to England, and maybe then some. He looked around, his alert brown eyes scanning the skies for intercepting Luftwaffe fighters. He saw none. But a sudden explosion off his starboard wingtip reminded him that German flak was on the job, the inky black puff of smoke immediately followed by another and then another. The flak bursts themselves weren't so unnerving but the sheer volume was another thing. The flak got so thick that McKavitt felt like he could get out and walk on it.

"Steady as she goes, gentlemen," McKavitt said over the R/T, trying to instill some confidence in his pilots. *"Loosen formation— spread out. Watch out for the Big Friends. Call out those bogeys when you see them, over."*

"Roger that, Uncle Leader," came the reply from the 435th's squadron leader Major Wilcox. *"Read you loud and clear."*

"Affirmative, Uncle Leader," Captain Haynes responded, C.O. of the 436th Squadron. *"Keeping a lookout for Nazi aircraft."*

Forty-eight metallic-silver Mustangs spread out evenly, expanding their flight formations, undulating on the air currents of 25,000 feet. The B-24's shuffled into the standard bomb-run formation. The pilot of the lead plane turned on the automatic pilot which controlled the altitude and direction of the bomber. The bombardier opened the bomb bay doors, ready to release the big bomber's 12,000 pound-plus bomb load. After opening the bomb bay doors, he made some minor level corrections by turning two knobs on his Norden bombsight, one controlling lateral movement, the other regulating altitude. The bomb-sight was connected with the autopilot; hence, during the bomb run, the bombardier flew the plane. The bombs were released automatically at a preset interval. This was a cue for the other B-24 bombardiers to release their bombs.

"Bombs away!" said the bombardier, and the bombs fell away.

Eighty-nine other bombers followed suit, and soon, the hapless German city below was alight with myriad 500-pound bomb blasts.

The pilots resumed control. The B-24 bomber formation flew to the prearranged rally point, then turned for home. The flak suddenly ceased and the airmen of the 8th Air Force knew what came next; another Luftwaffe attack. And right on cue, as if performing an encore, three formations of German fighters suddenly appeared. McKavitt saw their snow-white vapor trails lace the sky as they veered down from the oxygen-depleted altitude of 28,000 feet. He saw Bf-109's, FW-190's, and a four-plane flight of unrecognizable twin-engine planes, which seemed to be moving extremely fast.

"Uncle here... drop babies," Colonel McKavitt said into his throat microphones, instructing the 479th to jettison their external drop tanks. *"Bandits coming down—11 o'clock high."*

Forty-eight pairs of 90-gallon drop tanks wobbled off into the slipstream, then the Mustangs wheeled around in a fast turn, turning to meet the onslaught of approaching German planes.

"Falcon Red Leader," McKavitt radioed Major Wilcox. *"Intercept those 109's making for the lead box."*

"Roger, Uncle Leader," Wilcox responded.

"Eagle Red Leader," McKavitt said to Lt. Colonel Henderson, *"Head off those 190's making a play for the lower box."*

"Wilco, Uncle Leader. Heading off the 190's. We'll get 'em!"

"My flight will take that smaller Kraut schwarm trying to make an end-run around the trailing Liberators."

The Mustangs split up into three separate groups, soaring after the attacking Luftwaffe fighters. An intercepting force of one hundred-plus German airplanes attacked, the second fighter assault on the American formation that day. The initial strike had occurred a half-hour before the B-24's bomb run; one squadron of Messerschmitt Bf-109's appeared, and they were promptly chased off by the 436th. One bomber was damaged and one Bf-109 was shot down. Now the crafty Luftwaffe controllers had amassed a formidable force, and it remained to be seen how the 479th would fair against 2-to-1 odds, a rarity at this point in the war. The Mustangs' mighty Packard-Merlin engines thundered with maximum power pulling the U.S. fighters across the sky at a steady 430-miles-per-hour. The 435th intercepted the Bf-109's just as they were pairing off for head-on attacks. One Bf-109 burst into flames.

The much faster FW-190's tore through the lower box of bombers and one B-24 was seen to go down, two engines on fire, smoke and fire trailing after it. Once they were through the bomber formation, Lt. Colonel Henderson's 436th Squadron caught up with them, and one FW-190 went down in flames while another had its tailplane shot off by a blistering salvo from a Mustang's six .50-caliber machine guns, the German pilot bailing out soon afterward.

Meanwhile, McKavitt and his squadron pursued the four-plane German flight that was coming around for a stern attack on the trailing box of bombers, their twin engines propelling them across the sky at an incredible speed. As McKavitt and his squadron of Mustangs winged after them, red-lining their engines to 440 miles-per-hour, the four German airplanes continued to pull away much to their stunned surprise. McKavitt couldn't believe it. This flight of German planes was steadily outpacing the P-51 Mustang, and by a wide margin. As the four German fighters turned toward the rear of the B-24 formation, he got a good look at one. It was unlike any plane he'd ever seen.

It had swept-back wings and two engines; McKavitt swore those engines had no propeller—no propeller he could see. The slender fuselage gave way to a near pointed nose, and when that nose erupted in a blur of fire, he saw the unmistakable streaks of 30-millimeter cannon shells, not a single stream, but four. Some Bf-109's he had faced had 30-millimeter cannons mounted in their noses. This plane had four of them. Four! As he gazed at that awesome sight, he saw the result of that fiery fusillade; a B-24's outer right engine and wing exploded in a spate of twisted aluminum and engine parts. A second burst tore the wing off completely, then the B-24 rolled over on its back and fell into a twisting tailspin; two parachutes blossomed two seconds later.

"Jesus H. Christ!" he heard his wingman Lieutenant Pratt crackling in his headphones. *"That Nazi bastard just blew that bomber right out of the sky—with just two bursts!"*

McKavitt hardly heard him as he watched the four German planes angle up in a steep climb, still pulling away, the wingless B-24 but a faint blur amid the dun and gray earth below. He had the Mustang's engine churning at maximum speed, almost 450-miles-per-hour. But the German planes just kept climbing, swiftly pulling away. Unbelievable!

Moments later, they were gone from sight. Colonel McKavitt throttled back to three-quarter speed seeing his temperature gauge getting precariously close to the red zone, fearing his Mustang's engine was about to overheat. He soared above the B-24 formation seeing the 479th scattered all across the sky, winging after disengaging German fighters.

"Uncle to Group..." he ordered. *"Reform—reform formation."*

The 479th duly broke off their attacks on the fleeing enemy aircraft and reformed on McKavitt's four-plane Red Flight. Thereafter, he took damage control and found out that four German fighters had been shot down for the loss of two bombers—not the best ratio. One of those bombers had been gunned down by that mysterious two-engine German fighter. It caused quite a stir in his flight.

"What in the hell was that, Colonel?" Pratt asked. *"What kind of Nazi plane did we just encounter? I mean... jeez!"*

"Don't know Pratt," McKavitt radioed back. *"Some new kind of high-speed fighter, I guess? Man, those things must have been doing at least 500-miles-per-hour."*

"At least!"

"Maybe it was one of those newfangled rocket fighters HQ has been warning us about," Lieutenant Trotter chimed in, McKavitt's second element leader.

"No, I don't think so, Red Three," McKavitt replied. *"These were much bigger and had two engines—jet engines, I think? That little thing we saw over Merseburg three months ago had only one rocket motor, and it was mounted in the back."*

"Whatever they were, they were fast. Faster than a Mustang!"

Colonel McKavitt reluctantly had to agree. Those two-engine Nazi nightmares had outpaced his Mustang, and rather easily. Air Corps HQ had warned him during a top-secret intelligence briefing that his air group might expect to see some unusual aircraft whilst over France and Germany, rocket fighters and V-1 buzz bombs, mainly. But they'd said nothing of jet fighter planes.

According to British Intelligence, it was believed the Nazis had scrapped their jet fighter program in favor of cheaper more conventional aircraft. Not so. They had pressed on and produced a high--speed jet fighter with overwhelming firepower. If that were the case, Allied airmen were in for a very rude awakening.

AFTER THE 479TH landed at R.A.F. Wattisham, the pilots deplaned. McKavitt held a post-flight briefing in the ready room.

He glossed over the highlights of the mission and then dismissed the men for a 48-hour liberty. The weather was predicted to be bad for the next two days so no missions were scheduled. After leaving the ready room, McKavitt sought out the S-2, Major Hickok (the 479th's intelligence officer). He relayed his encounter with the German jets to Hickok in no uncertain terms, saying the Luftwaffe had something imminently superior to the P-51 Mustang, also saying that they were extremely deadly.

"Yes, I know, Colonel McKavitt," Hickok replied rather frankly. "The General Staff has known about it for quite some time now."

"Really? And when were they going to tell us?"

"Well, they didn't want to create any unrest among the 8th Air Force pilots and air crews. They had limited intelligence, and they didn't want to spread unfounded rumors. English Intelligence told our people the Nazis had canceled their advanced fighter program."

"Yeah, well, I knew about that. But I feared otherwise, and those fears were rudely reaffirmed today."

"I'm sorry about that, sir. The General Staff decided not to say anything until they had definitive proof."

McKavitt sighed. "Definitive proof? That figures. It's just like them to withhold information from us."

"If they had said something, do you think it would have made any difference, Colonel?"

McKavitt frowned. "Probably not. But it would've been nice to get a little heads-u, you know? let us in on what we're up against?"

"Yes, I know. You're right, sir. But with the buzz bombs and V-2 rockets harassing England and its people, the General Staff didn't want to add insult to injury. If the public got wind of these new jet fighters, it might create an even bigger flap. The English people are war weary, Colonel, and they just don't want to hear about another German wonder weapon. You can understand that, can't you?"

"Yeah, I guess so." McKavitt rasped the back of his neck. "But what if the Nazis have a whole bunch of these things? I mean, those jets are world-beating fighter planes—they'll fly rings around us!"

"That would be very bad for the 8th Air Force."

"Oh, bad is not the word, Major," McKavitt declared gloomily. "Downright disastrous is more like it."

"Hope it doesn't come to that, sir. We must prevail at all costs."

McKavitt left the airbase an hour later, and drove to his two-story flat in the village of Wattisham, south of Stowmarket in Suffolk, considering all of this. So the Nazis have jet fighters now? That's really depressing. How in the hell are we going to fight those bloody things if we can't even get near them? How are we going to protect the bombers from high-speed jet fighters with deadly 30-millimeter cannon? "Pray to God and hope for a miracle," he said aloud.

Within a few minutes after leaving the base, he parked the Willy's jeep in front of a block of row houses and went inside his flat, his soul bereft of hope, his worried mind clouded with thoughts of doom and gloom. The Germans were getting desperate and the war in the air was coming to a climax. The days of simple conventional warfare were coming to an end. Technological advances on both sides were turning it into a real bloodbath. McKavitt wondered what Europe would be like after the war; or would there even be a Europe to wonder about?

"Honey, I'm home!" McKavitt announced as he closed the door to the flat. "Safe and sound, once again."

"G'day, David!" said the shapely blond dressed in a lovely blouse and skirt. Her lips were daubed with bright red lipstick and her slender fingers were tipped in red as well. She smiled, displaying a perfect set of teeth. Her shoulder length hair was purely platinum; her eyes were bright blue; she had a mole on her left cheek.

"Gimme a kiss, babe." McKavitt seized the young woman by the waist, wrapping his arms around her, planting a great big kiss on her luscious red lips. She reciprocated, and they stood there a moment, kissing through an embrace, until she pulled away, catching her breath.

"Well, now!" she said, sighing blissfully, staring straight into his eyes. "Somebody is certainly glad to see me."

"You bet your sweet ass, I am, Rose. Had another rough day at the office and I really needed that."

"I bet you could use a drink too, aye?"

"Yes, I could. How about a cognac—on the rocks?"

"Right-o, luv. Coming up in a tick."

She strolled off to the kitchen and retrieved a glass tumbler from the cupboard, then seized the bottle of Hennessy on the countertop. A crystal-clear glass and two cubes of ice were soon conjoined with those needful spirits. A moment later, Colonel McKavitt was sipping an icy smooth cognac and staring at the most beautiful girl in the world, his sweet Aussie Rose—his wife of thirteen months.

After the disappearance of Captain Jack Knight, a heartbroken and dejected Rose Cresswell languished about Brisbane, her hometown, for a couple of months, wondering what to do about her marriage to the devilish Texas air ace. In the end, she decided to have the marriage annulled on the grounds of misrepresentation and deception. Jack Knight was not the man he said he was, and she couldn't go on living her life knowing she had married a liar and a fraud. She went back to her job at the *Brisbane Telegraph* and started reporting on the war and how it was effecting the citizens of Australia.

Later, at an Air Corps awards ceremony at Brisbane's Eagle Farm Airfield, she met the most celebrated American airman and the most eligible bachelor in all the U.S. military. Then, just a Lt. Colonel, David McKavitt was awarded the Medal of Honor for his daring exploits and his 28 aerial victories over Japanese aircraft. He had been Jack's C.O. and the only pilot to rival the lanky Texan's aerial prowess. Together, McKavitt and Knight lulled the masses with one victory after another, launching the "ace race" to break Eddie Rickenbacker's First World War record of 26 victories. In the end, McKavitt won the race. Knight was summarily shot down by Japan's ace of aces Hiroyoshi Nishizawa just after scoring his 27th kill. Knight was subsequently captured by the Japanese and packed off to a prison camp never to be seen or heard from again. Rose interviewed McKavitt after the awards ceremony and the two became fast friends. Much later, after a protracted war bond tour and the filming of the Air Corps' latest propaganda film, McKavitt, the star of the documentary-styled war flick, invited her to meet him in Los Angeles, California for a more in-depth interview. Her newspaper editor agreed to send her on an all-expenses-paid trip to America and bring back the story of the decade. Rose Cresswell got the story, and she got the engagement ring, as well. She was married three months later.

"Now that's what I call a drink." McKavitt sighed contentedly and sat down, crossing his legs. "So, how was your day?"

"Boring, compared to yours, I bet." She sat down next to him.

"Yeah, you got that right."

"Want to tell me about it?"

Well, uh... nah, I better not."

"That bad, aye?" She snuggled up close to him. "Did you lose somebody today?"

"Mmm," McKavitt bobbed his head. "But not from my group. We lost two bombers over Osnabrьck."

"Oh. That's... twenty men, isn't it?"

"That's right. Two whole crews."

"Sad. But that's happened before. Why so glum this time?"

"Because we lost one of the bombers to a... to a..."

"To a what? What happened? Tell me, David."

"To a—jet fighter. The Nazis have a new jet fighter, Rose. Faster than a Mustang, faster than a Mosquito, I'll bet... possibly by 100-miles-per hour. Maybe more."

"A *jet fighter?* You mean like one of those doodle bugs?"

"Yeah, like one of those *doodle-bugs,* but faster, and piloted."

Rose was referring to the V-1 pilotless bomb, or "buzz bomb," as it was more commonly known. The Germans officially called them the *Vegeltungswaffe,* or "Vengeance weapon" and they had been harassing England since July. It was a small jet-propelled winged missile that carried a high explosive warhead. But they weren't the real worry anymore. The terrible and eminently more destructive V-2 rockets where presently terrorizing London and its surrounding environs. It was basically a rocket powered ballistic missile with a one-ton warhead. They couldn't be stopped by conventional methods because they actually left the earth's atmosphere and then made reentry several miles above the target area. Destroying their launch sites was the only way to stop them. And that was a job for the 8th Air Force and the R.A.F.

"So you encountered one today?"

"Four of them, actually. One blasted a B-24 from the sky, and then just flew away. Couldn't catch any of them—too bloody fast."

Rose's face looked pained. "Crikey, are you serious?"

McKavitt nodded. "The war's getting unpredictable, Rose. The

Germans are getting desperate; they're resorting to all means within their power."

"Unpredictable? Has war ever been anything else?"

"No, I suppose not. But—"

"But nothing, David. You wanted this, remember? You wanted to go back into combat—you knew it wouldn't be easy. And I warned you not to go, remember that?"

"Yes, I remember."

"We must be careful for what we wish for, David, my mother always says. Sometimes we get what we want, but sometimes we get what we deserve." Rose took a sip from his glass and got up.

"Where are you going?"

"Dinner, my deary. You're hungry, aren't you?"

"Yeah, I could eat a bite. What's cooking?"

"Leftovers... meat and potatoes, and such."

"Ugh!" McKavitt made a face. "Again?"

"Well, what did you expect?"

Colonel McKavitt finished his drink and stood up. "As a full-bird Colonel in the Air Corps, I expect to eat like a king ever once in a while." He nodded smartly.

"Is that right?" There was a coy smile following that statement.

"That's right. Get your coat and hat. We're going out tonight."

"Where to—Tholly's Tavern?"

"Yeah. That's the place." McKavitt donned his service cap. "Dinner, drinks and... maybe a little dancing, afterwards?"

"Cor! What's gotten into you?"

"What's gotten into me, you ask?" He seized Rose by the hand and pulled her close and planted another passionate kiss on her lips. "The Colonel has a beautiful wife, and he thinks he ought to take her out once in a while. Show her off—wine and dine her."

"Oh, really? That's right nice of the Colonel."

"It's the least he can do for a pretty girl."

"Is it now? Well, you'll get no argument from me, my dear. I'll get my coat and hat then." Rose strode off for the coat rack, smiling.

McKavitt adjusted his uniform jacket, tugging on the tails, adjusting the waist belt, thinking about that German jet again, wondering how such an airplane could be beaten. Was there such a thing as an unbeatable fighter plane? He hoped not.

BRIGADIER GENERAL Thaddeus Huxley Truscott, III, Chief of Staff, 5th Air Force, Southwest Asia, eyed the intelligence report again and grunted dubiously, sitting in the passenger cabin of a C-54 Skymaster. He could hardly believe what he was reading. That annoying little thorn in his side had resurfaced again. And how had that happened, he wanted to know? How had that equivocating little bastard returned from the depths of perdition? How had he made it back from hell itself? He really didn't want to know, he decided. He only knew that he had a rather embarrassing problem on his hands that needed to be solved and solved rather quickly.

The Japanese pilot that had been shot down over Saipan three months ago by Navy Hellcats had suddenly recovered from his amnesia and was now claiming to be Captain John J. Knight. And according to the doctors at Navy Hospital Pearl Harbor, he certainly matched the physical description of the former American fighter pilot. Truscott well remembered the swarthy 6-foot-2 Texan with black hair, the pencil-thin mustache, the lanky 190-pound frame. But this man only weighed in at 148-pounds (an emaciated state) claimed the good doctors of Navy Hospital, caused by malnutrition, dehydration, and dysentery. All this, apparently, after spending fifteen months in a Japanese P.O.W. camp.

According to the man claiming to be John J. Knight, he had broken out of the Jap prison camp and stole an A6M5 Zero fighter from a nearby naval air station, then flew southeast from Yokohama and miraculously made it all the way to Saipan, only to be shot down by intercepting Hellcats. Unable to bailout because he had no parachute, he ditched the Zero in the sea, bashing his head against the cockpit canopy, sustaining a memory-erasing concussion and breaking his left arm in three places. He was fished out of the sea by a patrolling U.S. destroyer and taken back to Pearl Harbor, where he was placed in the custody of the Shore Patrol and Pearl Harbor's Navy Hospital, where he languished in a comma-like state for nearly six weeks before regaining full consciousness. Once he finally awoke from his delirium, he told the kindly nurse who'd been looking in on him that his name was Jack and that he was actually an American pilot, more specifically, Captain John J. Knight of the 35th Fighter Group, 39th Fighter Squadron.

"Seems unbelievable doesn't it, sir?" said the General's aide, Staff Sergeant Al Stabler, sitting across from Truscott.

"Unbelievable is an understatement, Sergeant Stabler," Truscott replied, looking up at the diminutive noncom, his mouth a hard line. "If this man really is John J. Knight, then we have a big, big problem on our hands. A *big* problem!" The General tucked the report back into the manila folder.

"How's that, sir?" Stabler asked.

"You know why."

"Because he impersonated an officer and made a mockery of the U.S. Army Air Corps?"

"Precisely." Truscott crossed his legs and sighed.

"What do you intend to do, sir?"

"I don't know just yet. But first I need to determine if this man is really who he says he is. And if he is, then I need to figure out what to do with him. Figure out what the Air Corps wants to do with him."

"What do you mean, sir?"

"You know damn well what I mean, Sergeant!"

Stabler winced.

"We just can't sweep him under a rug," the General went on, "He was a topnotch combat pilot and a national obsession for a time. People still remember him. Especially in this theater of war."

"Yeah, I recall. He almost broke Rickenbacker's record, right?"

"He actually did, Sergeant. But unfortunately he got shot down in the process. And since he never returned from his last mission, the kill was never confirmed. Then days later David McKavitt shot down two and set the official record, winning the Medal of Honor for doing it, if you well remember."

"Yes, sir. I remember."

"The galling fact that Knight—or Castillo—I should say, fudged his way into the fighter program by not only impersonating an officer. But stealing someone's identity is tantamount to a court-martial offense. If that bit of information ever reached General Kenney's desk, then my military career would be in total jeopardy, Sergeant."

"How's that, General?" Stabler asked innocently.

"Because I knew the despicable truth long before his dirty little secret was ever exposed."

"You did?"

Truscott nodded. "Unfortunately. However, I kept it quiet, you see. Because Knight was blasting the Japs out of the sky, helping us win the war. Regardless of his past or unsavory behavior, he was kicking the enemy's ass. When we were getting beaten down by the goddamn Japs, he was our only hope and salvation."

Sergeant Al Stabler evinced a scornful frown, remembering Jack Knight's irascible attitude and self-important personality. "Well, sir, I remember him as an arrogant son-of-a-bitch. A self-interested bastard who only thought of himself and his own accomplishments."

"Most egotists are, Sergeant. Arrogance and success almost go had in hand. He may have been a braggart and a bastard, but he was a brilliant pilot and a top-notch marksman. And no one could touch him in that respect."

"That Jap ace Nishizawa *touched* him, sir. Shot him down—"

"Humph! An even more arrogant son-of-a-bitch, I suspect."

"So what if this guy really is who he says he is, eh, General?" Stabler proposed querulously. "What then?"

General Truscott didn't answer right away, thinking, wondering, worrying what might happen if General Kenney or General MacArthur found out that he had basically aided and abetted a fraud, perpetuated his career, misled the U.S. Air Corps and the American public. Worse than that, he had allowed a simple noncom and an uneducated working-class thug to circumvent the tried-and-true codes of conduct of the officer corps. If the true story of one Jack Knight (James Castillo) ever became public, General Thaddeus H. Truscott could kiss his twenty-seven-year career goodbye. His name would be dragged through the mud and be forever tainted just like that rakehell Jack Knight. Truscott wasn't ready for that. He had to keep things quiet, suppressed, hushed; no one must ever learn the truth about Captain John J. Knight; no one must ever suspect that he'd duped the smartest minds of the Air Corps.

"Then I'll just have to pull some strings, Sergeant."

"Pull some strings, sir?"

"That's right. Fix it so no one's the wiser."

"How are you going to do that?"

Truscott smiled wickedly. "You'll find out soon enough."

Once the Skymaster landed at Hickam Field, General Truscott

and Sergeant Stabler were whisked away in a jeep and driven to the Navy Hospital where Jack was being kept. After a quick briefing by the chief surgeon, Truscott was ushered into Jack's room. Since his sudden return to his senses, and because of his incredulous claims about his identity, he'd been moved into a "special care" room which was actually a padded cell in the psycho-ward of the hospital. The good doctors of the Naval hospital didn't know what to make of the babbling ex-Air Corps pilot, so they decided to keep him in a separate wing and away from other patients. A burly chested S.P. was also posted outside the door of his cell; Jack was still considered an enemy combatant until his identity could be officially proven. When he was picked up by the U.S. destroyer, he had no dog tags around his neck as they had been confiscated by the Japanese upon his arrival at Camp Yomi. Yomi was a prison camp for high profile P.O.W.'s, and according to Imperial Japanese Headquarters, these prisoners simply did not exist.

Truscott entered the dimly lit cell and sat down on a chair near the foot of Jack's bed. Jack, who had been napping, sat up and eyed the mustachioed silver-haired staff officer with keen eyes.

"Well, well, well, now," he said, his voice thick with liquid. "If it ain't Col—*General,*" he corrected himself, "Truscott in the flesh."

"Hello, son," said Truscott, looking Jack over, grimacing, seeing the weathered and emaciated figure before him. He had a large bandage around his head and over the left side of his face, covering his eye, concealing a nasty cut and abrasion, one that had to be stitched up. His left arm was in a plaster cast and sling, supporting that broken arm. But despite his ragged and emaciated countenance, General Truscott could see it was definitely Captain John J. Knight (a.k.a. Sergeant James Castillo) which was his true identity, sitting right there before him.

"What brings you 'round these parts, sir?"

"You, Captain John J. Knight."

Jack smiled. "Boy, I'm sure glad you called me that. Been trying to convince these sawbones 'round here of that for dang near two weeks now. Nobody wants to believe me. They think I'm a Jap pilot. Can you believe that, sir? They think old Cap'n Jack Knight, the terror of the South Pacific, is a stinkin' Jap pilot. Gawd!"

"Well, you were flying a Zero and wearing a Japanese uniform, and you had no dog tags or any other identification on you. And with your tanned complexion and black hair... oh, hell! Never mind all that. I know who you are."

"Thank-ya, sir. I appreciate that."

Truscott gave a faint nod, then said: "That was a daring escape you made. I mean, escaping from the Japanese Home Islands and making it all the way to Saipan, that's goddamned unbelievable."

"Yup. I could have gone all the way to Guam if it hadn't been for them dang Navy fighters. I tried to get away from 'em, diving, climbing, looping, rolling, you name it. But there were just too many of 'em... and well, my old stick-hand ain't what it used to be."

Jack opened and closed his right hand, making an enfeebled fist, grunting. Truscott saw the jagged pink scar and surmised Jack must have been wounded sometime in the recent past, most likely when he got shot down over the Solomon Sea in '43. He looked frail and weak and his voice sounded hoarse and feeble. Jack Knight was a hollow shell of his former self; a war-weary specter; a long-forgotten hero living in the shadows of antecedent accomplishments; an airman with a long history of lies and prevarications; a man with a checkered past.

"You look like hell, son," Truscott said after a thoughtful pause.

"Well, sir, I've been through hell—escaped from it—and lived to tell about it. I'm here, barely."

"But here, nonetheless. Now the question is: what do we do with you? Where do we go from here?"

"I suppose I got a lot to answer fer, eh, sir?"

"Yes you do. But I don't give a goddamn about all of that."

"You don't?"

"No," Truscott replied equably. "You always were an extraordinary combat pilot and a sharpshooting daredevil. Regrettably, your past finally caught up with you... yet, I was willing to overlook it all in light of your spectacular achievements... and I still am."

Jack's bleary blue eyes brightened. "Really?"

"Really. Uncle Sam can still use men like you. It may not be from the cockpit of a fast fighter plane but it'll be something as useful, I can guarantee you that. I still know a few people in this man's Army, and they can find a place for you, Knight. You can still serve your country despite your fraudulent past... and your injured state."

"I can?"

"You can. There are different ways to fight a war. Your days as a high-flying ace are over, but you can still do something worthwhile to redeem yourself, get back in the good graces of your superiors.

"Hmm..." Jack frowned. "No more air combat."

"I know someone in the Office of Strategic Services, someone who could use a man like you. He'll get you squared away."

"Right. Sounds peachy."

"Just promise me you'll keep your mouth shut about who you are for the time being. Okay? And I'll get you out of this mess."

"Yes, sir. I'll keep it zipped."

"Good. That's what I like to hear."

"When will you know something, sir? About my new... *job?*"

"I'll let you know in due time. In the meantime, keep your fucking trap shut. You understand me?" General Truscott stood up.

Jack nodded, zipping his lips up in a mock gesture.

"All right, get some rest now, son. Get well. And we'll talk again soon." Truscott rapped on the door, and the S.P. unlocked it.

"Congratulations, sir," Jack said, grinning.

"Hmm?" Truscott replied, looking back at Jack, a puzzled look on his face, his hand on the doorknob.

"A one-star general, eh?"

"Ah, yes," Truscott replied, his puzzlement fading as he glanced at the silver star on the shoulder board of his uniform jacket. "Got it a year ago for my *steadfast service...* if you can believe that?"

Jack burst out laughing.

Truscott slammed out of the cell.

Jack laid back down, placing a hand behind his head, staring at the ceiling, thinking. That General Truscott's not a bad apple, all in all. He's really looking out fer me. He surely is. Then that devilish little voice inside his head warned him: *Don't you dare be fooled, Jack old boy. That lying son-of-a-bitch is just looking out for his own ass. He'll drop you like a hot potato as soon as he gets the chance. You bet your back pay on that!*

"Don't you fret none, old buddy. He's gonna get his comeuppance just like all the rest." Jack smiled devilishly. He was back in the saddle again. Ready to take on anything or anyone, the Japs, the Germans, the Air Corps, anybody—General Truscott included.

```
TOP SECRET

URGENT

PEARL HARBOR, 0800 10 OCTOBER 1944

FROM: CHIEF OF STAFF, 5TH AIR FORCE, SOUTHWEST PACIFIC
      BRIGIDIEIR GEN. THADDEUS H. TRUSCOTT (USAAC)

TO:(EYES ONLY) DIRECTOR, OFFICE OF STRATIGIC SERVICES,
    WASHINGTON, DC, MAJOR GEN. WILLIAM J. DONOVAN

REGARDING: Capt. JOHN J. KNIGHT,(erst)35th FG/39th FS

Dear Bill,

   Attached hereto is the personnel file of Capt.John J.
Knight, most recently a POW of the Empire of Japan. It
is the desire of the Supreme Commander General Douglas
MacArthur that Captain Knight be reassigned to the OSS
in lieu of his debilitating war injuries and be formally
trained in the areas of subterfuge and espionage for
duty in the European Theater of Operations.

   It is directed that you:

A. Acknowledge receipt of this message by teletype.
B. Immediately prepare suitable identity for this
   officer and advance him by the most expeditious means
   through appropriate channels, via Chief of Special
   Operations, ATTN: Col.Bruce (S.O. Branch) London.
C. Provide all identification papers and training.
D. Furnish copy of proposed ID papers by teletype at the
   time you begin to forward it through the appropriate
   channels. (SEE A. ABOVE)


                              Respectfully Submitted
                        Gen. Thaddeus H. Truscott
                        Chief of Staff, 5th Air Force
                                 Brisbane, Australia
```

CHAPTER 3

11 NOVEMBER 1944
FRIDAY, 0750 HOURS
RAF WATTISHAM, ENGLAND

COLONEL MCKAVITT and the 479th flew an escort mission on October 15th. All he saw on the trip to Cologne and the return flight were dense clouds and the inevitable German flak. Not one black-crossed fighter. Four days later, he climbed into his Mustang for a mission to Mainz. A thunderstorm closed in and visibility rapidly disappeared, and the 479th never got off the ground. On the 22nd, the Group escorted the 392 BG to Hamm. Nothing but flak. Neumunster, on the 25th, promised action. They encountered some FW-190's but had little chance to do more than chase them across the sky. Still, no kills, and McKavitt's combat tour was fast coming to an end. Nearly six months and not a single chance to rack up a kill. His time was running out and there would be no third tour. He'd applied for another one but it was summarily denied by General Doolittle, the Commanding General of the 8th Air Force. Once his tour was finished, Colonel David McKavitt was to return to the United States and become a flight instructor, lending his aerial expertise to the fledgling pilots that were now flooding into the Air Corps' fighter program.

A mission on the 26th to Minden looked promising, but the FW-190's and Bf-109's played coy. A few made halfhearted gestures several miles from the formation but turned tail when the Mustangs gave chase. At Krefeld, McKavitt took his squadron down to strafe a German airfield. It was a mistake, and the moment the Mustangs approached the field, all hell broke loose. Pratt's P-51 took a flak burst in the fuel tank. McKavitt shouted: *"Bail out, you're on fire!"* But Pratt was killed when his P-51 plunged to earth and exploded.

Colonel David McKavitt's disgust with the way things were going steadily mounted. On 29th, the 479th sortied out on a strafing mission to Denmark. Halfway there, they received a recall because a storm front was closing in, and they returned to base. A day later they flew an escort to Hamburg. The B-24's charged through the flak, bombed the hell out of the town, and then flew home. The Luftwaffe played coy again. Action had become so scarce that McKavitt was almost looking forward to the end of his tour and going back home.

Today, November 11th, the Group was to fly a bomber escort to Leuna—a massive synthetic-fuel works a hundred miles southwest of Berlin. And not only was it the largest producer of synthetic fuel but the most heavily defended. It was guarded by the largest concentration of flak batteries the Germans had ever amassed; it could also be shielded during a bombing raid by the dense black clouds produced by the smoke and fumes of the explosions.

By this time in the war, General Spaatz's oil campaign was in full swing, McKavitt knew well. Spaatz no longer had to concern himself with the Nazi's major imported source of oil, Ploesti. The Romanian oil fields, heavily bombed by the 15th Air Force striking from Italy, had been captured by the resurgent Soviet Army. With their advance into Eastern Europe, the Russians had also overrun a number of refineries in Poland. Germany's primary remaining outside supplier was Hungary. Whilst the 15th Air Force bombers raided the oil-rich area of Budapest, the 8th Air Force, flying from England, hammered the German's last bastion of oil production—some two dozen synthetic-fuel refineries situated inside the Third Reich.

Once the 479th got airborne and on its way, trouble soon began. The 436th Squadron's White Flight had mechanical difficulties. Then Major Wilcox's trusty wingman complained of engine trouble. Over the Dutch coast, Wilcox sent him home with his No.4 man and that left only Major Wilcox and his lead element to cover an area originally assigned to eight Mustangs. Over Göttingen the Germans decided to mix it up—at last! Sixteen Messerschmitt Bf-109's dived from high altitude, trying to pounce on the B-17 bomber formation, raising holy hell with their 30-millimeter cannons and machine guns as they slashed through the massive Flying Fortress formation. Drop tanks were jettisoned.

As the slender German fighters dived headlong through the bomber formation, they pulled up in sweeping right turns, suddenly rushing at Colonel McKavitt and his new wingman Lieutenant Spencer. Well, this was what McKavitt had been trying to get into for days. He and Spencer soared toward the Messerschmitts head-on breaking up their formation. Their Mustangs banked sharply, turning onto the Bf-109's tails when they rolled and dived for the deck. Spencer went after them. McKavitt's attention was diverted elsewhere. A *schwarm* of FW-190's flying top cover tried to bounce him, and McKavitt turned to face them. Lieutenant Spencer relentlessly pursued the Messerschmitts. Two FW-190's latched onto McKavitt's tail whilst he still struggled to jettison his stuck drop tanks. They wouldn't budge. He turned several times with the two snub-nosed German fighters, banking and rolling as they tried to blast him from the sky, their four 20-millimeter cannons and two machine guns blinking fiercely. Spencer radioed excitedly:

"Help, Colonel! Help! Get these bastards off my tail!"

But McKavitt had his hands full. *"Roger, Red Two,"* he responded. *"Hang on for a few seconds and I'll be right down. I'm kind of busy myself right now."* McKavitt rolled tightly to the left and skidded about, swinging his Mustang's wings around, bringing his guns to bear. He fired. The Focke-Wulf pilots lost their nerve and split-essed, diving away. McKavitt searched for Spencer but couldn't find him. Then two more FW-190's jumped him as he continued to struggle with his stuck drop tanks; they just wouldn't jettison! All the while Spencer was calling for help. McKavitt looped his Mustang and fired off a burst from all six .50-caliber machine guns. The Germans wisely dived out of range. And before McKavitt could descend and find Spencer, two more FW-190's attacked him. Things were getting hot!

McKavitt escaped the Focke-Wulfs with some fancy maneuvering, forcing them to break off once he got around behind them. He spotted Spencer, finally, some 12,000 feet below him, just above the Harz Mountains. Three fighters whirled around in mad circles, the Mustang out in front, the two Focke-Wulfs close behind, pressing hard, their tracer and cannon shells flaring menacingly.

"Hang on, Red Two," McKavitt radioed. *"Almost there."*

"Hurry, sir!" Spencer replied. *"These Krauts mean business!"*

McKavitt, diving at 480 miles-per-hour indicated airspeed, realized the drop tanks would never jettison; they reduced his speed somewhat and hindered his maneuvering, but for the moment, he was cursed with them. At 5,000 feet, McKavitt lessened the dive to normal speed. The two Germans were giving Spencer a really bad time. One clung to his tail, snapping off rapid bursts, getting perilously close with his tracers. The other FW-190 hung back, and every time Spencer came around, he rushed in for a head-on attack. McKavitt knew if Spencer straightened out for even a second to take a shot, the FW-190 on his tail would shoot him down. So Spencer just kept turning and turning. U.S. Air Corps doctrine stated that down below 6,000 feet the Focke-Wulf could easily roll inside the Mustang; any pilot who tried to turn with that speedy radial-engine fighter was basically committing aerial suicide. McKavitt wasn't sure Spencer knew that, him being new to the ETO. But he kept ahead of the pursuing FW-190, matching him turn for turn; he was even gaining on him!

McKavitt side-slipped clumsily onto the tail of the second Focke-Wulf, turning his Mustang hard-left, getting into that crazy turning circle, then pulled the nose up for a high-angled deflection shot. Once he had the German fighter properly sighted, he fired off a long burst. Six .50-caliber machine guns flashed torridly. The bullets slammed into the Focke-Wulf's engine cowling; flames erupted, a wing ripped off and a stream of slugs hit the cockpit. And that brought the curtain down. The flaming FW-190 spun down violently, smoke pouring out of its engine, its pilot dead at the controls. This unnerved the other German pilot, and he broke off his attack on Spencer's Mustang. He swiftly split-essed (rolling and diving for the deck) and shortly, disappeared in the dense cloud bank below.

Before McKavitt had settled back to watch the Focke-Wulf go down, habit brought his head around in a swivel to look behind him. It was just in time to see another FW-190 closing in on his tail, its nose twinkling with 13-millimeter machine gun fire. His left hand rammed the throttle forward, his right hand hauled back and right on the stick, his stomach came up in his throat. He jerked the Mustang into a sharp right climbing turn, staying just above and in front of the pursuing German fighter. The magnificent Packard-Merlin was doing its job!

To get hits on McKavitt's Mustang, the German first had to turn inside it, then haul its nose up steeply to get its guns in front of it for a deflection shot. The FW-190 just didn't have it. At 3,000 feet it stalled out as the Mustang soared onward. McKavitt flicked over and locked onto the Focke-Wulf's tail. Then it was coming at the Mustang! Whilst McKavitt had slipped into firing position, the German had whipped his plane around in a 180-degree turn. The American pilot had never seen a fighter turn tighter or quicker in his life, not even a Zero!

This Kraut pilot is good, he thought. Damn good! He didn't even turn—just reversed his flight and came at me.

Several times they rushed headlong at each other trading shots. Then McKavitt started firing inside bursts as the Focke-Wulf weaved across the sky. It worked. Twice, it ran into McKavitt's stream of well-aimed bullets. With white vapor streaming from its main fuel tank, the FW-190 winged over in a sharp turn and ran for its airfield. McKavitt didn't want this Kraut to escape. He closed to 50 yards and fired again. The canopy blew off into the slipstream as the German yanked the release, intent on bailing out. McKavitt flew closer, wanting to get his bullets into the man himself before he could get out of the airplane. He had one leg outside the cockpit when a volley of slugs chased him back inside. A moment later, he was crashing into the ground, dead before he hit. "That Kraut will never draw a bead on another Allied airman," McKavitt said to himself. "If I hadn't gotten him, he would've shot down many more of our planes. He's the best I've ever fought."

No. 30!

McKavitt turned back and rallied the Group. Once everyone had rejoined and was back on station, escorting the B-17's, heading to Leuna, he took visual inventory. No bombers lost; no fighters lost; two FW-190's shot down. Not a bad day, so far.

"Thanks, Colonel," Spencer radioed, expressing his gratitude.

"My pleasure, Red Two," McKavitt replied. *"But just remember to adhere to proper radio etiquette from now on. I know this is only your third time out, but keep it official. Okay, Red Two?"*

"Roger, Uncle Leader. Sorry. Will comply from now on."

McKavitt smiled. Good kid, that Spencer. And soon, 500-pound bombs were falling on the Leuna synthetic-fuel works. Bull's eye!

"SORRY, COLONEL," Major Hickok apologized. "Your gun camera must have malfunctioned.

"What? Malfunctioned?" McKavitt replied, his face looking pinched and perplexed. "How'd that happen?"

"Don't know, sir. Could have been a fuse, could have been a bad connection, battle damage. Could've been anything, really."

"So you can't confirm my two kills?"

"No, sir. I can only count them as probables."

"Shit!" Colonel McKavitt cursed. "Are you serious?"

"Yes, sir, unfortunately."

"Dammit! Those were the first two kills in months, Major. My first two since coming to this theater."

"I know, sir. It's a sorry situation. But there it is."

McKavitt frowned, shaking his head.

"I can submit an appeal to Fighter Command, see if they can overturn the ruling, but I doubt they will. General Doolittle is adamant about pilot over-claiming, Colonel. You know that."

"Yeah, I know. But—"

"If the gun camera can't capture at least twenty-four frames of gunfire, the kill is to be listed as a probable, or, as damaged."

"I know, I know. You need not remind me, Major."

"Sir, if you could've had one more witness other than Lieutenant Spencer—who actually wasn't sure how many you'd shot down—then I might be able to confirm them."

"More witnesses?" McKavitt scoffed. "Do you have any idea how hectic it is up there, Major? Planes zooming around the sky like crazy, flak going off, guns blazing, clouds obscuring the view... it's amazing all those pilots don't just run into each other much less see everything that's going on around them. It's a bloody three-ring circus up there!"

"Sorry, sir. I know how you must feel—"

"Do you?" McKavitt shook his head. "I don't think so."

Major Hickok sighed resignedly.

"All right, whatever," McKavitt acquiesced. "I've got exactly one month to catch Dick Bong—try to surpass his score. And at the rate I'm going, it's not looking too good."

"Well, I wish you luck, sir. Really, I do."

"Oh, shut the hell up, Hickok," Colonel McKavitt blurted out. He turned and stormed off. "I need a drink, by God."

"Ah, jeez," Major Hickok grumbled, frowning tightly. "What a frigging sorehead." He turned on a heel and returned to his office.

McKavitt headed over to the Officer's Mess in a stalking stride, intent on cooling off his temper with a shot of whiskey, or a beer, or both. He was hotter than a firecracker on the 4th of July. Those two kills would have made 30 for the war, a nice round number and a fitting figure to go with his Medal of Honor. It would've set him above the status quo of current American aces who were usually sent home after scoring their 20th or so kill, just as he had done after breaking Eddie Rickenbacker's record. It was a record he held until Major Richard Bong came along; he broke it whilst flying P-38's, fighting over the Pacific, serving in the 5th Air Force, very much like McKavitt.

Well, Bong had shattered that record. And aside from a couple of lesser Air Corps aces, McKavitt was the only high scoring American ace in Europe still flying air combat. And that would end in twenty-six days. He was also worried General Doolittle or General Spaatz might ground him before his tour was completed, which was quite possible. Doolittle had already made known his objections about having a Medal of Honor winner flying air combat. Even President Roosevelt had voiced his opinions about the subject. Indeed, nobody wanted to lose America's most decorated airman and West Point graduate to a Nazi hotshot, or worse, to plain old flak-fire, the latter of which had already claimed several American aces. McKavitt was running out of time. He needed to step up his efforts and start knocking down some Kraut planes if he wanted to be regarded as the American' "Ace of Aces." Not an easy task when things like bad weather, timid Krauts, equipment malfunctions, or the threat of grounding were factored into the mix. Yes, Rose had warned him, she knew it wouldn't be easy. He was just figuring that out.

"Afternoon, sir," said the barkeep, Corporal Hill. "The usual?"

"No. Give me a shot of Irish and a beer, please. I need to shake off this damn jinx with some heavy drinking."

"Coming up, sir." Hill nodded. "One whiskey—one beer."

"Thanks, Corporal" McKavitt removed his cap and sat down on a bar stool. He looked around the mess, seeing no one else around.

The Officer's mess was empty at that hour, the clock on the wall marking the time at 15:45 hours. Most of the officers were still on duty, or showering, or shaving, getting ready for the evening's usual festivities—drinking heavily and playing cards. McKavitt rarely lingered here after a mission now that he was a happily married man.

"I heard you had a tough time today, sir," Hill said as he poured the shot of whiskey and then filled a mug with beer, topping it off with a rich, sudsy head. "Weapons malfunction, sir?"

"Something like that."

Hill set the whiskey and the beer before the brooding Air Corps Colonel, wondering if he should keep his mouth shut and stay out of the Group Commander's business. Yet, he hazarded another word.

"Shot down two, I heard. But then—"

"Mind your own business, Corporal," McKavitt rejoined curtly. "I'm not in the mood to make small talk. Got some serious thinking to do. I don't need some nosy little noncom butting in."

Hill gulped. "S-Sorry, sir. I'll leave you alone—"

"Thank you, Corporal," McKavitt interjected coldly and shot the whiskey back, chasing it with a long gulp of beer, drinking half of it. He set the mug down heavily, sighing, stewing. "Another shot, please," he demanded, wiping his lips with the back of his hand.

"Yes, sir," Hill replied, and silently went about pouring McKavitt another shot. He slid the shot glass forward and then turned back to his barkeep duties: shoveling ice, polishing glasses, wiping the countertop.

McKavitt quaffed the whiskey down with equal gusto and finished off the beer in one gulp. He rasped the stubble on his chin and thought about the days events one more time, grumbling bitterly, wondering if he should call it quits and get out while he was ahead. No sense in sacrificing oneself to feed some sick sense of propriety. How many others had done that in the past, he asked himself? How many airmen and soldiers had fallen because of their own hubris? How many? Hmm... he could think of quite a few.

"Colonel, sir?" He heard the deep-base timbre of his personal aide Tech Sergeant Nate Williams beckoning him from his thoughts.

"Yes? What is it, Nate?"

"The General wants to see you."

McKavitt glared at the 6-foot-4 negro noncom with disbelieving eyes and asked: "General *Doolittle* wants to see me?"

Williams grinned, shaking his head. "Nah, sir. General Warlick, 65th Fighter Wing. He called a moment ago. Wants you over at Wing HQ at sixteen-hundred-hours for a meeting—he said."

"What about? Did he say?"

"Nah, sir. Just said for you to get to Wing by sixteen-hundred."

McKavitt nodded. "All right, Nate. Thanks."

"Yeah, sir." Williams saluted and left the mess.

"Hmm," McKavitt grunted, puzzled. "Wonder want he wants?" Then he scoffed. "Probably just another boring bomber-briefing."

McKavitt slid from the bar stool and exited the Officer's mess. Outside, he found Sergeant Williams sitting in an idling Willy's jeep, ready to take him to General Warlick's briefing.

"Need a lift, sir?" Williams asked.

"Sure, Nate. That would be much appreciated."

McKavitt hopped in. Williams jerked the jeep into low, then gassed the accelerator. The jeep lurched forward amid squealing tires. The burly noncom had the handsome Air Corps colonel there in ten minutes flat. McKavitt wished everything else was so easy.

BRIGIDIER GENERAL Joseph "Bulldog" Warlick, a redheaded fireball and a 5-foot-8, forty-eight-year-old ex-World War I fighter pilot and a man of unseemly profane utterances, sat at the desk in his office, an odious corona clenched between his teeth. The intelligence report VIII Fighter Command had sent over had set him off, upsetting him to the point of insane worries. It worried him so much that he called his best group commander, Colonel David McKavitt.

McKavitt strode into the General's office at 65th Wing, Elveden Hall, Suffolk, England, with the cool-headed confidence of the invited. His ragged and incessantly well-worn leather jacket reeked of the war zone and of hard service. In contrast to the clean-pressed uniforms of Staff, it seemed like a shabby afterthought. But the eyes of the General, raised suddenly from the reports on his desk, saw only the man.

"Ah, McKavitt!" the General rumbled, puffing the corona. "You're prompt. I'm glad to see you. Pull up a chair. Have some scotch?"

"No thank you, sir." McKavitt pulled up a chair and sat down. He wanted the scotch but decided he'd better not. It was quite enough that a West Point graduate should be the guest of a self-made American general; he did not want to press on hospitality. The General, a straight-shooting, heavy-handed Southerner whose every move was executed with parade-ground precision, was regarding him with appraising eyes.

"You look tired, McKavitt. Worn out, are you?"

A slow smile crept over McKavitt's mouth, his head turned slightly to the window. From twenty-five miles west there came a faint thrum of engines, a thrumming that was the overture of hell it-self when a man left the comfort of Staff and went up where the 8th's bomber groups assembled high above the Cliffs of Dover. The bombers had thrummed thus for over two years now, and ever since OVERLORD, McKavitt had been flying with those bombers during his daylight hours, trying to sleep in the wake of their onslaught be-tween sunset and dawn.

"We've been busy, sir," he answered.

McKavitt did not have to elaborate. He was a colonel in the Air Corps and the commander of the 479th by reason of the General Staff's interest in him; an interest that had blossomed out of their ap-proval of his philosophy. He was known from one side of the globe to the other as the all-American ace. He had blasted his way to repu-tation by gunning down the enemy's airmen where ever he found them, over the deep-blue sea, or over embattled blood-red earth. He had not fought for the thrill of victory, nor looked to see if a foe's parachute had deployed. He had fought to kill with the impersonal coolness of a spiraling bullet—and he'd been just as deadly. The ex-alting tone with which the press had hurled the word "hero" at him had changed now. McKavitt had made it a title of accomplishment, a word that merely meant he was a great pilot. He had 28 kills on the books, and he had left a few more, as the good Lord could attest, unaccounted for in enemy territory.

The General shuffled his paperwork. "I have direct authority, you know, in Air Corps matters. Indeed I do! And damn it, McK-avitt, I've gotten word from certain parties you're due for a rest. But son, I have a job for you—a dirty job."

McKavitt grinned. He knew it wouldn't be easy when he came

46

to Elveden Hall. A brigadier general didn't hand out routine missions.

Warlick rapped his desktop. "The Nazis have jets, McKavitt."

McKavitt's face darkened. He knew. He'd seen those propellerless wonders over Germany, experienced their awing superiority. "We can't touch 'em, General. They're too fast, too well-armed—"

The General's fist hit the desktop. "Bullshit! There are more ways than one to skin a cat, Colonel. We'll just get them before they get airborne. Before they can get to the bombers. Shoot them up on the tarmac and on the runway. Strafe them where they're parked."

"I've got to beg off, sir. I wouldn't know about ground attack."

The General glared, clamped down hard on his corona and blew some smoke. "No! But you're a goddamn genius at flying. And I'm going to use you. Your duty from now on will be interdiction, exclusively. The order will go out tonight. We've got to take out those jets on the ground, strafe their airfields, destroy their fuel dumps, kill their pilots."

"What about escort duty, sir?"

"Others can do it."

General Warlick got up and paced the floor, a long plume of smoke floating behind him as he puffed furiously. McKavitt leaned back in his chair. He knew there was more behind all of this than had been laid bare. He knew the General too well to believe otherwise. The General whirled around.

"McKavitt," he said, his blue eyes flaring. "Goddammit! We're losing a hundred men a day over the Third Reich. We're losing men like a bad gambler loses bets. It's insane! But the outcome of the war is in the balance now. So we can't get sentimental—there's no room for pity."

McKavitt's eyes met the General's. His jaw trembled a moment, then it stiffened. His mouth opened, but the words didn't come out.

"The bombers are our one and only hope, McKavitt," the General ranted on. "They can paralyze the Nazi's sources of industry. So they must not fail." His fist clenched. "I have shouted myself hoarse before the General Staff, trying to get your group reassigned to interdiction sweeps."

"Why?" The word left McKavitt's lips responsively. In his mind he knew the answer. General Warlick stood stiffly, his legs apart.

"Because," the General answered, "you're the only group commander I can depend on. You're the only one with enough guts and the iron will to sacrifice airmen as the Army sacrifices soldiers."

"So fighter pilots are expendable? Is that what you're saying?"

"At the moment one bomber is worth three fighters to our cause. Okay, you've got the men and you've got the job. So get those goddamn jets, Colonel!"

A grim smile spread over McKavitt's face along the chiseled contour of his jaw. He certainly knew what was in store for him and his men. Colonel McKavitt rose to his feet. His hand instinctively came to a salute—a salute that was more for the man than the stars on his shoulders. "We'll get them, General. You can count on it."

General Warlick did not fail to see the magnitude of that statement. "I do hope," he said, "the attackers won't become the attacked. But—" His head jerked forward, his jaw a hardened rock. "Those German jets must be destroyed at all costs."

"Yes, sir." McKavitt stepped forward. "I'll have that scotch now, if the offer is still open?"

"Of course." The General took a serious drag from the corona and gestured with it. "One for me too, if you'll be so kind."

McKavitt poured. They touched glasses. There was no toast; they knew each other well; they drank to things men never speak of.

ROSE MCKAVITT got up from the chair when her named was called, clutching her purse anxiously. She strode up to the reception desk and gave her name, confirming her appointment with the nurse on duty. "Yes, I'm Mrs. Rose McKavitt."

"Go right in, Mrs. McKavitt," the nurse replied, an elderly lady with gray hair and a friendly face. "The doctor will see you now."

"Thank you." Rose turned about and walked down the hallway to the doctor's office, a nervous look on her face. This was the moment she'd been waiting for, fretted about for days now, and she was anxious to get on with it, or more appropriately, learn the truth about her condition. She had been experiencing some nausea and queasiness in the morning and it was occurring more frequently. She had her suspicions, but she said nothing to her husband about it, who was flying quite regularly now that General Warlick had stepped up the campaign against the German jets. Rose perpetually worried about him, fearing he might be shot down and killed. It was a distressing concern and she couldn't wait for the last day of his tour, which wasn't long in coming.

She entered the doctor's office and closed the door behind her. The doctor, an elderly gentleman, sitting behind his desk, gestured to the chair in front evincing a placid grin.

"Have a seat, Mrs. McKavitt," he said warmly. "Please, make yourself comfortable."

"Thank you, Dr. Eddington." Rose sat down.

"So, how are you feeling this morning, Mrs. McKavitt?"

"Mmm, about the same, I suppose."

"As expected." Dr. Samuel J. Eddington, M.D. was a heavyset, fifty-eight-year-old man with snow-white hair and thick eyebrows. He glanced over Rose's examination results and nodded.

"Am I...?" Rose asked tentatively.

"Yes you are, Mrs. McKavitt. Eight weeks, actually."

"I thought so." Rose looked down at her hands.

"You sound as if you're unhappy about it."

"It's just the war and all. It's a terrible time to have a baby."

"Yes, I know. But a newborn baby can bring a lot of joy and happiness into an otherwise dreary war-torn world"

"I suppose so. My older brother was born during the last war, and I, soon after it."

"There you go. Bet your parents were overjoyed back then?"

"I guess so."

"Your husband is an American pilot, isn't he?"

"Aye, he is. He's with the 8th Air Force. Flies fighters."

"Ah, yes. That's right. He'll be overjoyed, too, I'll bet."

"He will. He's a family man—comes from a big family himself. Four sisters and a younger brother, he has."

"Is he the oldest?"

"He is. His sister Kate is two years younger, and an army nurse serving in Italy. His little brother Mike is a cadet at West Point."

"I see. Isn't David due to go back to the States soon?"

"Yes. He's got about three weeks left on his tour of duty, then we go back to New York where he'll take up an instructor's job."

"Well, a newborn baby will be a welcome change from the rigors of air combat and active service."

"I agree. I'll just worry myself to death until he's finished."

"I know. It's hard on the wife of a military man. There's always the fear of death lingering about."

"It's a terrible feeling. And being the wife of a pilot, there's always the extra fear of him being killed or badly injured in a crash—something that's totally unrelated to air combat."

"Yes, flying is a hazard unto itself."

"More pilots are killed and injured in training and regular flying than in air combat, he's told me many times."

"I've heard that, too."

Rose contemplated that prospect for a long moment, thinking horrid thoughts of airplane crashes and life without her husband. It made her tremble, and it made her think of her first husband Jack. The very day he'd been shot down, she had learned the awful truth about his past. Rose found out that Jack Knight wasn't who he said he was but someone named James Castillo, a man who'd finagled his way into the Air Corps fighter program by lying and impersonating an officer, but worse than that, stealing a dead man's identity. Rose was deeply disturbed after she learned the truth; she remembered how Colonel Truscott had warned her about wanting to know too much. It was something that bothered her for many weeks afterward, making her regret her decision to marry Jack. She eventually had the marriage annulled once it was determined he'd been captured and interned in a Japanese P.O.W. camp. That was a very dark time for her and she didn't know what to do at first. She'd been attracted to the man, Jack Knight, she remembered very well, not his social or military standing. And she wondered if he had been truthful to her, portraying himself by his true identity (a lowly, working-class noncom from West Texas) would she have felt the same about him? She couldn't decide at the time. But now she was quite sure. Rose knew she could never stay with Jack, not after all that had been revealed. No, it would be living a lie, and that, she couldn't do.

"Well," she said at last, "I guess I'll have to start eating properly and watch what I do from now on."

"Right. Having a baby is a major undertaking for a woman."

Rose stood up. "Thank you, Doctor. I'll see you again soon."

The doctor got up. "I suspect so. Goodbye, Mrs McKavitt."

IN THE COLD light of dawn, McKavitt took stock of his group. The 479th's Mustangs were forming up on the taxiway; each pilot sat in their cockpit ready to take to the air and do battle with Germany's infamous Luftwaffe once more as they'd done so many times before. But on this gray November morning, they wouldn't be shackled to the bombers, they'd be given free rein to pursue the enemy all the way back to his base if necessary. General Warlick had given them the authorization to do what they did best—kill German fighters. Not just any German fighter, but jets; those high-flying speed demons that had so lately become such a worry and a danger. Although they'd appear to stick close to the bombers whilst flying over enemy territory, they had been given license to leave their charges and pursue, pursue any aircraft that attacked and shoot them down (jets specifically) or follow them to their base and strafe them as they tried to land.

The 479th launched three squadrons—forty-two Mustangs— with McKavitt in the lead. He was leading 434 Squadron's Red Flight with Spencer flying on his wing. McKavitt was a bit anxious as he eased the throttle ahead for takeoff. After a few days off, because of inclement weather, he was more than ready to fly a mission over Germany. Only after the landing gear came up and locked into place he did relax again. It seemed he was always more comfortable sitting in the cockpit of a fighter than standing on the ground. The rumble of the Mustang's mighty engine was a calming tonic.

The weather over Germany was dreadful; layers of clouds extended up at least 30,000 feet. The B-24's of the 2nd Air Division were at 25,000 feet, flying in a ragged formation, drifting in and out of wispy cloud layers. It was impossible to keep them all in sight. A miasma of flak soon added to the already cluttered atmosphere. McKavitt worried the Luftwaffe wouldn't be able to find the bombers in all those clouds if, they ever got airborne.

It was an uneventful mission. The only sign of the Luftwaffe were long contrails pinpointing two fighters high above the bomber stream—10,000 feet above. They circled in a wide turn and then disengaged. McKavitt wanted to give chase but decided not to; the sky was too cloudy that day and the Group would only get lost in it.

The next day, the 479th took off on a fighter sweep. They were to patrol the area around Osnabrück, specifically the airfields of Achmer and Hespe. These airfields were jet fighter bases and were athwart the main American bomber approach route. B-24's of the 392 BG would also be operating in the area, bombing industrial targets near Rheine. The one-hundred-and-one-strong bomber formation would surely draw the Messerschmitt jet fighters out of their bombproof revetments, hopefully putting them on a collision course with McKavitt's Mustangs. The 479th took off at 10:00 hours, and eventually rose to 20,000 feet, cruising at 250-mph as they crossed over the Rhine River.

McKavitt closely monitored the R/T, listening to the 392nd's radio transmissions, hoping to hear of a Luftwaffe attack. The B-24's were being escorted by two squadrons of the 56th Fighter Group—a paltry sum of thirty-two Thunderbolts; enticing bait for the Luftwaffe. If the jets made an appearance there would probably be a *staffel* or two of FW-190's or Bf-109's flying top cover. And it would be the same over Achmer and Hespe. The Krauts knew their Me-262 jets were highly vulnerable whilst taxiing on the runway, so they usually assigned some piston-engined aircraft to protect them. If indeed a jet or jets appeared, the Mustangs were to give chase, follow them all the way to their air bases if necessary, strafing them as they landed. Along with the protective CAP, heavy flak would also be a major factor as well as every other high-caliber anti-aircraft gun that ringed those jet bases. It would be a hotbed of activity, but in McKavitt's mind, well worth the risk. If he could add a Me-262 to his victory total, then he would consider his duty finally done.

The sweep went without incident. But as McKavitt and the 479th turned back for home, he observed two flights of Thunderbolts from the 56th cruising about 5,000 feet overhead. A moment later, a Me-262 appeared out of nowhere and shot down the trailing Thunderbolt of the rear flight. McKavitt rammed the throttle to max-power and climbed to intercept. The other three men of the Thunderbolt flight apparently did not notice the absence of their "Tail-End Charlie," so the Me-262 slid into the No.4 position in their flight and started shooting at the No. 3 Thunderbolt. But when the Kraut saw McKavitt's flight coming after him, he broke away in a steep climb, heading west to the Rhine River.

Soon, the whole squadron was chasing him. The Me-262 pilot was obviously quite cocky and arrogant; he performed some masterful aerobatic maneuvers for the pursuing Mustangs, flaunting his superior speed and climb capabilities. He gradually winged down to 15,000 feet, diving and turning, maintaining a steady speed of 500 miles-per-hour. Then he did something very bold. He suddenly whipped around 180 degrees and came charging toward the Mustangs chasing him, firing as he went. McKavitt turned into him head-on, all six guns blazing.

Eleven Mustangs scattered helter-skelter, north, south, east, and west trying to evade those ruinous 30-millimeter shells. But not McKavitt, he held his position and saw the Me-262 jerk its wings to the vertical and go thundering by, just missing a fatal collision. He thought he'd hit the jet with his gunfire but he wasn't sure; the Me-262 had zoomed by so fast that he really couldn't tell. But once McKavitt got turned around, he saw the twin-engined jet streaming smoke from one of its engines. Yes—he had hit it! But that damned machine was so quick that just a mere three-second turnaround had cost McKavitt a couple of miles of sky. He was awed as much as he was angered. He duly radioed his wingman Lieutenant Spencer.

"Red Two!" McKavitt shouted. *"Where the hell are you?"*

"Coming around on your six, Uncle Leader."

"Well, close it up! I'm going after that jet. I hit him and he's trailing smoke. He's probably heading back to Achmer."

"Roger that, Uncle Leader," Spencer replied. *"Closing it up."*

"And that goes for the rest of you guys," McKavitt radioed his squadron. *"Get back in formation. Let's follow that bastard!"*

The 434th responded obediently, and soon, twelve Mustangs were winging after the jet, slowly closing in on it, Colonel McKavitt leading the charge. The Me-262 had obviously been badly damaged. Its left engine was streaming dirty black smoke and causing the jet fighter to slow down, making it yield to the pursuing Mustangs. Nevertheless, the German pilot kept the jet on a downward course, rapidly losing altitude, gradually making its way back to its airbase, which was Achmer, as McKavitt had correctly guessed. And once the smoking jet got below 1,000 feet, it turned for the far end of the runway and began its approach. A wall of flak greeted the American fighter planes.

McKavitt weaved through that storm of steel as he came around after the jet. He could see its flaps and landing gear were down, and he knew it was about to land. He only had a few seconds to catch it and shoot it down if he wanted credit for an aerial kill. Otherwise, it would just be tallied as a ground kill which wouldn't help his personal score. He gassed the throttle and zoomed down in a fast dive, registering 450-miles-per-hour on his airspeed indicator. Spencer was right with him. The rest of the squadron had pulled up in an abrupt climb, dodging the flak, watching out for enemy fighters.

McKavitt closed to 50 yards, sighted, and fired.

The Me-262 burst into flames just as its two back wheels touched down. Then it bounced, tail-over-nose, and exploded in an orange-black fireball, scattering all over the runway into flaming pieces. McKavitt winged over in a climbing turn, victorious at last.

"Got him!" he exhorted proudly, clenching his fist.

"You did it, sir!" Spencer responded. *"That's a confirmed kill!"*

"It sure is, Red Two! Number Twenty—" a loud bang and jolt interrupted his joyous affirmation. The Mustang's engine shuddered to a halt, then McKavitt saw the propeller blades windmill to a dead stop. He'd been hit by flak—a direct hit in the engine.

"Ah, hell!" he cursed. *"I've been hit!"*

He knew he was too low to bail out, scarcely registering 300 feet. He'd have to make a force-landing and hope for the best. He circled the lamed Mustang around in a gliding turn, flak going off around him. He saw an adjoining field and banked toward it, pushing the stick forward, his heart pounding in his ears, his lips spread wide across clinched teeth. *"I'm going down, goddammit!"* he announced. *"Crash landing!"*

The Mustang came down on its belly, skidding sideways. Dust and dirt billowed up in a dark cloud. The propeller blades warped backwards as the nose dug into the cold ground. Then the Mustang halted. German soldiers duly surrounded it, closing in on all sides.

CHAPTER 4

1 DECEMBER 1944
FRIDAY, 0700 HOURS
CAMP X, WHITBY, ONTARIO

COLONEL FAIRBAIRN'S office was heated by a potbelly stove and Jack stepped appreciatively toward it. An American named Major Ken Cartwright and a British-Canadian named Lieutenant Lipton lined up beside him facing the Colonel and another man who sat eyeing them carefully, his face expressionless.

"At ease, lads," Colonel Fairbairn ordered then pointed to the man in the Army uniform sitting next to him. "This is Colonel Bruce, from the S.O. branch. He's come from Washington. He has a job for you."

Lipton raised an eyebrow and glanced sideways at Cartwright and whispered: *"Special Mission."*

"What about our leave, sir?" Jack asked. "Will we get leave before or after this mission?"

"After." The Colonel's voice was cold and crisp. "Lipton and Cartwright have been on special missions before, of course. You, Captain, are included as a reserve... what you Americans call a 'back-up' man." He glanced at Cartwright. "Is that the right term?"

"I believe so, sir," murmured Cartwright.

Fairbairn looked to Colonel Bruce. "Okay, It's your show now."

Colonel Bruce was slender and his face angular and serious looking. Steely, blue-gray eyes gave him a forbidding expression. He said: "There's not much I can tell you right now, except that you'll all be flown to Scotland immediately. There's no need to pack, gentlemen. You will be reequipped at your destination. The job you are to carry out is one of great secrecy and urgency. You will, of course, tell no-one of this." He glanced at Colonel Fairbairn. "I don't think it's necessary for me to say anymore than that—a plane is waiting for them."

55

A thin smile creased Jack's lips.

"I'm sorry about postponing your leave, gentlemen. But you three are the best men for the job I have in mind. Perhaps... the only men who could bring it off. Shall we go?"

Colonel Fairbairn wished them godspeed; they left the office in a closed staff car. Thirty minutes later, they boarded a Douglas C-47 Dakota heading for Newfoundland. From there they took another plane and flew to Greenland, then nonstop to Scotland. It gave Jack time to catch his breath, reflect upon the past two months...

THE CANADIAN COLONEL had asked the straightforward question: "Would you be willing to jump from a plane behind enemy lines if you knew you would be tortured to death if caught?"

Jack answered with a resounding—YES! It was a question that'd been put to thousands of American G.I.'s during the war by recruiters for General William "Wild Bill" Donovan's Office of Strategic Services (O.S.S.) It was a highly dangerous job, one that required cool nerves, good physical condition and linguistic flair, so much so, that out of the one hundred volunteers who had sighed up that day, only five were accepted. Jack was one of those accepted.

The winnowing of this would-be agent began with a security check, a psychological exam, and some timed exercises designed to gauge his ability to think and act under pressure. One test required him to carry a heavy load across a deep creek with nothing to use for a bridge but wooden planks, all while enduring harassment from a gang of heckling bystanders. He passed that screening and went on to attend the secret "Camp X" in Ontario, for an (assassination and elimination) training program operated by O.S.S. Special Operations. He learned everything from camouflage to the art of silent killing, with still more advanced training in specialties like sabotage and communications.

Basic O.S.S. training was an unbroken string of twenty-one, eighteen-hour days of code work, interrogation exercises, memory tests, all designed to prepare him psychologically for the life of an O.S.S. agent, which was a constant gamble of detection. Jack zealously guarded his new identity during training (Nicklaus Daemon). And he was constantly watched; even the party at the end of training was an evaluation test.

Later, courses toughened him for special operations. Jack learned to live off the land, and to fight and kill with his hands, a thing he already had some experience with. By the time he had finished his training, techniques as varied as parachuting, blowing up bridges, operating radios, lock-picking, setting up booby traps and forging signatures, Jack was ready for operations. Perhaps he was ready for other things too. "If I make it through this dang war," he quipped on the final day of training, "I'll make a perfect gangster!"

Despite his background and his past history, Jack was the ideal candidate for the O.S.S. and he was suitably seduced by the idea of being a mysterious man with secret knowledge. He certainly was an unusual type of man. His insatiable appetite for the unconventional and spectacular went far beyond the ordinary. And with a good measure of abandon thrown in, he was a perfect fit for this type of work.

He was never told what was in store for him. After being released from the hospital and then sent stateside, he was put through a rigorous three-day screening of physical and mental agility tests at a suburban Washington facility known only as Station S. Once he passed the tests, he was sent to Camp X for training in techniques of survival, sabotage and espionage. If he had failed the tests, he would have been sent to an Army prison camp to serve out a sentence for the remainder of the war, perhaps longer, according to General Truscott's terse estimations.

Jack had learned to send Morse code and to repair radio transmitters; to kill silently by garrote, knife, and with bare hands, to parachute into almost any kind of terrain, and to handle Allied and Axis firearms—skills needed to work behind enemy lines. One veteran O.S.S. officer marveled at the speed in which Jack had learned his trade. Indeed, he'd come among them, this aspiring spymaster, like an innocent girl from finishing school anxious to learn the seasoned demimondaine ways of old professionals. But the initial feelings of awe and respect soon evaporated, and it turned out that this sly finishing school byproduct had learned all the tricks and devices of the old professionals in no time at all. And all the screening and training would pay off handsomely one day, Jack knew well. He would need all of it to accomplish his task. He was a new man with a new name. He felt different, he even looked different. Gone was the long hair and sideburns, gone was the mustache.

THE NEXT TEN days were ones of intense advanced training. They were billeted in a makeshift camp of wooden huts in the Scottish Cairngorm Mountains. Fresh winter snow lay sprinkled on the slopes and all three men spent some extremely long days training on boats and dinghies. Lipton and Cartwright were expert sailors, and they were surprised to see Jack was almost as good as they were.

"I've got a bit of experience, you see," he told them. "Spent some time in dinghies earlier in the war."

"Must be why they picked us for this mission," said Lipton. "I suppose we're the three best men for the job."

And so they were. And during those ten days when they weren't honing their sailing skills, they were instructed in Danish geography; they learned a smattering of the Danish language (Cartwright was fluent). They spent many hours getting in and out of a rubber dinghy and paddling across Scottish lochs. It was dull work, but it made them very proficient. They'd not seen much of Colonel Bruce from Special Operations, but one evening he appeared and briefed them on their mission.

"All right, gentlemen,"he said, settling himself on the corner of the table. "Briefly—this is what you'll be doing. You will board a destroyer which will take you to the Danish coast by nightfall. You'll leave the destroyer by dinghy and go ashore. A Professor Nils Johansen will be waiting in a safe house near a coastal town, and you will contact him and bring him back to England. That, basically, is your mission."

There was silence in the hut. Outside, the wind whistled eerily.

"Now for the details. Professor Johansen wants to defect to our side. He's a scientist—an atomic physicist—to be exact. His work is top-secret, and he now wishes to lend his expertise to the Allies, not the Nazis, in exchange for asylum in England. He's contacted one of our agents in Nazi-occupied Denmark and has asked to be extricated... and we've told him we'll do it."

"Where is Johansen now, sir?" Cartwright asked.

"In the township of Thisted, not far from the coast where you'll land... some fifteen miles inland. Once you get the Professor, the destroyer will be waiting off-shore to pick you up."

"How will we get to the house once we land?"

"One of our agents in the area will have a car at your disposal, hidden in a garage near the place where you'll come ashore. Use it to drive to the house where Johansen is staying."

"What about me, sir?" Jack asked. "You said I was a *back-up* man. What'll I be doing, huh?"

"You'll go as far as the coast—stay aboard the destroyer. You'll only go ashore if either Cartwright of Lipton are unable to continue for whatever reason. If that happens, you'll take that man's place."

Cartwright was looking thoughtful. "This Professor Johansen, sir, is he the same atomic physicist who won the Nobel Prize?"

"Yes, that's the man. He won the Nobel Prize in 1922 for his contributions in furthering atomic structure and quantum theory. He recently met with Professor Heidelberg, a noted Nazi physicist in Copenhagen for an atomic conference. We sent one of our agents to attend the conference carrying a pistol, with orders to shoot Heidelberg if his lecture indicated the Nazis were close to completing a bomb. You were picked, Cartwright, because you met him once. Remember?"

"Yeah, I remember. That's why I asked."

"It's important we get the right man, you understand?"

Cartwright nodded. "I get the picture."

"What if Cartwright gets killed or something?" Jack interjected querulously. "Lipton and I don't know Johansen from Adam."

"You'll be shown photographs of the Professor. In the event of Cartwright dropping out, God forbid, you'll have to rely on photographs for identification. But we'd rather Johansen be recognized by someone who's met him. It's safer." Colonel Bruce sighed. "It wouldn't be beyond the Germans to try a trick such as substituting someone in Johansen's place, especially if they're aware that an attempt to abduct him might take place. So, are there any questions?"

No one spoke. The silence seemed to last an eternity.

Colonel Bruce stood up and glanced at his watch. "Okay, gentlemen, let's get a move on now. The destroyer that takes you to Denmark is waiting. You sail at once."

Jack watched as Colonel Bruce walked out of the hut, mumbling bitterly, wondering why he'd been relegated to a "back-up" slot. He had not joined the O.S.S. to play second fiddle to other agents.

AT 02:30 HOURS, the sporadic moonlight that appeared momentarily from time to time from behind thick dark clouds, the dim coastline of Denmark suddenly appeared dead ahead. The destroyer Jack and his comrades were aboard plowed through the ice-cold waters, getting ever closer. There was ice on the rigging and wire stays, and on all the other metal fixtures of the exposed deck of the British destroyer. They were dangerous to touch, so cold were they.

Jack, Lipton, and Cartwright were bundled up in their cold weather survival gear, the fur-trimmed hoods of their anoraks raised around their heads. They stood in a close group at the base of the ladder leading to the bridge where two Royal Navy officers watched the shoreline slowly drifting by. They gazed through binoculars, searching for a landmark that would signify that they'd arrived in the right place to launch the rubber dinghy in which the two men would go ashore.

Jack rubbed his gloved hands together and shivered. "Can't s-say how s-sorry I'm about staying aboard, f-fellers," he chattered. "It's colder than a well-digger's ass in wintertime."

"Maybe you *will* go," said Lipton, grinning, turning his steely eyes to Cartwright. "I think I got me a bum leg."

"You mean you can't go and I—" Jack broke off once he realized the Canadian was just joking. "Ah, shut up, you crazy Canuck. Stop screwing around already."

A voice above them called out softly: "Stand by, chaps. We expect to reach the proper coordinates in twenty minutes. Better check your gear once more. Make sure that dinghy is shipshape, aye? If that thing springs a leak, you've had it. That water is freezing cold."

The destroyer's engines which had registered a steady thrum of power since they had left port, died away and the forward momentum slowed down ever so slightly. On the deck, Lipton and Cartwright checked off their equipment from a list they'd been given. Each man had a bulging O.D. green rucksack which contained rations, flashlights, spare clothing, cigarettes, fighting knifes, compass and maps, and other necessary items. Propped next to each rucksack was a .45-caliber M3 sub-machine gun, also known as the "grease-gun," each with a fixed silencer and bandoleers jam-packed with extra 30-round magazines.

Jack held three sets of web gear, and he adroitly inserted the extra magazines into the pouches while the other two men inspected the rubber dinghy which was lashed against the guardrails of the ship. It had been inflated an hour earlier and was still firm and stiff. Looking forward, they could see the outline of two 4-inch anti-aircraft gun turrets on the foredeck. The gun crews were closed up at that hour and even as they watched, they noticed the guns were slowly rotating, aimed at the dark clouds above. A naval officer in a peacoat suddenly appeared.

"Expectin' some trouble, mister?" Jack asked, jerking his head in the direction of the anti-aircraft guns.

"No. No chance of that, mate. Too much cloud cover," the naval officer replied. "Just routine action stations," he explained. "We're well within enemy waters. Don't want to be caught napping, see?" He glanced at his wristwatch. "We've spotted the landing ground. You'll go in ten minutes. Just checking if you blokes are ready."

"We're ready," Cartwright affirmed. "And sooner the better."

"Right," Lipton agreed. "Will you be the ship picking us up?"

"Aye." The officer nodded. "We'll wait off shore every night for the next three nights at the same place, time, and location. Flash the Morse code letters 'P.O.D.' and we'll send a cutter in for you."

"P.O.D.?" Jack questioned.

"Professor on Delivery," came the reply accompanied with a wry smile. "Our skipper's got an odd sense of humor."

The destroyer turned slightly inshore and the coastline came into shadowy relief; it was near. A muted call came from the bridge.

"Attention On Deck.... Standby To Embark Passengers. Agents Lipton And Cartwright Report To Gangway With Gear."

Jack bent down and picked up the third set of web gear which had been laid out. "Well, won't be needin' this, I guess," he murmured. "I'll stow it below. Good luck, you guys."

He put out a paw to shake hands with Cartwright and Lipton—and the destroyer blew up amidships as a result of a violent explosion. The ship seemed to leave the water with the force of the blast. A great column of flame burst through the deck forward of the bridge and Lipton saw the bridge crumple and totter sideways. Then the geyser of water that had been thrown up by the explosion fell in a smothering deluge that forced him to his knees. In the same instant the destroyer tilted sideways at a frightful angle and everything loose on the deck rolled and jolted toward the dipping guardrails. Another explosion devastated the interior of the vessel of the already broken hull, and it buckled precariously. Then Lipton caught sight of Cartwright lying with his head through the guardrails, about to fall into the sea below. Lipton threw himself full length and grabbed the American's ankle, hauling him back in. Cartwright was dazed but unhurt.

"We must have hit a mine. Two of them!" Lipton declared. "The ship's sinking!" And just to confirm his words, the destroyer suddenly settled lower in the dark water.

"What's the skipper doing?"

Lipton shook his head. "We don't have a skipper anymore. The bridge went up when the first mine exploded. He's dead, I'm sure."

Another explosion rocked the destroyer from stem to stern. The bow dipped and went under and Lipton and Cartwright went sliding down the steeply pitching deck. They both scrabbled at a hatch cover as they slid by and barely grabbed hold of it.

"The crew? Where are they?"

"Don't know." Lipton steadied himself and got to his feet. "Don't see anyone. That officer we were talking to... he just disappeared. Blown over the side, I guess."

The bow dipped further, and the stern rose clear of the water.

"Where's the dinghy?"

"Gone."

"We'd better be gone, too. This boat's going to the bottom."

They struggled to the side. With the bow under water and the stern raised high, the water seemed a long way off to them.

"It's going to be cold," said Lipton.

"It's our only way out. Stay put... and we go down with it."

"And Daemon?"

"No sign of him. C'mon, man. Let's jump. I figure we've got about a minute or two left. She's sinking fast!"

They both had one leg over the guardrails and were taking deep breaths before jumping when they heard a familiar voice. It shouted:

"Okay, fellers, jump! I gotcha."

"What the heck?" Cartwright turned to look behind him.

"Down here!" came the same voice. It was Jack.

They peered down. Floating on the swirling swell amid a grow-ing mass of flotsam that had drifted out of the doomed destroyer, they saw the rubber dinghy. And sitting securely in the center, Jack. He had a paddle in one hand and was waving with the other.

"Fer Heaven's sake, jump you idiots!" Jack yelled hoarsely. "I've been paddlin' around looking fer you two! If'n ya don't get off that dang thing—yer going down to the bottom with it."

The ship lurched precariously and Cartwright and Lipton hesi-tated no longer. They pushed off and dropped into the sea. The wa-ter was liquid ice, and it beat the breath from their bodies. It squeezed their lungs in a vice-like grip. It almost felt as if it were crushing their skulls. They surfaced a moment later, mouths agape for air. They both would have surely have gone under a second time if Jack, leaning perilously overside of the dinghy, had not grabbed their collars and held them up. That brief respite enabled them to catch their breath, enabled them to gather their wits, made them re-alize that if they did not get out of the freezing water quickly, they would die.

They recovered and grabbed hold of the dinghy. Its fat swollen sides didn't help much. But they scrambled and struggled, and with Jack pulling them in, managed to squirm themselves over the side and to safety. A paddle slapped Cartwright on the side of his face.

"Git going, fella. Move it!" Jack was yelling frantically. "Git that paddle and row, by Gawd! It'll warm ya up. And it'll git us away from *that* dang thing!"

Cartwright gathered himself. The freezing-cold water had numbed his senses completely, but he was recovering. Above him, he saw the towering menace that was the sinking destroyer. The dinghy had drifted close and under the stern and right above them were the still turning screws of the twin propellers. They looked like giant revolving blades of a threshing machine. Then the dinghy was moving away. Jack was paddling like a madman, flailing away at the water. Lipton was working hard too, and the rubber dinghy floated away from the black threat of the dying ship. And just in time too. For they were only fifty feet away when the stern rose even higher above them, and on a high-pitched crumpling sound that echoed on the night air like the shrieking wail of a banshee, slid downward. Within seconds, the ship vanished beneath the waves. Giant air bubbles floated to the surface and burst. Boxes, planks, chairs, tables, detritus of all sorts, everything not lashed down on the deck came bubbling to the surface and spread like an ominous stain of death. As if transfixed by the same thought, the three men paddled toward the now gently undulating flotsam. Back and forth they went, calling out, but no one answered.

Many minutes later, Jack stopped paddling and said, "If anybody survived allthat, well... they'd be frozen stiff by now. Dead."

"No survivors. No one," Cartwright commented glumly.

"Except us three." Lipton sighed heavily. He sat in the dinghy's stern, a paddle laying across his knees. "Now what?"

"Yeah, it's a long way home from here."

"We don't go home, fellas." Jack looked to the Danish coastline and pointed. "We go—that-a-way!"

"Ashore?"

"If we're caught, we'll end up in a P.O.W. camp."

"To hell with that!" Jack growled. "That ain't a gonna happen, brother. Naw siree! Been there—done that."

Jack's bold words held the other two riveted for a moment.

"Look, why don't we go ashore as planned, hmm? Get on with our mission." Jack gestured across the debris-strewn water, his lips a hard line. "I reckon Colonel Bruce would want us to do that... he didn't send us out here fer nothin', right?"

Cartwright nodded. "Right! Let's do it. Let's get the Professor."

"What about you, mate ?" Lipton said to Jack.

"Me? I'll do whatever you guys do," said Jack with a snort. He rummaged around in the bottom of the rubber dinghy and pulled out two rucksacks. "I wouldn't mind having a crack at the Germans."

"Whoa! Where in the hell did you get those?" Cartwright gazed at Jack with bewildered eyes.

"Fished 'em out of the water, that's where." Jack groped further in the hidden recesses of the dinghy. "When all hell broke those— the first explosion—I was blown straight over the side, you see. And everything went over with me. All our gear. And I got most of it before it sank."

Cartwright and Lipton exchanged incredulous glances.

"The rucksacks, the web gear," Jack waxed on, "most of the stuff, anyway. All except our grease-guns, unfortunately. They sank like hundred pound sacks." He almost sounded apologetic.

"Well, I'll be damned," Cartwright replied, stroking his jaw. "Then we go—get on with the mission." He plunged his paddle into the water and rowed. Jack and Lipton quickly followed suit.

They were feeling cold again; a little exercise would warm them up. And soon, the rubber dinghy scooted across the water at a heightened speed. High in the sky came the first hints of dawn, and the gray coastline looked as ominous as ever. As they drew near, Jack wondered how they would accomplish their mission now. But he didn't care at that point. He was just glad to be alive right now.

THERE WAS NO BEACH or foreshore, only a fortified shoreline; a stark gray seawall jutted out from the shore obstructing the mirror-surface of the sea. They stopped paddling and let the dinghy drift forward silently. All three men looked searchingly.

Jack was the first to put into words what the others were think-ing."That's one seawall we ain't gonna penetrate," he said. "Look at it. No place to squeeze through, no break in the line of concrete, not a dang thing! No beach to land on either. Take it from me, fellers... if'n we're going ashore, it ain't here."

Cartwright sadly had to agree, but he didn't give up that easily. He paddled the dinghy closer and closer until they were right next to the seawall. "We'll paddle along the edge of the wall. There's got to be a break in it somewhere. An inlet of some sort; something we can slip through easily."

Paddling and pulling themselves along and against the wall, they covered some three hundred yards when Cartwright put up his hand to stop them. "Listen!" he whispered "Engines!"

They stopped, holding on to the stony seawall, motionless in a pool of shadowy darkness cast by the wall. They could all hear the noise now; the steadily throbbing *blub-blub-blub-blub-blub* engine noise of a sizable diesel-driven boat.

"Sounds like something big," Lipton uttered. "Like an E-boat."

They waited anxiously. The boat came closer. And then sudden-ly, they saw the dark silhouette of a long, slender E-boat, just as Lip-ton had suspected (one of the S-100 class) by the looks of its three anti-aircraft guns and forward wheelhouse. A cutting curve of white water foamed at the bow, and above the steady drone of of its diesel engines, they could hear voices and the occasional pinprick of light as though someone were smoking a cigarette on deck.

"Gawd!" said Jack. "You were right, Lipton... it's an E-boat."

The three agents watched silently as the vessel motored past them. It was almost out of sight in the half-light when it turned in toward the wall and disappeared.

"Bloody hell! Where did it go?" Lipton looked to Jack and then to Cartwright in astonishment. "It just... vanished."

Jack and Cartwright plunged their paddles in the water, surging the dinghy forward. "C'mon, Lipton!" Jack spouted. "Get with it, fella! We're following that boat."

"Yeah. It didn't just vanish, man," Cartwright explained. "It turned into an inlet—between that rocky seawall up ahead, I'll bet."

"And what will be on the other side, I wonder?"

"Don't ask me. I've never been here before."

"A harbor," Jack surmised plying his paddle with the will of a man possessed, and the rubber dinghy skimmed over the glass-like surface. "Why else would an E-boat turn to an inlet in the seawall?"

"Makes sense," Cartwright agreed, smiling. "Glad we don't have to screw around trying to get over that thing." He gestured to the stony seawall, shaking his head.

They had reached the inlet now, following the wake of the E-boat; the rocky seawall rose high on both sides of the inlet, enclosing them. The dinghy rose and fell uncomfortably, tossing and pitching on the churning backwash of the German E-boat.

"Hang on, fellers," Jack urged. "We gotta keep up with that thing, follow it to its dock."

"They'll see us," Lipton returned.

"Naw, keep paddling. They cain't see us even if they were looking fer us," Jack declared. "The closer we get the better. These breakwaters twist and turn and narrow. We don't wanna get lost."

They hunkered down and paddled harder, moving swiftly, riding the recurring waves of the E-boat's wake. Nearby, they could hear the water slapping the sides of rocks. And as a half-hour passed, all three men were beginning to tire. Then in the next moment, they rounded the edge of the second seawall and saw the E-boat, moving slowly, less than a hundred yards ahead. Beyond that, they saw a concrete quay. Further on, were a assorted collection of gable-front-ed houses and long sheds. They formed a neat pattern against the emerging dawn skyline.

"What now?" Lipton traded glances with Jack and Cartwright. "If we hang about, it'll be daylight and someone's going to see us."

"We'll go ashore." Cartwright pointed to the right-edge of the waterfront town before them. "Over where those houses end."

Ten minutes later, they were wading toward land through a jumbled mass of jagged rocks carrying the gear Jack managed to salvage. It was still dark, not quite daylight. When the packs and gear were ashore Cartwright said, "Let's sink the dinghy. If the Krauts find it, they'll start looking for whoever landed here, meaning us!"

Jack and Lipton hastily heaped in some rocks and then slashed the rubber hull below the waterline. Within seconds, their mode of arrival disappeared beneath the watery surface.

"We gotta hide somewhere, dry out, eat something," Jack evinced with a stolid expression. "You fellers gotta a better idea?"

Lipton and Cartwright shook their heads.

Cartwright pointed to Jack. "You go and find a place, okay?" he ordered. "An empty shed, or something similar. If you're not back in a half-hour, we'll move on... assuming you've had it." His puffy eyes were bleak as he added: "Remember, we're here to locate Professor Johansen and get him back to England. That's our prime objective, not start a private war with the Germans." He was looking right at Jack when he said that.

Jack nodded in agreement. Then he clambered over the rocky berm ahead of them, half-crouching, and vanished in the half-light, heading toward the waterfront houses of the little coastal town. Cartwright and Lipton began to take stock of their equipment. Their extra clothing was soaking wet and the packets of biscuits were soggy. Their dining was confined to the few tins of bully beef they carried in their rucksacks.

"Damn! Everything is soaking wet," Lipton grumbled.

"It'll all dry out given time," Cartwright replied optimistically. "And the Danish people will help us. They hate being occupied by the Nazis, believe me."

There wasn't much they could do until Jack came back, so they settled in, sheltering themselves among the rocks. They sat there fighting the cold that was slowly sapping their will and motivation.

"IT'S AN OLD storage shed for fish," Jack explained. "It stinks to high heaven and its dark but it'll do." He was back now and helping the others carry their gear across the rocks. "And what's even better, it ain't been used in a coon's age."

"How do you figure that?" asked Cartwright.

"Dust and cobwebs—all over the place. Take my word, no one's been in that shed for a long time."

The shed was a tall, wooden structure with a tar-covering on the outside. Inside, there were staves of broken barrels and piles of rotted rope lying around. The windows were covered in dust and emitted little light; but it was a sanctuary from the cold—warm and dry.

They opened up three more tins of bully beef and ate ravenously, scooping out the meat with their fighting knives. Hungry as they were, none of them could stomach the saltwater-soaked biscuits. To slake their thirst, they put handfuls of snow in the empty tins and drank it once it melted. Jack found a pack of cigarettes and matches that hadn't been soaked by the sea and they all lit up once they finished eating and drinking. They sat there silently for a while.

"We'll light a fire once it gets dark," said Cartwright. "Can't risk it yet. If someone sees smoke billowing from this shed, a shed that's supposed to be empty, they'll come over and investigate."

And so they praised the Northern latitudes that brought nighttime so early, because by the time they considered it safe to light a fire, they were shivering in their boots from the cold. They lit a fire in an old bucket, filling it with splintered staves, and soon, the fire was glowing red. They laid out their extra clothes and dried them by the fire and heated two cans of bully beef. By the time the fire had heated the old shed, and warmed them up, they were contemplating their next move.

Cartwright pulled out a map. It was ragged and wet and stained with seawater but still quite readable. His forefinger jabbed at a certain spot on the map. "We're right here—Hanstholm." He moved his finger, tracing a line southeast across the damp map. "And this is the town where Professor Johansen is staying—Thisted. It's a fishing village about fifteen miles south from here; we can walk it."

"Walk?" Jack groaned. "Thought we was driving?"

"Change of plans, Daemon, due to extenuating circumstances.

We were supposed to have landed five miles southwest of here and commandeer a hidden car. But since we were blown off course, literally, we've got to hoof it now, on foot."

"Right," Lipton agreed. "Hanstholm is the last place we wanted to come ashore. This place is a fortified Nazi fortress, part of the Atlantic Wall defenses. There's two large naval guns near the northern shore—as big as a battleship's, I'm told. They can blast any ship out of the water several miles away."

"Maybe that's what sank our ship, huh?" Jack proposed.

"No," Cartwright replied. "I'm sure our ship hit a couple of mines. The explosions came from beneath the waterline."

"Let's pack up and get going," Lipton put in. "We need to find the Professor, figure out how we're going to get him out of here."

"Right. We can use the main road. Keep our eyes open; if we see a German patrol, we can hide. It'll be faster."

Jack, who was standing near the door, stubbing out his cigarette, an eye peering through one of the many holes in it, said: "Reckon there are many Krauts around these parts, Cartwright?"

"Not too many. A company of infantry and a platoon of artillery gunners, I think? A small garrison, considering it's a Nazi fortress. But it's able to call on support from the bigger towns should they need it." Something about Jack's sudden preoccupation with the hole in the door made him say: "Why do you ask?"

The lanky Texan turned about with a sly grin on his face. "Because there's two Krauts coming straight for us," he whispered. "Looks like a couple fellers on patrol—stoppin' off for a smoke."

They could hear heavy jack-boots on the pavement getting louder and louder. A shadow passed over the door, then a sudden thud as though something heavy was propped against the shed wall.

"That's a g-gun, I'll bet," Lipton said in a nervous whisper.

They heard the faint, guttural tones of two Germans, then the acrid smell of cigarette smoke wafting through the planking. Jack jerked a nod and winked. "Told ya so."

"Hey, we could use their weapons," Cartwright said in a low voice. "What do say we grab them, eh?" He unsheathed his knife. "Won't take too long. No noise, okay?"

Jack nodded in approval. "Yup, we need their guns, alright. Let's get 'em, Cartwright."

With that said, he eased the door open and stepped gently outside, waiting until Cartwright made the long walk around the far end of the shed. They now had the two German soldiers standing between them. Simultaneously, they edged around the corners of the shed. The two Germans, preoccupied by cigarette smoking and conversation, never knew what hit them. Jack and Cartwright's long fighting knives made quick work of their victims, killing them soundlessly. Within seconds, the bodies and machine pistols were being hauled inside the shed.

"The sooner we go now, the better, chaps," said Lipton. "Those two Germans will be missed as soon as they fail to check in. Maybe two hours from now... maybe in two minutes." He kicked one of the rucksacks with a boot. "What about this stuff?

"Leave it," Cartwright replied carelessly. "We don't need it. We should rendezvous with Professor Johansen—ASAP. Hopefully by this time tomorrow night we'll be on our way back to England."

"Yeah? How?" asked Jack quarrelsomely. "We slashed and sank the dingy, remember?"

"We'll just have to steal a boat. There are dozens of fishing boats in the harbor. We'll nab the Professor and then head back here. He may even have friends who can help... arrange for a boat to be waiting for us. C'mon, let's get moving."

All they took with them, apart from the recently acquired MP-40 machine pistols, were the fire-dried clothes on their backs. Their white trousers and fur-trimmed anoraks would make them virtually invisible in freshly fallen snow. Ten minutes later, they were walking along a narrow darkened road heading southwest for Thisted.

CHAPTER 5

AFTER HIS CAPTURE, they marched Colonel David McKavitt an hour until he reached the town of Osnabrück. As he walked down the center of the main street, the German population turned out to gawk and utter murmurs of hatred at the sight of the American airman. He was then coaxed into the back of a truck and driven south near Frankfurt, to the main Luftwaffe interrogation camp at Wetzlar, known as Dulag Luft; it was the first stop for U.S. Army Air Corps personnel captured in German occupied Europe. The camp had four large wooden barracks, two of which were connected by a passage and known affectionately to the prisoners as the "cooler." Two of the barracks contained two hundred cells eight-feet-high, five-feet-wide, and twelve-feet-long. Each cell held a cot, table, a chair and an electric bell for the P.O.W. to call a guard. The third barracks contained the administrative headquarters. The fourth barracks, an odd, L-shaped structure, held the interrogation offices, files and all the records. Dulag Luft was surrounded by a ten-foot barbed wire fence and the perimeter was equipped with floodlights and watchtowers. Upon arrival at Dulag Luft, Colonel McKavitt was stripped and his uniform searched. Then they put him into a cell described as solitary confinement. There, the Reception Officer visited him, along with an interpreter, because the Reception Officer was not fluent in English. Yet, he endeavored to persuade McKavitt to answer all the questions on the "form" then transmitted this form, together with his assessment of McKavitt's character, to the Chief of Interrogation, a Major, who, in turn detailed the most suitable member of his staff to conduct the questioning.

71

The interrogations were held in McKavitt's cell, but more often than not, in the office of the Political Interrogator. The interrogations were short, and they continued for four straight days, often twice per day. The political interrogation officer compiled, in the form of basic statements, the information which he had gleaned as a result of his oral examination of Colonel McKavitt, and these statements were then forwarded to the Luftwaffe Operations Staff in Berlin

The interrogators often used threats and violent language, calling McKavitt a "murderer of children" threatening him with prolonged solitary confinement or half-rations unless he talked. He was threatened with death, considered a spy unless he identified himself as an airman by revealing technical information on the subject of radar and Air Corps combat tactics. Confinement in an unbearably frigid cell and fictitious shootings of comrades was resorted to in the early phases. But intimidation yielded inferior results and the "friendly approach" was soon considered best by the Germans.

Colonel McKavitt's interrogations at the hands of Dulag Luft personnel was "correct" as far as physical violence was concerned. One insistent interrogator, exasperated by polite refusals to give more than his name, rank, and serial number or, more precisely because of an exceptionally smart remark on McKavitt's part, lost his temper and struck the American officer. But it didn't go beyond that angry slap on the face—one dealt in the heat of the moment; physical violence was not employed as a standard policy. On the other hand, no amount of calculated mental depression, privation and psychological blackmail was considered excessive. After the final unsuccessful interrogation, Colonel McKavitt was forced to undress and issued wool coveralls and sent to the "cooler" as a punitive measure for ten days; the full amount permitted by the Geneva Convention was thirty days.

For the majority of each day, he exercised, keeping himself fit as he could. He pretended he had a jump rope, and he "skipped" for hours. Then he rested, exercising his brain by trying to remember all the songs he was taught in school. After three days, he could sing them perfectly. Then he tried to remember every date he'd had with Rose, starting from the time he left the house until he arrived at the restaurant, and everything he'd said to her during those magical dinner dates.

After eight days, his boots were worn thin from skipping on the gritty floor. So he decided to do calisthenics. He did push-ups; he did sit-ups; he laid on his back and cycled his legs. He slept very little. When he marked the tenth day, he felt weak and listless in spite of all his efforts to stay fit. And he hoped the other two men he'd arrived with had tried to keep themselves fit, too. He knew the R.A.F. officer would survive but he worried about the Lieutenant.

He was not released on the tenth day, nor the next. There were thirteen marks on the wall before the cell door opened and the guard told him to step out. Without a word, he was led down a long corridor to the Office of the Chief Interrogator. As he trudged down that lonely corridor feeling tired, hungry, dejected, and some ten pounds lighter, he had time to reflect upon the events that had brought him to this sad situation. A new chapter in his military career was about to begin, one he had not expected: enduring the war as a P.O.W.

A STARK RED swastika flag hung menacingly on a flagpole above the door of the Chief Interrogator's office as the American pilot was ushered inside. He was hand-cuffed and was then taken into a dimly lit room where a lean-faced Luftwaffe Major sat behind a desk. He studied McKavitt in a trance-like silence for a moment, twiddling an ordinary pencil between his fingers, then said:

"Für Dich ist der Krieg vorbei!" quipped the Major in a spiteful German tone. (For you the war is over!)

McKavitt didn't say a word.

"Now then, tell me the name of your unit and its location."

McKavitt spoke up, reciting his name, rank and serial number. "I am not obliged to tell you more than that, Major. Although I will say one more thing. I came here to shoot down your aircraft. And that's just what I did—did a pretty good job of it, too."

The Major scoffed softly and made a notation on the piece of paper laying in front of him. "You almost killed yourself taking down one of our fighter jets, Colonel. Was that also part of your orders?"

Silence.

"Come, come now, Colonel. Speak up!" the Major insisted. "Let's not play dumb, *ja?*"

More silence.

"We know who you are. You are regarded as quite the extraordinary Air Corps officer. A group commander and a Medal of Honor recipient, no less. A very valuable prize. So, you shall be sent to Stalag Luft V, forthwith. Have you ever heard of it?"

"No. But I suppose it's just another one of your P.O.W. Camps." McKavitt sneered. "I've never been a prisoner before. And I don't aim to be one for very long. I'll be out of your Stalag Luft V and on my back to England before you know it, Major."

The Major ignored the wisecrack. "Stalag Luft V is also known as... *Camp Totenkopf.* It is in central Germany and it's a high security camp. We use it to hold top priority P.O.W.'s, officers and non-coms of the R.A.F. and the U.S. Air Corps who have special jobs and abilities. I assure you, Colonel, you will not like it there."

McKavitt shrugged. "Whatever."

The Major gestured to one of the guards standing at the door. *"Raus! Take him away. Put him with the others. Transport to the Stalag Luft V will leave shortly."* McKavitt was passing through the door when the Luftwaffe Major spoke some final words, grinning evilly. "By the way, Colonel, no one has ever escaped from there. Ever!"

McKavitt and two other prisoners (one an R.A.F. Officer, the other an Air Corps Lieutenant) were driven from Dulag Luft and deeper into Germany in a small open truck, sitting uncomfortably on the floorboards in the back. Every time the truck drove over a pothole, and there were plenty of them, they were tossed around like eggs in a basket. Behind them, always keeping a close distance, some ten yards back, a half-track followed. Seated in the cab, they saw three German soldiers. One was driving and the other two were manning a menacing looking MG-42 machine gun which jutted out over the windshield. They trained it on the three Allied airmen, and the muzzle of that fearsome machine gun never wavered from its threatening position.

"Do you believe what that Luftwaffe chap said?" said the R.A.F. officer sitting next to him; a stout, red-haired man with a pencil-thin mustache, swaying to the motion of the truck.

"What's that?" McKavitt replied indifferently.

"That Stalag Luft V is escape-proof?"

"Not one damn word."

"I'm Flight Leader Clifton Hawthorne, III, by the way." The Brit proffered a clammy hand. "Mosquito Squadron 139, Marham."

McKavitt shook the hand offered. "Colonel David McKavitt... 8th Air Force," was all he was willing to say aware that the Germans often planted informants in the midst of prisoners in order to glean vital information from them. He trusted no one at this point.

"Oh, don't worry, old boy," the Brit returned, grinning. "I won't give away your airbase or squadron. I know who you are, Colonel."

"Is that so?"

"Indeed, so."

Indeed, he did. He knew McKavitt was the group commander of the 479th and one of the top-scoring aces of Pacific Theater. He also knew what airbase he operated from and what kind of airplane he flew. He easily recognized the American airman from his publicity photos. But he was wary of pressing him for too much information. He realized McKavitt might be reluctant to divulge anything.

"What do you say about jumping off of this thing, Colonel?" said the man wedged in the corner, his legs hunched up close to his body. He and McKavitt had been introduced earlier when they first boarded the truck. He was a short, blond, slightly built Lieutenant and a B-24 bombardier named Tommy Gunston.

"We wouldn't get very far, Lieutenant," McKavitt replied glumly. "Those Krauts behind that meat-grinder are itching to do some shooting. They'll cut us down before we got ten paces away."

"I don't like the sound of this—Camp Totenkopf," said Gunston. "I mean... that German Major said no one has ever escaped. It must be a really harsh place, Colonel."

"We'll escape," McKavitt said with a snort.

"We'll have a go at it, anyway," agreed Hawthorne. "I don't fancy being locked up behind bars. And who knows how much longer this bloody war will go on. Another year maybe? Nao! Not for me!"

"No." McKavitt sighed heavily. "Not for me, either."

Late the next evening, the three Allied prisoners arrived at the notorious Stalag Luft V. It was snowing and the wind was blowing hard; they were shivering in their boots. The prison camp was built on a hilltop some 2,000 feet above sea level, near the town of Halle, in the southernmost part of Saxony. Downhill and practically all around it lay the vast Thuringian Forest and the Saale River. It was an isolated camp. However, Leipzig, one of Germany's major cities, was only twenty-two miles away. And just as the Dulag Luft Major had said, they knew they weren't going to like it there.

There was a narrow bridge spanning the river and a long gravel road snaking up to the hilltop, flanked on both sides by dense tracts of towering fir trees. Atop this tree-covered hilltop, situated in a flat area surrounded by eight watchtowers and the usual double-barbwire fence that formed the camp's perimeter, McKavitt saw his new home. He wondered how a man could escape from a place like that, especially now that winter was setting in. And as far as he could tell, the only way up or down the hill was the gravel road they were currently going up.

Once they reached the top of the hill the truck and the half-track came to the entrance of Stalag Luft V and halted. They were greeted by a squad of Germans who were guarding the entrance leading into the camp. McKavitt, Hawthorne and Gunston were ordered out of the truck and were marched into the center of the camp. It was roughly a square divided into three main compounds, which in turn, were subdivided into small stockades. All around them they saw the barracks—rectangular wooden buildings divided into two sections. As the barbed wire gates swung closed, the sounds of barking dogs and bolts being slammed home echoed chillingly. With prods and pokes of their rifles, the guards herded the three Allied airmen into the central compound. Then they backed them up against a barracks wall and stood facing them, rifles slung over their shoulders. After a minute or so, the three airmen began to talk softly among themselves. Gunston lit a cigarette and kept it carefully hidden in a cupped hand.

"What now?" he muttered. "Do we just stand here all night?"

One of the guards snatched the rifle from his shoulder and cycled the bolt, then pointed it at Gunston. *"Halts Maul!* He bellowed in German, then added: *"You are not to speak. That is the same as trying to escape. We will shoot you for that, understand?"*

McKavitt's eyebrows rose questioningly as he gazed at his fellow airmen, but decided not to say anything, getting the essence of what had just been said. Hawthorne and Gunston duly followed his example and kept their mouths shut. They just stood there, quietly eyeing their captors with cool impassive eyes, wondering what would happen next. Ten minutes had passed when the guards suddenly bolted to attention.

"Achtung!" shouted the senior guard, then in plain English: "Allied prisoners—attention!"

From out of the centrally located headquarters office, stepped a heavyset German officer. His uniform was immaculately pressed; his knee-high riding boots glistened. His face was big and round and his eyes were small, red-rimmed and watery. His peaked cap was rakishly tilted, and he strode fastidiously between the puddles as he approached them. Behind him walked another officer, shorter and thinner. He walked with quick little steps, treading carefully the ground as if on sore feet.

The heavyset officer stopped in front of Colonel McKavitt. They were nearly the same height and their eyes met, the German staring reproachfully, McKavitt glancing back noncommittally. The German walked on and looked at Hawthorne and Gunston. He then about-faced and stepped two paces away before turning to face them again. He gave a commanding nod to the shorter, thinner officer.

"Now hear this," said the little German in near perfect English. "You are now prisoners of Stalag Luft V. I am Hauptmann Becker, Security Officer of this camp. No one escapes from this place. If you try, you are shot. No one talks in this compound, if you do, you are shot." He gestured to the heavyset officer. *"Herr Kommandant..."*

Hauptmann Becker stepped back and the Kommandant came forward. He stared bleakly at the three Allied prisoners before him, saying softly: "My name is Oberst Hartwig von Warnstadt, Kommandant of Stalag Luft V." He raised a gloved hand to his adjutant. "As you heard Hauptmann Becker just say, you will be shot for any wrong-doings, mainly, trying to escape. I encourage this attitude. I have a proud record to uphold; there has never been a successful escape from Stalag Luft V. Never. And I wish to keep that record."

Although the Kommandant's English was heavily accented and hardly comprehensible, McKavitt and the other two airman got the gist of what he was saying. He glared at the big German with hateful eyes now, his lips cocked in a prideful sneer.

Von Warnstadt stepped closer, his eyes gleaming.

"I hold over you the power of life and death," he said, frustrated. "You are sneering at me, Colonel. Why? Why are you sneering?"

McKavitt didn't answer, he just glared back at the Kommandant. "Hauptmann Becker! This man is insubordinate. Correct him!"

"Jawohl, Herr Kommandant!"

Becker clicked his heels and stalked over to Colonel McKavitt and slapped his face, backhanding him rudely. The next second Becker went tumbling backwards as McKavitt hit him with a right-hook that came so fast the German never saw it coming.

"Ach! Du Schweinehund!" Becker raged, scrabbling at the flap of his pistol holster. The guards lunged forward as McKavitt and the others poised for a fight, a fight that might see them to the hereafter.

"If this is how it's going to be, the sooner you shoot us the better. But I'm going to knock a couple of you Krauts out before I go!"

As the first guard rushed forward, McKavitt swept his foot and kicked him on the knee, then he dropped his shoulder and charged. He rammed the second soldier in the chest and sent him reeling head over heels into the guard behind him. Hawthorne, gave a lusty war-cry and leaped into the fray and punched the fourth guard in the ear with a balled fist just as he raised his rifle to shoot. The rifle dropped to the ground and Tommy Gunston kicked it away.

By then, McKavitt had deftly sidled sideways from the first three guards. Another guard ran up, cocking his gun, and fired off the round from the hip which chipped away a chunk of wood from the barracks behind the scuffling prisoners. Hawthorne slammed into him, head down, charging like a rowdy rugby player, bowling the German over backwards and knocking the wind out of him. McKavitt picked up the fallen rifle and held it with both hands, knees bent, finger on the trigger, ready to drop the next man who moved. He trained it on the Kommandant who had by this time, reached for the Luger sidearm in his holster. McKavitt sucked his teeth and shook his head.

"You're staring at me with a sneer, Kommandant," grated McKavitt. "Wipe it off your face before I blow it off."

The Kommandant raised his chin defiantly, dropping his hand away from the holster, gazing at the American officer with half-closed eyes. "You will never get away with this, Colonel," he said. "Look around you. You are surrounded. My men have you completely covered. They can shoot you down anytime they wish."

"Then why don't they, hmm?" McKavitt returned, keeping the

rifle trained on the Kommandant, yet allowing his eyes to scan the eight watchtowers of the camp's perimeter. A trio of German soldiers stood poised at every watchtower armed with an MP-42 machine gun, about thirty men in all. The gun crews stood stiff and ready for action.

"They are waiting for my order," von Warnstadt replied.

"Then give the order!" McKavitt snapped. "And I'll make sure you get the first bullet, Kommandant."

"And Becker gets the second," Hawthorne put in drolly. He had snagged Becker's Luger and was twirling it nonchalantly around his finger by the trigger-guard like an old west gunslinger.

The Kommandant scoffed softly, conjuring up a wry expression.

"I want to see the senior Allied officer in charge of the prisoners," McKavitt demanded hotly. "Get him out here, Kommandant, now—and his second-in-command."

Von Warnstadt sighed bitterly and turned to Hauptmann Becker. "Fetch Group Captain Hawker, and his second, Squadron Leader Lawford. Bring them out here, please. Immediately."

Becker dutifully strode for the innards of the camp, two guards trailing after him. A couple of minutes passed, then the sounds of footsteps emanated from the darkened recesses of another barbed wire compound. Two British officers stepped out, one a Group Captain (Colonel), the other a Squadron Leader (Major). They were ragged looking and their uniforms were threadbare and patched.

McKavitt popped off a crisp salute seeing that Hawker was the senior officer. "Evening, Group Captain... I'm Colonel David M. McKavitt," he said crisply, then very angrily: "I was just assaulted by that man, there," he pointed at Becker, "and I defended myself. We all did. I'd like you to bear witness to what happens next."

Hawker was a cadaverous man of middling height, black-haired and mustachioed; his face was wan and unshaven. He returned the salute. Hawker looked around and then remarked rather dryly: "You seemed to have acquitted yourselves quite well, I see. But I'm afraid it was all for naught, Colonel. You can't get out of here, I'm sorry to say. There's no way to get down this bloody hill without being shot, and I can assure you, you'll find only more Jerries waiting for you at the bottom. And they'll have surely rung up the nearest Wehrmacht battalion for assistance."

"I figured as much, sir," McKavitt replied. He unloaded the rifle and tossed it on the ground at von Warnstadt's feet. He motioned to Hawthorne, and the redheaded Englishman relinquished the Luger sidearm, flipping it back to Becker in the most offhanded way.

"Your my witness, Group Captain," McKavitt said. "We have surrendered. And we are unarmed. I think these bastards would like to shoot us now. If that happens, I want you to know... so the Kommandant and his little German cronies will be named as war criminals when the Allies get here. And they'll get here all right, and sooner than later. Warnstadt's knows it'll happen, too."

"You have your witness, Colonel." Hawker turned and looked around at the surrounding barracks. "And more than just myself and Mr. Lawford. Every prisoner is watching and witnessing as well."

From every window of every barracks one could see a dirty-faced prisoner gazing out at the scene just enacted. They had seen everything from start to finish; there was no denying what they had all saw. And the Germans knew it too.

Von Warnstadt huffed derisively. He was furious and seething inwardly with rage. But he remained calm nevertheless. He said:"I will take control of these prisoners now, Group Captain. Thank you. You may leave us now."

Hawker gave McKavitt a reassuring nod. "I think you've saved your arse for now. But you're not going to like what happens next. I certainly hope I'll see you again soon." He nodded, touching the visor of his ragged peak cap. He stepped off sharply, his second-in-command Squadron Leader Lawford following closely, and both walked away from the central compound.

Von Warnstadt turned on a heel and stamped back to his office, gesturing crossly "Lock them up in solitary confinement, Becker, all three of them," he said over a shoulder. "Thirty days!"

"Jawohl, Herr Kommandant!" Becker replied.

Colonel McKavitt, Hawthorne and Gunston were led away. And the guards kept a respectful distance. However, each man had a finger on the trigger. The three airmen were taken to a small stockade and escorted into a narrow wooden hut with numerous iron doors on each side. Three doors were opened, and the three airmen were shoved inside. The doors slammed, and the guards locked them in. Then there was terrible silence.

SEVEN DAYS LATER, Colonel McKavitt was taken to the Kommandant's office. It was late in the evening and the heavyset German was sitting behind a large oak desk eating an apple. He kept McKavitt waiting until he finished, then tossed it into a wooden waste basket. He smiled glibly, clasping his fingers atop the desk.

"I've decided to suspend your thirty-day sentence, Colonel," said von Warnstadt. "Do you promise not to make any trouble?"

"Not unless someone slugs me again... or I think of a way to escape this damned place."

"Is that so?"

"It's the duty of every soldier to try to escape."

Von Warnstadt picked up another apple from the bowl on his desk. He nodded and took a bite. "I hope you do try, Colonel. Then I will have a superb reason to shoot you, *ja?*" He leaned back in his chair grinning smugly. "But not before we interrogate you thoroughly. Berlin wants answers, and I shall give them answers. Before we are finished with you, Colonel, you will wish you were dead."

"Go ahead, Kommandant. Do your worst."

"Los! Weggetreten!" von Warnstadt barked, dismissing McKavitt with a testy wave of the hand, ordering the guards to take him away. "Compound A!" His eyes were filled with animosity as he watched McKavitt go. And one by one, the other two airmen were released. The newly arrived prisoners were searched, medically examined, and then promptly deloused. Flight Lieutenant Hawthorne was duly sent to Compound B (British Compound). Stalag Luft V housed P.O.W.'s of other Allied nationalities as well: French, Polish, Yugoslav (Serb), Canadian and Russian. Although the nationalities were segregated by barbwire compounds, communication existed between. The Germans made no effort to keep the prisoners from consorting with each other.

Colonel McKavitt was reunited with Gunston in Compound A (American Compound). Officers and noncoms alike gathered around in the compound's main barracks as he introduced himself to everyone. McKavitt and Gunston spoke of their recent war experiences. Shortly, bowls of food were brought out which the prisoners had been cooking.

"Here... dig into this, Colonel," said the burly Air Corps Sergeant Major named Boggs. "That grub they give you in solitary couldn't feed a damn mouse." He handed McKavitt a bowl of hot barley soup and some German issue bread. Gunston was also fed. Boggs was the barracks chief, and he went around clapping the two airmen on their shoulders, urging them to eat. After a time, he waved everybody off.

"C'mon, men. Let's leave it to 'em now. We'll talk later."

The two men ate in silence for a few minutes. They were hungry, and the food was satisfying. However, McKavitt soon pushed his bowl away, unable to finish it.

"Sorry, fellas," he apologized. "My stomach just can't handle so much food at once. I'll eat some more later."

After so many days without solid rations, McKavitt's poor stomach had shrunk considerably. But considering his recent ordeal, he looked to be in good shape, as was Lieutenant Gunston.

After they ate, they shaved off their beards. Boggs gave them some old fatigues to wear while their uniforms were being washed.

"We thought you'd had it, sir," Boggs said, "when you cold-cocked that little twit Becker... No one's ever done that before."

"Yeah," another man spoke up. "We all would've liked to!"

"It was a foolish thing to do," McKavitt admitted.

"You did the right thing when you called for Hawker, sir. Warnstadt would've had all three of you shot, then dumped your bodies in the river. And that's the last anybody would've seen of you."

They chatted on, and soon, McKavitt filled them in on the progress of the war. They were eager for news of the outside world. They'd heard some news on a home-made radio set. But more often than not, the reception was weak and garbled and it frequently faded out during crucial broadcasts. When Colonel McKavitt had answered all their questions and satisfied their demand for tidings, Boggs said: "So, what are you going to do now, sir?"

"I think I'll get some shut-eye, Sergeant," McKavitt replied, standing up. "The bunks in here look a lot softer than that concrete slab I was sleeping on the last seven days."

"Yeah, good idea," said Gunston, stretching his arms, yawning.

"Well, you go right ahead, Colonel." Boggs nodded. "Warnstadt's guards won't come around for two more hours yet, then it's only to take evening roll-call. After that, we're allowed an hour of exercise in the central compound. We have an old volleyball we hit around sometimes—keeps the muscles toned and limbered up."

"Right." McKavitt nodded.

"You can have Captain Gordon's old bunk, sir," Boggs offered.

"Captain Gordon? And where is he?"

"Dead." Boggs sighed gloomily. "He *was* the senior American officer here... before they shot him while trying to escape."

"Oh," McKavitt replied with a frown

Boggs led him over to the small corner room where Gordon's old bunk was and McKavitt sat down. He inspected the wooden bunk and the gunny-sack mattress filled with excelsior.

"This feels nice." He took off his boots and jacket and laid down, then pulled the tatty wool blanket over his shoulders. "When I wake up, we'll talk more, Sergeant. I don't like Warnstadt and I don't like this place. The sooner I escape, the better. Good night."

ROSE MCKAVITT returned to the airbase for the third time in as many days hoping to get some more news about her husband David. She had heard General Warlick was going to be at RAF Wattisham for a mandatory inspection and a Group briefing. He was the commander of the 65th Wing and the man directly above her husband; no one had been able to tell her anything, not even Air Corps Intelligence. She had no idea if David was dead or alive. She'd heard her husband mention the General's name many, many times over past six months, saying he was an extraordinary officer and a man who got things done. She hoped he would be able to give her some answers. If not, she decided she would have to go to the British authorities at Whitehall to plead her case; she was that desperate. She needed to know something one way or the other.

The taxi cab pulled up to the front gate at Wattisham, and the M.P. standing guard duly halted the four-door sedan. Rose rolled the window down and flashed her dependent I.D. card begging entry. The M.P was already familiar with the routine and he handed her a clipboard where she promptly signed her name and collected her clearance pass—a cardstock badge with a numerical code on it. The M.P. raised the red and white striped barricade and then waved the taxi cab through.

A moment later, Rose exited the cab and headed for the Operations HQ of the 479th FG. As she walked over to Operations, she noticed a squadron of P-51 Mustangs parked on the hangar apron nearby; they were lined up neatly, wingtip to wingtip, the morning sun spanking off their silver wings. It made her heart skip a beat seeing those warplanes parked there, all polished and glistening. Her husband had flown a Mustang, it being affectionately named "Aussie Rose" after her. One of his mechanics had daubed a red rose on its nose with her likeness painted over it—a real work of art some had said. Colonel McKavitt thought it was a vast improvement over the half-naked pin-up girls he'd seen painted on too many of the 8th Air Force's big bombers. Rose thought it was a bit maudlin herself, but it boosted morale, and that's what was important.

As she turned her head back to the direction she was walking, she ran into an Air Corp officer—a General—to be more precise.

"Son-of-a-bitch!" he cursed; it was General "Bulldog" Warlick.

"Crikey!" Rose gasped, nearly losing her balance.

"Whoa there, young lady," General Warlick said grabbing her arm and steadying her, his own service cap a turned askance from the collision. The two Air Corps officers walking with the General chuckled coyly, seeing some humor in the little accident.

"I'm so sorry, General. I wasn't looking where I was going!"

"That's quite all right, ma'am. I was a bit preoccupied myself." General Warlick readjusted his cap and puffed his corona. "And where were you going in such a damn hurry, hmm?"

"To see you, General. I'm Rose McKavitt—"

"Good God! You're Colonel David McKavitt's wife?"

Rose nodded. "That's right."

General Warlick shook his head. "I sorry Mrs. McKavitt. David was a damn good officer. I was very upset when I heard he was shot down, and so close to the end of his tour. A fucking shame, it is."

"Yes, a... a shame it is, all right. Have you heard anything?"

General Warlick puffed some smoke then turned to one of the officers standing behind him. "Major Hickok? That's your department. Anything on Colonel McKavitt's whereabouts yet?"

"Well... um—"

"C'mon, Major!" General Warlick snapped. "Out with it! This woman is worried sick about her husband. What's the word?"

"He was s-shot down—crash-landed near Achmer, sir, just after destroying a German j-jet. That's what his wingman reported—"

"Goddamn-it!" General Warlick rumbled. "You, knucklehead—was he killed or did he survive? That's what she wants to know."

"Y-Yes, sir. He s-survived the crash-landing. He was then captured by German troops and taken into custody."

Rose breathed a sigh of relief. "So he *is* alive?"

"Yes, ma'am," Major Hickok added. "But that's all we know. We're still waiting on word from our Intelligence people in—"

"Jesus Christ, Hickok!" General Warlick spouted, his face getting red-hot all of a sudden. "What the hell am I paying you people for, huh? Get on the fucking horn and find out what happened to him. Now! Call the folks over at British Intelligence if you have to."

"Y-Yes, sir." Major Hickok nodded nervously. He doffed his cap and then excused himself. "Ma'am." He about-faced and stalked off for the Communications center in the building, his tail between his legs; the General's reproach had left him feeling quite emasculated.

"My apologies, Mrs. McKavitt," said General Warlick. "Major Hickok will find out something shortly, I assure you."

"Thank you, General," Rose replied, still feeling a bit euphoric; her husband was alive and her faith was suddenly restored!

"David's alive, I'm sure of it, Mrs. McKavitt. He's a damn good pilot and a survivor. He's probably in a P.O.W. camp by now."

"A P.O.W. camp?" Rose cringed, thinking this was the second time this had happened: her husband being kept in a prison camp.

"A Luftwaffe P.O.W. camp, Mrs. McKavitt," General Warlick imparted. "They'll usually a lot better than the regular ones."

"Really?"

"Yes. Not as strict and better managed. There is an honorable code of conduct, if you will, between airmen of the combatant nations, especially the German Luftwaffe. As much as I fucking hate to admit it, they're a descent bunch of Krauts, Mrs. McKavitt."

Smoke whirled around the General's head as he puffed furiously on the corona. He really didn't give a damn about all of that kind of stuff (honor and decency between airmen), it was all a bunch of hogwash as far as he was concerned. But there was a grain of truth in it, he knew. The Luftwaffe was manned with more than a few noble officers, a few even from the Great War—generals by now—

much like himself. They typically treated Allied airmen with respect and honor and didn't abuse them unnecessarily. If Colonel McKavitt was indeed in a Luftwaffe camp by now, he was most likely in good hands. But General Warlick also knew the changing fortunes of war made men do desperate things sometimes, things they would never have done before, especially when they were losing a world war. He hoped that wasn't the case.

"Well, that *is* reassuring, General," Rose replied, feeling a little better now. "I can rest easier knowing that."

"Yes, ma'am, Mrs. McKavitt, you can rest easy now. Your husband will be fine, I'm absolutely sure of it." General Warlick turned to the officer standing beside him and gestured with the odious corona. "Isn't that right Colonel Henderson?"

"Yes, sir," replied Colonel Henderson. "Absolutely."

"Oh—by the way, Mrs. McKavitt," General Warlick added rather arbitrarily, pointing with his smoky corona. "This is Colonel Tom Henderson, the 479th's new C.O. He took command after your husband was, uh... well, shot down. He's an ace in his own right. Not a big gun like your husband but an ace, nonetheless"

"Mrs. McKavitt," Colonel Henderson said, inclining his head politely. "Glad to make your acquaintance. I knew your husband— flew with him. He was a fantastic pilot. Better than me, apparently." He gave the General a sidelong glance, a sour look that the General chose to ignore; Warlick had flubbed his dub, and he knew it.

"Thank you, Colonel." Rose replied. "Nice to meet you. I'm sure the 479th is in good hands now. David would surely approve."

"He surely would," General Warlick put in. He puffed his corona, thoughtfully. "Say, Mrs. McKavitt... would like to join us for breakfast? We were just heading over to the Officer's mess. We can have some coffee and talk a while, wait on word from Major Hickok. What do you say, huh?"

"Well, okay. I suppose so. If it's not an inconvenience to you—"

"Hell no! No inconvenience at all. The more the merrier, I say. Isn't that right Colonel Henderson?"

"Yes—sir. The more the merrier." Colonel Henderson smiled mechanically, a little irked by the General's constant profanations.

"Great!" General Warlick seized Rose by the arm, locking his arm in hers, and spryly escorted her across the apron, pacing toward the Officer's mess, Colonel Henderson following closely, listening.

"I'm glad to hear David is all right, General," Rose was saying.

"Don't you worry, Mrs. McKavitt. He'll be fine. Those Luftwaffe camps are a cakewalk, to be sure."

"Happy to hear it."

Colonel Henderson's frowned; he knew the General was just placating Rose McKavitt with glib blandishments, trying to make her feel better about the whole rotten situation. He knew the Germans were losing the war and they weren't beyond doing some desperate things, the Luftwaffe included. He only hoped Colonel McKavitt was in a better camp already, not some damn, dirty hellhole.

THISTED, THE FISHING village where Professor Johansen was hiding, was as quiet and still as a graveyard. Jack, Cartwright, and Lipton crouched amid the tree line of tall firs on a hill above the village, watching and waiting in the dim twilight. They had been in position for fifteen minutes, and so far, had seen nothing more than two people in brightly colored anoraks walking down the waterfront street. No lights beamed from any of the windows. The village seemed deserted.

"Which one is the Professor's house?" Jack asked.

"The one standing alone, there, next to the church." Cartwright pointed. "Can't miss it. No lights and no movement though."

"That doesn't mean there's trouble," Lipton put in. "Anyone with any sense will be indoors at this hour." He shivered. "We'd get inside too if we weren't so barmy."

"Better safe than sorry, my friend," Cartwright remarked. All the same, he had to agree with the Canadian. There was little to be gained from further observation. The sooner they got down that snowy hill and rendezvoused with Professor Johansen the better. Cartwright was reasonably sure there were more than a few Germans garrisoned in the village.

They moved silently through the streets like a trio of ghosts, skirting the wood-boarded houses; each house had a narrow, stepped porch leading up to the front door. Wisps of smoke rising from several chimneys alluded to the only signs of life. The house near the church was just as quiet. Cartwright motioned to Lipton, directing him to the cover of the low brick wall that enclosed the little churchyard, and he took up a position near the end of the house.

"Find out what's going on, Daemon," Cartwright whispered. "If it looks like trouble, hit the deck. Lipton and I will open up."

"Got it."

"We'll fire half a dozen rounds and then stop for one minute. That's when you high-tale it back over here, all right?"

Jack nodded smartly. He drew a quick breath and stepped out into the street, then ran swiftly to the door of the lone house. Without hesitation, he rapped his knuckles on the door. Cartwright raised the MP-40 and aimed at the front door, an inch above Jack's head. Not far-off, Lipton was doing the same thing. Ten seconds elapsed...

Twenty seconds... and then the door finally opened a few inches. Cartwright heard the low murmur of Jack's voice on the cold air. The door opened wider and Jack, in a brief moment, was outlined by the dim light of the doorway, turned and raised his right arm—waving. Cartwright motioned to Lipton, and the Canadian dashed forward, his MP-40 held ready. He, too, paused at the door, and then exclaimed: "Okay, Cartwright, this is the place!"

Cartwright leaped up and ran to the door.

Inside, a burning log fire cast a cozy glow around the room which gleamed with polished woodwork. Two comfortable looking armchairs were pulled up close to the fire where a little table also stood; bits of uneaten food lay on plain ceramic plates, the remnants of a late meal. The man who had opened the door, an elderly Dane with fearless blue eyes, peered at them above a straggly white beard and tatty turtleneck.

"Would you care for something to eat or drink?" he asked in his native Danish tongue, smiling. *"Please, sit. My wife will prepare something for you."*

Jack and Lipton looked to Cartwright with questioning eyes.

"He wants to know if we want something to eat," Cartwright interpreted, then articulated in Danish, *"We've come for Professor Johansen, sir. Where is he?"* As he said this, he gestured to Lipton, signaling him to go upstairs and search. He wanted to make sure they weren't walking into a trap though he knew it was unlikely. The old man allowed Lipton to climb the stairs without protest.

"I'm afraid you've come too late, my friends," he explained,

frowning, his hands upturned. *"Professor Johansen is not here. He was taken by the Germans yesterday morning."*

Cartwright sighed frustratedly. *"Taken? Taken where?"*

"To Spøttrup Castle," The old man answered, shaking his head. *"It is further south, about sixty kilometers from here. Northwest of Skivie in northern Jutland."*

Jack happened to notice the pained look on Cartwright's face and asked, "So what's he sayin', huh? Where's the Professor?"

"In some goddamned castle, that's where!" Cartwright blurted out. "About sixty klicks from here."

"When's he comin' back?"

"He's not coming back. The Nazis got him."

"Sumbitch!" Jack cursed. "That just tears it."

"My wife and I are the Professor's servants, you see," the old man elaborated. *"Hired to look after him while he worked here."* He gestured vaguely to the rear of the house. *"He had a laboratory back there where he conducted his experiments."*

Lipton came down the stairs. "It's clear," he said to Cartwright.

Cartwright nodded. "Good." He then resumed his interrogation. *"So why did they take him? Did the Germans say?"*

The old man nodded. *"I overheard them say he was in danger here in Thisted. He would be safer in Spøttrup Castle."* He sighed. *"But the Professor didn't want to go, I tell you.. He asked how he would continue his work. The Germans told him the castle had much better facilities than here."*

"Did they say what kind of danger he'd be in if he stayed?"

The old man nodded again. *"The Germans feared the Allies would try to kidnap him."* He smiled amusedly. *"They were not so far from the truth, eh?"*

"Not here to kidnap him, damn you!" Cartwright riposted edgily. *"The Professor wanted to flee to England. He wanted the Allies to benefit from his experiments, not the stinking Nazis."*

A woman came out from the kitchen holding a tray of cups half-filled with brandy. She set them down on the table without a word and withdrew back to the kitchen.

"Please... drink," said the old man.

"First—how do we get to this castle?" Cartwright pressed. *"You said sixty kilometers."*

"You could go by Route 26 but that is regularly patrolled. Take my old fishing boat, it is nearby. It will take you across the fjord and to the far shore near the castle."

"Oh, great," Jack muttered halfheartedly. "More boats."

Cartwright nodded. *"That's the way we'll go then."* He sat down and picked up a cup of brandy and took a sip.

Lipton and Jack each picked up a cup and drank heartily.

"Sorry. Wish I could be more helpful," the old man apologized, shrugging. *"I can only wish you luck at this time."*

"Yeah, well, here's wishing us luck then, old man," Cartwright returned churlishly. He raised his cup high and was sailed: *"Skol!"*

CHAPTER 6

THE NEXT DAY, McKavitt devoted himself to getting back into shape. That morning in Barracks A-1, he led his fellow prisoners in calisthenics, going through the entire gamut of exercises typically called for by the U.S. Army P.T. manual. During the afternoon break, he and some men romped around the compound playing volleyball. The Englishmen in the nearby Compound B watched idly; it wasn't what they considered as sporting as soccer. Later, the prisoners received their Red Cross parcels which contained items such as chocolate, can goods, and dry food. The food at Stalag Luft V wasn't terrible, but indeed, far from the best. So the parcels augmented the prisoner's diets to a large degree. And McKavitt behaved himself. The camp's guards kept a close eye on him at first, but then relaxed their attentions once they realized he wasn't going to cause any more trouble. Kommandant von Warnstadt spoke to McKavitt during the morning roll-call, wondering if he was planning on escaping soon.

"No," he replied. "Because you'll have me shot. You said so."

Becker, who had been standing nearby, enjoined curtly, "You will address the Kommandant as *'Herr Kommandant'* understand?"

"Herr Kommandant," McKavitt duly returned.

Becker and von Warnstadt exchanged satisfied glances and walked on. McKavitt had figured out what all the others already knew; there was no escape from Camp Totenkopf. It was just better to bide one's time and wait for the war's end. However, the Kommandant would have been very unhappy if he could have eavesdropped on Colonel McKavitt's conversation later on that night.

91

McKavitt was talking to Group Captain Hawker and Squadron Leader Lawford. McKavitt had crept through a "hole" in the wire and quietly skulked over to Hawker's barracks once lights-out had been declared. Although McKavitt and Hawker were essentially equivalent in rank, Hawker had three year's seniority over the recently brevetted American Colonel. Hawker would continue as the senior Allied officer whilst McKavitt would act as co-commander, and of course, as a liaison to the American P.O.W's. He told Hawker of his plans to escape, basically requesting his approval.

"I want to know all the details, Colonel," Hawker said, "before I give my permission." He gestured, his hands gesticulating with grave intent. "You do realize that there have been ten attempts to escape from here before? And not one of them has succeeded."

"I heard that, sir."

"I've seen far too many courageous men gunned down whilst trying to escape from this bloody place, and I will *not* sanction any plan I deem foolhardy or improperly conceived."

"I've thought it out thoroughly, sir. I think it has a good chance to succeed. I'm willing to stake my life on it."

"You may well being doing that, Colonel," Hawker rejoined, a dire look in his eyes. He sighed. "All right then, let's hear it."

McKavitt settled himself on the wooden bench seat.

"You probably know there's a Luftwaffe airfield less than a mile north of here, right?" he began. "We all hear the planes taking off in the morning. A guard told me they're Junkers Ju-88 bombers on their way to bomb our troops in France and Belgium."

Hawker and Lawford exchanged amused glances.

"To cut a long story short, sir... my idea is to get to the airfield and steal a German bomber and then fly to France."

Lawford chuckled. "That's not a new idea, Colonel. Others have thought of that."

"Aye," Hawker had to agree. "And no one has ever gotten that far. They were either shot by the guards or drowned in the river trying to cross. One lad reached the barbed wire downriver. But that's as far as he got. The wire is rigged with trip-wires, you see—connected to mines."

"Has anyone ever tried going... upriver?"

"Upriver?" Hawker was stunned. "That's bloody impossible."

"You think so?"

"The current is far too strong. No one can swim against it. Plus, the water is freezing cold by now. You'd surely die of hypothermia before you ever reached your destination."

"If I could find a way upriver," McKavitt pressed, "would you give your consent for the escape?"

"Hmm..." Lawford interjected thoughtfully. "There are fewer guards patrolling the banks upriver."

Hawker shifted in his bench seat. "All right, Colonel. What would you do *if* you reached the unpatrolled bank, eh? Tell me."

"I'd make for the airfield," McKavitt explained. "Then I'd steal a bomber and fly it to France."

"Can you fly a German bomber, Colonel?"

"Yeah, I think so. Can't be much different than our own."

"You make it sound so simple," said Lawford. "It may not be as easy as you think. That airfield is under constant guard, I daresay."

"Probably so. But if I go at night, there will be a lesser chance of detection. There might even be fewer sentries."

"Humph!" Hawker grunted. "Then you'd fly the German bomber out of there... in the dark? A plane you've never flown before? No, no, Colonel. Sounds too bloody reckless if you ask me."

"Reckless indeed," Lawford agreed.

"Maybe so. But I think I can do it."

"Well, it all depends on your ability to get beyond the wire without getting shot, and then, upstream, Colonel."

"Precisely," Hawker put in. "There's the rub, old man."

"All right then, Group Captain," Colonel McKavitt replied, sighing resignedly, standing up. "I'll work out all the details in a day or two, put more thought into it. Then I'll get back to you."

"Jolly good, Colonel," said Hawker, rising from his bench. "If you can prove that your plan has a good chance of succeeding, I'll approve it. And if you need any help with your plans, or need information about the camp or the surrounding area, get with my man Lawford here, he'll be glad to help you."

"Thanks, sir." McKavitt proffered a hand. "I appreciate that."

"Think nothing of it," Hawker replied, shaking the hand offered.

McKavitt saluted, then exited the barracks through Hawker's secret exit—a concealed opening in the floorboards. Once the boards were back in place, and activity returned to normal, Hawker paced the barracks floor a moment, thinking. He gazed out the window and saw the shadowy figure of Colonel McKavitt scurrying back to the American Compound, seeing him skirt the probing searchlights and knife-like barbwire as he went.

Hawker turned to his second-in-command.

"What do you think, Lawford?" He asked. "His chances are slim to none, I say... even if he gets beyond the wire."

"The Yank's confidence certainly borders on the insane, sir," Lawford answered. "He's got more guts than sense, I think."

"My thoughts exactly, Lawford." Hawker sat down and lit a cigarette. "Well, let's see what he comes up with, what? Then we'll go from there. If it sounds like bloody cock-up, I won't approve it."

"I concur." Lawford strode over to the stove. "More tea, sir?"

AT DAWN'S early light, the wind on the water was bitterly cold. The men's hot breath froze in little droplets on their fur-trimmed hoods. Cartwright stood in the open-door wheelhouse of the little trawler steering it across the fjord. Jack and Lipton stood on the bow and stern of the trawler, keeping watch, trying not to look suspicious, trying to look as much as possible like a common Danish fishermen; their weapons were concealed beneath their anoraks. Not only had the old Dane supplied them with the keys to his boat, he'd given them some dry clothes, gloves and scarfs, too, and a Mauser carbine and ammunition he had confiscated some time ago during the German invasion of Denmark. Although he never had cause to use it over the preceding four years, he kept it nonetheless. Now Jack had it, and he was finally glad to have his own weapon besides his fighting knife.

It had taken the three men a better part of the night to reach and secure the old man's trawler. The most dangerous part of the journey, they'd been forewarned, would be the first two hours after they boarded the trawler and guided it through the tortuous inlets of Limfjord. German sentries would surely patrol the area around the trawler's launch. But they saw no one; they pretended to be early morning fishermen going out to catch oysters, and no one seemed the wiser. It was a quiet, roundabout journey for the most part. Only when they passed under a traffic bridge near Glyngore did they encounter Germans. As the old trawler puttered by slowly, a couple of sentries on the bridge's western checkpoint took notice of them.

"Hej venner!" Cartwright called out to them in Danish, waving. *"Det er en god dag til fiskeri! Ja?"*

One of the Germans waved back, nodding.

Jack, standing on the stern of the boat, sneered and gave them the 'finger' and shouted: *"Gå til helvede, du beskidte nazister!"*

The Germans just laughed and went back to their conversation.

"Jesus Christ, Daemon!" Cartwright chided in a low voice. "You'll blow the whole goddamn operation with that kind of crap. Knock it off already!"

"Sorry." Jack grinned mischievously. "Couldn't resist it. It's the only Danish I cared to remember."

"What the hell did he say?" Lipton wanted to know.

"He told the Nazis to go to hell," Cartwright explained.

Two hours later, they reached the far shore of Limfjord near Spøttrup Castle. They anchored the small, two-masted trawler about a thousand yards offshore, still perpetrating their deceptive ruse, but pretending to be fishermen with engine trouble now. Cartwright gazed through a pair of binoculars he'd found in trawler's dash-box, looking at the tall, dark silhouette that was Spøttrup Castle.

Beyond the pebble-strewn beach, he saw the 16th century moated castle surrounded by a high earthen rampart, a well-preserved hall and chapel, a small semi-frozen lake, and a large field overlooking the fjord which was currently teeming with drilling German soldiers. The large arched windows of the castle were walled up, leaving only narrow sighting slits. The ramparts and the double moat served to defend the castle from cannon fire back in olden times. Near the shoreline, he saw a wooden pier jutting out over the water—that's where they would go ashore. But not in the hours of daylight, later that night. They'd have to wait until darkness to circumvent the castle's defenses, which in this day and age, consisted of at least a full battalion of German soldiers. A daunting task lay ahead of them, one that couldn't be easily achieved.

"Okay, men," said Cartwright, turning away from his careful observation, the binoculars dangling from his neck now. "We'll go ashore at night, around twenty-hundred-hours, okay?"

"Twenty-hundred-hours?" Lipton questioned.

"There's a hell of a lot of Germans protecting that castle. And the only way to get in undetected is under the cover of darkness."

"Right, right"

"How many men, you think?" Jack asked.

"A battalion? Five hundred men? Maybe more?"

"That's quite a lot for one man—the Professor," said Lipton.

"Maybe they're expectin' some company, huh?" Jack proposed.

"Could be. But I seriously doubt it. The Nazis typically use any old castle or fortress as a base camp or headquarters. That castle is no exception, Daemon."

"I hope yer right, hoss."

"So what do we do then until dark, Cartwright?" Lipton turned and looked across the fjord and at the castle, sighing.

"Well, first off, let's weigh anchor and find a little cove to hide in. Let's not attract the attention of the Germans. I think our little *engine trouble* charade is about played out. If the Germans get suspicious, they'll send a boat out here to investigate."

"Good enough fer me," Jack said, nodding. "Let's eat something and cop a few Z's. I think we could all use some sleep."

"Yeah, that's what I had in mind."

Cartwright toggled the anchor chain and then started the engine. The ragged little trawler sputtered back to life. Jack and Lipton monitored the anchor chain as they reeled it in, and when properly secured, the trawler motored away, making for the headland that lay close by. Once they rounded the headland and found a suitable cove to hide in, they dropped anchor and ate. The old Dane's wife had given them some meat and bread to eat, and they scarfed it down ravenously. It wasn't the best food but it was good enough.

Once they finished, they stretched out in the trawler's cabin where it was a good deal warmer. Cartwright took the first two-hour watch, standing guard in the wheelhouse, looking out for German patrol boats whilst the other two men slept. And for the next twelve hours, the men would rotate watch, sleep, eat, drink, get some much needed rest. As Jack lay there in a sleeping loft in the cabin, covered in a tatty old blanket, he thought about Rose, wondering what she was doing at that moment. How was she, he wanted to know?

"How are ya, my sweet Aussie Rose?" he whispered.

ROSE WAS FEELING sick again. Not just from her pregnancy but from sheer dread. As she sat in the lobby of Air Corps Intelligence, her feelings of anxiety multiplied by the second. There was still no official word on her husband's whereabouts. So far, Intelligence had only told her that David had been shot down near Achmer and was then taken to the Luftwaffe interrogation center at Wetzler. She was told that he had been "processed" and from there was sent to a P.O.W. camp. General Warlick had been most kind and accommodating, polite even, but he had not been able to light a fire under anybody's ass. Major Hickok had been doing his utmost to get more details. However, his job as the 479th's S-2 Officer took precedence; the Group was in the midst of a violent air war with the Luftwaffe, and his primary job required him to have the latest intelligence. Not just about current German combat strengths and casualties, but about their locations and sphere of operations. It was a thankless job and one that required his complete and undivided attention.

"Mrs. McKavitt?" said the operations clerk. "Major Hickok will be with you in just a moment. He's wrapping up an intelligence briefing with Colonel Henderson."

"Hmm?" Rose replied, scarcely hearing what was said. "I'm sorry. What did you say?"

"I said," the clerk repeated, "Major Hickok will be with you shortly. He's wrapping up a briefing."

"Oh, yes. Thank you."

"You're welcome, Mrs. McKavitt."

"I was just... daydreaming—thinking. Not paying attention."

The clerk smiled. "I understand."

Rose uncrossed her legs and sat more upright. She gazed at the clock on the wall and noted the time (08:25) and then reached into her purse for her cameo powder case and re-powdered her nose. She felt nervous and nauseated, a bit shaky, too. Rose hadn't eaten breakfast that morning, only drinking a cup of very strong coffee, which seemed to be burning a hole in her stomach at the moment. After she powdered her nose, she pulled out a pack of saltines and tried to eat them. But the dry, tasteless crackers only made her want to gag; she was that ill.

A minute later, the door to the Major's office opened, and out stepped Major Hickok and Colonel Henderson. Hickok was in his customary shirt, tie and jacket. Henderson was dressed in his flying kit; he wore khaki trousers, ankle boots, a leather jacket, his silk scarf, and had his gloves, goggles and flight cap in hand. He was a tall, handsome figure, dashing even, and it made Rose think of Jack Knight, of all people. Why she suddenly thought of him, she had no earthly idea. He had been out of her life and out of her mind for a very long time. What had made her think of him all of a sudden, she wondered? She supposed it was because she had gone through a similar upheaval when Jack had been shot down. The same feelings of remorse and regret were tugging at her heartstrings again. But Rose promptly dismissed those vexing feelings, and she got up and strode over to where Hickok and Henderson were standing, holding her little clutch purse with both hands.

"Major Hickok," she said. "It's Rose McKavitt again."

"Ah, yes, Mrs. McKavitt," said Major Hickok, turning to face her, nodding. "I was just about to call you in."

Colonel Henderson smiled politely. "Mrs. McKavitt... How are you, ma'am? Good to see you again."

"Gentlemen." Rose evinced a friendly nod. "Please, call me, Rose, if you would? 'Mrs. McKavitt' sounds so—so formal."

"Okay—Rose," Hickok replied. "That's easily done—"

"Have you heard anything about my husband yet? Do you know where he is? What camp he's been sent to? What do you know?"

"Well, uh..." Hickok replied evasively, then faced Henderson. "All right, Joe. You're clear on all of that stuff, right?"

"Yeah. I got it."

"Good. Get with General Clagett of the 392nd and shore up the details. There's bound to be heavy fighter opposition over Rechlin. We've got to smash those jet warbirds where they're hatched."

"Right. I get the picture."

Hickok saluted. "Good luck, Colonel."

Colonel Henderson reciprocated. "Thanks, Major. We'll certainly need it." He turned to Rose McKavitt. "Ma'am..." He bowed his head. "Good to see you again. Hope you find out something today —something good."

"Right-o, Colonel," Rose replied. "I hope so, too."

Colonel Henderson turned on a heel and made for the exit, a look of grim determination on his face. Hickok placed a gentle hand on Rose's shoulder, beckoning her into his office, a glib smile on his lips. "Please, come in, Mrs. McKavitt—"

"Rose—call me Rose, please."

"Oh, yes, Rose. My apologies. Please come in and have a seat."

"Thank you, Major."

Rose went into Hickok's office as he shut the door behind her. She sat down on the chair parked in front of his desk, leaning forward, knees together. Major Hickok sat down behind his desk and sat stiffly, upright, his elbows on the desktop. He seemed nervous.

"So, Rose. How are you feeling today?" He asked.

"Not so good, I have to admit."

"I understand. You're worried about your husband."

"Very worried."

"You're pregnant now. I'm sure that's causing you some—"

"Please, Major," Rose interjected. "Let's cut to the chase, shall we? I want to know what's happened to my husband. Do you have *any* new information about him? As to his whereabouts or what the Germans might have done with him? Please, I need to know."

Major Hickok sighed. "Well, the only information I have, Rose, is what I got from British Intelligence."

"And what's that?"

"That your husband is being held at a high security P.O.W. camp in central Germany—a special camp—according to the British."

"Where is it? What's it called? Does this camp have a name?"

"It does, but..."

"But what, Major? What's it called?"

Hickok hesitated, his lips a hard line.

"Major? Please, I need to know!"

"Camp Totenkopf, ma'am. That's what the Brits are saying."

"Totenkopf? Why, that means—"

"Death's head," Hickok interjected. "That's the camp's unofficial name. The Brits haven't been able to get more than that, unfortunately. It's a kind of nickname or a morbid code name, they say."

"General Warlick told me the Germans would most likely send David to a Luftwaffe camp—they're better than the average German P.O.W. camp. Is that right, Major?"

"That's right." Major Hickok settled into the backrest of his chair. "You see, the Germans keep their camps segregated. Pilot's and airmen go to Luftwaffe camps, navy men go to a Kriegsmarine camp, while regular army types go to the standard German Stalag."

"I see."

"Typically, they separate the officers from the noncoms, even keep them in different camps. And in each camp they segregate the different nationalities. But since Germany's losing the war now, they're lumping them all together into one camp."

"So, is this Camp Totenkopf a Luftwaffe P.O.W. camp, Major?"

"I believe so."

"Was General Warlick correct when he said American airmen get better treatment in Luftwaffe camps?"

"Yes, ma'am, he was." Major Hickok leaned forward. "There is a certain unwritten code of conduct between Allied and German airmen, a gentlemanly way of doing things. The Luftwaffe, although they're a part of the Third Reich and take their orders from Hitler and the Nazis, they're still a cut above the rest. They adhere to chivalry and gallantry like the knights of olden days, and they treat their defeated foes with dignity and honor. Much the same as they did in the last war."

"Right." Rose glowered, then retorted: "Look, Major. I used to be a reporter back in Australia, not so long ago. I know all about what goes on between prisoners and their captors. The Japanese are especially ruthless, I found out. Downright sadistic, they are. And that's not all—"

"The Luftwaffe camps aren't like the Japanese ones, ma'am. The Germans are civilized and genteel, not pitiless Asian devils."

"Do you really believe that, Major?"

"Yes." Major Hickok sighed. "Granted, they are always a few individuals who abuse their power and commit questionable acts. But as a whole, that's very rare."

"Huh! You sound quite convinced of that, Major."

"Yes, ma'am. I'm quite convinced." Major Hickok folded his arms over his chest. "Look, I'm aware of the Nazis' hatred of the Jews and of other ethnic groups they deem inferior. But I'm certain the Luftwaffe is an honorable organization. I'm certain of it. Your husband is in good hands, Rose. I assure you."

Rose sighed and sank stiffly into the backrest.

"So, when will you know something definitive?" She persisted. "Like where this camp is, and what the situation is, Major? I'm not so convinced the Luftwaffe has better camps than the rest. The Germans are losing the war and they're getting desperate. They'll resort to all means possible soon enough, if they haven't already done so."

"I going to London in a couple of days, Rose. And among other duties, I will meet with the Red Cross director when I'm there. He'll be able to tell me more about your husband's whereabouts and his situation better than British Intelligence or Air Corps Intelligence can."

"Then I'll hear something about David when you return?"

"Yes, ma'am. You have my word. I promise you."

"Good." Rose stood up. "I thank you for your time, Major."

"My pleasure." Major Hickok got up from his chair.

"I'm sorry I've been so pesky and edgy lately. But I'm worried sick about David. I need to find out what happened to him, find out if he's all right and not in imminent danger. You understand that?"

"I understand perfectly." Major Hickok came from behind his desk and saw Rose to the door. "I'll find out something from the Red Cross, I'm certain of it. They're typically in contact with all the prison camps and handle all correspondence between P.O.W.'s and their families. As a matter of fact, the P.O.W.'s are indebted to the Red Cross for almost all their food, clothing and medical supplies."

"I've heard that."

"A Red Cross representative makes a routine visit to the different camps every six months. And food parcels arrived regularly, I'm told, and in sufficient quantity. Well...most of the time, anyway."

"Right-o." Rose nodded. "All right, Major. I'll expect to hear from you in a week or so then?"

"Yes, ma'am. I'll telephone you as soon as I get back."

"Thank you." Rose waved. "G'day, Major. See you soon."

Major Hickok waved back. "Goodbye, Rose."

He returned to his desk and sat down. He glanced over the intelligence flimsy lying on his desk again, the one from British Intelligence. A new Nazi jet fighter had just been discovered by one of their undercover agents, something far more advanced than the Me-262 or the Me-163 Komet. Something faster and more dangerous.

COLONEL McKavitt and Lieutenant Gunston stood by casually in the American compound watching some prisoners hit a volleyball around when a bitter outcry echoed from a window of Barracks A-1.

"Jeez! What the heck was that all about?" Gunston asked, staring at the nearby barracks.

"Don't know?" McKavitt answered. "Maybe somebody got hit by a guard." The Colonel looked to Barracks A-1, wondering.

Suddenly, a windows flew open and Corporal Hall's head popped out. "Listen up, men!" he exclaimed. "The Germans have launched a surprise attack through the Ardennes! Our army is falling back! It just came over on the radio."

"Looks like the Krauts aren't finished yet," Sergeant Major Boggs added glumly, standing in the doorway. "Tanks galore—pouring over the front lines. New ones, big ones. Our boys are getting slaughtered!"

McKavitt and Gunston stood there in stunned silence a moment thinking about that. Gunston shook his head and stared at the ground, grumbling bitterly. McKavitt sighed heavily, worrying that this might mean the war could continue for a while longer still—maybe indefinitely. Then he and Gunston hustled into Barracks A-1 and huddled around the homemade radio. And soon, other prisoners crowded around and listened to the reports coming over the airwaves. And true enough it was, the Germans were not beaten yet.

On the foggy morning of December 16, 1944, twenty-six German divisions amounting to some two million men attacked the weakly held Allied front in the Ardennes. Their goal was to smash through to the Meuse River, capture Allied fuel depots and carry out an all-out drive on Antwerp and the Channel coast. U.S. troops were caught completely off guard due to a colossal intelligence snafu. No one in the Allied High Command had anticipated a German counteroffensive, especially at the onset of winter. The swiftness of the Wehrmacht's breakthrough was startling and alarming. The gods of war seemed to be on the German's side because miserable weather over the battlefront played havoc on the Allied air forces; the foggy conditions kept the 8th Air Force and the R.A.F grounded. Not even the 9th Air Force could get off the ground. It was a sorry situation.

The disparaging grumbling went on for a while, rising to a muted crescendo of doom and gloom. The news quickly spread over the entire camp, and soon, the hopes of the men getting back home by Christmas were summarily dashed. Alas, those hopes were never fully realized though; the prisoners knew it was a fanciful pipe dream; a fantastic but vain hope. Even if the war had ended yesterday, they knew they wouldn't see home for many more months to come. To Colonel David McKavitt, it was the impetus to step up his plans for escape. And soon enough, the guards came around and quelled the disturbance, ordering everyone back into their barracks, Becker leading the charge.

"Return to your barracks immediately!" he bellowed, waving his Luger. "Get inside! You have one minute to clear the compound!"

Swiftly the men still in the compound shuffled through the doors of their assigned barracks. The doors were slammed shut and the moaning and groaning died away to an eerie silence.

Becker turned to his men. "Search all the barracks! There's a radio hidden somewhere. Find the men responsible for it and bring them to the Kommandant's office."

Inside Barracks A-1, Sergeant Major Boggs and a few other men crouched around the homemade radio set, blatantly ignoring Becker's order for a search. They listened intently to the news of the German offensive which was still being broadcast.

"Jesus Christ!" Boggs cursed. "The Germans aren't whipped yet, looks like. Our Army is in full retreat, fellas. The war goes on."

"You better get that radio set hidden away," McKavitt warned, his brown eyes looking worried. "Becker and his goons will be in here any minute. They'll tear this place apart looking for it. And they'll keep looking until they find it, too."

Boggs switched off the radio and stood up. "They've made searches before, Colonel. And they never found it."

"They'll rip everything apart, Boggs," said McKavitt. "They'll pull up the floorboards, tear out the cupboards, smash up anything that looks like it could hide a radio set."

"Yeah, like all our escape gear," Gunston threw in.

"Right," Colonel McKavitt concurred. "All the gear you fellas have been hording the past few months. Things we need to make our escape."

"Escape, sir?" Boggs replied, pulling a face. "Now?"

"Why not, Sergeant?"

"Because our army's in full retreat, sir. We don't know how far they've been pushed back—could be all the way back to Paris."

"No, I don't—"

"Yeah! That's a long way to go, sir," another man spoke up. "Even for a Kraut plane... if you could get your hands on one."

"The war is going to go on for a while longer, men," McKavitt declared. "And the way I see it, our Army will regroup and beat the Germans back before that happens. I'm sure of it. The Wehrmacht is running out of gas, literally, and the Luftwaffe can't stop our air force. This new offensive won't last, I tell you. The Germans are played out. Beaten."

"But the Germans will keep on fighting irregardless, sir, you can bet on that. Old Adolf still has a few tricks up his sleeve."

"Hell! The war could go on for another year," Gunston whined.

"Maybe. But whatever happens, we're still stuck on the side-lines, right? Waiting, watching, hoping, stuck in this damn place un-til God knows when?" McKavitt took off his crush cap and ran clammy fingers through his dark hair. "Escape is still our best bet. It's our duty. We—"

"Heads up, guys!" said Corporal Hall. "Looks like Becker and his goons are on their way." Hall had been keeping watch, peering out of the window. "Get that aerial down and hide that thing. Now!"

"Forget it. There's no time." McKavitt bent down and picked up the set. "I'll pull it down and chuck it out the window." He hefted it to the window, Gunston jumping up behind him. The little Sergeant unhinged the window and threw it open.

"What are you doing, sir?" Boggs asked. "If they see you with that radio, you'll be booked solid in the cooler for forty-five days."

McKavitt raised the radio set shoulder-high. "They'll have the set, Boggs, but they won't know who had it. Maybe Becker will be satisfied and call off his search."

For a second, the radio teetered in his hand. McKavitt leaned back like a quarterback about throw a long bomb, then he threw the radio set out the window. It went flying into the compound and landed on the hard, frozen ground, smashing into little bits and pieces of metal and shattered tubes, scattering in a sparkling heap.

The noise attracted the guards, and they came running, Becker in the van of that blue-gray gang of enraged German guards, his Luger still drawn. He was the first man to see it laying on the snowy ground, realizing what the scattered remnants signified. Then he looked around and saw nothing but silent barracks and closed windows. But Becker had found the radio set.

Von Warnstadt ordered an immediate roll-call, and the prisoners shuffled out of their barracks and into the compound again and stood anxiously in ranks while they were counted and their names checked off the list. Becker stalked up and down the ranks hoping to provoke someone into doing something foolish. But no one said anything or did anything; Becker had to content himself with glaring angrily and yelling himself hoarse. Colonel McKavitt, his eyes cold with bitterness, stared ahead impassively until Becker just gave up and walked onward. And von Warnstadt let them stand there for a full hour before he finally made his appearance. He stepped up onto a little wooden crate so everyone could see and hear him.

"The radio message you *schweinehunds* just heard... is true!" he shouted. "Our glorious German Army has broken through and is routing the Allied forces in the Ardennes. The tide has shifted in the favor of the Third Reich once again. Total victory will soon follow!"

He gestured and a squad of guards armed with machine pistols took up a position in front of him, their barrels trained upon the amassed ranks of prisoners. "We have found your little radio set and collected its smashed remains. I warn you, if I find another such contraption, I will personally hold the senior officer responsible." He pointed directly at McKavitt. "I will not tolerate disobedience from you—or any of you! As punishment, *all* of you be put on half-rations for ten days."

A low murmur of discontent swelled from the ranks of P.O.W.'s. as von Warnstadt stepped down. Becker took his place in front of the prisoners, and at his order, everyone was dismissed. They shambled back to their barracks disgruntled and disgusted. It didn't matter what was happening at the front, Camp Totenkopf was still being run true to form. Freedom was still a long way off and escape seemed just as impossible. But Colonel McKavitt wasn't discouraged. He'd continue on with his plans of escape regardless of what happened; he would not let the tide of war dictate terms to him.

JACK SAT QUIETLY on the deck and ate his rations, finishing the last pieces of meat and bread. It was almost time to go. In a few minutes he, Cartwright, and Lipton would embark on the next phase of their mission: assailing the Nazi-held Spøttrup Castle and rescuing the Professor. It would undoubtedly be a formidable task, maybe even suicidal. Some five-hundred German soldiers occupied that castle and the surrounding areas, maybe more. It would be a feat of cunning and daring to get in there undetected, a dangerous undertaking that might end in their deaths. But getting killed had never worried Jack too much. He was used to the threat of death hanging over him. Dying was always the last thing on his mind. Doing something meaningful, getting things done, achieving his goals were the main thoughts on his mind. Circumventing a Nazi stronghold and rescuing a Danish physicist was just another road he had to travel to reach his final destination. Jack always remembered where he came from and he never forgot about his humble beginnings. Anything he achieved after those forgettable bygone days was icing on the cake —a great victory. He had been given a second chance and he would not squander it; his star would rise again, much higher this time. And Rose would love him for it.

"Okay, gentlemen," said Cartwright, starting the trawler's engine. "Here we go. Time to go get the Professor."

"You square with that German carbine, Daemon?" Lipton asked Jack as he shouldered his own weapon, an MP-40 machine pistol."

"I'm square," Jack replied, slapping the cartridge home. "No problems here. It'll be like shooting fish in a barrel with this thing."

"Just make sure that trigger-finger of yours doesn't give us away before we get near that castle," Cartwright warned. "Use your knife if you have to. Gunfire will just alert the whole goddamn garrison."

"Right." Jack nodded. "Nice and quiet like—I gotcha."

A few minutes later, they reached the pier. The tide had come in and it made it easier to maneuver the trawler closer. As they approached, Lipton scanned the shoreline for enemy activity. He saw no one. A bone-chilling wind abruptly rose, and with it the first few flakes of snow. It settled on their clothes, and within minutes, it covered them. Visibility diminished. Soon, it was snowing very hard.

"If the Jerries d-don't get us, this bloody weather w-will," Lipton chattered. "We'll be frozen s-stiff by morning."

The shoreline had all but disappeared in the flurry of snowflakes. Cartwright steered the trawler closer, more carefully, realizing that this sudden deluge wasn't as bad as it seemed. "This weather is really what the doctor ordered," he quipped. "I hope it gets worse."

"Worse?" Jack glared at him in bewilderment. "Why worse?"

"Because if the snow falls harder no one's going to see us come ashore or hustle up closer to that castle."

Jack's face split into a big grin. "Hey, yer right, hoss! I never thought of that. It's better than a dang smokescreen."

The snowfall did get worse. An hour later, it was blowing like a blizzard; but the three agents had made their way beyond the beach and up the shore road leading to Spøttrup Castle by then. When they spotted the main entrance—a stone-arched gatehouse and causeway—they saw the old medieval castle up close. It was a well-preserved defensive structure, a stately family home these days, with towers and a ballroom built on an expansive 800 acre piece of land. It had stone ramparts and a double moat that had protected it from attack several centuries ago. Presently, it had a garrison of German soldiers protecting it; the three agents could see some of them standing guard near the foot bridge adjacent to the gatehouse. They counted four men in all; two in the front and two in the back, one on each side of the gatehouse.

"This is where it gets dicey," Cartwright said, gazing through the binoculars, eyeing the four Germans. "We've got to get past those four Krauts without a lot of fuss." He looked beyond the causeway, focusing on the entrance of the castle—a set of wooden, studded double-doors. "As far as I can tell, there's no one guarding the two doors into the castle. They might even be unlocked."

"How do you figure that, mate?" Lipton asked.

"Because there's more Germans on the other side."

"You think?"

"We've gotta take out those four Germans first," Jack spoke up. "Get them outta the way."

"Yeah. But how?"

"Leave that to me, fellers." Jack hopped up, shoulder-slinging his weapon, reaching for the fighting knife at his waist. "I'll take out the two Krauts on the outside. Then you fellas sneak up afterwards and take out the other two—all nice and quiet like—alright, Cartwright?"

"Right." Cartwright nodded. "It's snowing hard enough now, our approach won't be detected until it's too late."

"That's what I was figuring, too," Jack replied, then bolted off into the darkness across the road.

"Okay, Lipton," Cartwright said, crouched on a bent knee, his MP-40 slung across his back now. His fighting knife was drawn, and he was ready for action. "When Daemon takes out those two sentries, we haul ass across the road and to the gatehouse."

"Right-o."

"Don't know how he's going to do it yet, but let's wait and see what happens first."

Lipton nodded, clutching his knife with a tentative hand.

Jack crept up to the gatehouse, approaching from the north, along the outer moat. The snow was really coming down and the wind was howling loudly, and it covered his approach. He paused near the foot- bridge, crouching behind a bushy shrub, and saw the German sentry standing nearby. He couldn't even see the other sentry on the other side of the foot-bridge—it was snowing that hard. When the German turned away, shielding himself against the frigid wind, Jack pounced on him. He reached around his head, clamping his mouth shut with a hand, and slit his throat with one quick motion. A moment later, Jack was dragging him into the moat by his boots leaving an ugly trickle of blood in the snow. Jack snatched the man's helmet off and swiftly removed his army greatcoat, then ditched the anorak and donned the helmet and topcoat. Then he got up and nonchalantly walked back over to the foot- bridge, his collar turned up high shielding his face. He ambled up to the other sentry who was by now standing under the cover of the gatehouse's arch, smoking a cigarette.

"*Komm!*" Jack rumbled. "*Eine Zigarette fuer mich, bitte!*"

The German sighed irritably and reached into his hip pocket for his cigarettes—only to be savagely waylaid by the tall Texan in the stolen greatcoat. Jack jumped on him and spun him around so fast and cut his throat that the man never even had a chance to cry out much less defend himself. Jack dumped him in the moat and was soon puffing contentedly; he really wanted a cigarette. And by that time, Cartwright and Lipton were coming up alongside him gasping for breath from running, but more in awe of Jack's handiwork.

"Good work, Daemon!" Cartwright whispered appreciatively.

"Aye, that was right handy," Lipton added.

"Nothin' to it, fellers." Jack pointed. "Now for the other two."

The three men slunk quietly into the gatehouse where the last two sentries were standing, Cartwright leading the way. The snow was really coming down now and the two Germans were huddled close together trying to stay warm. As Cartwright crouched there, waiting for the two Germans to separate so he could pounce on one of them, the double-doors opened and another soldier stuck his head out and shouted beseechingly. The taller sentry muttered something in reply, something that sounded like a gleeful response, and he gladly tramped off down the causeway and went inside.

Only one German now!

Cartwright waited a moment, then leaped up, his knife flashing. As he lunged forward, he lost his footing on the icy causeway and slipped and fell. The German spun around, hearing the noise. And before his frigid mind could register what was happening, a bullet split his brow. He fell backwards off the causeway, falling into the icy inner moat, a muffled splash swiftly following. Jack had shot him right between the eyes.

"For Christ's sake, Daemon!" Cartwright barked in a savage whisper. "I told you to be careful about shooting off that thing."

"Sorry, hoss," Jack replied. "That Kraut was about to plug you. Had no choice but to shoot him."

Cartwright and Lipton looked to the double-doors expecting to see a whole platoon of Germans come pouring out. But no one came out. The wind was howling so loudly that no one had heard the gunshot. It was a miracle. But to Jack, it was nothing. He knew the Germans were probably three sheets to the wind by now, this being the Christmas season and all. A sudden gunshot in the middle of a raging snowstorm whilst toasts and libations were being exchanged would not be heard. And he was right. For they crouched there a full minute by the double-doors, waiting for Germans to appear... but none ever appeared.

"Okay, Cartwright," Jack spouted. "What now?"

Cartwright took a deep breath and hustled down the causeway. When he reached the doors, he grasped hold of one of the handles and slowly pushed the door open, just a crack, and peered in. He looked around quietly, seeing it opened up into a cobbled courtyard. Cartwright could see the courtyard was deserted. Seeing no one was around, he waved Jack and Lipton in, and both men skirted past the big wooden doors and slunk into the courtyard, closely hugging the walls, staying in the shadows. It was considerably warmer and less stormy inside, Jack noticed right away.

"By jingo!" he quipped a few seconds later as they stood in the shadows of the courtyard. "It sure is good to be out of that freezin' snowstorm. If'n I get some leave when we get back, I'm gonna spend it in front of a real hot fire, with some real strong whiskey."

"Right-o, mate," Lipton replied. "But we gotta get back first."

"Shh!" Cartwright shushed. "Someone will hear you guys."

Cartwright dashed up to a brick-arched doorway, stepping down into a stone foyer. Beyond it, he could see a long, dimly lit hallway, whitewashed walls and a stone-flagged floor. He went inside, waving the other two men inward, and then rested against a wall.

"Listen up, men," Cartwright whispered, "There's no sense in rushing into this place and trusting to luck we'll find the Professor. This is a big castle and he could be anywhere—it has at least a hundred rooms, probably more. So here's what we'll do." He paused a moment, collecting his thoughts and his breath, then said: "We've got to find a German and take him, take him alive, then force him to talk. Every German in here must know where the Professor is, I'm sure of that. Then we go find the Professor and get him."

"Sounds like a plan," Jack concurred.

"I hope we can find someone quickly," Lipton remarked, "before the Jerries discover we just killed three of their mates."

"Yeah," Cartwright affirmed glumly. "Okay, men. Let's go!"

CHAPTER 7

SS STURMBANNFÜHRER Emil Dietrich read the intelligence communique with delighted blue eyes, reveling in the information it brought forth; the German offensive in the Ardennes was going as planned and the Allied forces were in full retreat. The tall, blond SS-Major clenched the communique into a tight wad and grunted elatedly; the winds of war had shifted again, and in the Third Reich's favor once more. He opened the back door to the Mercedes-Benz staff car and exited the four-door sedan, not waiting for his driver to do it for him. Rottenführer Wenzel was too slow for his personal taste; the poor man had a bad limp that slowed him down, caused by a nasty shrapnel wound he got whilst serving on the Russian Front. He was a stocky, loyal man, a decorated hero even, but just too slow to keep up with the much younger SS-Major.

"Relax, Wenzel," Dietrich said as he traversed the turf tarmac to the aircraft hangar looming before him. "I'll be a few minutes."

"Jawohl, Herr Sturmbannführer," Wenzel replied, saluting, clicking his heels, then seized the cigarette pack laying on the dash.

Dietrich saw the big, black-stenciled letters on the two large hangar doors, which read: FLUGZEUGHALLE (EprSt) FOCK-E-WULF, and knew he was in the right place. He stepped to the side door, snatching it open with a strong arm, and entered the hangar office. Inside, he found the man he was looking for, engineer Hans Multhopp, the man responsible for one of the Luftwaffe's latest warplane design—a jet engine fighter purportedly capable of 600-mph.

"Herr Multhopp?" said Dietrich, finding the lean, bespectacled engineer stooped over a drafting table looking at a blueprint. "It is I... Sturmbannführer Emil Dietrich, again. Are you ready to go?"

"Hmm?" Multhopp replied absently, staring down at the blueprint, his forefinger hooked around his chin. He looked up and then said quite blandly: "Uh, yes... Dietrich. I suppose so."

"The flatbed truck will be here momentarily, ready to transport the prototype to REIMAHG—"

"REIMAHG?" Multhopp gasped. "I thought that was an Me-262 manufacturing facility?"

"It is. But Reichsmarschall Goering wants your new prototypes assembled there as well now. After today's bombing, this facility is no longer safe. It just missed getting bombed to kingdom come."

Multhopp sighed. *"Ja,* I know. I spent three hours in a bomb shelter earlier today... But REIMAHG? That's, that's so far from here. Let's see, it's near, uh...um..."

"Near Kahla, south of Jena, Herr Multhopp. The old sand mine in the Walpersberg Hill."

"What? Isn't that being used for porcelain production?"

"It was." Dietrich nodded.

"Is is safe there? I mean, can it accommodate an advanced production facility? An old porcelain mine, really?"

"It's safe. The existing tunnels in the Walpersberg have been enlarged, and others are being dug, and massive concrete bunkers are also being built outside the tunnels. The top has been leveled off and concrete was poured—an ingenious construction effort—to form a 1,000 meter long runway."

"That's not sufficient for my prototype, I'm sure of that."

"Quite." Dietrich nodded. "Small rockets will have to be fitted to it for take-off. The runway is also too short for any jet to land, so leaving the Walpersberg is an all-or-nothing proposition: there can be no emergency landings. Your jet, like the Me-262, will be flown from the Walpersberg to Lechfeld Air Base, 130 kilometers away, to be fitted with weapons and radios, and to undergo final testing."

"Well, you certainly seem to know a lot about it, I see."

"I have to. I'm in charge of the whole operation."

"But... I thought the Luftwaffe was handling all of this?"

"Not anymore. The SS has taken over the operation."

"Gott! So I see. Is the SS also handing the construction, too?"

"No. The work is done by forced laborers, Herr Multhopp."

"Forced laborers?"

"Poles, Jews, P.O.W.'s, mostly, and other troublemakers. That's why the SS is handling everything now."

"Wunderbar." Multhopp sighed distressingly.

"Laborers from nearby Buchenwald concentration camp, and others, are put to work excavating the tunnels. Harsh conditions—"

"Silence!" Multhopp snapped. "I don't want to hear anymore."

Dietrich chuckled.

Hans Multhopp turned away and stalked out of the office and made his way into the main hangar bay where a futuristic jet plane with a short stubby nose and a bifurcated air intake, mid-mounted 40-degree sweptback wings, and a sharply raked vertical tail, sat parked. The air intake angled under the cockpit and tapered to the rear where the highly advanced Heinkel HeS-011 turbojet engine was housed. That engine would give it a projected speed of 620-mph. The pressurized cockpit had a bubble canopy, which would provide an excellent view for its pilots. The primary armament of the aircraft consisted of four 30-millimeter cannons arranged around the air intake. It would also be able to carry a sizable bomb load of 1,100-pounds, or four Ruhrstahl X-4 wire-guided missiles. A reconnaissance camera could also be fitted to it if need be. It was a highly advance airplane, Multhopp thought proudly, one that would hopefully turn the tide of the air war over Germany. The only problem was time. If he could get the prototype to production and then see it deployed, there was an excellent chance it would make a meaningful impact on the war.

"So, this is your latest, eh, Herr Multhopp?" Dietrich said as he ambled in behind the German engineer. "It looks... deadly."

"Yes, that's a very good description, Dietrich. Deadly, indeed."

"What do you call it? What is its production designation?"

"Well, under the original Project V guidelines, it stills bears RLM airframe number 8-183. But I call it the *Huckebein.*"

"Huckebein? Why that?"

"From an old children's book, written by Wilhelm Busch called: *'Hans Huckebein der Unglücksrabe.'* It's about a cartoonish raven who makes lots of trouble for others."

"Hans Huckebein, The Unlucky Raven?"

"That's right. A book I once read as a child, many years ago."

"Hmm, how obscure," Dietrich remarked. "But... very fitting. It will undoubtedly make a lot of trouble for the Allied bombers."

"It certainly will. I just hope it hasn't come too late."

"Nah! The Third Reich is far from being beaten, Herr Multhopp. As we speak, our Army is smashing thru the Ardennes and pushing onto Antwerp. Then to Paris and beyond. If the Allies don't sue for peace too soon, the war will go on for another year. Maybe longer."

"Lieber Gott, I hope not."

Dietrich walked up to the jet fighter and ran his hand across the leading edge of the sweptback wing. He made a pained face.

"Why, this is made of... wood, is it not?"

"It is," Multhopp replied with some regret. "A chronic shortage of war materials nullified my first option of using aluminum in the construction of the main spar, which led to a necessary reappraisal. I chose to use wood instead of metal throughout the entire wing structure. Wooden ribs attached to the front and back of the I-beams gives the wings their overall shape—then I covered them with plywood."

"So I see." Dietrich nodded doubtfully.

Rottenführer Wenzel came limping in. "Herr Sturmbannführer?"

Dietrich turned around. "Yes, Wenzel, what is it?"

"The Tatra flatbed is here."

"Ah!" Dietrich turned to Multhopp. "Okay, Herr Multhopp, your transportation has arrived. Is this thing ready for transport?"

"Almost. The wings still have to be removed, an easy enough task though. Then you can begin loading procedures."

"How long will that take?"

"My engineers can accomplish the task in a couple of hours, I should think. Maybe less. They're only made of wood, remember?"

"Of course." Dietrich gestured. "All right, Wenzel. Tell the transportation crew to take a supper break while Herr Multhopp and his engineers remove the wings. Then we'll load it and transport it."

"Tonight, Herr Sturmbannführer?" Wenzel grumbled.

"Yes, tonight, Wenzel." Dietrich nodded. "We can't travel by day. Too many Allied fighter-bombers flying overhead. We can only move under the cover of darkness these days. It's the safest time."

"Right." Wenzel saluted, stiff-armed, and then hobbled away.

"Okay, Herr Multhopp," said Dietrich, bowing stiffly, his head inclined. "Have your engineers remove the wings, posthaste—they have precisely one hour. Then we'll begin the loading procedures."

"One hour?" Multhopp sighed, then said: "Oh, all right."

"Do you have a problem with that, Herr Multhopp?"

"No, not really. But—"

"But what?"

"Well..." Multhopp began, then trailed off miserably. "Never mind. It's not important. I'll have the prototype ready in an hour."

"Good." Dietrich's smirk was accompanied by a mocking wink. "After all, the wings are only made of wood, as you said."

"Regrettably."

"I shall return in one hour." Dietrich clicked his heels smartly and saluted, stiff-armed. *"Heil Hitler!"* He traipsed off and left the engineer to his brooding thoughts.

"One hour?" Multhopp said with a resigning sigh, then shambled back to his office. "Alas, the wings are only made of wood."

KEN CARTWRIGHT crept down the stone-flagged corridor, clutching his machine-pistol firmly, Jack and Lipton following soundlessly. The corridor was illuminated with burning firebrands held in iron brackets fixed against the walls. The flickering flames left dark pools of shadows between each firebrand. The three men darted from one shadow to the other. Jack had ditched the greatcoat and helmet, and in his black turtleneck and knit cap, he was no more than a shadow himself. Cartwright and Lipton looked about the same, having taken off their cumbersome anoraks, leaving them in a hidden place. They knew they were on borrowed time, and they had to move swiftly, because when the Germans discovered that three of their guards were missing, all hell would surely break loose. They had to find a German quickly, and then make him talk, force him to tell them where the Professor was being held; a long-shot gamble, at best. But it was the best they could do at the moment. The entire mission had been an ad-libbed operation so far. Ever since the destroyer had struck the German mines and then cast the three O.S.S. agents into the cold sea, they'd been struggling to carry out the mission. Jack found it all rather amusing and stimulating, and interesting, too. This is what he'd signed up for: danger and adventure;

sneaking around an old medieval castle; killing Nazis soldiers; searching for a noted Danish physicist. It was just what he wanted to be doing. And after spending fifteen grueling months in a Japanese P.O.W. camp, he was glad to be back in action once again. But through it all, he wondered if he'd ever get back into the cockpit of a fast fighter plane. To fly and fight had been his only reason for living once. Then of course, there was Rose. Would he ever see her again?

They came to a flight of steps that led to a landing that angled and went higher. Here, they found luxury. Electric light bulbs lighted the way through the ever-widening hallway before them, then to a marble- floored gallery with a broad strip of plush carpeting.

"What now?" Lipton whispered, putting his thinning lips close to Cartwright's ear, gazing at the brilliantly lit gallery before them. "Do we still snatch a German and make him talk?" The Canadian jerked a thumb over his shoulder. "It's a bloody long way back now. Dragging someone who won't be keen to go along is asking a lot."

Cartwright was thinking the same thing. "Change of plans," he replied. "We'll just politely ask someone where the Professor is."

"Politely?"

"Yeah, with this..." Cartwright patted the barrel of his MP-40. "If we don't get a quick answer... we'll just ask someone else."

Jack chuckled.

"Your barmy, mate," Lipton protested.

But Jack understood; Cartwright heard the metallic sound of his Mauser carbine being cocked. Then Lipton cocked his weapon, acquiescing to the inevitable. Then the three men moved out into the gallery feeling like actors steeping into the spotlight, totally exposed suddenly. Naked may have been a better description.

When they reached the center of the lengthy gallery, they heard footsteps coming toward them. The echoing footfall of heavy jack boots got louder, and at the far end of the gallery appeared a German officer; the tabs of a Wehrmacht Oberleutnant (1st Lieutenant) clearly visible on his shoulder boards. He walked onward, totally engrossed in a slip of paper, perhaps a communique, his head bent, reading as he walked. He was no more than ten paces from the three agents before he became aware of their presence. He looked up, his jaw dropping as he took one more step before realizing something was wrong. Terribly wrong.

"Guten Abend, Herr Oberleutnant," Cartwright uttered politely, his MP-40 machine pistol raised and trained on the German officer. *"Wie gehts es ihnen, hmm?"*

The German froze in his tracks, gaping fearfully.

"Sprechen Sie Englisch?"

The German gulped and replied: *"Ja...* er, yes, I mean. I s-speak English."

"Then it's yer lucky day, *amigo,"* Jack chimed in.

"Or unlucky day—if you don't cooperate," Cartwright added, re-cocking the MP-40. "You get my meaning, chap?"

The German nodded wordlessly.

"Where can we find Professor Johansen?"

The German's eyes widened incredulously realizing why three enemy agents were there in the castle. *"Mein Gott!"* he uttered anxiously, then replied, pointing: "U-Up the stairs there. T-Third floor."

"He's lying." Lipton's voice was grating. "I don't trust him."

"It is the truth, I tell you! I want no trouble, please."

"Turn around. Put your hands on your head." Cartwright jerked the barrel of the machine-pistol menacingly. "Do it—now!"

The German officer jerked to life. He turned around and placed his hands behind his head. The paper he had been carrying fluttered to the ground. He hesitated.

"Move it!"

The three agents and the German officer walked forward slowly.

"W-Where to?" asked the German.

"Up the stairs," Cartwright growled. "Third floor. We'll find out in a moment if you're lying or not."

"And if you are, Jerry, old friend," Lipton quipped. "You die."

They traversed the gallery and came to a large dining room. A huge vaulted ceiling with an enormous chandelier opened up above them. Ornate, red-paned windows lined the room. Below, they saw the courtyard with the double doors on the far side. Wide wooden doors on all four sides branched off into separate rooms; all the doors were closed.

"Hey," Jack spoke up, peering out of a window, gazing at courtyard below. "That's the way outta here. Worth remembering."

"Yeah," Cartwright answered. He prodded the German with the muzzle of his machine pistol. "Keep moving, Jerry. Third floor."

The German led them upstairs, rounding half the landing before turning into a narrow doorway where a short flight of stairs rose upwards. He mounted the steps, hands still behind his head.

"Wait!" Cartwright pushed the muzzle into the German's back.

He happened to glance out a window. Below, in the courtyard, he saw four armed guards marching stolidly across the cobbles heading for the causeway. Damn! He knew the German's were about to go on high alert now. Cartwright shoved the German officer, and he continued up the stairs. At the top, they came to a corridor. The German turned right, and they followed until he halted in front of a door.

"Professor Johansen's room?"

"*Ja*—y-yes."

"Go inside. Walk into the middle of the room. Don't turn around and don't take your hands off your head."

Jack grabbed Cartwright's arm. "Whoa, hoss. If this is the Professor's room, why ain't there a guard on the door, huh? He's a dang prisoner, ain't he?"

Cartwright leveled the MP-40 at the German. "Well? You heard him. Why no guard, Jerry?"

"It is not necessary. No one can escape," the German explained. "No one can cross the causeway without encountering guards."

Cartwright believed him; the German was sweating profusely and his eyes flickered with fright. He stared back at the three agents, his pale face an abject mask of fear.

"Okay, go in!"

The door was unlocked, and it opened easily. The German obeyed the instructions and marched into the middle of the room.

There was no sound from inside the room and Cartwright motioned to the others. "Okay. Inside."

They burst in like the well-trained men they were. Lipton stepped past the door and took position with his back against the wall, his machine-pistol moving slowly side to side, covering the room. Jack went straight across to the far side and dropped to a knee. Cartwright closed the door behind them and stood with his back against it. He reached for the switch and turned on the light, flooding the room with electric illumination. It was a small room with a trussed ceiling. It was sparsely furnished with a bed, a chest of drawers, and a tall wooden wardrobe. In the bed, staring up in bewilderment, sat a middle-aged man with graying hair and a neatly trimmed goatee.

"Is he the Professor?" asked Jack. "Is that really him?"

"Yeah," Cartwright answered. "That's him all right." He walked over to the bed and proffered his hand. "Hi-ya, Professor Johansen. Remember me—Ken Cartwright?"

"Ken... Cartwright? Oh, yes, Ken, I remember you." Professor Johansen sat up straighter and shook Cartwright's hand, nodding sleepily. "Zurich, '39, wasn't it?" His English was halting but understandable.

"That's right. I heard you give a speech on quantum physics. We talked at length afterwards, several hours, as I recollect."

Professor Johansen smiled. "I recall the day. Your knowledge was quite impressive if I remember correctly." He looked at Jack, then at Lipton. "But what are you doing here? Who are these men?"

"We're here to rescue you and take you back to England. We'd have had you sooner, sir, only the Germans got wise to it, somehow, and took you from Thisted and brought you here—"

"Hold on, mate," Lipton interjected. "You know something about quantum physics?"

"I studied it in college. I was going to be a physicist myself one day, but, the war came along so I enlisted in the Navy instead."

"No wonder they picked you for this bloody mission."

"Listen, fellers," Jack interceded. "Can we save the idle chit-chat fer later? We gotta get the Professor outta here. Like now! Before the Krauts cotton to our presence."

"Right-o," Lipton agreed. "Let's get cracking, what?"

"How many are there of you?" the Professor asked. "Have the Allies taken Spøttrup Castle?"

"Well, that's a matter of opinion, sir," Cartwright answered with a smirk. "We like to think we've taken the castle... but the Krauts just don't know it yet." He pointed at the German. "Except him."

"There's just the three of us, sorry to say," Lipton added. "And I think we'd rather be pushing off sooner than later, aye?"

"Heck, yeah," Jack threw in. "The sooner the better."

Cartwright walked over to the wardrobe and jerked it open. He took out some trousers and a thick sweater and tossed them on the bed. "Get dressed, Professor. Quickly. We're leaving now."

The Professor swung his pajama-clad legs out of bed. "Yes, yes. Right away. I'll only take a minute." He stood up. "There are papers I must take—papers relating to my work. You understand?" He pointed to the chest of drawers. "You will find them in there. A briefcase is in the bottom of the wardrobe. Please put the papers in the briefcase. All of them." He took off his pajama-top and put on the sweater.

Cartwright motioned to Jack; the Texan leaned his rifle against the wall, then reached into the wardrobe. He found the briefcase and filled it with documents. By the time the case was full the Professor was dressed; over the sweater and trousers he wore a fur coat.

"What about old Jerry here?" Lipton queried, looking at the German, his MP-40 trained on him. "Lay him out? Kill him?"

"Tie him up—use the bedclothes... gag him. We don't want him yelling his head off when we're gone."

"Right-o."

The German officer was bound up tighter than a Christmas goose ready for the oven. He lay on the floor glaring at them. Unsatisfied with the job, Jack walked over to the German and whacked him on the back of the head with the rifle butt, harshly, knocking him out cold. Cartwright and Lipton exchanged disturbed glances.

"He ain't gonna yell out now, is he?" Jack quipped.

The three men stepped out of the room and into the corridor.

"What are your plans," the Professor asked, "for getting me out? You realize the only way out is across the causeway."

"Yeah. We know." Cartwright nodded. "We came in on it."

"Right. And that's how we'll leave, Professor," said Lipton, jerking his head toward the staircase. "We'll go back the way we came, through the courtyard and out the front door."

"There's a blizzard blowing outside," Cartwright imparted confidently. "No one will see us, Professor."

"So sure, are you?"

They made it all the way to the lower hallway and foyer. Then all hell broke loose. The Germans had found their dead comrades and the whole castle was now in a frantic state of alarm. Soldiers were yelling and hollering, bustling back and forth through the double doors of the castle. The sounds of angry Germans and heavy jackboots seemed to be everywhere.

"Shit!" Cartwright cursed. "The Krauts know we're here!"

"Oh, that's just ripe," Lipton muttered glumly.

"Not to worry, fellers." Jack disappeared for a moment, then reappeared with the German greatcoat and helmet on, the same out-fit he had ditched earlier before going upstairs. He smiled fiendishly. "Alrighty then. I'll slip out into the courtyard and siphon off some of these Krauts, okay? Get 'em moving away from here—"

"How the hell you gonna do that, mate?" Lipton asked

"Just wait and see—and listen up for my signal, okay?" Jack gestured to Lipton's MP-40. "Lemme have that banjo there, and a spare magazine. I might need to play a fast tune on some of these Krauts. Maybe a special request." Jack chuckled.

"W-What?"

"Deamon?" Cartwright interjected. "What the heck are you up to? This ain't no time for heroics."

"Just give me the dang machine-pistol, Lipton!" Jack insisted. "We gotta move fast now, while the gettin's good. With all the com-motion going on the Germans will never suspect I'm an American."

Cartwright sighed worriedly; he really had no idea as what to do at that moment. But whatever Jack was planning on doing was bet-ter than doing nothing, he wisely realized. He puffed out his cheeks and nudged Lipton on the arm. "Go on, give it to him, Lipton. We gotta do something, and fast. Before it's *really* too late."

Professor Johansen frowned; these men had no plan at all.

"Bullocks!" Lipton grumbled, handing off the MP-40 to Jack.

"Thanks." Jack motioned. "And a spare magazine, please?"

"Shite! We're just going to blast our way out of this place?" Lip-ton rumbled as he reluctantly gave Jack the spare 32-round maga-zine. "This is mad, Cartwright. Right bloody mad, 'tis!"

Cartwright shrugged. "Got a better idea?"

"Heaven help us," Professor Johansen moaned.

Jack hopped up. "Okay, fellers. I'm ready. How do I look?"

"Good enough, I guess," Cartwright muttered.

"Like a half-arsed Nazi," Lipton rejoined, holding the carbine.

Jack winked. "It'll pass mustard, you'll see."

He darted out the foyer and stalked into the courtyard, the great coat buttoned up all the way up and the collar turned up high. The gray coal-scuttle helmet was pulled down tight over his brow, the chin strap firmly fastened around his jaw. He held the machine-pistol at the ready, his finger on the trigger. As he went out into the courtyard, a squad of Germans suddenly pushed through a door on their way outside.

"Geh wieder rein, ihr Idioten!" he shouted in German. *"Get back upstairs! Secure the Professor! Los! Los! Mach schnell!"*

The Germans turned around obediently and went back inside the castle. Jack darted to the outer doors and peered out. He saw a squad of Germans, about eight men, standing around, nervous looks on their faces. He grinned; he also saw a German Kübelwagen parked and idling in front of the gatehouse, blocking the entrance, an officer standing upright on the floorboards brandishing a Luger. It had stopped snowing and the wind was blowing calmer now.

"Sweet! That's our ride outta here," he said to himself, nodding assuredly. "Yup, Lady Luck sure is lookin' out fer us."

Jack turned back to the others and whistled. "C'mon out, ya'll. The coast is clear."

Cartwright, Lipton and the Professor emerged from the darkened recesses of the foyer, curious looks on their faces. Cartwright immediately scurried over to the double doors and pulled one open, just a crack, looking out. He got a big shock.

"What the hell, Deamon!" Cartwright gasped. "The coast is clear? There's got to be at least a platoon of Krauts out there!"

"Just eight. Don't get yer boxers in a wad over it. I got this."

Jack jerked a nod and slammed out of the double-doors, stalking down the causeway, his hands on the MP-40, his trigger finger itching to do some shooting. He walked right up to the squad of Germans leering fiendishly, his eyes flaring. A guard turned about and faced him, his chin up, his eyes inquiring.

"Was is los?" he asked.

"Just this, Jerry," he uttered in English and let fly a blistering volley of 9-millimeter rounds, spraying the surprised Germans, mowing them down. They spun off in all directions, blossoms of blood spouting from their greatcoats, stunned looks on their faces. None of them ever got off a shot. And Jack's aim was good. When he'd completely emptied the 32-round magazine, eight Germans lay dead or dying on the causeway. He ejected the empty and reloaded the extra in one swift motion. The officer standing in the Kübelwagen was dumbfounded, and in a momentary state of shock, just stood there aghast as Jack stepped over the dead bodies and came toward him. Three seconds later, he composed himself and fired a shot, but missed, then fired again, missing again while Jack steadily stalked toward him. He finally hit Jack, grazing his shoulder, shearing off the greatcoat's right shoulder board. Jack just laughed and opened fire; he hit the German officer with a rapid six-round burst, literally upending him and knocking him out of the Kübelwagen, killing him instantly. Jack glanced sidelong at his smoldering shoulder and scoffed carelessly.

"Close... but no cigar, *signor.*"

By that time, Cartwright and the others had scampered past the double doors and ran down the causeway, sidestepping the dead Germans laying about, incredulous looks on their faces.

"Jesus Christ!" Cartwright swore, gazing wide-eyed at the mayhem Jack had just perpetrated. "You, you... k-killed them all?"

"Yup," Jack replied laconically, then pointed. "Got us some transportation, too. Looky there. A Nazi jeep—compliments of the German Wehrmacht. Running and ready to go."

"Bloody hell!" Lipton muttered. "You're regular assassin, Deamon. I mean... a damnable devil, you are."

"Yeah, I've been called that once or twice."

The Professor sighed miserably, looking around; he hated war.

"Okay, let's mount up, men," Cartwright ordered waving everyone onward. "Let's get the Professor in and head down to the pier. God, I hope the boat's still there."

"You came by boat?" Professor Johansen asked, surprised.

"How else?" Lipton replied.

"I thought maybe you men parachuted in, like commandos?"

"Nah," Jack said with a crooked grin, sliding in behind the steering wheel of the Kübelwagen, then remarked sarcastically: "Why jump out of a perfectly good airplane when you can take a boat ride—in style!"

Everybody got into the Kübelwagen.

That wry bit of sarcasm was not lost on Cartwright's sharp mind. True, the mission had been a dicey undertaking thus far, ever since the destroyer sank and them nearly with it. Now they had to board yet another boat and navigate some narrow fjords all whilst angry Germans pursued them. He knew they'd be on high alert by the time they got to the pier; this was the critical part of the mission. Success depended on the next two hours. Yet somehow, Jack's bloodthirsty heroics had bolstered Cartwright's waning spirits. This guy was a one-man army, he thought; a human wrecking ball; a devil of man; one audacious rakehell!

"Okay," Jack declared calmly. "Everybody in?"

"Punch it, mate!" Lipton exclaimed. "Gas this banger, already!"

Jack stamped the accelerator and wheeled the Kübelwagen onto the icy roadway and sped away, its snow-chained tires digging into the snow. And just in time. An angry mob of Germans came pouring out of the castle doors and stomped down the causeway, shouting and shooting, cursing the men who had killed their comrades.

IT WAS ALMOST six o'clock in the morning when Rose finally got home. She'd spent the better part of the evening at Tholly's Tavern eating and drinking with some of her girlfriends—the last three hours in a bomb shelter. The air raid sirens had sounded just as she and her two friends were leaving the tavern, forcing them to scurry to a nearby bomb shelter, where they sat and waited, fretting, being told by an air raid warden that some V-1 buzz bombs had been spotted in the area. Well, they heard no explosions, so they assumed none had struck nearby. At about 5:30, the all-clear was finally given, and she went home.

As she sat down on the bed and peeled off her nylon stockings, she thought about Jack again. Strange it was to her, if not a little unsettling, that she'd be thinking about him instead of David. Perhaps it was just a byproduct of her relief. Major Hickok had telephoned her from London earlier that day with some promising news. The Red Cross director had informed him that David was being held at Stalag Luft V, a Luftwaffe camp near Halle, Germany, and that he was in good health. Rose was told she'd probably be receiving a postcard from him very soon. Major Hickok had also told her that during their stay at the prison camp, transient P.O.W.'s were allowed to send one postcard, usually their first, in which they informed next of kin of the camp's number and address. P.O.W.'s permanently at Stalag V drew two postcards and letters per month. Incoming mail, judiciously censored by the Germans, was unlimited in quantity but sporadic in arrival, especially at high security camps like Stalag Luft V, which received no incoming mail for months at a time. Both outgoing and incoming letters could up to take two or three months in transit as did personal parcels. And the flow of such parcels was light. Yet Rose was hopeful—a little less worried now.

That's why she thought of Jack again.

As far as she knew, he was probably still in a Japanese P.O.W. camp suffering ungodly privations and enduring horrific physical abuse. No official word had ever been relayed to her by General Kenny of the 5th Air Force, or for that matter, by Colonel Truscott (who was now a General she'd been told) as of his whereabouts. Jack had mysteriously disappeared from the face of the earth just as he'd mysteriously appeared, without warning, why or wherefore.

But Rose knew there had been a cover-up, she knew Truscott had swept the shocking truth about John J. Knight under the rug. And how convenient it was, she recalled, that he had been shot down and captured precisely when his true identity was coming to light; that old rascal Truscott had known all along, too. But he continued to use Jack as a publicity tool, marketing him as the all-American working-class hero and hotshot air ace, touting him as the next Medal of Honor winner. Howbeit, when Jack was unexpectedly shot down, so was his problematical past. And there it was left to languish quietly in a Japanese prison camp until the end of the war... along with poor old Jack himself.

She suddenly felt sorry for the man she once loved. Jack had only done what he thought he needed to do to get where he wanted to be; a fighter squadron serving in the Pacific. There was no shame in wanting to become something bigger or better than himself. And taking advantage of an accidental opportunity was really the only crime he'd committed. But stealing another man's identity was a serious crime in the eyes of the law, and in Rose's eye, an unforgivable act. Not because it was outright unlawful but because he had deceived her in trying to win her hand; he had lied about who he actually was. Once the truth was known to her, she felt cheated, taken advantage of, used, and her love for him justifiably waned. She lingered for a while, though, wondering what she should do. Divorce him? Have the marriage annulled? In the end, she chose the latter, deciding the whole thing was a farce to begin with and the wedding nuptials meant nothing at all. And when she became involved with David, she forgot all about Jack. So why now had she thought of him? Why did she care all of a sudden? What part of her heart still pined for the dishonorable devil, Jack Knight?

Crikey! I must forget him and think of David, she told herself. *He's the man I truly love. Not Jack. Jack never really existed.*

Rose got up from the bed and unbuttoned her blouse. As she stood there in the dim lamplight of the room fumbling with the buttons, she heard a strange sound (an odd pulsing that sounded something like a two-stroke motorcycle engine) and it was getting louder and louder by the second. She stepped over to the window and gazed out, wondering what it could be. When she looked up into the dawn sky, she saw a pulsing flame moving across the sky in the general direction of her two-story flat, and this stuttering rattle of some peculiar sound. She froze, abject fear shooting through her body. When the pulsing sound abruptly stopped, and the flame disappeared, she knew what came next.

"God! No!" Rose moaned as she leaped to the floor as a massive explosion went off outside her window. The building quaked and glass and plaster went flying. She felt the floor buckle beneath her feet, then the lamp went out. A great crashing sound rumbled in her ears as she slid across the floor, feeling the place collapsing around her; she felt pieces of wood and plaster hit her body and head. But she felt nothing. She cried out. Then darkness engulfed her.

THE LITTLE TRAWLER puttered onward across the fjord, two of its four passengers huddled together in the wheelhouse. Cartwright and the Professor stood shoulder to shoulder whilst Jack and Lipton stood at the bow and stern respectively, keeping a lookout for German patrol boats. They'd gotten to the trawler in good time, racing along the coastal road that led to the pier. They clambered aboard and threw off the mooring lines. Within minutes, they were chugging for the western inlet making good their escape. As far as they knew, no Germans had followed them. But Cartwright was sure the Jerries had put out the word, alerting the entire area of their escape.

Soon enough, he soberly realized, German E-boats would appear on the scene; the Luftwaffe might even make an appearance. He wasn't worried about that. The weather was too bad for most aircraft and the nearest Luftwaffe airfield was many miles away. But the dreaded German E-boats were sure to show up and make trouble. If that happened, Cartwright wasn't sure what could be done. To fight off an E-boat in a derelict old trawler was just plain suicide. So, he kept the little six-cylinder motor going at full speed, hardly exceeding 15-knots, in hopes of making it past the inlet and then to the open sea. And from there? France? England? He knew not. He had used the trawler's shortwave transmitter several times to contact the Royal Navy using frequencies he knew they used. But so far, no one had responded.

"You men are very courageous, I must say," the Professor said to Cartwright, watching him drive the boat with knowing hands.

"Courage is often confused with having nothing to lose."

"Ah. Is there a ship waiting for us beyond the fjord?"

"Maybe. Maybe not? I don't know. We've been playing it by ear since the destroyer sank days ago."

"I see." The Professor frowned.

"If we can get to open sea before this fog dissipates, we'll have a good chance of eluding German patrol boats. I hope this little trawler holds together until then."

"Are you a Navy man, Ken?" The Professor asked.

"Yes, sir. I am. Joined the U.S. Navy right after the Pearl Harbor. attack. I transferred to the O.S.S. later on... after I got—discharged."

"Discharged?"

"Yeah. Mouthed off to an admiral, then got arrested by the Shore Patrol for starting a fight with a sub-captain. They were going to jail me for the duration when I was approached by an O.S.S. recruiter. He got me off the charges and had me discharged from the Navy in return for joining the O.S.S. as a special agent."

"Interesting."

"I miss the Navy, though."

"I'm sure you do." The Professor smiled. "One day you'll leave the service. Take a wife, father children. See less and less of the sea, until she becomes like a painting on the wall, static and irrelevant. But she'll keep calling you. And when she does, you'll step into that painting and feel the swell beneath your feet once again. It'll come back to you like it was yesterday."

"You think so?"

"I've watched you men handle this boat since you rescued me, accomplish unbelievable things. From what I've seen, if we reach the open sea, we just might survive this ordeal."

"I hope you're right—"

"Heads up, mates!" Lipton shouted from his lookout on the stern. "We've got trouble. Look!" He pointed to the slender silhouette astern of them. "German E-boat coming up fast—behind us!"

Everybody turned around and looked. About a half-a-mile away, they saw a German torpedo boat cutting the waves behind them, cruising at least 40-knots, maybe more. Cartwright knew it carried four torpedoes and two 20-millimeter cannons mounted on the forecastle and midships, plus a 37-millimeter cannon aft, more than enough firepower to obliterate the little trawler several times over.

"Damn!" Cartwright cursed. "What now?"

"Yeah, what now?" Jack echoed.

"We just keep going until we can lose them in that fogbank ahead," Cartwright returned. "They must know the Professor is aboard by now. So they won't fire on us for fear of killing him."

"And if they overtake us?" Lipton wanted to know.

"We let 'em have it!" Jack retorted cockily, cocking his newly acquired machine-pistol for effect. "Mow those bastards down—"

"You're bloody daft, man!" Lipton shot back. "They'll cut us to pieces before we even get off two shots."

"He's right, Daemon. Shooting it out with the Germans is crazy. Your hell-for-leather heroics can't save us now. There's at least thirty armed crewmen on that E-boat, and their cannons can blast us right out of the water—easily."

"Then what will you do, Ken?" asked the Professor.

Cartwright didn't answer. He he no idea what they should do.

"Well?" Lipton asked. "What *are* we going to do, hmm?"

"We just keep heading for that fogbank ahead," Cartwright said, finally. "Try loose them in it if we can. It's all we can do right now."

"You could surrender, Ken." the Professor proposed. "No sense in all of you dying on my account—"

"No way, Professor Johansen. We didn't come all the way out

here to rescue you, only to hand you back over to the Krauts in the end. We'll keep going until we get free of this place or we can't go any further. Meaning: we fight it out in the end... if we have to."

"Now yer talking my language," Jack quipped devilishly.

"God help us." Professor Johansen groaned.

Cartwright leaned on the throttle trying to milk a few more knots out of the little trawler. But he knew full-well it was already at maximum rpm's; 16-knots was all she would do. He kept his eyes forward and focused on the approaching inlet hoping he could get out on open sea and escape into the vast fogbank that seemed to engulf the ocean beyond. The small slow-going trawler could lose the bigger E-boat in the dense fog, it's smaller, quieter motor easily drowned out by the German's noisy diesels. He knew the E-boat didn't have radar so finding a fishing trawler in a large fogbank might be a haphazard game of cat and mouse. So he hoped.

The E-boat was getting closer. In a few minutes it would overtake the little trawler. Although its guns were already within range, the crew held its fire knowing the Professor was aboard. Their orders were to overtake the trawler, board it, and take the Professor alive, along with all the crew, if possible. Under no circumstances were they to open fire on the trawler, unless, of course, they had to defend themselves. But as the trawler traversed the narrows of the inlet and broke out into the open sea, the motor began to sputter and smoke. Then it just quit.

"God-dammit!" Cartwright cursed. "Our goose is cooked now."

"Bloody hell! And here come the Jerries now."

Jack shook his head, half-grinning, half-laughing. "Looks like we gotta fight it out now—"

"No. No!" Professor Johansen protested. "You will not fight. I cannot allow you men die so needlessly just to spare my life."

"It wouldn't be needlessly, Professor. It's our job, sir. We're O.S.S. men. It's what we signed up for."

"Nothing doing, Ken. I won't let you do it—"

"ATTENTION CREW OF DANISH TRAWLER!" a voice boomed from the E-boat; a German officer stood on the deck with a bullhorn, barking out orders in English, oddly. *"SURRENDER IMMEDIATLY OR WE WILL BE FORCED TO FIRE ON YOU!"*

"Christ!" Cartwright bemoaned fumbling with the ignition.

"They know who we are. We've had it now."

"I say we let *them* have it," Jack riposted. "We go out shooting —die with our boots on."

"You blasted Yank cowboy!" Lipton snarled. "This isn't some ruddy Hollywood western—this isn't some cowboy and red Indian movie. Use your bloody loaf, man!"

"No! No!" the Professor continued to protest.

The E-boat was almost on them, its 20-millimeter guns trained on its hull and wheelhouse, its forward torpedo tubes open and ready to launch. In a matter of seconds it would be alongside them, primed to grapple and its crew spoiling for a fight. Cartwright shook his head, realizing he only had one real option—surrender. It was a dirty shame, he thought. So close and yet so far. He laid his gun down and raised his hands, then urged the others to do the same.

"C'mon, men," he implored. "It's over. We've run out of luck."

"That is a wise decision, Ken," Professor Johansen agreed.

"To hell with that!" Jack refused. "Let's fight it out—"

"Please, don't be foolish, gentleman," the Professor adjured. "You did your best. But it's over now. We must surrender."

"Never!" Jack growled. I ain't going to no P.O.W. camp. Naw, sir. Been there, done that. I'd rather die than be a prisoner again."

"Forget it, mate," said Lipton. "We're finished."

"Get below, Professor," Cartwright enjoined. "If this goes sour, I don't want you in the line of fire."

"Get below? Listen, Ken—"

"Just do it, Professor. It's for your own safety."

"No. Listen, I must—"

"Please, sir," Cartwright insisted. "Get below. Do it, dammit!"

Professor Johansen sighed resignedly and did as he was told. Reluctantly, he went into the wheelhouse and went down below, descending the wooden steps that led to the trawler's lower cabin.

"ATTENTION CREW OF DANISH TRAWLER!" the voice boomed once again. *"DO NOT ATTEMPT RESISTANCE. LAY DOWN YOUR WEAPONS AND SURRENDER IMMEDIATLY!"*

"Drop your weapon, Daemon," Cartwright ordered. "It's no use to resist now. We can't win."

Jack shook his head, wagging it back and forth dolefully. "Naw. Naw. I cain't surrender, man, I just cain't. I don't wanna go to another prison camp. No way in hell!"

"Just do it, mate!" Lipton cut in sharply. "We've had our chips. Cartwright's right, we can't win." He tossed the carbine and raised his hands up high.

"Horsefeathers!"

"Drop your gun, Daemon!" Cartwright barked. "I order you!"

Jack muttered bitterly and laid his weapon down, glaring hard at Cartwright, shaking his head, he couldn't believe this was happening; he couldn't believe he was going to be a prisoner again. All the miscues and mishaps they'd been through together just to find and rescue the Professor, it was all for naught now. They were simply giving up without a fight. Jack felt disgusted, disheartened—defeated. This was not what he'd signed up for; surrender was not a thing he was accustomed to; giving up in the face of the offered odds was not something he cared to do. It was against his principles and a rude kick in the balls. It was a slight against his honor.

"WE ARE COMING ALONGSIDE NOW," the voice repeated but more sternly. *"RAISE YOUR HANDS IN THE AIR! DO NOT ATTEMPT TO RESIST! RESISTANCE IS FUTILE!"*

Cartwright, Lipton and Jack stood there with their hands raised.

The E-boat pulled alongside, its deck brimming with stolid German sailors armed with StG-44 assault rifles and hostile expressions. Jack refused to believe this was happening. He stood there, a dejected look on his face, glaring at the Germans with virulent eyes.

Once the two boats were side by side, six German sailors boarded, each armed with an assault rifle. The Commander of the E-boat, a lean, middle-aged man with a blond mustache, drew his Luger sidearm and also boarded. Two Germans seized Lipton and escorted him over the gunwales. The Commander approached Cartwright.

"Where is the Professor?" he asked, his English clear enough but heavily accented. "We know he is aboard this boat."

"Don't know what you're talking about."

"Hah-hah-hah!" The Commander chuckled.

He turned to one of his men and barked a command in German, ordering him to search the cabin of the trawler. The sailor cocked his assault rifle and went below. In the meantime, two other sailors grabbed Jack by the arms, manhandling him roughly. Jack threw off the sailors' arms and leered at them hatefully.

"Back off, Jerry!" he snarled angrily. "Git yer dang dirty Nazi paws off me, ya hear?"

"Stand down, Daemon!" Cartwright snapped, he himself now in the custody of two German sailors. "Don't do anything stupid."

"To hell with this!" Jack raged and turned on the other German, throwing an elbow to his jaw, knocking him over. The other German promptly whirled around and tried to hit Jack with the butt of his rifle but missed. Jack ducked and cold-cocked him with a vicious left hook, literally sprawling him out. Then a shot rang out that spun Jack around and knocked him to the deck; he felt a bullet pierce his right forearm, stinging him, hurting him, drawing his blood. He laid there moaning, bleeding.

"I told you resistance is futile!" the Commander growled, holding the smoking sidearm, ready to shoot again if necessary.

"B-Bastard," Jack grumbled. "I'll see you in hell first before—"

His retort was cut short by a massive explosion. The E-boat bent in half as a spouting geyser of flame and foam shot up in the air, lifting it out of the water. Then it broke in two and rapidly sank amid a whirling wake of flotsam and fire. And amidst that violent explosion, Cartwright threw off his two captors and grabbed his gun. In a quick coordinated motion, he rattled off a quick burst that struck the E-boat Commander and killed him instantly. Then he shot the two Germans nearest him. Jack, although wounded, managed to trip up a German and clobbered him with his rifle stock, smashing his skull —all this whilst the trawler rocked and rolled in the wake of the explosion, almost sinking itself.

But one German managed to get off a shot. It was the sailor who had been ordered to go down into the cabin and find the Professor. He came staggering out of the wheelhouse, his StG-44 cocked and loaded. He hosed down the deck with a blistering volley, catching Cartwright full-force, bloodying him, spinning him around, knocking him over backward. Cartwright gasped a bloody spate, mumbled something, then expired, his eyes frozen in a dead man's stare.

Jack fired. He hit the German with a rapid-fire burst, wounding him, making him drop his weapon. The young sailor grunted and dropped to a knee, holding his bloodied side. Jack stood up as the smoke of the gunfire and explosion dissipated, coddling his right arm. He strode over to the sailor, the assault rifle trained on him.

"Easy now, fella." Jack quipped grimly. "It's all over now."

The Professor came up from the hold, a disturbed look on his face, his hair wet and tousled, his eyes wide with disbelief. He walked up to Jack and looked around, seeing dead Germans everywhere. "My God!" he exclaimed. "W-What happened?"

"There, Professor." Jack pointed. "That's what happened."

The sea bubbled up nearby as a British submarine surfaced, its conning tower rising high above of the water. A moment later, the hatch opened and two Royal Navy officers appeared. One waved.

"Ahoy, there!" he shouted. "We received your transmission. Got here as quick as we could."

Jack waved back. "Ya got here just in time."

"Sorry about the mess, old boy. Hope everyone's all right?"

"We're fine. As well as can be expected, considering."

Lipton suddenly materialized, clambering over the gunwales, soaking wet and freezing cold but nonetheless alive. "B-Bloody Royal Navy," he grumbled bitterly. "Nearly k-killed us all!"

The Professor knelt down beside Cartwright's prostrate body and wept. "Poor, poor boy," he muttered. "Dead. And for what?"

PART TWO

CHAPTER 8

C HRISTMAS EVE AT STALAG Luft V was a grim affair. The men of Barracks A-1 just sat around the wood-burning stove reminiscing about Christmases long past. Colonel McKavitt spent his time writing postcards and plotting his escape, waiting for the tide to turn on the battlefront. Things were still looking bad for the American troops dug in around Bastogne. A new prisoner had relayed news of the battle. The Germans practically surrounded certain units of the American Army. And the weather was so deplorable that the Air Corps remained grounded; air drop was the only way to resupply the troops. The war, it seemed, had become as static as it had been in World War I. But the course of the war didn't bother McKavitt as much as the weather did. If he could really escape the confines of Camp Totenkopf, he faced the bitter prospect of traversing unfamiliar territory in the dead of winter. Group Captain Hawker had already warned McKavitt that no escape plan would be approved unless he deemed it foolproof. The American Colonel had to agree reluctantly; an escape had to be thoroughly thought out and carefully planned if there was going to be any chance of success. So, in the meantime, he'd busied himself by seeing to the men's well-being making sure they were getting decent food and winter clothing. He met with the Kommandant several times demanding better conditions, more privileges, clean bedding, hot showers, medical supplies and faster mail service. But Warnstadt's hands were tied; supplies were limited and anything extra went to the German troops fighting on the front. McKavitt felt helpless and disillusioned.

Although the men lacked basic necessities, their overall health was good. Several American army doctors captured early in the African and Italian campaigns, attended to the P.O.W.'s and were able to treat some of their aliments and administer simple remedies. Stalag Luft V also had a few British doctors as well as some French. The men reported to the dispensary, and if considered ill enough for hospitalization, were kept in the camp infirmary which could accommodate around a hundred patients in ten rooms. More serious cases went to Lazarett IV near Leipzig. This field hospital-like installation consisted of twelve barracks, two of which were equipped for surgical operations. Emergency dental treatment could also be obtained at the German Lazarett. The doctors complained often to McKavitt about the serious shortage of medical supplies. At first they used German medicines and any equipment they could get. Later, the Red Cross sent supplies which alleviated the shortage but did not totally satisfy the doctors' demands.

Despite delousing, lice and fleas troubled the men a great deal. The Americans P.O.W.'s, however, unlike the Russians, had not contracted typhus. Some men suffered from skin diseases brought about by acute uncleanliness. The washing facilities in the camp were altogether unsatisfactory, and a man was extremely lucky to take a shower every two weeks. And the latrines were always a source of contention between McKavitt and the Kommandant. The same complaint was constantly issued that the pits were only emptied when they threatened to overflow, and there was no chloride of lime to neutralize the odor which permeated the surrounding area.

In spite of recent events, McKavitt found the men's morale to be rather high. The noncoms repeatedly showed their disdain toward the Germans by often refusing to salute, by failing to come to attention when a German officer entered the barracks, and by their apparent careless, slouching, hands-in-pocket walk; after their sojourn in Italian camps some men captured in '43 were unpleasantly surprised by the treatment they received in Stalag Luft V which had been described to them as a model camp and a prison with better living conditions. Morale slumped even lower when the camp grew overcrowded due to the influx of hundreds of new prisoners. The Germans were consolidating their P.O.W. camps because of supply and manpower issues.

The men had neither decent living quarters nor satisfactory sanitary facilities nor sufficient clothing. Earlier that week, Sergeant Major Boggs reported that stealing among the prisoners had become rampant and a few fights had broken out because of it. McKavitt alleviated the problem with the best morale-enhancer he had at his disposal, food; it was made available for the Christmas celebrations. Although the camp was more crowded than ever before, the P.O.W.'s spirits remained high. Red Cross parcels kept coming in and the arrival of veteran N.C.O.'s with strict work ethics did much to prevent their spirits from declining.

A representative of the American Red Cross made a routine visit on the 19th. Afterward, he said he would make a special trip whenever summoned. McKavitt was permitted to talk to him privately, and despite oral and written protests by the Red Cross to the Kommandant about both general and specific affairs of the camp, very little improvement was effected. Von Warnstadt repeatedly said that his hands were tied and there was nothing he could do about it. After petitioning the Red Cross for swifter action, and still nothing happened, McKavitt began to feel the Red Cross was characterized by indifference and inertia—until the arrival of the Christmas food shipment. Afterward, his attitude changed for the better. He knew the men were indebted to the Red Cross for almost all their food, clothing and medical supplies. Although food parcels arrived regularly and in sufficient quantity—most of the time—the camp still suffered a chronic clothing shortage; the stocks shipped from Geneva were not quite enough to equip the many hundreds of transient P.O.W.'s who passed through the camp every day.

The men's morale was truly boosted with the arrival of Captain Harold Jenkins, a Chaplain from Atlanta, Georgia. He quickly won the hearts of both Americans and British. He was given complete liberty to look after P.O.W.'s in Stalag Luft V. Once a month he'd be allowed to visit the work detachments near Birkhahn, a sub-camp of Buchenwald. He also received permission to visit Lazarett IV. In addition to Jenkins, Major Atwell of the Church of England held services for the Protestants. Roman Catholic prisoners were allowed to attend weekly masses held by French priests. Jewish P.O.W.'s were segregated in separate barracks. Otherwise, they were not discriminated against. But they were not offered any religious services.

HANS MULTHOPP stood outside the REIMAHG production facility, gawking at the giant bombproof doors again, staring at them a bit more awed; they were an impressive sight. He'd just been given a tour of the facility. It was indeed located in an old sand mine in the Walpersberg Hill just as Sturmbannführer Dietrich had said. It bore the odd code name "Lachs" (Salmon). It had been built for quicker assembly line manufacture. Due to the setup at the main Messerschmitt factory, fast assembly line production was not possible. Furthermore, the factory was extremely vulnerable to Allied bombing attacks, so accordingly, a new aviation company named *Flugzeugwerke Reichsmarschall Hermann Göring* (REIMAHG for short) was formed. It was a subsidiary of the Gustloff Nazi industrial complex. It was typically concerned with the production of Me-262 jet fighters. Herr Multhopp's new jet prototypes would also be constructed there.

He'd keenly observed how the existing tunnels in the Walpersberg had been enlarged while others were still being dug, and two massive concrete bunkers were being built outside two of the tunnels. Me-262 sub-parts were being manufactured and partially assembled in these tunnels, then moved outside to the concrete bunkers where final assembly took place. The assembled jets were then raised to the top of the mountain via an aircraft lift that moved along a railed ramp by a powered winch. The top of the Walpersberg had been leveled off and concreted in an impressive construction effort to form a runway 1,000 meters long and 30 meters wide. The runway had a narrow gauge railway running along one side and various buildings, huts, and hangars on the other. The runway wasn't nearly long enough for a Me-262 to take flight, Multhopp knew; even with jet engines takeoff was fairly slow. So, small rockets would be fixed to assist takeoff. The runway was also too short for the jets to land on; leaving the Walpersberg was an all-or-nothing proposition: there could be no return landings. The jets would be flown from Kahla to Lechfeld Airbase, 130 kilometers away, and equipped with weapons and radios, and then undergo final testing.

Multhopp also found out from Dietrich that a hillside of slate boulders along the Elster River was chosen as the site of a tunnel system that would produce fuel from coal. Laborers from nearby Buchenwald concentration camp and other P.O.W. camps were being put to work excavating the tunnels under extremely harsh conditions, Multhopp had noticed. And according to Dietrich, some of these laborers were soon to include American airmen and soldiers who'd been captured during the recent campaign in the Ardennes.

"Well, Herr Multhopp," the awed engineer heard the grating voice of Sturmbannführer Dietrich droning in his ears. "What do you think?"

"Impressive," Multhopp replied. "Quite impressive."

"I thought you might like it. This facility, once operational, will produce one hundred and fifty jet fighters a month, perhaps many more. Each aircraft being produced in 2,500 man hours."

"Hmm, as long as the Allied bombers don't interfere."

Dietrich scoffed derisively. "This facility is impervious to high explosive bombs, Herr Multhopp. Nothing can penetrate these concrete bunkers." He pointed. "See those concrete buildings there? They have reinforced walls four meters thick."

Multhopp looked, adjusting his glasses. "Ah, I see."

"You will be well-protected, Herr Multhopp. You'll be able to continue your work without interruption."

"Good." Multhopp nodded. "As soon as my engineers have finished setting up shop, I'll begin construction on the next prototype."

"Excellent." Dietrich smiled glibly. "Your new prototype will be a superior alternative to the Messerschmitt fighter jets. Perchance a bit more reliable, I hope?"

"I should think so." Multhopp glowered. "Herr Messerschmitt chose the temperamental Jumo-004 engine for the Me-262. And that engine's paltry lifespan of fifty operating hours is now severely decreased due to shortages of war material, especially those metals made of ferrite heat-resistant steel. With the addition of silicon or aluminum, such steel can resist temperatures up to 1700° Celsius."

"Interesting—"

"However," Multhopp waxed on, "even with regular maintenance between major overhauls, Me-262 mechanics can only expect an engine life of twenty to twenty-five hours from the Jumo. The BMW and Junkers axial compressor turbojet engines are characterized by a more sophisticated design and can offer considerable advantages. Alas, the lack of rare war materials for the Jumo design have put it at a serious disadvantage compared to the better axial-flow BMW turbojet, which despite its largely centrifugal compressor-influenced design, provides between operating overhaul intervals of sixty to sixty-five hours, for an overall operational life span of, um—let's see," Multhopp did some figuring in his head. "...one hundred twenty-five hours!"

Dietrich made a face. "I have no idea what you're talking about, Herr Multhopp. Withal, you'll be working side by side with some of Messerschmitt's top engineers. You don't have issue with that?"

"Not at all. We can all benefit by working together."

"I'm glad to hear it."

The two men walked to Dietrich's idling staff car.

Multhopp cleared his throat pridefully, continuing his discourse on jet engines. "The Heinkel HeS-011 turbojet engine, which all my jets shall eventually be equipped with, will give them a top speed of 595 miles per hour, maybe faster. My Design III prototype may even reach speeds of 620 miles per hour, Sturmbannführer."

Dietrich pursed his lips approvingly. "Hmm, *most* impressive."

"Initially, a total of sixteen shall be built, allowing the tail unit to be interchanged between the Design II and III variations. Of the experimental test series aircraft, the I-183, only it will be powered by the Jumo-004 turbojet. However, all future aircraft will be designed according to plan, pending delivery of the HeS-011 turbojet engine, of course. The I-183 was only intended to be a pre-production prototype and a static test aircraft. Combat deployment for the HeS-011 equipped jet fighters is projected for May 8, 1945."

"May 8th?" Dietrich's brow narrowed. "Well, I hope the Allies haven't surrendered by then. I'd like to see this jet of yours take to the air and blast the American bombers and fighters from the sky."

"So you shall, Sturmbannführer. So you shall."

"All right, Herr Multhopp," said Dietrich, waving. "I'll leave you to your plans and ideas now. I must take a little trip to a nearby Stalag and round up some more workers. This facility must be fully operational by March 1st. It must!"

"Where are you going? To which Stalag are you referring?"

"Why, to Stalag Luft V, of course. Where elese?" Dietrich saluted, stiff-armed. *"Heil Hitler!"*

SHE LAID THERE in the hospital bed feeling drowsy and weak. The painkillers the doctor had given her had only succeeded in putting her out, diminishing very little of the pain. Her head ached and her legs felt numb, and to add insult to injury, she was still experiencing plenty of morning sickness. But she was glad to be alive. That buzz bomb had not killed her, although for a brief moment, she thought it had. Rose remembered nothing of what happened after the bomb exploded, blacking out after a thick piece of ceiling plaster fell on her head. She awoke a few hours later in a hospital bed in the Wattisham infirmary, scared, bleary-eyed and semi-conscious, wondering where she could be. She blacked out again and woke up only to find herself in yet another hospital, this time in London's Queen Alexandra's Military Hospital.

"Well, Mrs. McKavitt," said the doctor, a lean, distinguished-looking English Lt. Colonel. "How are you feeling today?"

"About the same, I suppose. Groggy, mostly."

"I figured as much. Those painkillers I gave you earlier can really make you sleepy. But rest is what you need right now."

"So how am I, doctor? What's the prognosis?"

"You suffered a serious concussion and both your legs were broken, Mrs. McKavitt. You also suffered multiple cuts and bruises."

"Oh. That's all?"

"Isn't that enough?" The doctor chagrined. "Had that ceiling beam fallen on your back instead of your legs, you might have been paralyzed from the waist down."

"Ooh... Well, I don't remember that happening. I remember getting hit in the head that's about it."

"You were lucky, Mrs. McKavitt. I was told both of your next-door neighbors were killed by that buzz bomb. So were twelve other people." The doctor picked up Roses' bed chart and glanced over it.

"You mean Mrs. Allenby, my landlord—she was killed?"

"I don't have the details, Mrs. McKavitt. You'll have to check with the Wattisham Constabulary for that answer. When you're up and about again, that is."

"And when will that be, doctor?"

"That's totally up to you. Your concussion will heal soon

enough. But your legs will take a little more time, I'm afraid."

"How much time?"

"Six to eight weeks?"

"Crikey! I'll be seven months pregnant by them."

"But you needn't worry, Mrs. McKavitt. Your baby is fine. We ran some tests when you arrived. Everything is still as it should be."

Rose sighed. "That's a relief. I should have realized it when my morning sickness returned yesterday."

"Indeed." The doctor laid the bed chart down.

"So tell me, doctor. Why am I here in London in a military hospital instead of a civilian one in Suffolk?"

"You can thank a chap named General Warlick for that. He insisted you have the best care. He arranged for your transport here."

"That was nice of him."

"Quite nice." The doctor reached into his lab coat hip pocket and produced a small, postcard-sized envelope. "One of his subordinates stopped by this morning whilst you were sleeping—a Major Hickok, and he dropped off this postcard." The doctor smiled. "It's from your husband, I believe? Colonel David M. McKavitt?"

Roses' eyes widened. "David McKavitt, you say?"

"That's right." He handed Rose the postcard. "From Germany via the Red Cross. I take it your husband is a P.O.W.?"

Rose nodded ruefully. "He was shot down over Germany over a month ago. This is the first I've heard from him."

"Shot down? That's bloody awful."

"No worries. He's alive and well now—I think?"

Rose hungrily tore the envelope open and read the post card, immediately recognizing her husband's dreadful scrawl. A little tear suddenly coursed down her cheek. It was a tear of joy.

"Well, I'll leave you to it then, Mrs. McKavitt." The doctor nodded and turned for the door. "I'll check in on you again later this evening, see how you're doing."

"Thank you, doctor," Rose managed with a little sniffle.

She read the five inky lines once more reveling in a sudden moment of bliss. David was alive and doing fine! He had not been wounded or injured after he was shot down, and was in a Luftwaffe P.O.W. camp in central Germany, and he missed her more than he could say.

Rose laid there in bed, her eyes swelling with tears, thinking about David. He was so faraway and locked up in a prison camp, and who knew for how long? If the news reports she'd heard were true, then the war would go on for another year, maybe longer. To be without David for that long could be a burden too hard to bear. To live everyday knowing he was stuck in some hellish P.O.W. camp suffering ungodly privations and starvation, stuck there unable to do anything but bide his time, waiting for the end to come, an end that was nowhere near in sight, was a thing more painful than all her injuries. She knew David would be out of his mind with boredom not being able to participate in the war anymore. She worried that he might try to change his situation by enacting drastic measures, which meant trying to escape. Rose had read about other men who had done so; most had failed in the attempt and then suffered even greater punishment after being caught. Only a few had actually escaped from Germany, and most, sadly, were just killed in the attempt. The latter outcome frightened Rose to the point of sickening worries. To lose him in such a dreadful and needless way would haunt her for the rest of her life. She wondered if she could go on living if such a thing ever happened.

As she thought about all of this, a strange thing happened. There was a bit of a commotion going on outside the door of her room; someone was talking and laughing very loud. The voice was familiar, and it sounded like someone she knew. But she couldn't place a name or a face to the voice. Who was it, she wondered? Who was loitering outside her room? It was a man's voice, she knew, but which man? It began to bother her so much she decided to call out and see who it was.

"Hello?" Rose uttered in a loud voice. "Who's there?"

The laughing stopped.

"Hello!" She yelled out louder. "Who is outside my door?"

No one answered; there was only silence.

"Please, sir, answer! I know that voice. Who are you?"

A tall, slender, swarthy figure then appeared in the doorway. It was an U.S. Army Captain in a dress uniform; his arm was in a sling. His eyes were shielded by a pair of gold-rimmed aviators. His jaw was lean and angular, his lips thin and straight, his face clean-shaven and calm.

Rose gasped. "J-Jack?"

"Beg your pardon, ma'am?" he said, removing his cap. "Yer mistaken. I'm Captain Nicklaus Daemon, O.S.S. Nick, for short."

"No, you're not." Rose sat upright in the bed, her eyes aflame. "You're J-John J. Knight—Jack. Jack Knight, for God's sake!"

"Sorry, ma'am," he said. "Must be a case of mistaken identity."

"No, it's not. You're Jack Knight, the Air Corps fighter pilot. But, but... how, I mean, you were captured by the Japanese."

"Me? A pilot? Captured?" Daemon laughed. "Oh no. Not me. I'm just a regular Army officer serving in the O.S.S., ma'am."

"Stop it! You're my ex-husband, and you know it."

"Ex-husband?" Daemon shook his head. "I ain't ever been married in my life. I hope to be one day. When I find the right girl."

Rose scowled. She glared at the man before her. It was Jack, she was sure of it. His black hair was much shorter, cropped high-and-tight. The mustache was gone, and he looked a lot thinner, and there was a long, jagged scar above and below his left eye. But it was Jack all right. There was no mistaking it. Or was there?

"You look different, yes, I'll admit that," Rose reluctantly conceded. "But you're Captain John J. Knight, I'm sure of it."

Daemon gushed bashfully. "Captain *Jack Knight?* The Air Corps fighter ace? That pilot who got shot down over the Pacific?"

"Yes!"

"Oh, no, ma'am. I know who yer talkin' about. But I'm not him. You're right when you said he was captured by the Japs. I read about it. He was going to break an old war record I heard, and—"

"Damn you, Jack!" Rose snarled, getting frustrated.

"I'm not Jack Knight, ma'am. No siree. My name is Nick Daemon. Maybe I look a lot like that fella yer talkin' about. But I'm not him, I tell ya. And I've never flown a plane in my life. Never."

"Liar!" Rose spouted. "You're Jack Knight, goddammit!"

Daemon donned his cap and nodded. "Okay, ma'am. Yer gettin' a little flustered, I can see. So I'll be leaving now. Nice to meet you, Miss—what was your name? I never got your name, ma'am."

"Rose McKavitt!" she blurted out, highly perturbed now.

"Rose...*McKavitt?*" he echoed. "Ah, well, nice to meet you, Mrs. McKavitt. Hope you get to feelin' better. And I hope you find this Jack Knight fella one day. Goodbye now." He turned about and walked out of the room. As he turned off into the hallway, he heard her shout: "You lying son-of-a-bitch! I know it's you, Jack! I know it's you! Come back here! Face me like a real man, damn you!"

Daemon shook his head and snorted softly as he walked on. Well, that crazy bitch, he thought. Who in the hell did she think he was? Jack Knight, the fighter ace? Deamon chuckled as he paused at the reception desk at the end of the hallway. "Excuse me, ma'am," he said to the nurse on duty. "There's a woman down there in Room 23 who's having something of an awful fit. You might wanna check in on her."

"Room 23? Mrs. McKavitt?" replied the nurse.

"Yes, ma'am. Room 23. She seems really upset."

"Right." The nurse stood up and paged an orderly. "She's in a lot of pain—heavily sedated, too."

"That explains it. What happened to her?"

"Buzz bomb, you know."

"Ah, I see. One of those Nazi flying bombs, eh?"

"A bloody nuisance, they are."

"Yup. They sure are—"

"And to be pregnant on top of all her injuries. Poor girl. No wonder she's so delirious half the time."

"Pregnant, you say?"

"Three months."

"Three months?" Daemon blinked incredulously.

"And her husband's in Nazi P.O.W. camp. That poor, poor girl!"

"You don't say?" Daemon rasped his chin, thinking. "Hmm, that's too bad. Terrible." He doffed his cap. "Well, goodbye, ma'am. I gotta be going now. Duty calls."

"Right-o, sir," replied the nurse. "Cheerio."

"Cheerio." Daemon waved and stepped off, then headed for the exit. His eyes were misty and his heart was beating fast. Rose, pregnant? And married? Married to someone named McKavitt? Colonel David McKavitt? He'd seen the ring on her finger—an expensive looking solitaire. Not the ring he remembered. The world had turned a few times, he realized. Rose had moved on with her life.

Don't you sweat it, Jack old boy, said that little voice inside his head. *"She's still your girl. Nothing will ever change that. Nothing!* Captain Deamon wiped the tear from his eye and smiled.

THE NEXT MORNING, Jack met with Colonel Bruce of the O.S.S. Special Operations Branch and Major General William Donovan. Jack was due to go on leave that day but was instead summoned to the O.S.S. Headquarters on Grosvenor Street. He was expecting to be debriefed about his recent mission in Denmark. Although the mission had been deemed a success (Professor Johansen had been brought back to England alive) there were still a few questions that needed to be answered. He reported at 0800 hours sharp still wearing his Army dress uniform, and of course, his arm still in a sling.

He marched into the office, half-saluted, then stood at attention.

"Captain Daemon, reporting as ordered," he said crisply.

"At ease, Captain," Colonel Bruce said. "Have a seat, please."

"Thank ya, sir." Jack sat down in the chair offered.

"This is Major General William Donovan, Captain," Colonel Bruce gestured. "He is the O.S.S.'s Director and Commanding Officer. He'll be sitting in on our briefing this morning."

"General," Jack acknowledged Donovan with a stiff nod.

"Captain Daemon," Donovan returned.

Colonel Bruce clasped his hands on the desktop. "We called you in here this morning, Captain, to get more feedback on the mission —to find out what went wrong as well as what went right. I read yours and Lipton's reports and I noticed several distressing things."

"Oh? Like what, sir?"

"Well, for one, how you men became... how should I say it— cast into the sea? Nearly drowned after the destroyer sank?"

"Oh, that, sir." Jack nodded grimly. "The destroyer hit a couple of German mines, and yeah, sank afterwards."

"A bad business, I'm sure," Donovan added.

"Yes, sir. A rotten situation alright."

"Nevertheless, you men went on with the mission, but without most of your equipment, namely your weapons. Is that right?"

"That's right. Our grease-guns went down with the ship."

"But you later acquired German weapons, correct?"

"Correct."

"I understand you were instrumental in making the mission a success, according to Lieutenant Lipton's report. You even took charge on several occasions. Is that true?"

"Yes, sir, it's true."

"Major Cartwright, according to Lipton, was slow in figuring things out sometimes. Is that right?"

"Well, sir," Jack explained "Things didn't go as planned, not at all. We had to constantly ad lib, as they say, in order to get things done. He wasn't too good at that. But he got us through it, though."

"I see." Colonel Bruce nodded. "But you, on the other hand, had no qualms about *ad-libbing*, did you, Captain?"

"Naw, sir. I did not."

"I read in Lipton's report... at one point, you stormed a whole squad of German soldiers and ruthlessly mowed them down, killing all of them, including their officer."

"Yes, sir, I did."

"Lipton described that as rather reckless and unnecessary. Do you agree with that statement?"

"Naw, sir I do not. It had to be done."

"Really?"

"Really. There was no way out of that castle, sir, but the cause-way spanning the moat. It was crawling with Germans. Because at that point they knew we were there. They knew something was up."

"Of course."

"I had to do something drastic. Yeah, it was foolhardy. But we had to get the Professor out of there before the whole Kraut garrison came down on us. Cartwright, well, he was at a loss as what to do."

"That's what Lipton said, too."

"Sounds like you did a hell of a job to me," Donovan said. "Drastic measures are what's sometimes."

"I agree, General," Jack replied. "You gotta take the bull by the horns now and then. Take some risks and keep the ball moving."

"I also agree, Captain," Colonel Bruce put in. "You did what had to be done. You salvaged a bad situation and saw it through."

"I did, didn't I?" Jack smiled.

"How is your arm, by the way? Healing okay?"

"Yes, sir." Jack nodded keenly, propping up his wounded arm. "It is. Doc says it ought to be fine in a couple of weeks. That Kraut skipper only winged me, ya see. Bullet went right through my arm. Bled like crazy but it didn't hinder me much. Really."

"Good," Colonel Bruce replied with a sympathetic nod. "Because when you return from leave, you'll be going on another special operation—behind enemy lines, again."

"Into Germany this time, Captain," General Donovan added. "Deep into the heart of the Third Reich."

"Really? Where to, General?"

"To a Nazi production facility, that's where."

"That's right," Colonel Bruce concurred. "It's a top-secret production facility for the Luftwaffe, somewhere in Saxony."

Jack winked. "Ain't much of a secret if we all know about it."

General Donovan grinned. "No. Not much, Captain. They're building fighter jets there. The Me-262 jet fighter, specifically."

"The Me-262?" Jack looked puzzled. "Well, I'll be damned."

This was the first he'd ever heard of the Me-262. He'd been stuck in a Jap P.O.W. camp for the better part of a year, then in O.S.S. training thereafter. He was surprised to hear about it. But not too surprised. He knew the Germans were a race of highly intelligent people who could produce something as miraculous as a jet fighter plane, or even more impressive, a V-1 or V-2 rocket, the latter being something right out of a Buck Rogers movie. He'd heard stories of what seemed ages ago now about jet technology but never realized it had come to a reality. Professor Johansen had spoken to him about quantum physics and atomic energy aboard the submarine on their way back to England, and Jack realized almost anything was possible through scientific research. But half of what the Professor had said just went over his head. Today, he was being told the Nazis had jet fighters. The war was getting unbelievably sophisticated. Oh how he wished he could fly again. Flying a jet fighter would be a fantastic achievement, he bemused. Jack Knight: jet fighter pilot. That sounded like something he really wanted to do.

"Anyway," General Donovan went on, "these jets are being built inside of a small mountain, in a bombproof factory, protected by 10-foot-thick concrete, imperious to 1,000-pound bombs, even."

"And so far, unbelievably," Colonel Bruce elaborated. "Our heavy bombers haven't even put a dent in it. So, Captain—"

"...you want me to go in there and blow up the place up, right?"

Colonel Bruce and the General exchanged pleased glances, both grinning, both realizing they had picked the right man for the job.

"That's exactly right, Captain," Donovan said, nodding. "You will lead an Operational Group of handpicked men, parachute in and infiltrate the factory facilities, plant high explosives, and destroy those jets and the facility itself, if possible. Nothing is to be spared."

Jack smiled.

"We can't allow those jets to make it to the deployment stage, Captain. Because we have nothing in our current arsenal to combat them. Our own jet prototype, the Lockheed XP-80, is still a few months away from being fully operational. So you must destroy that factory. You must!"

"XP-80? You mean... we have jets, too?"

"We sure do, Captain," Colonel Bruce interjected. "We even have a second jet fighter under development back in the U.S. Built by Bell Aircraft. But it won't be ready for at least six more months, possibly longer. That's why we need to destroy that facility."

"Yes, sir. I see what yer sayin'."

General Donovan cleared his throat.

"If the Germans can amass enough of these goddamned Me-262's, Captain, and concentrate them against our bomber formations, then our air force will be in for a very bad time. Our conventional fighters can't match them in speed and armament. And trying to catch them on the ground has been a fruitless catch-as-can effort. That factory must go, and soon, by God!"

"I get yer drift, General," Jack replied. "We gotta hit the dang Nazis where it counts—on the assembly line—git those jets before they git into the air, before they can cause some real trouble."

"Correct again," said Colonel Bruce. "And that's why we've chosen you for the job. Because you're ruthless and cunning, because you're fearless and unfailing, because you're an ex-pilot and you know what our airmen are going through right now. You're the man of the hour, Captain. We believe in your abilities."

"Thank ya, Colonel Bruce. I appreciate that. I really do."

"All right, Captain Daemon. When you get back from leave, we'll brief you with all the details. That is all. Dismissed."

Jack stood up, grinning broadly.

"Okay, sir. I'll be ready. You can count on me." He half-saluted and then about-faced. He paced out of the office and closed the door behind him. And when he was gone, General Donovan said:

149

"Well, now you have a leader for your special Operational Group, Colonel. Daemon will get the job done, I'm sure of it."

"Yes. I think he will."

"It's something of suicide mission though, I have to admit. If he comes back, it'll be a miracle."

"I know. But you remember what General Truscott said?"

"What's that?"

"That Captain Daemon is expendable. It's better if he dies, sir. Because his sordid past must never come to light."

"Yes, I remember Truscott saying something about that. The true story of Jack Knight must never be told. But, I still think he's a damn good soldier, Colonel. Good enough to lead this operation."

"Agreed. And the rest are all good men as well."

General Donovan scoffed and got up. "There isn't a 'good' man among them, Colonel. Not anymore. Some of them may have been before the war. Some of them may be again come the end of it. But right now 'good' men are not what is needed. These times call for dark men to do dark things. And Captain Daemon will not be afraid to lead them to it." The General slammed out of the room.

CHAPTER 9

COLONEL MCKAVITT and Sergeant Major Boggs were standing outside Barracks A-1, Boggs smoking a cigarette, McKavitt deep in thought, his arms folded over his chest. They were discussing the recent news they'd heard. American ground forces had rallied and the encirclement had been broken. General Patton's 3rd Army had smashed through the German lines near Bastogne and the 101st Airborne Division was no longer surrounded. Supplies were once again pouring in and the Allies were going back on the offensive. Despite not having a homemade radio, the news had come to them via Group Captain Hawker. A German farmer who regularly delivered produce to the Stalag's Officers' Mess, and who was sympathetic to the Allied cause, told one of the British mess stewards, who in turn, told Hawker. The tide was turning and McKavitt was plotting his escape again.

As they stood there talking, a Mercedes-Benz staff car suddenly appeared outside the front gates. Once it was waved through, McKavitt could see the SS death's head insignia stenciled on its door and the red swastika pennants fluttering from its fenders. It stopped and parked near the Kommandant's headquarters, and a tall, slender SS officer got out and stalked up the steps to Von Warnstadt's office.

"What's this, huh?" Boggs said exhaling some smoke.

"The SS, looks like," McKavitt replied, hands on his hips now.

"What the hell do they want, I wonder?"

"Can't be anything good, that's for sure."

"Interrogations, maybe, Colonel?"

151

"Maybe. But I doubt it." McKavitt shook his head. "They've given up on that. He's here for another reason, Boggs."

"I wonder what, sir?"

"When the SS shows up at a P.O.W. camp, it's usually for the transfer of a high-profile prisoner. Or... for a special work detail."

"You think that guy is here for you, Colonel?"

"Could be, Boggs. Von Warnstadt warned me Berlin might want to question me further. The SS is Berlin's errand boys, you know. I don't relish talking to any of those characters. Not one damn bit."

"I hear that, sir."

It had been a while since Colonel McKavitt had been interrogated by the Germans. Once he left Dulag Luft at Wetzlar, he was sent to Stalag Luft V and basically left alone. And since he was just the commander of a fighter group and not a bombing group, he had little to offer to the Nazis in the way of information. The Luftwaffe already knew all they wanted to know about the P-51 Mustang. They wanted to know about the Norden bombsight more than anything else, and Lieutenant Gunston had already been interrogated many times since his capture, six times whilst being incarcerated in Stalag Luft V. And after each interrogation von Warnstadt locked him up in the "cooler" for a few days, threatening severer punishments if he didn't cough up some pertinent information soon. But 2nd Lieutenant Tommy Gunston held his tongue and never divulged a damn thing, much to the frustration of von Warnstadt. McKavitt commended the young Lieutenant on his steadfast defiance and perseverance, always reassuring him and telling him to hang in there. Soon enough, McKavitt told him, the Germans would lose interest and leave him alone. And they did. But now the SS had made an appearance and that was troubling. What in the hell did they want, he wondered? What did the goddamn SS want with a bunch of American P.O.W. airmen? He was about to find out.

Shortly, a stout-looking Luftwaffe Feldwebel approached McKavitt and Boggs, his face stern, his Mauser carbine shouldered.

"Komm, Colonel McKavitt," he said in a thick Bavarian accent. *"Der Kommandant möchte Sie sofort in seinem Büro sehen."*

"What for, Sergeant?" McKavitt returned in English; he understood German well enough by now, most of it anyway. But he liked to taunt the guards ever now and then, let them know he was still an

American and proud of it. "What does the Kommandant want?"

"I do not know, Herr Colonel," the Feldwebel returned, his English quiet good, actually, then jerked his head in the direction of the Kommandant's headquarters. "Let's go. Move it."

"Does it have anything to do with the SS officer that just arrived?" McKavitt stepped off in front of the Feldwebel.

"The Kommandant does not confide in me, Herr Colonel. So your guess is as good as mine."

"Why not? You're a good man, Feldwebel. He ought to."

"Please, Herr Colonel. Do not patronize me. I am just doing my duty. You will find out soon enough what the SS man wants."

"Thank you, Feldwebel. You just answered my question."

The Feldwebel growled. *"Los! Los! Gehen! Beweg dich!*

McKavitt laughed as the German prodded him in the behind with the rifle barrel, urging him on insistently. Most of the guards were just regular Luftwaffe noncoms, not hard-boiled officers like von Warnstadt or Hauptmann Becker. They laughed and joked with the American prisoners from time to time, even shared a cigarette or two, as well as some of their personal observations. The guards were inasmuch prisoners themselves at Stalag Luft V just as the Americans were, rarely getting leave or time off. Most of them were conscripted from the dregs of the Luftwaffe and were considered inferior soldiers by their commanders. A few were there because of some serious infraction, or a minor misdeed, even. And serving in a P.O.W. camp was an alternative to fighting on the Eastern Front. It wasn't glorious work but it was better than dying in some frozen godforsaken place like Russia.

A moment later, McKavitt was standing in the Kommandant's office, staring at the SS officer seated beside von Warnstadt's desk.

"Welcome, Colonel McKavitt," said von Warnstadt. "I'm glad you could join us this morning."

"What's this about, Kommandant?"

Von Warnstadt motioned. "This is Sturmbannführer Dietrich from the *SS-Totenkopfverbände*—Thüringen Regiment."

"Charmed, I'm sure, Sturmbannführer," McKavitt quipped.

Dietrich grinned amusedly.

"This is the senior officer of the American P.O.W.'s, Dietrich," von Warnstadt stated, glaring at the American officer. "Colonel

David M. McKavitt, formerly of the 479th Fighter Group."

"I'm charmed as well, Colonel," Dietrich rejoined.

"Dietrich is here to select some prisoners for a special work detail, Colonel," von Warnstadt explained.

McKavitt scoffed. "You mean a *hard labor* detail, don't you?"

"Something like that," Dietrich answered. "It's for a new mountaintop factory. We need more laborers to finish the work."

"Well, forcing P.O.W.'s to work is against the Geneva Convention, pal. Or haven't you heard?"

Dietrich sighed. "I am aware of it, Colonel."

"Some of my men have already volunteered for several work details," McKavitt explained, "just to get beyond this camp's barbed wire and have more liberty. Something I advised them against. But they do it willingly and by my permission only. Not at the whim of some Nazi taskmaster. They see it as a privilege and a chance to get out of here, do something constructive, instead of waiting around biding their time."

McKavitt wasn't lying when he said that. The original group of Air Corps P.O.W.'s—composed mostly of noncoms—was not allowed or dared not work. Nevertheless, after coming to Stalag Luft V, many later P.O.W.'s volunteered for work detachments, simply to go beyond the camp's confining environment and get away from the mind-numbing boredom of prison life. However, the Germans insisted that only basic airmen be assigned to labor details. Later on, Von Warnstadt "coaxed" the N.C.O.'s to volunteer for these duties, a practice McKavitt advised against except in the case of farm work, which was less unpleasant than labor work detachments.

Attached to the camp were some eighty work detachments, ranging in size from five men (sent out to local farms) to five hundred men. The three major work detachments were situated in Leipzig, Weimar and Jena. After the heavy bombing of Leipzig, a work detachment of nearly one thousand P.O.W.'s was formed. This detachment consisted of sixty percent Americans and forty percent British. It left the Stalag at 05:00 and returned at 20:00. The P.O.W.'s traveled in cattle cars from the Halle train station, standing up all the way to Leipzig and back.

The time spent in the train going to and returning from work, was two hours. During their eight hour working day, P.O.W.'s cleared debris, filled bomb craters, and dismantled damaged railroad tracks. The men received two meals at Leipzig and their regular ration at the camp. In the event of air attacks, adequate shelter was provided. There were a few instances of guards pricking them with bayonets and hitting them with rifle butts to make them work faster and harder. But that was rare. Some guards knew the war was coming to an end soon, and they didn't want to be perceived as ruthless war criminals, fearing reprisals from liberating troops as well as the prisoners themselves.

"Well, Colonel," Dietrich replied haughtily, "They will be given a chance to volunteer for this work detail."

"I'll forbid them, Dietrich. No man under my command will work in a Nazi factory, above or below ground. It's against the Geneva Convention and the Articles of War."

Dietrich chuckled. "How pompous you sound, Colonel. You are in no position to make such high-and-mighty statements. You are a prisoner of war; a vanquished foe; a defeated enemy, and you will do whatever is required by your captors, wherever, and whenever they decide."

"Over my dead body!"

"Careful, Colonel," Dietrich warned. "That can be arranged."

"Murder me, Dietrich, and you'll hang, for sure. Once—"

"Silence!" The SS-Major stood up. "I do not have time to bandy with arrogant Air Corps officers today. If none of your men volunteer for the work, Colonel, then they will be chosen at random."

McKavitt snorted, folding his arms over his chest.

"I need three hundred and fifty men to excavate the hillside tunnels along the Walpersberg. Laborers from Buchenwald and other camps will also be put to work excavating the tunnels."

"If you're just going override my authority, mister, why bother asking me, huh?"

"I'm not asking you, Colonel. I'm simply informing you of what will transpire in the coming days. Certain enlisted men and noncoms will be chosen to work, along with officers below field-grade."

"*Certain* enlisted men and noncoms?"

"Those identified as Jews—those considered troublemakers."

"Jews? Troublemakers? Whatever. But officers are not required to work, according to Article 49 of the Geneva Convention."

"You and your smug hypocrisy, Colonel. It carries no weight or basis at this stage of the war. There are no more 'rules of war.' Your bombers have murdered thousands upon thousands of innocent German civilians, laying waste to cities like Cologne and Hamburg."

"Just like your bombers murdered thousands upon thousands of innocent Londoners during the Blitz, eh?"

"*Touché,* Colonel." Dietrich stood up and then added rather arbitrarily: "The officers, in effect, will only be overseers. They will not be required to do manual labor."

"And nor will *any* P.O.W., Dietrich. My men will not contribute to the Nazi war effort. No, sir. No way in hell will they."

"Perhaps not in hell, Colonel. But here on earth, yes."

"Never!"

"Well, they will probably come to regard it as a living hell after a time, once my men exert their extraordinary skills of persuasion."

"You're a fucking bastard, Dietrich. A rotten lowlife, you are."

"*Hah, hah, hah, hah, hah!*" Dietrich laughed.

"Pure insolence!" Von Warnstadt exclaimed, jerking up from his chair. "You have just earned yourself twenty-four hours in the cooler, Colonel."

"Twenty-four hours? I can do that standing on my head."

"*Verdammt!* Ten days!" Von Warnstadt rumbled. "Guards!" he yelled out. "Take this man to the cooler. Ten days—half-rations!"

Two guards, including the Luftwaffe Feldwebel, seized Colonel McKavitt by the arm and escorted him out of the Kommandant's office, then marched him over to the cooler at gunpoint. Sturmbannführer Dietrich turned back to von Warnstadt and donned his peak cap, nodding assertively.

"I'll be back in two days, Herr Kommandant," he said. "And I will select a three-hundred-and-fifty-man work detail for the tunnels around the Walpersberg. Some will also be chosen for the Elster River as well. The work must be completed by March 1st, as the Führer has decreed it. In the meantime, I must investigate Colonel McKavitt's background. He has a very... Jewish look about him."

"Indeed, he does," von Warnstadt agreed. "I always thought so. He has a very inferior look about him, like a typical Jew—"

"Good day, Herr Kommandant." Dietrich saluted. *"Heil Hitler!"*

OPERATION BODENPLATTE (Baseplate) was late. It should have been launched the day of General von Runstadt's Ardennes offensive. But bad weather meant the all-out air attack could not be coordinated with the ground forces. In hindsight, it was madness to proceed with the operation. Nonetheless, with a respectable strength still available to the Luftwaffe, the order of battle was impressive; some 900 front-line fighters were on hand to participate. Hitler had ordered the fighters to stage a massive surprise aerial attack on Allied forward airfields in Holland, Belgium and France, then provide cover for von Runstadt's Panzers. The attack was mounted at precisely 09:20 hours, and things started to go awry soon after take-off.

Ground fog caused delays at some airfields, hampering the coordinated effort. Many of the pilots were ill-trained, and some of the veterans were hung over after the New Year's Eve celebration, a celebration they believed would be their last. As a result, many pilots never found the Allied airfields. But some did, and they caught several airfields by complete surprise. They shot up and bombed the Allied aircraft parked on the ground, destroying over a hundred. But lamentably, many of the Luftwaffe planes skimming the snow-covered landscape came under fire from German flak guns. The gun crews had been duly warned but the sudden appearance of so many low-flying aircraft at the unexpected hour caused massive confusion; many fighters were shot down.

Elsewhere, American and British fighters rose swiftly to do battle, and furious air combat ensued. At Asch, in Belgium, a group of Mustangs was taking off shortly before 10:00 hours when fifty Focke-Wulf FW-190's swooped down and attacked. The P-51 Mustangs, led by Colonel Tom Henderson, the recently transferred and new commander of the 352nd FG, were not following the official orders of the day. The pilots should have been in their squalid little snow-covered tents preparing for a bomber-escort mission over Germany. But on a hunch that the Germans might attack that morning, Henderson got permission from his wing commander to stay back and fly a tactical combat patrol.

Colonel Henderson was leading his Mustangs off the runway when he looked up and saw a FW-190 bearing down on him. He quickly retracted his landing gear and gave the Mustang full throttle.

The FW-190 open fired and missed just as Henderson thumbed the firing button on his control column, rattling off a quick burst—but he also missed. The FW-190 veered off, banking away in a steep climb. Henderson turned and went after him.

"Red Leader to Fox-George," he radioed the Group. *"Rhubarb in progress. Leaders attack—pick targets. Wingmen, hang tight."*

"Roger that, Red Leader," came the quick reply.

"Wilco, Red Leader," replied another. *"Attacking now!"*

Henderson came around in a tight turn and lined up his gunsight, targeting the rolling FW-190 in front of him. At less than 50 yards, he fired, opening up with all six .50-caliber machine guns. The German fighter staggered and flamed under that fiery onslaught, slewing in an awkward roll, then pitched straight down in a nosedive. It hit a couple of seconds later, crashing right into a dense tract of trees, exploding in a surging fireball. Henderson zoomed over the orange-black flames, his propeller's backwash cleaving and curling the rising smoke into a swirling cloud. He climbed to 500 feet and sought out another foe, seeing two FW-190's bearing down on a hangar. Henderson eased the stick forward and saw his airspeed indicator advance to 400 miles per hour. A moment later, he was a 100 yards away and firing. The trailing FW-190 pulled up sharply as its pilot felt Henderson's fiery volley hit his tailplane. He curled away, leaving his leader to deal with the Mustang. Henderson accelerated and bore down on the German leader, his gunsight's pipper edging out in front of the FW-190's nose. At 60 yards, he thumbed the trigger and fired a two-second burst that sawed off the left wing. The one-wing Focke-Wulf flipped over and went careening into the snowy ground, bouncing once before erupting in flames.

Henderson had just bagged two FW-190's in less than a minute, rounding up his personal score to 10 victories. And he wasn't done yet. His guns were still hot and loaded, and his fuel tank read full; a winter shootout was in the making and he was up to the task at hand. And all around and above the snowbound airfield, he could see Mustangs and Focke-Wulfs whirling about the sky, locked in bitter air combat, some men fighting for their country, others just fighting for their lives. It was a bloody scene of mayhem; a low-level dogfight not seen since the bygone days of the Great War. Germans and Americans alike died hard.

Colonel Henderson suddenly came under fire. But it wasn't a Luftwaffe fighter, it was an American antiaircraft battery. The sky was so full of aircraft that morning that the ground gunners took a shot at any plane they saw. Henderson lost a chunk of his wing to one determined battery, almost losing control of his Mustang in the process. He got clear of the barrage by zooming away from the airfield at full speed, then came back at a higher altitude, and found two Bf-109's strafing the airfield, shooting up the C-47's Skytrains parked on the tarmac. He side-slipped and got behind one of the Bf-109's, his thumb cocked over the firing button. When he had the German fighter properly lined up in his gunsight, he fired. The .50-caliber stream of lead punched out nasty holes in the Messerschmitt's wings, prompting the pilot to break off his strafing run. As he turned away, trying to escape Henderson's second volley, the German's fuel tank ignited. The flames quickly flared out of control and he was obliged to bail out. The canopy flew open, and the pilot leaped into the air, tumbled twice, deployed his chute, swayed once, and then slammed into the hard frozen earth in a sickening thud. The flaming Bf-109 hit a second later and blew up, barely twenty yards from its ejected pilot, spewing wreckage in a hundred different directions, killing him where he lay prostrate on the ground.

Henderson pulled up in a climb and went after the other Bf-109, but lost him in low-hanging clouds a moment later. And when he got turned around, and headed back to the airfield, he found that all the attacking German aircraft had left the scene. As he guided his blue-nosed Mustang around in the landing pattern, he saw the black smoke clouds billowing up from at least twenty shot down planes. He knew most of them were German planes, and he also realized some of them might be American planes, too. But once he landed and deplaned, he found out that only one of his men had been shot down and killed. However, his squadron had shot down sixteen FW-190's and three Bf-109's, the latter German fighter appearing after his hasty retreat from his own antiaircraft. The Luftwaffe had rolled the dice and came up empty; its preemptive air strike had cost it at least three hundred fighter planes with over half the pilots posted as killed or missing, with sixty-seven taken into captivity. In comparison, only one hundred and thirty-four Allied aircraft were lost. The Luftwaffe was a spent force now—decimated.

JACK SAT on the edge of the bed in the dim lamplight, smoking a cigarette, gazing at the half-empty bottle of Old Crow sitting on the nightstand. Behind him a drunken, naked, semi-conscious girl laid sprawled out over the bedsheets, her pale skin glistening with sexual afterglow. He'd met her at a New Year Eve's party in some grotty little tavern in London's east end, and spent the night drinking and dancing with her. Later, around 3 a.m., he took her back to his hotel room and ravished her, pumping and pounding her willing young body until he practically passed out. He slept the entire next day and through the night, only waking to ravish her once more, and then ordered something from room service. She was an attractive English girl of twenty-four or twenty-five: short, shapely blond, big-breasted, sensual, erotic, and best of all, hungry for male companionship. It was the first time Jack had been with a woman since his marriage to Rose.

After seeing Rose in the hospital that day, Jack couldn't get her out of his mind. He'd wanted so badly to tell her that it was he standing there before her. But he just couldn't do it. It wasn't about the O.S.S.'s strict policy of identity secrecy; it was more about him feeling ashamed of his past and him not feeling like his old self. General Truscott told Jack what had happened the day he got shot down, how Rose came to him and inquired about his past and how she felt afterward. Truscott, though, hadn't mentioned that Rose had remarried. And based on her current surname, Jack had to assume it was his old C.O. Colonel McKavitt that had married her.

Jack also assumed that Rose had somehow gotten a divorce or had their marriage annulled. That hurt most of all, he lamented. Rose had moved on and remarried, and most of all, not waited up for him. Yet, he really couldn't condemn her for that. When he was captured and then dispatched to Camp Yomi (a high-security prison camp for high-profile prisoners), he all but disappeared from the face of the earth; the Japanese High Command did not acknowledge the existence of any prisoner incarcerated there. So as far as anybody knew, he had died there. But Truscott knew better, Jack bitterly realized. That old son-of-bitch knew where John J. Knight had been sent; Truscott knew the Japs had locked him away in their most super-secret P.O.W camp.

Rose had totally given up on him. So had General Truscott and a few others. His inconvenient identity was simply, and very conveniently, relegated to the dustbin of fate; packed off to the garbage heap of kismet; condemned to the darkest depths of hell, never to trouble anyone ever again. But Jack returned, he had come back and fooled the fates, and he had changed his destiny—it was almost like returning from the dead. But his new life was very different from what it had been before. Jack was no longer the famed air ace and a hotshot fighter pilot; he was no longer a national hero or a household name. He was, instead, nothing but a nondescript O.S.S. agent with a bogus name and a clandestine occupation. His exploits would never be heralded in any newspaper or newsreel. Any significant act or heroic deed he perpetrated would, instead, be kept secret. Only he and his immediate superiors would ever know. And to a lonesome, piss-poor farm boy from West Texas, that was something very hard to stomach.

All his life, Jack had only wanted to fly. To fly a fast fighter plane like his idol Eddie Rickenbacker; to slip the surly bonds of earth and dance the skies on laughter-silvered wings; to fight and kill an aerial enemy; mark his progress with an unending string of victories; flaunt a uniform full of glittering medals; become a legend in his own time. It was something he had nearly achieved. Two missteps had prevented him from becoming what he had always dreamed of: a history of prefabricated lies, and a run-in with Japan's ace of aces. The latter was something he could have prevented. In hindsight, Jack should have fought Nishizawa with greater respect and caution, he should have taken the Japanese ace more seriously.

But the sky was so full of opportunities that day he ended up taking the easy kill instead of dealing with the "Devil of Rabaul" (as Nishizawa was better known). It was a mistake on top of a mistake, one that would haunt him for the rest of his life. How many Allied pilots had faced the "Devil" and had come out the loser? Sixty? Seventy? Eighty? A hundred even? And how many of those pilots knew who they were up against when the bullets started flying? Not too many, Jack surmised. Only a few pilots probably ever knew they were facing Japan's greatest fighter pilot. And how many of those pilots had been shot down? All of them. Nishizawa was a paragon of aerial excellence.

Jack stubbed out the cigarette in an ashtray and got up. He was feeling restless again. His right arm was still smarting a bit from that German's bullet but it seemed to be healing nicely now; it was getting stronger by the day. It would have to be fully healed before he went on his next mission because parachuting into enemy territory at night was no joke. It would take every ounce of his being to get through this next operation. Blowing up a mountaintop factory deep in the heart of Germany was a perilously difficult task, one that required a healthy body and s nerves of steel. Sixteen other men would accompany Jack, sixteen men of varying skills and abilities. Most of them were O.S.S. veterans and all were highly trained experts in demolitions and hand-to-hand combat—and Jack would be leading them; Colonel Bruce had already told him that much. And in a few short days, Jack would find out exactly where and when he was going and what he'd be doing. Until then, he was on his own time, and so he wanted to enjoy himself.

Jack had no illusions of surviving the operation, he knew he might not return. So before he embarked on this most dangerous of all operations, he'd have to come clean with someone, he'd have to tell her how sorry he was about deceiving her, tell her that he still loved her and that would never change. She had been the love of his life and he wanted her to know it. It wouldn't change the fact that she had married somebody else or had become pregnant by another man. But it would satisfy his conscience and give him the quality of feeling honorable and having a good name finally; a man not inclined to lie or defraud; a man not prone to deception or duplicity, but a man deserving of esteem and respect. Captain Jack Knight: a man of honor.

"What you doing, luv?" asked the girl laying on the bed.

"Just doin' some thinkin'," Jack replied.

"Thinking? About what?"

"About the war. About my life." Jack turned around slowly and grinned. "And about *you*, babe. How about another romp, huh?" He crawled back onto the bed on hands and knees and hovered over her.

The girl chuckled "Again, aye? Well, ain't you the randy little devil. All right. Let's have another go then. Let's do it!"

Jack seized her by the thighs and threw her legs over his shoulders as his manhood swelled to full size, then he plunged straight in.

THE YOUNG HOSPITAL orderly parked the wheelchair facing a large window in the recreation ward so Rose McKavitt could look out and admire the Thames. It was just after breakfast and she was feeling better now that her bouts of morning sickness had finally subsided. After the orderly departed, she sat there with a shawl draped over her shoulders, quietly watching the snow flurries out-side, thinking about David and wondering what he must be going through at that very moment. She'd had read the one and only post-card he had sent several times over, and each time she read it, it brought yet another tear to her eye.

It was an awful predicament, him being locked away in a prison camp, her being laid up in a hospital half-pregnant and with two bro-ken legs. Her legs would heal in about two month's time, so said the doctor, and then she would be well into her pregnancy. But the war could go on for many months more; German resistance was still very strong according to the newspapers. Hitler and the Nazis would not give up anytime soon, even if defeat looked imminent, which ac-cording to several Allied generals and a few members of the press, was probably going to be the case. With the massive Red Army ap-proaching from the east and three Allied armies advancing on the Western Front, Germany was hemmed in and fundamentally sur-rounded. Whilst her cities were being bombed to the ground and her industry and infrastructure systematically laid to waste, the Wehrmacht and the Luftwaffe fought a losing battle, utterly unable to stem the tide. The end was near. But how near? How much longer could Germany fight on? When would the German people surrender? When would Hitler admit defeat?

She shook her head, shaking off those depressing thoughts. She didn't want to think about the war anymore and how it was ruining everything sacred and good, her life included. The world had gone perfectly mad, and no one seemed to care or could do anything about it. Death and destruction would go on until one side was utter-ly destroyed; there seemed to be no other alternative. In the mean-time, life would have to go on, albeit a very tenuous life. People would have to go about their everyday lives in spite of the mayhem being enacted in practically every corner of the globe. Rose wanted to cry. If David perished, could she go on living without him?

Rose thought about Jack, or the man she thought was Jack. This Captain Daemon fellow, or whoever he was, looked and talked just like him. Sure, there were some minor differences, but she was positive it was Jack Knight—her ex-husband and the man who had lied and cheated his way into the Air Corps. But how had he come to be in this hospital? How had he escaped from the Japanese? And how was it that he was still in uniform and serving in the Army? If he had indeed escaped from a Japanese P.O.W. camp, then he would, according to General Truscott, have a lot to answer for, namely his felonious identity and his surreptitious behavior. Impersonating an officer and stealing someone's identity was a capital offense, one that deemed investigation and prosecution. And that name 'Nicklaus Daemon' what was that all about? Why had he changed his name, yet again? And how had the Army allowed that? How had Jack gotten away with it? Perhaps he really wasn't Jack at all. Maybe in her narcotic state of mind she had only imagined him? But he seemed so real and so much like Jack it was eerily uncanny. If he truly was Nicklaus Daemon, then Jack had a twin brother that no one knew about, including Jack himself. Although Rose was mystified, her intuition told her it really was Jack. There could be no other—Captain Jack Knight had returned. But how?

"Howdy, stranger," Rose heard a voice say. She turned around in her wheelchair and saw who was addressing her. It was an Army Captain in a dress uniform and he was holding a bouquet of roses.

"J-Jack?" She replied, a little stunned he was suddenly standing there, then quickly recovered, quipping bitingly: "Or should I call you by your latest name, hmm? 'Captain Nicklaus Deamon?'"

"Aw shucks, no, Rose," Jack replied shaking his head. "It's me alright, Jack Knight in the flesh." He gestured with the bouquet. "Hey, I brought you some flowers, to cheer you up. I hope—"

"Keep them," Rose retorted. "I don't want them."

Jack frowned. "I'm sorry, Rose. I'm sorry for lying, sorry for leading you on, sorry for hurting you... sorry for everything."

"So you thought you can just come waltzing in here with a bouquet of roses, eh?" she returned, "and make everything okay again, make me forget what an awful liar you are, make me take you back again? No, no, Jack. Never. I'll never take you back. You made me love you, and then you broke my heart."

"I'm truly sorry for that, Rose. I really am. It was never my intention to do that—to break your heart. I loved you. I still do."

"Do you? Well, I remarried, Jack. I married your former commanding officer, David McKavitt... and I'm pregnant with his child. I moved on, Jack. I got over you and got on with my life. After Truscott told me everything, I had to. I had no choice." Rose sighed lugubriously. "I'm sorry Jack, but I don't love you anymore."

Jack nodded. "I deserve that, Rose. I sure do. You did what you thought was best. You moved on and forgot about me. I don't blame ya one bit, I really don't. You remarried and now yer gonna have a kid, I'm happy for you... and for your husband, Colonel McKavitt."

"Oh, really? Humph! I thought you'd be jealous, angry, hurt—all the things I felt when I found out about you. Hurt badly. But I got over it. I got over you." Rose shook her head. "What's wrong with you, hmm? Did you think everything would work out somehow? Did you think you could fool everybody? Did you really think you could get away with all of it? What do you have to say about that? What say you, eh? What's your story, *Jack Knight?* Tell me."

Jack stepped to the window and laid the bouquet on the windowsill, then stared out of the window, contemplating all of that. He lit a cigarette and stood quietly for a moment, smoking, thinking of what he should say. "Well," he said in a smoky sigh, speaking finally. "I have no story to tell, Rose. I know it seems as though I tried to conceal everything, but... truth is... there is no story to tell."

"Oh, c'mon, no one's past is that ordinary."

"Not ordinary, just... without relevance." Jack took a puff and then exhaled. "A long, long time ago, I freed myself from the obligation of finding any. No need to account for all my life's events in the setting of a story that somehow defines me. Events, some of which no one could determine any meaning from, other than the world is a place of everlasting misery. I've come to peace with the knowledge that there is no storyteller imposing any connection, or sense, or grace upon my life's events. Therefore, there's no obligation on my part to search for it. You know of me all I can dare to be known—all that is relevant to be known. That is to say, you know my friendship and my love for you. Can that ever be enough and there still be some trust between us?"

"I don't know, Jack. Only time will tell."

"Then there is hope, I see." Jack nodded, a faint smile on his lips, the cigarette perched betwixt pleasure and pain. "And I hope you'll forgive me one day for all I've done. I don't expect any sympathy from you, nor do I want it. I just want you to know whatever I did or said in the past, my intentions were always good: to only love you and always cherish you. Whoever I may have been—James Castillo, Jack Knight, and now, Nicklaus Daemon—my heart has always been the same, the one part of me that is genuine and true."

"I think I always knew that, Jack. I never doubted it. But you deceived me and I can't forgive you for that. It hurt me to know that you lied to me about who you were. You fooled me into thinking you were somebody different, somebody special, somebody unique. When in reality, you were somebody quite simple, quite unremarkable. Ordinary. And yes, your heart was genuine and true; that part of you was always the same whoever you were. Perhaps that's the part I fell in love with. But all the same, Jack. I couldn't allow myself to be taken in like that. I just couldn't. I'm too smart for that."

"Yeah, you are. I don't blame you." Jack turned, placing the cigarette between his lips and buried his hands in his pockets. "I just wanted you to see you one last time—come clean before I'm gone."

"Before you're gone? Where are you going, Jack?"

"To where I really belong."

"Where you really belong? What are you talking about?"

"A place where everyone knows my name—who I really am."

Jack walked away, puffing contently. He had said his peace and his conscience was clear, his honor was redeemed. He could go to his just desserts knowing he'd said what needed to be said. Rose would never love him again, he knew that now, but she would hopefully see him in a better light. A man worthy of respect and honor, someone she could abide by and believe in.

"Jack? What do mean: *where everyone knows my name?*"

"To hell, Rose. That's where. The one place where I truly belong." Jack laughed and strode out the room, smoke trailing after.

"Jack, please, come back. Don't go. Jack. Jack! Please!"

He smiled. Now he could go on being who he truly was.

CHAPTER 10

8 JANUARY 1945
MONDAY, 1705 HOURS
O.S.S. HQ. PARIS, FRANCE

COLONEL BRUCE locked the door, the operations briefing was officially in secession. Seventeen men dressed in combat fatigues sat in a semi-circle facing a pull-down map of Germany and a dusty chalkboard. One of those men, Captain Daemon (Jack), reclined anxiously, awaiting the beginning of the briefing. Today he'd learn the time and location of his next mission; a nocturnal parachute jump followed by a demolitions operation. That's all he knew at the moment. Shortly, Colonel Bruce would conduct an in-depth briefing detailing the men on every possible aspect of the operation.

Jack had met all the men taking part in the operation days before; the only one he knew was Lieutenant Lipton, his (X.O.), the very same man that'd accompanied him to Denmark for the Professor Johansen operation, who incidentally, was now in the United States working on a project known only as "Manhattan." The other fifteen were all Americans and all of them were noncoms of varying ranks, the highest being a Tech Sergeant, the lowest a Corporal. Unlike O.S.S. Special Operations teams, an Operational Group (O.G.) always operated in military uniform. The fifteen men were trained in infantry tactics, guerrilla warfare, foreign weapons, demolition, parachuting and had attached medical personnel. Typically, an O.G. had four officers and thirty enlisted men. But for this operation, only one section was being sent in—a unit half the size of a regular O.G. Jack would be the leader of this reduced group. A smaller team would be ideal for infiltrating the mountaintop facility at night.

The highest ranking N.C.O. was a guy named Tech Sergeant Frank Davis. He was a beefy, 6-foot-3 ex-linebacker from Ohio State. He had fought in North Africa during Operation Torch serving as an infantry platoon sergeant. He suffered serious wounds during the ill-fated Battle of Kasserine Pass. Inexperienced and poorly led American troops suffered many casualties and were quickly pushed back over fifty miles by Rommel's Afrika Korps. As a result of the battle, the U.S. Army instituted sweeping changes of unit organization and replaced commanders and certain types of equipment. Davis was sent home with a supposedly war-ending wound. Not so. Upon his return to the States, he was promptly recruited by the O.S.S. He was an able leader and an expert marksman, and would be Jack's platoon leader.

Staff Sergeant Bob Justice, was a tough former Marine who'd been drummed out of the Corps on charges of insurbordination. According to the court martial transcripts, Justice had struck an officer who had ordered him to fight on during the bloody Battle of Edson's Ridge on Guadalcanal. On the night of September 12, 1942 Japanese regulars attacked the Marines between the Lunga River and ridge, forcing his Marine platoon to fall back to the ridge before the Japanese halted their attack for the night. The next night the Japs attacked Justices' forty-plus Marines with one thousand troops and an assortment of light artillery. The Japanese assault began just after nightfall with a veteran battalion attacking Justices' right flank just to the west of the ridge. After breaking through the Marine lines the Jap battalion's assault was eventually stopped by Marine units guarding the northern part of the ridge, but not before suffering heavy casualties. Justices' commanding officer, a Captain and a "ninety-day wonder" had called for a counterattack. Justice refused and retreated, winning the admiration of his decimated platoon but earned himself a court martial after an informal field hearing. Despite his righteous namesake, he was sent stateside to a military prison to serve out a ten-year sentence. Less than a week later, he was approached by General Donovan, and was inducted into the O.S.S. Justice was a specialist in heavy weapons, most notably the U.S. Army's M1918 Browning Automatic Rifle (B.A.R.).

Staff Sergeant "Boomer" Hentges was a combat engineer and demolitions expert from Shreveport, Louisiana. He was a diminutive fellow but a giant of a man when it came to high-explosives and other demolition charges. His compact little M1 demolition kit contained everything from half-pound blocks of TNT (the standard explosive that could accomplish most jobs) as well as Composition-C, dynamite, and even one-pound blocks of TNT. Staff Sergeant Hentges was obviously the key man in the operation; his demolitions know-how would get the job done. His survival was extremely important. Jack would have to take special care in keeping him alive.

His assistant, Tech Corporal Carl Schmidt, was the only other man who knew how to rig explosives. He was a trained army engineer and recent O.S.S. recruit. Although he might have been considered too young or too green to participate in such a critical operation, he spoke fluent German, being a first-generation American. His father had immigrated from Germany after the Great War and married a woman from Philadelphia. Despite his blond hair and Germanic looks, Schmidt was the all-American boy; he spoke with a sharp South-Philly accent.

Then there was Sergeant Hank Hassler. He was a well-built, compact piece of human machinery. Once a semi-professional boxer and formerly the Army's middleweight champion, Hassler could take down any man of bigger size with just a few punches. He was also very handy with a commando dagger. He'd be the go-to man in close-quarter actions; he was a silent killer when he needed to be.

Sergeant Sparky Powell, the radioman, a onetime Madison Avenue accountant, was the team's radio operator and communications expert. Sergeant Powell was especially proficient with the SSTC-502/SSTR-6, popularly known as the "Joan-Eleanor." The SSTC-502 (Joan) was a three and a half-pound hand-held radio that ran on compact long-life batteries, eliminating the need for a heavy charger. The SSTR-6 (Eleanor) was mounted in an aircraft. This revolutionary system allowed the ground operator to talk with O.S.S. personnel in an aircraft thousands of feet up and miles away from their location, greatly reducing the chances of detection.

Sergeant Melvin Bryant was the O.G's medical corpsman. He was from Stockton, California and a former fireman. He didn't like killing but didn't want to be seen as a conscientious objector, so he joined the medical corps at the onset of the war, and later transferred to the O.S.S after a chance meeting with General Donovan.

The seven remaining men were all riflemen holding the rank of Corporal or Technician 5th Grade. They were: Hays, Carter, Russell, Sims, Ames, Foster, and Ricci. All were expert paratroopers and able marksmen. Foster and Ricci was the team's .30-caliber machine gun crew. They were on hand to add the heavy suppressive fire often required in operations such as these. And they were all deemed expendable by the O.S.S. Jack thought of them as good little soldiers ready to die for king and country—that's what Lipton had to say about it.

"All right, gentlemen," Colonel Bruce said, standing before the group, a map pointer in his hand. "The code name for this operation is: OPERATION NEMESIS, after the Greek goddess of divine retribution and vengeance... and this is where you'll be going." The map pointer stabbed at a location in Saxony, central Germany. "Kahla— south of Jena. The Walpersberg Hill, the REIMAHG Me-262 production site."

Some of the younger men blinked dumbly. Tech Sergeant Davis just grunted. Jack nodded, remembering Colonel Bruce's prior briefing. Most of the senior N.C.O.'s sat quietly unawares of what the Colonel was talking about. They'd heard of Kahla and Jena and the Walpersberg, but they didn't have the foggiest idea what he meant by "REIMAHG" or "Me-262."

"REIMAHG, or *Flugzeugwerke Reichsmarschall Hermann Goering,* code named 'Lachs' by the Nazis," Colonel Bruce went on, "is a top-secret production facility for the German jet the Messerschmitt Me-262."

"The Me-262, sir?" Staff Sergeant Justice questioned. "I thought the Germans had scrapped their jet program?"

"Not so, Sergeant. They have been in production for nearly a year now, along with a few other prototypes."

"Damn, that's kind of depressing."

"Very depressing." Colonel Bruce nodded. "That's why you've got to destroy that facility." He gestured to the calendar on the wall. "We go in two days, gentlemen (20:00 hours) on the night of January 11. A full moon will aid you on this most important of all operations. A C-47 Skytrain from the 91st Troop Carrier Squadron will fly you to the drop zone—here," he pointed, "and you'll parachute in from 600 feet and rendezvous, here, at point Alpha-Peter-One."

"Uh, 600 feet, sir?" Sergeant Hentges interrupted, his little face screwing up anxiously. "That's kind of low, isn't it, sir?"

"It is, Sergeant," Colonel Bruce replied. "But due to terrain features and the late hour, it will be necessary to jump at 600 feet. It will be easier to keep everyone together that way."

"Yes, sir." Hentges grimaced uneasily.

"You got a reserve chute, right, Hentges?" Jack cut in.

Hentges nodded. "I do."

"Then there ya go, fella. No worries, huh?"

"Y-Yes, sir. No worries."

Although Jack exuded a great deal of confidence, he was feeling a little anxious himself; 600 feet *was* low for a combat jump. But it wasn't unheard of in the annals of parachuting, especially during D-Day and Operation Market Garden, although the latter a grand Allied undertaking, failed miserably. It was risky but not impossible.

"The C-47 will take off from Châteaudun Airfield at 20:00 hours and proceed on a direct course to Kahla at low altitude, staying under German radar." Colonel Bruce paused, and then said: "It's four-hour flight, gentlemen. So you'll have plenty of time to think about what's ahead. However, don't think too much. Stay loose but focused, okay?"

"Easier said than done," Hentges muttered in a low voice.

"But before all of that, men," Colonel Bruce went on, "a three-man Jedburgh team will take off from Harrington Field, in England, aboard a B-24 Carpetbagger a day earlier. They'll parachute into the area and make a thorough reconnaissance of the facility, making sure nothing has changed in the way of defenses or terrain."

"Uh-huh. And what if things *have* changed, Colonel?" Tech Sergeant Frank Davis asked. "What then?"

"You will be notified accordingly."

"So the operation will commence irregardless of any defensive changes, sir? Is that what you're saying?"

"That's exactly what I'm saying. Barring a sudden snowstorm or something equally cataclysmic, this operation *will* proceed."

"Right." Davis nodded.

"And what will we be facing, Colonel?" Staff Sergeant Bob Justice inquired suspiciously. "In the way of enemy defenses, I mean?"

"Yeah," Hassler chimed in, his chin cocked in leery consternation. "What kind of Kraut outfit will we be facing?

"I was just getting to that, gentlemen." Colonel Bruce pointed to the dusty chalkboard. "The *SS-Wachbattlion III 'Südwest'* of the *Totenkopfverbände Divsion* (rendered in English as SS Guard Battalion III, Southwest, Death's Head Division). Five infantry companies and one heavy weapons platoon—about 600 men, I believe."

Justice shuddered. "What... 600 men? Jesus Christ!"

"Most of them will be asleep by the time you arrive. A nocturnal contingent will be in place—maybe 50 to 75 guards?"

"Maybe? Jeez, I hope so."

"Don't worry, Sergeant. Most of the guards aren't elite SS-troops, meaning: they're not from the Waffen-SS. They're the dregs of the service, so to speak. Prison guards. Not as sharp as the rest."

"Sharp or not, they're still SS, Colonel—"

"Hesh up, Justice!" Jack enjoined. "If'n you ain't got the guts to go, then bow out now, okay? I can easily replace you."

Justice glared at Jack, seething bitterly. "No—I'm going. I've got plenty of guts, Captain. I sure do. I just want to know what the hell I'm up against here, that's all."

"Well, now you know, Sarge," Jack quipped. "Feel any better?"

Sergeant Justice sighed heatedly and averted his gaze, looking back at Colonel Bruce. He had no patience for crack-brained operations or arrogant officers. He already didn't like this Captain Daemon character one bit and he hoped he wouldn't come to regret it.

"There is one caveat, though."

"What's that, Colonel?"

"This battalion in commanded by a topnotch SS-officer. His name is Sturmbannführer Emil Dietrich, (that's a Major in normal military jargon). He's a hard-boiled Nazi and a veteran of Stalingrad and Kursk, a real soldier, so says the Intelligence Branch. He's also a winner of the Knight's Cross of the Iron Cross, with Oak Leaves, Swords and Diamonds, mind you. That's the highest Nazi Germany can give, gentlemen. He's a coldhearted bastard and killer. *Do not* underestimate his abilities or his arrogance. I'm sure he'll be onsite, monitoring the work on the factory complex. Be on the lookout for him. He's tall, blond and real mean, with blue eyes. A regular Aryan... if you believe all that nonsense. Kill him if you can. But be very careful... please."

"It'll be my pleasure, Colonel," Jack interjected. He looked around at the sixteen seated men, grinning coolly. "Leave him to me, fellas. I'll kill that Nazi sumbitch myself, no problem."

Some of the men stared with incredulous looks on their faces wondering if this Captain Daemon fellow was for real, especially Staff Sergeant Justice. He was beside himself, simmering in utter distaste. But Lieutenant Lipton wasn't put off, he knew Daemon wasn't kidding when he said that. He knew the man was capable of some serious acts of bloodlust, he seen it firsthand.

"So what's the weather forecast for January 11th, Colonel?" Tech Sergeant Davis wanted to know. "More snow?"

"The weather over the drop zone will be overcast in the morning with light snow in the afternoon. But it will be clear at night. That could change though as you well know. But as I said earlier, barring a sudden winter snowstorm, the operation goes on, regardless."

"I figured as much."

"Now... for the sordid details," Colonel Bruce continued, "this is how you're going to infiltrate the production facility, gentlemen." He turned off the lights and flicked on the AP-5 opaque projector. The first picture he inserted was an aerial photo of the facility.

"This is an aerial photograph of the site, taken by British photo-reconnaissance on December 8, 1944. See the hilltop runway at the top of the Walpersberg? An Me-262 can be seen just at the top of the ramp, beside the runway. Various bunkers and assembly buildings can also be seen along the cleared area at the bottom of the slope... here, to the right of the ramp bottom. Those dark blotches on the runway, to the right of the ramp, are an incomplete attempt at painted camouflage."

The men looked on in silence as Colonel Bruce went through the photos, and for the next half-hour, he explained the actual assault in painstaking detail. It was an ingenious plan that would rely on expert timing, surprise, and the darkness of night. Essentially, after parachuting near a key road junction south of Kahla, the team would make its way toward the Walpersberg and to the factory complex neutralizing certain German defenses as they went, firstly eliminating a barracks full of sleeping SS-guards. Then they'd proceed to the assembly bunkers and plant TNT charges. They would also place charges along the steel tracks of the aircraft lift as well as the runway itself. When Colonel Bruce finally finished talking, he asked: "Questions, any one?"

The O.S.S. men sat in stolid silence, numb looks on their faces.

"Okay then, that's all for now, gentlemen, " Colonel Bruce concluded. "We'll have another briefing tomorrow at 07:00 hours sharp and discuss ex-filtration method from the Walpersberg complex. You are dismissed."

The men rose to their feet muttering quietly to one another. Jack remained seated a moment and lit a Players. He watched the men slowly exit, smoking. As Sergeant Justice strode by on his way out, Jack got up and walked after him and intercepted him at the door.

"Sergeant Justice..." Jack called out.

"Yes, sir?" Justice paused, turning around to face Jack.

"I know what happened on Guadalcanal."

"Oh, do you?"

"I read your dossier, I know you struck your C.O. "

"Yeah?" Justice bristled. "What about it?"

"Well, the same thing ain't gonna happen again, is it?"

Justice's face tightened. "I hope not, sir."

"You *hope not,* Sergeant? What does that mean?"

"It means, I can't say for sure."

Jack leaned in close, nose to nose with Justice. "Listen, you old jarhead. When I give you an order you better follow it to the letter. Because if you don't, I'll knock every gol-danged tooth outta yer swollen little head. You git me, mister?"

"Y-Yes, sir," Justice returned, a bit unnerved. "I hear you loud and clear. To the letter, sir."

"Good." Jack backed off, inhaling some smoke. "Because I ain't like any officer you ever served under before. Do like I ask and we'll git along just peachy—we might even be friends. But screw up, hoss, get on my bad side, and you'll have hell to pay. *Comprender?*"

"Yeah, I understand."

"Alright then." Jack clapped Justice on the shoulders. "Let's git some chow, eh? Let's see what this fancy French mess has to offer the fine young men of the O.S.S. "

Lipton winked as he walked past Justice.

"He means it, mate," he said with a wry smile. "Get on his bad side, and you've had it. Give the devil his due, aye?"

COLONEL MCKAVITT sat on the concrete slab that was his bed, listening to Chaplain Jenkins, the only man allowed to visit him whilst he was incarcerated in the cooler. McKavitt listened attentively as Jenkins filled him in on the camp's goings-on, mainly of the labor detachments leaving for work on the REIMAHG production facility. Some men were also being sent to the hillside tunnels along the Elster River. Despite McKavitt's bitter objections, 350 P.O.W.'s had been dispatched to the Walpersberg complex and the hillside tunnels, all at Dietrich's direct command. Most of the men had volunteered. But the officers did not. Under strict orders issued by Colonel McKavitt forbidding them to work, the officers "politely" declined. However, two were made an example of and were summarily beaten down by six of Dietrich's men, then dragged off to the cooler to spend the rest of the week in solitary confinement. Begrudgingly, if not reluctantly, the remaining officers boarded the work detail trucks and rode off with the men. And true to Dietrich's word, they were only on hand to act as overseers. But that didn't stop the SS guards from occasionally ordering them to fetch this or that, now and again, and it didn't stop them from abusing them, either. One officer returned from the facility one day with a busted lip and a bloody nose; an SS-guard had hit him with a rifle butt.

"So, how are the men holding up, Chaplain?" Colonel McKavitt asked. "Morale-wise, I mean?"

"Pretty good, Colonel," Jenkins replied. "Lieutenants Callahan and Matthews are a little bruised and banged-up. But they'll recover soon enough, according to the M.O."

"That's good to know. I hope they don't begrudge me for ordering them not to go. I feel responsible for their beatings."

"Not at all, sir. Callahan and Matthews understand what's at stake here. They'll abide by your orders. They told me so."

"Well, I might have to rescind that order, let the officers decide at their own discretion. I don't want anybody's beating—"

"Nonsense, Colonel," Jenkins interjected. "Article 49 of the Geneva Convention specifically states that officers do not have to work if they don't want to. You're the C.O. and what you say goes. If you order it, they have to do it. No ifs, ands, or buts about it, sir."

"Well, I can't do much about it in here." McKavitt looked around the four concrete walls, as small as they were, and grimaced inwardly, thinking: What is it with the Germans and concrete? Why must every jail, prison, or bunker be made of it? Nowhere else in this camp can you find a concrete structure like this!

"Von Warnstadt says you'll be out of here in a couple of days," said Jenkins sitting down on the slab next to McKavitt. "Then you can take up your grievances with the SS-Major yourself."

McKavitt grunted dubiously. "A lot of good it'll do me."

"You never know, Colonel." Jenkins evinced a wry smile. "God works in mysterious ways. This SS-Major might be moved to do the right thing. Miracles do happen."

"I doubt it, Chaplain. He's a hard-boiled Nazi. He's part of the SS that handles concentration camps and labor camps. That man has no conscience or scruples. Besides, Germany's losing the war. And the Krauts, whether they be Wehrmacht, Luftwaffe, or SS, will stop at nothing. They'll even using American officers as laborers."

"I don't think you have anything to worry about, Colonel." Jenkins laid a consoling hand on McKavitt's shoulder. "So far, only junior officers have been ordered to the tunnels and factory. You're a Colonel—a Group Commander—for Heaven's sake! That SS-Major wouldn't dare order you off on a work detail."

"Oh, he can, and he will." Colonel McKavitt sighed. "He'll do it to prove a point, Chaplain. Just to show everybody how much power he really has over me."

"You can refuse him, Colonel. Show him how much power *you* have. You might suffer the consequences, but God will protect you. He won't let you die or suffer needlessly. And if he does, it'll be because of some higher purpose."

McKavitt frowned. "That's not very reassuring, Chaplain. But it doesn't matter anyway."

"Oh? Why not?"

"Because if Dietrich assigns me to a work detail, I'll go."

"You will?"

McKavitt nodded firmly. "Yeah. Just so I can get out of this rotten P.O.W. camp for a little while and see what's what. Have a look around. Maybe plan my escape even. You never know, Chaplain. My *brain* works in mysterious ways."

Chaplain Jenkins chuckled. "That's the spirit, Colonel. Even you can be God's instrument, believe or not."

"Yeah, well, I hope God is rooting for the Allies instead of the Nazis, Chaplain. Because the way it's looking, divine intervention will be the deciding factor in this war."

"Never underestimate the power of the Lord, Colonel."

"Yeah. And never underestimate the power of the Germans—"

"In Ordung! Deine Zeit ist abgelaufen!" the Luftwaffe guard barked. *"Komm heraus, Kaplan!"* The guard unlocked and opened the door, ordering Chaplain Jenkins out, at gunpoint, much to the dread of the young Baptist clergyman from Atlanta.

"Well, I gotta run looks like, Colonel," Chaplain Jenkins uttered nervously, getting up. "Guess I'll see you in a couple of days, or at morning roll call."

"I suppose so." McKavitt stood up. "Thanks for stopping by, Chaplain. I really appreciate it."

"My pleasure, sir." Jenkins bowed his head. "Anything to ease the pain of war and general misery."

The Chaplain and the Colonel shook hands, and then the former departed, being herded down the corridor like a mindless beast of burden. McKavitt returned to his slab and sat down as the iron door slammed shut behind him, stroking his week-old beard, wondering what lay in store for him. If Dietrich had plans to assign him to a work detachment, then he decided wouldn't fight it. If going to some Nazi tunnel complex or mountain factory as a laborer was the only way an Air Corps Colonel could get outside the barbed wire confines of Camp Totenkopf, then so be it.

So far, it was the only plausible way he could think of, and it didn't need the approval of the Escape Committee (id est, Group Captain Hawker). He wasn't worried about being ordered around or abused by the SS; he knew they valued him as a high profile prisoner. He worried more about being locked away in solitary confinement and kept out of the loop of camp happenings and the war at large. Stalag Luft V may have appeared to be a high-risk escape at first glance, but it was positively inescapable now. With the weather worsening and the SS making regular visits an escape attempt seemed untimely now. Better to bide one's time and get assigned to a labor detachment, see what one could see, then make a break.

"OKAY, MRS. MCKAVITT," said the doctor, taking off his rubber gloves. "you can step down now."

"So is everything okay, doctor?" Rose replied.

"Yes. Based on your current health and well-being, Mrs. McKavitt, you'll give birth to a healthy baby when the time comes."

"That's good to hear."

Rose McKavitt scooched off the examination table and carefully placed her legs on the floor. Her legs were still in casts and she had to be cautious when she moved about. A nurse helped put on a hospital robe and then guided her into the wheelchair. She had just completed a prenatal exam and was feeling a little better about herself today. Having two knee-high plaster casts on both legs and constantly being wheeled around the hospital in a wheelchair was a dreadful feeling; her self-esteem was at an all-time low. She felt ugly and helpless, and lonely. Jack's visit reminded her of that wretched feeling. She felt guilty for forsaking him for David, even though her conscience told her it was the right thing to do at the time.

Somehow, Jack had escaped from the Japanese prison camp and rejoined the Army. But which branch had he joined? She saw no golden Air Corps wings above the breast pocket of his uniform the day he visited her. Rose only saw the silver Airborne wings over his left breast pocket; she had seen them many times on other soldiers around Wattisham and London. David had explained to her that they were paratrooper wings, and they denoted that the wearer was a jump-qualified expert. So was Jack a paratrooper now, she pondered? Why not a pilot? And he no longer called himself Jack, much less, John J. Knight or James Castillo—but Nicklaus Daemon? How had he managed that? Had he duped the U.S. Army once again, this time with a crewcut, a clean-shaven face and an ugly scar? And where had that come from?

Too many questions, Rose, she said to herself. Too many questions! Jack was an enigma that no one could figure out. He'd apparently disappeared and reappeared without causing a stir in the ranks of the U.S. Army or the General Staff. He was like a ghost returning from the dead, and now he was haunting her thoughts and dreams once again. Rose was baffled, and it made her head spin just thinking about it.

"All right, Mrs. McKavitt," said the elderly hospital nurse. "I'll take you back to your room now—"

"No," Rose insisted. "Take me to the telephones, please? I need to make an urgent phone call."

"Oh?" The nurse replied, surprised. "Can't it wait until—"

"It cannot. I must make a call right now. Or I fear it might have come too late already. It's about... my husband, David, you see?"

"Yes, yes, of course, my dear." The nurse changed direction, turning the wheelchair about and heading for the hospital courtesy phones. "If it's about your husband, then by all means."

"Thank you."

The nurse pushed Rose's wheelchair down the lengthy hallway and to an area adjacent to the recreation ward. A long row of partitioned telephones stood against the wall opposite the large windows of the ward. There were six telephones set in place for use. But currently, five were being used, and the sixth had a sign on it that read: "out of order." The nurse parked the wheelchair nearby and patted Rose on the shoulder in a consoling kind of way.

"Oh, dear," she said with an anxious sigh. "They're all in use currently. Do you wish to wait for one? Or should—"

"Yes!" Rose hissed. "I'll wait."

"Very well. I'll leave you to it then. I'll be back in a moment."

The nurse scuttled off, heading for the nurse's lounge. Rose sat and waited impatiently as she watched two men in hospital robes jabbering away whilst an orderly sat cross-legged talking on another. An R.AF. officer was perched near the fourth telephone smoking a filtered cigarette. He just stood there listening as his party blabbed away whilst he only got in a word in edge-wise every few seconds. A ruddy, heavyset man in striped pajamas and with a bandage on his head occupied the last working telephone. He was arguing with someone, perhaps his wife, Rose wondered? He kept saying phrases like: "My dearest deary," and "Oh, come off it, Clara," and "Me lovely old wifey."

Rose sat and waited, arms folded over her bosom, huffing edgily. The telephones were never so much in use as they were right now. She had passed by them many times in the days before, never seeing more than one in use at any given time. But now, when she really needed to make a call?

"Cor!" She spouted. "Will you people finish up already!"

The R.A.F. officer turned about and made a pained face.

The orderly cupped the mouthpiece and said: "What'd ye say?"

The two robed men seemed to have not heard her, for they continued their loquacious conversations unabated. The heavyset man looked over his shoulder and smiled stiffly, not really hearing Rose's snappy remark for all his wife's chatty complaining. Rose was getting angry.

"Somebody! Please! Get off the bloody blower! Push off, what!"

"My word," said the R.A.F. officer, a rather distinguished, mustachioed gentleman of elderly age. "How very rude of you, ma'am."

"I'm sorry, sir," Rose apologized glibly. "I'm in a bit of a hurry you see. My husband's been missing-in-action for quite some time now, and I need to call the... War Office, posthaste. I worried sick."

"Well, in that case, ma'am, I shall conclude my call, forthwith." The R.A.F. officer politely begged off and hung up the handset. "It's all yours. You may place your call now." He turned on a heel and calmly walked out of the ward.

Rose wheeled herself over the telephone and seized the handset.

The orderly had also concluded his call by now. He strode over to Rose and shook his head. "Bloody hell, ma'am. Do ye even know who that was ye just chased off?"

"No!" Rose flared. "Who?"

"Air Chief Marshal Hugh Dowding. The bloody leader of Fighter Command during the Battle, that's who. 'Stuffy' they called 'im."

Rose's face turned bright red. "Oh."

The orderly sauntered off, chortling.

Rose grumbled, chiding herself, then placed her call.

"Yes, ma'am?" the operator responded.

"Would you connect me with Supreme Allied Headquarters in Portsmouth, Southwick House, Personnel Section? Hurry, please!"

JACK LIT A cigarette and got up from the mess table. He carried the half-eaten tray of ham and eggs and took it to the garbage can where he emptied it and then stacked it on top of several others. It was almost 07:00; time for Colonel Bruce's final briefing. Today, Jack would find out the exact ex-filtration method from the Walpersberg facility, information he probably wouldn't need anyway.

That and other things. Like the rendezvous coordinates of the ex-filtration point—the place where the team would be picked up by an O.S.S. flown Lockheed C-40. The Lockeed was a stripped-down, twin-engined plane that could carry ten people, not counting the pilot and navigator. Jack as well as the rest of the men knew a few of them would not be coming back. In fact, Colonel Bruce had told Jack and Lieutenant Lipton he was counting on a fifty percent casualty rate. Jack thought it was a rather conservative figure; he didn't think anyone was coming back, himself included. An operational group of seventeen men infiltrating a heavily defended production facility deep in the heart of Germany was just plain suicide in his estimation. But he didn't care. He'd never planned on living a long life, anyway.

After exiting the mess, he headed over to his billet to fetch some paperwork. He needed to amend his Army life insurance policy, file his last will and testament, and give Colonel Bruce an important envelope, a letter meant to be opened after embarked on the mission. Going up against Jap Zeros and escaping from a P.O.W. camp in Japan was one thing. But going up against a fanatical group like the SS with a handful of men, deep in German territory, without combat support, was something he didn't consider survivable. He wanted to make damn sure he didn't leave any loose ends this time, make sure everyone and everything was taken care of, leave nothing behind that would incriminate himself... but inculpate those who had left him for dead the last time.

After dropping off his life insurance papers and will at the Personal Office, the envelope stashed in a hip pocket, Jack hurried over to the briefing room. He wanted to get there before the others arrived so he could talk to Colonel Bruce privately. But when he got there, he found the Colonel already talking to someone else—a tall, slender and eagle-eyed looking man with tanned and rugged facial features, with a receding hairline and sideburns that were mostly gray, his pencil-thin mustache nearly the same. He was wearing a plain black tie and a double-breasted suit and a gray fur-felt fedora, which sat perched upon his head at a rakish angle. Even though he used a cane to prop himself up, he still appeared to be a strong and virile middle-aged man.

"Ah, Captain Daemon," said Colonel Bruce as Jack came in.

"You're early again, I see. And just in time to meet someone."

"Oh, yeah?" Jack replied, saluting and closing the door behind. "And who would that be, sir?"

Colonel Bruce gestured to the man standing next to him. "Captain Daemon, this is... Herr Willi Wissemann, a former pilot, just like yourself, and a special liaison officer for the *Bureau Central de Renseignements et d'Action,* and for the O.S.S. here in Paris."

"The Willi Wissemann?" Jack said, grinning, proffering his hand. "The Black Eagle of Bavaria? Well, pleased to meet ya, sir."

Wissemann shook Jack's hand. "Oh, please. That was so long ago, I'd almost forgotten about that silly old nickname" Wissemann smiled awkwardly. "Nice to meet you, Captain Daemon."

"Likewise, sir. I've heard a lot about you. Yes indeed, I have," Jack gushed. "Man oh man, you shot down 33 Allied planes during the Great War. You were the top scoring Bavarian ace and a winner of the Blue Max."

"Uh... no." Wissemann blushed, the awkward smile suddenly become thin and crooked. "I was neither."

"No?"

Wissemann shook his head. "Rittmeister Eduard von Schleich held both of those honors, not I. I was... second, you might say?"

"Wissemann defected to our side four years ago," Colonel Bruce elaborated, "and gave the Brits some of their first insight on Germany's secret weapons. Now he's working with France's Central Bureau of Intelligence and Operations lately, coordinating and communicating information with our own intelligence agencies."

"Interesting," Jack replied, nodding slowly. "It's funny how things work out sometimes, eh, Herr Wissemann? Once a German ace and now a French liaison officer—that's quite a different path."

"Indeed," Wissemann replied. "We had similar paths, it seems."

Jack reached into his hip pocket and gave Colonel Bruce the envelope. "Here, sir. This is the letter I spoke of earlier."

"Right." Colonel Bruce took the envelope and slyly pocketed it.

"Wartime intrigues?" said Wissemann with a crafty grin.

"Mmm, something like that," Jack replied, winking.

CHAPTER 11

C OLNEL DAVID M. MCKAVITT stood before the formation of America P.O.W.'s, his legs spread apart, his collar turned up against the cold air as roll call was being taken by a Luft-waffe Feldwebel. Hauptmann Becker and Kommandant von Warn-stadt stood by listening as each prisoner's name was called. The Kommandant was smiling this morning for some strange reason; his typical Prussian scowl seemed to have been replaced by a gleeful expression. McKavitt wondered what it could be. Germany was los-ing the war, bombed into submission by the 8th Air Force by day, and bombed by the R.A.F. at night. Their great winter offensive had been soundly repelled, and the Wehrmacht was falling back on all fronts. What could make the Kommandant so happy this cold, snowy morning?

"Alle anwesend und verantwortlich, Herr Kommandant!" the Feldwebel announced, esentially saying every prisoner was present and accounted for. He saluted crisply, clicking his heels.

The Kommandant returned the salute, and then stepped up on his wooden soapbox, hands clasped behind his back, nodding, eye-ing the American P.O.W.'s keenly. When his eyes fell upon Colonel McKavitt, they narrowed, sharp and piercing. He cleared his throat.

"Good morning, American prisoners," he began in an affable high-pitched voice. "Today we will continue our good work on the production facility at the Walpersberg."

A chorus of grumbles arose from the assembled P.O.W.'s.

"Yes, yes, that's right, gentlemen. It's back to work today."

McKavitt frowned. "Why so cheerful today, Kommandant?"

"You will please address the Kommandant as '*Herr Komman-dant*', Colonel McKavitt," Hauptmann Becker enjoined hotly.

"*Herr Kommandant,*" McKavitt duly replied, grinning. "Since you said please, Becker."

The men guffawed spontaneously.

Becker scowled, clenching his fist.

Von Warnstadt stepped down from his soapbox and walked over to Colonel McKavitt, hands still clasped behind his back.

"To answer your question, Colonel," von Warnstadt said, "I am smiling this morning because a certain someone will be accompany-ing his men on a work detachment today. A certain someone who thinks he's above doing common labor."

"Would that someone be *me*?" McKavitt replied, still grinning.

"It would."

"Aw, I'm touched, Herr Kommandant. I thought you'd forgot-ten about me," McKavitt uttered in snide supplication. "My hands got all soft sitting on them in the cooler these past ten days."

Some of the men chuckled. However, a few of the senior non-coms did not. They realized what was about to happen; a senior offi-cer was going to be sent out on a work detachment.

"And soft they shall remain, Colonel. You will only accompany the work detachment as overseer—as I have said before."

"Well, that's ashamed. I was hoping to get my hands dirty."

The men laughed.

"Silence!" Hauptmann Becker shouted. "One more outburst and it's the cooler—for all of you!"

The P.O.W.'s booed defiantly. They knew Becker was bluffing.

"I see your odd sense of humor has not been affected, Colonel, by ten days in the cooler. Perhaps a few more days might—"

"Nah, nah, nah" came the rasping voice of Sturmbannführer Emil Dietrich. "That won't be necessary." He walked up to von Warnstadt, simpering, cloaked in a double-breasted motorcycle coat made of rubberized cotton, his death's head peaked cap tilted rak-ishly over a brow. "He'll accompany his men today, and he *will* en-gage in manual labor."

"Like hell I will," Colonel McKavitt swiftly refused.

Dietrich snorted, reared back, and backhanded McKavitt across the right cheek, snapping his head to one side, bloodying his lip.

"Your insolence grows tiresome, Colonel," Dietrich snarled.

The P.O.W.'s groaned and lunged forward in protest, only to be forced back as the guards unshouldered and cocked their rifles.

McKavitt grimaced painfully and shook his head, coddling his bloodied lip. But he stood erect and defiant again. "Striking a superior officer... hey, that's a court martial offense. Isn't it, Dietrich?"

"Shut up, Colonel," Dietrich returned coldly. "Your outdated notions of wartime etiquette are no longer applicable. You will do as you are ordered, or you will be shot."

"Is that a promise, *Herr Sturmbannführer?*"

Dietrich drew his Walther sidearm and cocked the bolt. He pointed it at Colonel McKavitt's face. "Yes, it is. Would you like to me oblige you right now, Colonel?"

The P.O.W.'s gasped.

McKavitt raised his hands in mock surrender, blood dribbling from his lip, his mouth a crooked line. "Uh, no thanks, Dietrich. That won't be necessary. I believe you."

"Good." Dietrich nodded, holstering his sidearm. "I'd hate to gun you down so coldly in front of your men, Colonel. It would be bad for morale."

McKavitt reached into his pant's pocket and pulled out a handkerchief and proceeded to clean the blood from his mouth.

"Very bad for morale," he quipped, snorting

"All right, gentlemen," the Kommandant interjected, a bit unnerved by Dietrich's savagery. "Let's get the men organized into separate work detachments, shall we? Then get them loaded onto the trucks. They've got a long drive ahead of them."

"Indeed they do," Dietrich concurred.

"Hauptmann Becker..." the Kommandant said, gesturing. "See to it, immediately."

"Jawohl, Herr Kommandant." Becker motioned to the guards, and they began dividing the men up into work gangs of fifty men.

Dietrich motioned to his men, the drivers of ten Opel-Blitz troop trucks, and ordered them to prepare for loading and departure. He turned back to Kommandant von Warnstadt and saluted, stiff-armed.

"Heil Hitler!" he bellowed, about-faced, and then stalked off.

"Yeah. *Heil-fucking-Hitler,"* Colonel McKavitt grumped, wiping off his mouth, then turned to his face men and winked coolly.

THE TWIN-ENGINED Skytrain shuddered and shimmied at the buffeting blasts of German flak. There sounded a series of deafening bangs and smoke began to seep in the fuselage where the O.S.S. paratroopers sat facing each other in two rows, bodies bulky with parachute packs and drop bags. Staff Sergeant Hentges, the smallest man aboard the airplane nudged Captain (Jack) Daemon in the ribs, trying to keep his voice from sounding frail.

"Gawd! What the hell, sir!" he exclaimed. "Is this thing starting to come apart or what?"

The Skytrain banked violently on a wing and stayed there a few heart-stopping seconds before it slowly returned to an even keel.

Jack's teeth flashed in a grin of realization. "I wouldn't be surprised, Sergeant. Seems like something's wrong." He jerked his head, indicating the forward part of the fuselage. "Lieutenant Lipton is going up front to the cockpit. He'll find out what's going on."

"You think we're near the drop zone, Captain?"

"Not yet. Miles away, I'm sure. Must be another thirty or forty minutes flying time before we get there."

"The Krauts seemed to be waiting for us." Hentges glared at the metal fuselage of the Skytrain. "Sounds like they're throwing everything they got up at us." As he said that, the flak outside seemed to get louder and more frequent.

"Nothin' we can do about it, Sergeant," Jack replied calmly. "Just take it easy, okay?"

"Huh! That's easy for you to say, sir," Hentges grumbled, wiping beads of sweat from his forehead with the back of his hand. "Nothing seems to bother you. You sit there looking cool as a cucumber. And I don't mind telling you... I'm scared. Flak! You never know when it will hit. You can't fight back. You Just have to wait and sweat it out."

"Ah, heck, you'll be okay in a spell. Soon as you jump out that door, you'll feel peachy. Like you said, there's nothing you can do about it, so why not just take it easy, hmm?"

Jack reclined on the bench seat and closed his eyes. He could feel his own heart pounding wildly and he could feel his pulse quicken every time a flak burst exploded nearby. But his face remained calm. No point in getting jittery over a little flak.

"You must have ice water in your veins instead of blood," Hentges uttered. He laughed tensely and added: "Wish I was like you."

Hentges glanced at Captain Daemon. He was a six-foot-two perfectly trained fighting man. Even sitting down he gave the impression of being able to jump up into instant action. He had a strong jawline and eyes that made Hentges shiver in his boots when he looked into them. His elbow nudged into Jack's ribs again.

"Hmm?" Jack grunted. "What's up now, Hentges?"

"Were you... sleeping, sir?" the little Sergeant asked.

"Snoozing. Might be awhile before we get the chance again."

Hentges lapsed into silence. He looked at the other members of the group. They sat quietly, talking in low voices. The cockpit door through which Lieutenant Lipton had passed through a few seconds before was still closed. However, Hentges was relieved to see that the smoke in the fuselage had disappeared finally.

"Hey, why do they call you the Devil, sir?" he asked. "Odd kind of nickname to have. Never heard of a name like that before."

"Because I'm just that—a devil," Jack replied without opening his eyes. "I'm a handful, that's why. I do things my own way, you see." He opened his eyes and Hentges felt a cold shiver go up his spine as that ice-blue gaze fixed upon him. "Anything wrong with that, Sergeant?"

"N-No, sir. Not at all," Hentges agreed quickly. "Nothing wrong with that at all. Not at all—"

Their conversation was cut short as Lieutenant Lipton pushed open the cockpit door, then slammed it shut behind him.

"Hook up, lads!" he barked. "At the double! Stand by to drop!"

"But we're nowhere near the drop zone," Hentges grumbled as he and the rest of the men stood up and fastened their parachute hooks on the static line of the overhead rail. "We're miles away!"

"Twenty miles—or thereabouts," Lipton replied. "If we hang about here, well, we've had our chips, lads." The Brit-voiced Canadian yanked a thumb towards the cockpit. "The pilot and co-pilot have had it. The pilot's hanging by a thread and the co-pilot's dead. The pilot's going to try to make an emergency landing after we jump." Then Lipton's voice raised to that of a drill sergeant's roar. "So hook up and jump, you dozy lot! C'mon! C'mon! Move your bloody arses now! Jump! Go—Go—Go!"

The fuselage door opened, and the noise increased to a deafening roar. Flak was still coming up at them; red and yellow lights filled the night sky. The men shuffled together toward the door as they yanked the static lines tight to make sure they were secure on the overhead rail. The first man, Sergeant Hassler, went out headfirst, then the next and then the next. Jack's turn came, and he went out without hesitation, and, Hentges, who was right behind him, took a great gulp of air and followed him out, although rather reluctantly. Bryant jumped last.

Jack felt the sharp jerk of the harness on his shoulders as his parachute deployed above him, blossoming into a gray-green mushroom. Below, he could just see other parachutes drifting down in the darkness, and above, he saw the swaying body of Sergeant Hentges. Flak was still filling the sky, but it seemed to be far away now. Then a great mass of icy green rose from the ground towards him, and he pulled on one of the harness straps, spilling some air from the parachute, causing it to fall away from the big tree that was suddenly beneath him. The ground came up so fast that Jack assumed he'd just jumped from less than 600 feet. Even so, he came down, elbows close to his body, knees and ankles together and hit the snow in a compact ball, rolling forward, then leaped up and gathered his collapsing chute. He crouched there, his .45-caliber "grease-gun" locked and loaded, straining his ears and eyes, probing the frigid darkness. They'd come down on the edge of a great forest. Jack hid the parachute and pack in the snow.

The tall Texan retreated into the trees and stood with his back against a huge tree trunk. Like scurrying ghosts, the others members of the "stick" that had just dropped from the sky moved into view, all of them with weapons drawn, backing up slowly toward the cover of the forest. Low-level jump, Jack surmised; they'd jumped rapidly one after the other from the Skytrain, and their decent had been swift owing to the low altitude at which the twin-engined plane had been flying. Within a minute the entire group had assembled in a defensive circle.

"Where's Lieutenant Lipton?" Jack asked softly.

Bryant moved forward into the beam of moonlight filtering down through the branches, his grease-gun shoulder-slung, his first aid pack strapped to his back. "Lieutenant Lipton didn't jump, sir," he replied. "He told me to tell you—he's staying with the pilot."

"Dang Canuck!" Jack griped bitterly. "Always playing the gentleman-fool, I see."

"Who's second-in-command then?" came the excited whisper.

"Sergeant Davis, that's who," Jack returned.

"Davis, eh?" Justice's voice had a note of protest in it.

"That's right. I'm the platoon sergeant, Justice. You know that."

"Yup," Jack agreed. "Got any objections, Justice?" The words, sharp as steel, cut like a dagger.

"S'okay with me, sir." Justice's nod seemed reluctant.

"Now that that's settled." Jack moved forward to the edge of the forest, moving with the grace and power of a panther. "Now we decide what to do... and that, depends on mainly where we are."

"Lieutenant Lipton reckoned we were about twenty miles from our proposed drop zone," Davis declared. "That was about two or three minutes before we all jumped."

"Let's say... twenty-five miles, okay?" Jack took out a folded map from his hip pocket and spread it out over the frozen ground in the moonlight. "That'd put us about—*here.*" His forefinger stabbed at the map. "Somewhere close to the village of Gehlberg, I'd say."

"All right," Justice waved aggressively, "so we know where we are. What I want to know is... where the hell do we go from here, huh?" He stepped forward, his chin jutting forward, his B.A.R. held high. "Let's hear your plan, Captain. I hope it's got some teeth. I surely hope so."

Jack folded the map and tucked it in his pocket. "Yup, it's got teeth alright. You up for some real fightin', Justice?"

Justice nodded truculently. "I am! And if you think I'm taking orders from a jumped-up jackass like you, well, you've got it all wrong, brother."

"Well, you *better* take orders, Justice, and take 'em quick. I saw a light over there just now." Jack pointed across that snowy field before them. "It's my guess the Krauts are out lookin' fer us. Someone must have seen us drop in and already reported it."

The men looked and saw a faint light near the next wood.

"Now, here are yer orders, men," Jack declared firmly. "Davis and Hassler, move out to the left flank. Hays, Carter, and Powell, out on the right. The rest of you take cover in the trees. If'n the

Krauts don't see us... let 'em keep going, okay? If'n they do, I'll give the signal and we'll cut 'em down. Now move out, all of ya."

Jack and Sergeant Justice stood there for a moment, glaring, eyes locked. Then Justice turned away, chortling snidely and melded into the darkness.

"He's a real nut-job, that Justice," Davis whispered as he strode off to take up cover in the snow-covered trees.

"Yup," Jack had to agree. "A real nut-job, alright. And one who better follow my orders."

The men of O.G. NEMESIS waited in absolute silence. On the snowbound field before them a shadowy figure appeared, then another, then another. The coal-scuttle helmets of the Germans offered no doubt as to their identity. However, they were moving across the ground parallel to the trees, and after a long moment, they disappeared from view again. Everyone breathed a sigh of relief.

"Gone. They didn't see us, thank God," said Hentges, grinning, his little teeth showing white in the gloom. "We're in luck, sir."

"Luck?" Jack humphed softly. "Give 'em another five minutes and then we'll move out."

Five minutes went by...

When the five minutes were up, Jack sounded a low whistle and the men came back quietly, forming in a semi-circle around him.

"Sergeant Justice asked me what I was planning to do," Jack told them. "Well, this is the plan. It's a simple one. We make our way to the drop zone and carry out our operation to blow up the jet production facility. It's important we knock it out tonight. Because according to our three-man Jedburgh team, the Krauts are bringing sixteen Me-262 jets on-line tomorrow. That's a whole friggin' squadron of Nazi fighter jets, gents. They're flying 'em out one by one to be equipped with weapons and radios and undergo final testing." Jack paused and eyed every man standing before him. "It's up to us they never make it to their destination. We must succeed at all costs. Y'all understand, right?"

Everyone nodded. Everyone but Sergeant Justice that is.

"Hell! We can't get from here to Kahla... before dawn tomorrow," Justice argued, "with snow, ice and the whole German Army around us? We might have to fight Nazis all the way there, *sir.*" The last word was inflected with some heavy irony.

"Well, that's just what we're gonna do, *Sarge.*"

"What if we don't get there on time?"

"Then we just blow up the facility itself—sans sixteen jets."

Justice moved forward, standing alone, facing Jack. "I say it's a botched job already. What we ought to do is try to get back to our rendezvous point at Saalfeld, get the heck out of Germany. Not continue on with this washed-out suicide mission." He jabbed a stubby finger out at Jack. "I know your type," he growled. "You want fame and glory. You're just looking for a fucking medal, buddy."

"You'll do as yer ordered, Justice." Jack's voice sounded like a wipe-crack. "Or you and I can settle this right here and now."

"Knock it off, Justice—" Tech Sergeant Davis warned.

"Hush!" Jack said, waving Davis off. "Let 'em have his say."

A broad grin spread over Justice's rock-hard features. He unbuckled his ammo belt, then he tossed the B.A.R. at his feet.

"Yeah. We'll settle it this right *now,* sir!" With those words said, he slipped out of his webbing and flung it at Jack's head.

But the ice-blue eyes hadn't wavered from Justice's leering grin. The webbing went flying over Jack's head as he ducked down, and within the same movement, he launched himself forward, his head enclosed in his paratrooper's round helmet, and crashed into Justice's midsection, knocking the man over on his backside. Justice lay dazed for the split-second it took Jack to stand over him and grab him by the lapel of his jump-jacket, hauling him up bodily to his booted feet. Then found himself shaken until his teeth almost rattled out of his head.

"I need you, dammit! I need every man here!" Jack shoved Justice away from him. "If I didn't, I'd take you apart. Now let's cut the crap and git moving. We've gotta long way to go."

Justice stood frozen, eyes flaring hotly, fists clenched.

Jack gazed at each man standing around him, one by one. "Unless there's any other objections, that is?"

Hentges' soft southern drawl broke the silence. "We're with you, sir. We were sent out to do a job like you said... so let's do it."

"C'mon, let's move out then," Davis added.

"Yeah! Let's do this thing, sir," Hassler threw in.

Everyone took up a chorus, and Justice knew he was alone. He grabbed his gear and strode off. Jack nodded. "Okay. Move out."

"AHA! WORKING LATE again, Herr Multhopp?" asked the emaciated looking Messerschmitt engineer Herr Bölkow

"Ja," Multhopp replied absently, staring at the clipboard in his hand. "I want my prototype ready to go when the other jets go."

Bölkow chuckled. "Does that thing really fly?" He said in a sarcastic tone. He gazed at the stubby fuselage and exceedingly sweptback wings, chortling, shaking his head doubtfully.

"It does. And quite well, too. Better than your Me-262, I think."

Bölkow scoffed. "I seriously doubt that, Herr Multhopp. Willi Messerschmitt's jet is the best in the Reich right now. Nothing can surpass its high-speed and climbing ability. Nothing! It is the fastest plane in the world, I can assure you."

"Aren't you forgetting about the Me-163 Komet, sir?"

"Ach! That's not an airplane. That's a rocket. It doesn't count."

"Well, my new Ta-183 prototype will reach speeds of 600-mph in level flight. And it basically has the same engine as the Me-262."

"Quatsch!" Bölkow spouted. "Nothing can fly faster than the Me-262, Herr Multhopp. Nothing."

"Nothing?"

"Nothing!"

"We shall see about that, sir."

"Humph!" Herr Bölkow waddled away, half-laughing, half-scoffing, hands in his coat pockets, shaking his little bald head.

Herr Multhopp smiled and turned back to his swept-wing prototype, admiring its aerodynamic lines and T-shaped tailplane. It really was a magnificent piece of machinery, and on its very first test flight, it reached 593-mph, armed with a full war load of one hundred fifty 30-millimeter cannon shells. It certainly impressed the Reichs Air Ministry inspectors when they saw it zoom by overhead that day at Rechlin, impressed enough to give Herr Multhopp the go-ahead for full production. Once REIHMAG's current production run of sixteen Me-262 *"Schwalbe"* jets were completed and flown to Lechfeld and equipped with armaments and radios, Herr Multhopp and his engineers could begin work on twelve Ta-183 jet fighters. They'd be the first dozen of two hundred ordered by RLM with a deployment date set for May 8th.

Multhopp glanced at his wristwatch and noted the hour; it was almost midnight! He looked up at the white electric lighting of the hangar workshop and sighed. He could never tell if it was day or night in here. The thick concrete walls and heavy steel doors made time stand still somehow. No sunlight, no moonlight. No clouds, no stars. It was a stale hermetically sealed environment—a subterranean hell. Even with the ventilation system working at full capacity day and night, the air inside the facility workshops always seemed damp and musty. It was a dank place to work in and it made Herr Multhopp yearn for the wide-open spaces of the Aeronautical Research Institute at Brunswick; its vast one thousand acre landscape, its five wind tunnels, administration buildings, canteen, telephone exchange, guard houses, generators and other needful facilities, gave him a deep sense of purpose and belonging. But now that the Reich was under constant bombardment and aerial observation, such luxuries were nonexistent.

Things were so different now.

How had the incredible might of German industry and engineering been forced underground, he wanted to know? How had Hitler and his Nazi cronies let things get so bad? He knew why. It was the same reason for his very existence, his life's work even. War. Without it, he would have never been able to pursue his dreams of jet-powered flight. Without the war, Herr Multhopp would be just another engineer at Focke-Wulf working on some simple, insignificant aircraft of propeller-driven design. The very thought of war, and the weapons designed for it, often made his conscience tingle with thoughts of guilt and moral consequence; he was basically creating weapons designed to destroy things and kill people. But he never let it bother him. He was an engineer, and above all, a scientist—a man with an advanced knowledge of things so intricate that they would ultimately be a benefit to mankind. To him war was a normal act carried out by human societies, and it was up to the engineers to make it as efficient as possible. Alas, people always died because of it but that was the nature of the beast. Without the accelerated imperatives of a country at war, certain technologies couldn't have been advanced so far and so fast. War, as ugly as it was, put technology on the fast track to the future. Without it, the world would simply wallow in a suspended state of arrested development.

"Will it be ready tomorrow, Herr Multhopp?" asked the strapping young SS-guard who had just walked up, his MP-40 machine pistol slung over a shoulder, a cigarette burning in his lips.

"I think so," Multhopp replied, pushing his glasses back. "The ailerons and trim tabs might need to be adjusted, along with the engine compressor, but It will be ready to fly out tomorrow."

"Will you be flying it, sir?"

"Heavens no!" Multhopp said with a chuckle. "The Luftwaffe is sending over a contingent of pilots to fly it and the Messerschmitt jets to Lechfeld Airbase tomorrow morning."

"Oh. *Can* you fly it, Herr Multhopp?"

"Yes, I can fly it. I am a licensed pilot as well as an engineer."

"Really?" The SS-guard replied skeptically.

"Indeed," said Multhopp, then added proudly: "And as you can plainly see, my jet fighter is armed with guns."

The SS-guard looked but saw no guns of any kind.

"Where? I don't see any guns?"

Multhopp sighed irritably and jabbed his finger at two of the four gun ports just visible on the nose of the jet. "There! See those gun ports right there? Those are MK 108 30-millimeter cannons, my friend. Powerful enough to knock down an American bomber with just one burst."

The SS-guard looked again, pursing his lips, squinting just a bit. "Ah, I see what you mean now. The guns are... inside the nose?"

"Yessss!" Multhopp hissed exasperatedly, wondering if the guard's skull was as thick as the helmet he wore.

The SS-guard shrugged. "Well, whatever works, I suppose?" He took a drag from his cigarette and sauntered off humming thickly.

Hans Multhopp shook his head woefully, rasping the back of his neck, questioning the intelligence of the SS-guard and a few others working in the facility. How did some people get through life with such simple minds, he asked himself? What made them do and say such stupid things, he wondered? It amazed him that even truly smart men like Herr Bölkow could be so block-headed at times. Oh well, so be it, Multhopp chagrined. Sadly, the world was yet full of fools, and that would never change. Would he ever meet a man with raw courage, common sense, and true genius, he wondered? Did such men still exist these dark and dismal days?

THEY MOVED eastward following a snowy track through the forest. Sergeant Justice was on point while Sergeants Davis and Hassler brought up the rear. Jack and "Boomer" Hentges walked together, side by side. Hentges was his usual talkative self.

"You showed him up all right," he said admiringly. "That's the first time I've ever seen Justice back down."

Jack seemed to have lost interest in the little episode. He walked onward with eyes fixed forward, trying to stay focused for the job ahead. "It ain't gonna be no joy-ride, Hentges," he said softly. "There's a lot of Krauts between us and the Walpersberg, and we may run into them at any time." He looked up at the moonlit sky through the canopy of frozen branches above. "We've got to make up a lot of distance before daylight. And at the rate we're going, it ain't gonna happen."

"We'll make it, sir," Hentges replied. "Don't you worry."

But progress was slow. The track through the forest thinned out very quickly, and soon, heavy snowdrifts and icy patches reduced the operational group into a cursing, ill-tempered gang.

"You sure we're going in the right direction, sir?" Davis asked. "Shouldn't we be out of this forest by now. It can't go on forever."

Jack glanced at the compass strapped to his wrist, checking their heading. "We're okay. In about ten minutes we'll break clear of this." He looked over his shoulder, glaring cold-eyed. "Our real troubles will soon begin. It'll be dawn in a few hours. People will be up and about. We'll be lucky if we can steer clear of the Germans once it's light."

The tall trees thinned out but the ground underneath became more and more snow-covered; every now and again a trooper sank to his knees in the dense snow, then had to jerk himself out, cursing angrily. By the time they broke cover, tempers were short. Not far away, about a half-mile, the high-gabled roof of a farmhouse jutted darkly against the sky which was growing lighter by the minute. Ahead, the ground sloped sharply to a white valley. Nothing moved; the air was cold and still. The men gathered around Jack. They seemed relaxed but their eyes darted all around, ever watchful and alert. Jack pointed ahead.

"We'll move down this valley. Let's stay out of the light, okay? If you see anyone, whistle softly. Then hit the deck. Questions?"

Heads bobbed in agreement.

Sergeant Davis said: "And hold your fire, men—if you can. We don't want to attract any unnecessary attention."

"Uh, when do we eat, sir?" Corporal Schmidt asked almost sounding apologetic. "I didn't eat anything before take-off. Flying makes me sick, you see. I, um, well..."

Schmidt's voice trailed off into an awkward silence. The austere faces before him glared back with icy contempt. His hunger pangs didn't interest them. They were cold, damp, and pissed off.

"Alright, let's move out." Jack waved Sergeant Justice forward with his grease-gun. "Yer on point, *Sarge.*"

"I'm on point," Justice echoied, nodding reluctantly. "Right."

Jack turned to Hays and Carter. "You two hang here a spell until the rest of us have gone ahead. Then follow about a hundred yards behind us. If we're gonna travel out in the open, so to speak, we need sharp eyes and ears in front and in back of us."

Hays and Carter both gave agreeing nods. They were lean, good-looking guys from a small town in Georgia. Neither of them ever spoke much; they were good soldiers who obeyed orders first... and saved the questions for later. Jack knew he could rely on them.

The group moved rapidly through the valley through ankle-deep snow. There was enough light from the moon so they could see where they were going. The valley appeared to be deserted. There wasn't a house nor an animal, and best of all, no Germans. Jack sent Corporals Russell and Ricci ahead to seek out the easiest path, and the two men from the American Midwest moved stealthily and speedily. By 4 o'clock, the sky was starting to glow with the first hints of light. The heavily laden column of men began to tire; they'd covered nearly ten miles from the forest where they had parachuted, but Jack reckoned they were still at least fifteen miles from their destination. They were going to have to find some transport if they wanted any chance at that Nazi production facility before daylight.

Suddenly, Corporal Russell, half-hidden amidst a copse of snow-covered shrubs, whistled softly, then dropped in his tracks. The column immediately flopped to the ground. On elbows and knees, Jack crawled forward and met Russell as he came crawling back himself.

"What's up, Corporal?" Jack asked.

"Kraut road-block ahead," Russell whispered.

"Can we go around it?"

"Yeah, I think so... but we gotta cross the road whatever we do, it stretches right across our path."

"We'll try to avoid it," Jack decided. "We'll move off to our right, quarter of a mile. If it's clear, we'll cross the road there. Alright, let's move out." The men hopped up and trudged onward.

Every few seconds, Jack could hear the engine of a car or truck as it drove by on the road ahead. Occasionally he caught sight of headlights glaring into the roadside but he felt reasonable secure himself, hidden as he and the men were by the snowy bushes that lined the side of the road. When he judged they'd moved more than a quarter mile from the place where Justice had seen the German roadblock, he halted the column with a wave of a gloved hand, then crept on alone to the road's edge. They had apparently reached a place where the road curved in a wide turn. The roadblock was out of sight. Jack looked right and left before signaling the others forward. They went across in pairs, running swiftly and disappearing into the undergrowth on the far side of the road. As one pair men made the crossing and then vanished, the next pair ran across. Jack waited to go over last with Hays and Carter. When at last every man was safely across, they moved off quietly, following the road east, hiding in the undergrowth and staying off the shoulder.

Jack set a blistering pace. They walked on the side of the road keeping a lookout for Germans and a potential vehicle, or vehicles, that they might commandeer because Jack knew they weren't going to make it before daybreak. He radioed ahead several times, trying to contact the Jedburgh team, trying to get a status report on the production facility; he wanted to know if the Germans were preparing the finished jets for departure yet. He figured it would be a long, drawn-out process since the facility had only one lift to bring the jets up to the mountaintop runway; it might be an all-day affair. But he couldn't make radio contact. The Jedburgh team was either out of range, somehow, or worse, out of commission; captured, wounded, or dead. So far, Jack's operational group had been very lucky considering the circumstances. But he knew their luck could run out at any given minute.

The column continued on its way. At 04:05 hours Corporal Russell, who was far up front, came running back suddenly, his eyes keen with good news. He stopped in front of Jack, panting, smiling.

"There's a farmhouse ahead. Light on inside and two vehicles in the barnyard. German trucks! Opel-Blitz 3-ton transports."

"Trucks, eh?" Jack smiled. He turned to the others and told them to remain hidden whilst he and Russell went forward to check out the situation. Once hidden in the trees around the farmhouse, Jack could see what Corporal Russell was talking about. The farmhouse showed blackly like a silhouette against the sky. There were two buildings, the house itself and a large barn behind it. Both buildings showed the ribs of roof rafters where the tiles were missing. Close to the barn Jack saw the trucks Russell had spoken about.

"What's the capacity of one of those trucks, Russell?" Jack whispered. "Do ya know?"

"Usually, two drivers and room for about fifteen men."

"So maybe... thirty-plus Krauts altogether?"

"Yeah. Maybe more, maybe less, give or take a few."

Jack nodded. "Well, It don't matter if there's fifty Krauts in there. We need those trucks. We need some motorized transport to get to the Walpersberg if'n were gonna make it before daylight."

"Yes, sir. I hear that."

An occasional light shined through the farmhouse windows were the sacking which covered the broken panes, fitting badly. A low murmur of voices emanated from those broken windows, the sounds and smells of German soldiers just waking up to face the day's duties.

"If'n there's just a dozen or so Krauts in there, we could do for 'em," Jack said softly. "Then get their trucks and ride out of here."

"Hopefully just a few inside." Russel inclined his head toward the dimly lit courtyard. "There's two sentries over there."

"Yup. I see 'em." Jack patted Russell on the helmet and gestured, jerking his thumb back over his shoulder. "C'mon, let's go tell the others."

Silently, they retreated.

"That's fucking crazy!" exclaimed Sergeant Justice when Jack explained his plan. "You want to storm a Kraut farmhouse and then steal the trucks? Jesus! And they outnumber us too, Captain."

"You'd be surprised what a determined bunch of G.I.'s can do together, buddy." Jack grinned devilishly. "We're all killers here."

"Don't call me *buddy,*" rasped Justice. "I'm a sergeant!"

"You're a pain in the ass too!" Davis rejoined. "I suppose we ought to let you handle this, eh, *sergeant?*" He nudged the B.A.R. "Send you in there by your lonesome? I bet a brave old ex-Marine like yourself could deal with all those Krauts in no time at all."

Justice glared venomously but decided not to reply.

"Well... what's the plan of attack, sir?" Hassler asked.

"You and Davis take out the two sentries near the barn." Jack's eyes beamed through the darkness. "Silently, Hassler. Take out 'em silently. I want those two Krauts knocked out before me and Justice here go into the farmhouse. This is gonna be a four-man operation."

"What about the rest of us men?" asked Sergeant Sparky Powell, the radioman.

"I want you men to spread out around the farmhouse and barnyard—set up converging fields of fire. If'n things go sour, you'll be there to cut the Krauts down. You guys know the drill, right?"

The men nodded affirmatively.

"Good." Jack glanced at his wristwatch. "Let's hot-foot it. We're burning daylight."

The group moved out with purpose.

Foster and Ricci set up the .30-caliber machine gun on the hillside overlooking the farmhouse. Davis and Hassler skulked through shadows and took up a position near the two patrolling sentries, getting ready to pounce on them. Jack and Sergeant Justice crept up in the darkness, edging up to the front door of the farmhouse. Jack fingered his grease-gun, making sure it was cocked and ready for action. Justice cursorily checked the B.A.R. seeing that it was locked and loaded. The silhouette of the farmhouse was now in full view as they crouched down to the ground.

"When Hassler and Davis have dealt with the sentries, you and I will go into the farmhouse, Sarge. We'll go in shootin'. An the sooner it's over the better. Yeah, we're gonna make some noise alright, but let's do it as quick as possible."

Justice looked troubled. "Look, Captain, don't think me yellow for not storming in with you, but I think we could easily bypass these Krauts and—"

"Horsefeathers!" Jack replied sharply. "We need those trucks, 'Cause the closer we get to the Walpersberg the more Germans there'll be. I doubt we'll find another isolated group like this again."

"*If* they're isolated," Justice argued. "I mean, how can we be sure there isn't a couple hundred Krauts further on down the road?"

Jack smiled in agreement. "Yeah, well, I've thought of that, too. If'n there are Krauts all around us, we've had it anyway. We either get lucky right here and now, get ourselves equipped with German trucks... and go on to the Walpersberg before it's too late... or we lose here and now. At least we'll go out fighting, eh?"

Sergeant Justice grimaced anxiously and nodded, acknowledging the gumption of Jack's argument. It was all or nothing.

Nearby, Sergeant Hassler rose from his crouch, his commando dagger clutched firmly in his right hand; he asked Davis for two minutes to to deal with the two sentries, stepped off silently, then vanished into the darkness. The two minutes ticked by. Jack and Sergeant Justice lay flat on the ground, eyes fixed on the farmhouse. They'd already decided to open up on anyone who came out while Hassler went about his grim business. But nothing happened. Once, a rumble of laughter came from inside the farmhouse but the door remained closed.

From the direction of the barnyard there was no sound at all. Five minutes passed... six... seven... eight, then ten. Sergeant Justice glanced enquiringly at Jack. The lanky Texan just smiled, holding up a finger, asking for patience.

And then came a whistle. A low wolf-whistle, one like the American troops used to express their admiration for an attractive girl. Jack clapped Justice on the shoulder and they rose together, then moved at a fast run, heading for the farmhouse door. Justice veered to one side to cover the windows as Jack went straight for the door. It was a flimsy door with a thumb-operated latch. All six-feet-two-inches of Texas fighting man hit the door squarely and smashed it wide open. The shattered boards swung backwards and hit the inside wall with a resounding crash, and at the same moment Jack, opened fire with his grease-gun. Ten Germans sat around a long wooden table with plates of steaming-hot breakfast laid before them. The raking fire of the .45-caliber grease-gun knocked three of them backwards off the bench seat.

At the window, Sergeant Justice's head and shoulders appeared and his B.A.R.'s muzzle spurted flame, dispatching four more Germans. Two Germans reached for their MP-40 machine pistols and tried to return fire only to be mowed down by another blistering volley from Jack's grease-gun. The last German dove under the table and tried to hide from the smoking volley. Jack could have easily killed him, too, had his gun not been out of ammo. He ejected the empty magazine and loaded another, seating it with a brisk slap.

"There's got to be more somewhere!" he shouted to Justice as he kicked the table over, revealing the cowering German. He plugged him with a short burst, then wheeled around on a heel. He leaped over the fallen bodies of Germans and kicked open the door on the far side of the room. Beyond it, he glimpsed a stove, a white enamel sink and two Germans. One still held a rag with which he was washing dishes. The other, the quicker-witted of the two, was bending over to pick up his MP-40 from a corner. The withering fire from Jack's grease-gun bowled them over. The sink shattered, sending slivers of white enamel slicing through the air in all directions.

Sergeant Davis and Hassler came running in, grease-guns at the ready. Jack exhaled in a soundless whistle and ejected the spent magazine and slammed another in its place. They all stood there listening intently for a minute. There was no noise; no sound of alarm outside. The assault had lasted less than a minute. Then they heard Hentges' voice. He said: "I'm coming in. All clear of Krauts?"

"C'mon, Hentges," said Jack. "The coast is clear, little buddy."

Hentges came in and looked around. "Good God! You guys clobbered them. I mean, the poor bastards never had a chance."

"Yup, that's how it's gotta be. Kill or be killed."

"You're damn handy with that thing, sir," Justice commented, a bit awestruck by Jack's hell-bent actions. "Downright murderous."

"That's right, Sarge. No mercy fer the dang Nazis. And I'm thankful there weren't as many as we thought." Jack motioned to the door. "Okay, let's collect what we came for and git out of here."

The four men went outside and met up with the others. They split up into two groups and climbed into the two trucks. Sergeant Davis took the driver's seat in one whilst Jack rode shot-gun. Hassler and Justice took control of the other. Then they drove off in a mad hurry, the clock still counting down the seconds until daylight.

"IT IS AS I suspected, Colonel McKavitt," said Sturmbannführer Emil Dietrich. "You are indeed of Jewish ancestry."

"Oh?"Colonel David McKavitt replied, and then scoffed carelessly. "And how do you figure that, huh?"

"Your great-grandmother Hanna Wójcik-McKavitt was a Polish Jew from Lodz. She immigrated to the United States in 1864, then met and married your great-grandfather Mack Michael McKavitt, a Scottish-American officer in the Union Army."

"My great-grandmother? Jewish? So what if she was?"

"That makes you Jewish in the eyes of the Third Reich."

"Yeah? Well, that's pretty thin, Dietrich. Pretty fucking thin."

"Is it? Your name David is a common Jewish first name. You even look like a Jew, Colonel. Dark hair, dark eyes, that big—"

"Oh, come off it, Dietrich!" McKavitt spouted. "So what's that got to do with anything anyway? I'm still an honorable, long-serving American officer. And I expect to be treated accordingly."

"Hmm, yes... you'll be treated accordingly, all right."

Dietrich sat in a chair next to von Warnstadt's desk in the Kommandant's office, a brown file folder on his lap. The folder was essentially an intelligence report from the RSHA (Reich Main Security Office). It was part of *Reichsführer* Himmler's SS and its activities included intelligence-gathering, criminal investigation, overseeing foreigners, monitoring public opinion as well as Nazi indoctrination. Its list of "enemies" included Jews, communists, Freemasons, pacifists, and Christian activists. McKavitt had been thoroughly investigated by the RSHA and they had discovered his Jewish roots. Although he wasn't considered a "pure" Jew, he had a Jewish great-grandmother, which was enough to incriminate him in the eyes of the SS and the Nazis.

"What's with you SS-thugs, anyway? Why do you persecute the Jews so vehemently? What's that got to do with this war?"

"Thugs, are we?" Dietrich grinned. "We are ridding the world of a detestable pestilence, Colonel. Europe cannot find true peace until the Jewish question has been solved. Only when the Jews have been totally removed can we hope to establish a co-operation among the nations which shall be built on everlasting understanding."

"What-ever." McKavitt shook his head and rolled his eyes. "You sound just like your beloved little Führer, Dietrich. But it's all nonsense, and you know it. And me being—one-quarter Jewish according to your precious RSHA—is laughable. It's bloody ridiculous!"

"Ridiculous or not, Colonel, it is the truth. You are of Jewish decent and you will be dealt with accordingly."

"Yeah? And what does that mean?"

"It means: you will be sent to the Walpersberg production facility as a common laborer, Colonel. You will do backbreaking work, and you will be subjected to any and all punishments administrable if you don't cooperate with my men or anybody else."

"If I don't cooperate? You mean... shot."

"Precisely."

Colonel McKavitt glared at Kommandant von Warnstadt, who had been sitting behind his desk quietly, listening intently to what was being said. Although he basically detested Colonel McKavitt for his arrogance and his supercilious temperament, von Warnstadt still regarded him as an honorable officer and a fellow airman, the latter of which was a special bond that no other branch of service could even begin to understand. Combatant pilots had a courteous brand of comradery that hearkened back to the days of knightly behavior and chivalry. It had began with the aces of the Great War and had, for the most part, been adhered to by the pilots during this war. McKavitt knew von Warnstadt was an old Great War pilot, not a fighter pilot like himself, but one who flew bombers and one who fought with honor and respect. He would defend Colonel McKavitt for just those reasons. Wouldn't he?

"Well, Kommandant," said McKavitt. "What's your take on all of this, hmm? Am I despicable Jew—or am I an American officer and pilot who deserves some degree of respect and honor?"

Von Warnstadt sighed nervously. "You're an American officer and pilot, I'll give that. And you've served your country honorably, even winning its highest award for bravery and courage. But..."

"But what?"

"Well, you're Jewish, according to that report. And that comes down from the highest authority of the Reich. So, I must—"

"Bullshit, Kommandant!" McKavitt raged. "You're not a Luftwaffe officer. You're stinking Nazi, that's what you are. A dirty, rotten, Nazi! No better than that piece of shit sitting next to you."

"Colonel!" said Dietrich, bristling, his little grin fading into something reminiscent of a scowl. "I warn you, if you insist on using such language, I will be compelled to silence you—forcibly."

"Go ahead, Dietrich," McKavitt returned defiantly. "Shut me up, why don't you? Shoot me now you slimy, blond-haired bastard."

Dietrich nodded faintly, his lips thinned to a bitter scowl. He stood up, drew his Walther, cocked the bolt, and pointed it straight at McKavitt's head. "With pleasure, Colonel. With pleasure!"

Von Warnstadt bolted to his feet and stepped between Colonel McKavitt and Dietrich, "Gentlemen, gentlemen! Please!" he implored, his hands raised beseechingly. "Let's be civil about this. We're all officers and gentlemen here. Can't we talk this out?"

"No," Dietrich replied flatly. He holstered his Walther sidearm and stepped to the door, opened it, then gestured for his guards. "We're going to the REIMAHG facility now, Kommandant. We have work to do. Hard, laborious, backbreaking work. Don't we, Colonel McKavitt?"

McKavitt sneered.

Two burly SS-guards came in and seized him roughly and escorted him out of the office. They took him out to a line of parked Opel-Blitz trucks where other P.O.W.'s had gathered waiting to embark, hands in their pockets, collars turned up against the elements, cigarettes burning in their mouths. Shortly, Hauptmann Becker barked heated commands and the loading procedure began in earnest. It was 4:50 in the morning, and it was cold and it was snowing. Another winter norther clawed at the countryside. God! Just another dark and dreary day in Nazi Germany.

Inside the Kommandant's office, Dietrich and von Warnstadt concluded their business. "Well, I guess that settles that, eh, Herr Sturmbannführer?" von Warnstadt said, glowering nervously.

"It does—for now." Dietrich picked up the brown RSHA folder and tucked it under his arm. "I will deal with this later. Right now I must get to the facility and oversee the next phase. The finished jets are flying out to Lechfeld Airbase this morning. *Heil Hitler!*" he exclaimed lustily, saluted stiff-armed, then stalked out of the office.

Von Warnstadt collapsed in his chair, sighing. *"Ja, Heil Hitler."*

CHAPTER 12

AFTER A TIME, they were forced to leave the main road. The sky had clouded over considerably but the pale light of dawn emanated from up high hinted at a sunny day. If they didn't get to the Walpersberg before daybreak and destroy the jets, thought Jack, there would be no more sunny days for anyone. But destroying those jets was the least of his worries. That could be handled easily enough with well-placed explosives, and if not that, with some random destruction, something he was really good at. What really worried him was dealing with a full battalion of SS-troops who would be waking up very soon. O.G.NEMISIS would not be able to get into the facility without first neutralizing the barracks where they were billeted. Taking on 600 or so SS-men was something Jack wasn't looking forward to. Storming a squad of German soldiers single-handedly with just a machine pistol was one thing, but taking on a whole battalion of Nazi Germany's finest was quite another. They'd be outnumbered nearly 70-to-1. Bad odds for a cold snowy day in hell.

Jack nodded, it was going to be that proverbial cold day in hell he had so often spoke of in jest. Well, there was nothing funny about it; it was no joke or laughing matter. It was, without a doubt, a suicidal undertaking, a deadly and dangerous mission, one that would lead to a lot of men's death, his own included. He had no illusions of surviving nor had he ever. He knew it was going to be a dicey operation from the get-go, one of zero survivability. He realized Colonel Bruce had sent him out on a fool's errand. But he cared not. He had lived long enough and well enough. It was time to dance with the devil again. Time to meet Satan's angels—the SS.

When they neared the objective, Jack ordered the trucks halted along the roadside, he then climbed up a tree to get a better view. The pale light revealed to him his main objective—the Walpersberg —the REIMAHG production facility. It rose abruptly above the flat plain they were traversing, dark and sinister, a half-mile away. By no stretch of the imagination could it be called a mountain. But Jack knew its height was just a shade over a thousand feet, and high enough to be a great obstacle in the way of his projected task. With binoculars, he could see the top of the Walpersberg was leveled off for the concrete runway of some three thousand feet in length and one hundred feet wide. Although not visible from his current vantage point, he knew the runway had a narrow-gauge railway running along one side with various buildings and hangars on the other. And massive concrete bunkers were built outside the tunnels where subparts were made and partially assembled in the tunnels and moved outside to the concrete bunkers where final assembly took place. Then the assembled jets were moved to the top of the hill via a lift that moved along a railed ramp by a high-powered winch. All along the perimeter of the complex, Jack saw a thick-gauged barbed wire fence about ten feet high, not an insurmountable obstacle but one that could not be easily circumvented from sloping sides of a snowy hill. Near the eastern end of the Walpersberg, he could see the main road leading into the facility and the SS-checkpoint at the entrance. And with the whole place draped in a fine white blanket of snow and ice, the facility had an air of cold invincibility about it—impregnable. Jack smiled keenly. So here was his quintessential "Waterloo"—the site of his last battle. He climbed down the tree and approached the men who had been waiting along the roadside.

"Well, sir," Sergeant Davis asked as Jack walked up. "What's it look like? How are we going to get in there?"

"Through the front door, Davis," Jack quipped. "Where else?"

"You mean... the front gate?"

"That's right. There ain't no other way in that I can see."

"Did you see a lot of SS-troops moving around yet?" Sergeant Justice wanted to know.

"Naw, not yet." Jack glanced at his wristwatch. "But I reckon they'll be up and about soon enough. So we need to hoof-it, gents."

"What's the plan, Captain?" Hassler asked.

"We're gonna pose as Germans, Sergeant," Jack replied with a sly grin. "With these German trucks and those Kraut helmets we saved, we're gonna pretend we're a squad of Luftwaffe troops complete with a contingent of ferry pilots." Jack pointed to the front bumper of one of the trucks. "See that insignia stenciled on the bumper there? This truck belongs to a Luftwaffe outfit... Erg. JG-2, to be exact. Looks like Lady Luck has been lookin' out fer us."

The men looked and saw the yellow letters and number stenciled on the blue-gray bumper. But they were clueless, it meant nothing to them.

"How do you know that, sir?" Hentges asked.

"I know a little something about air forces and aircraft, you see. Spent some time around that stuff for a spell." Jack reached into the cab and pulled out a flight helmet and a pair of goggles. "This gear belonged to one of the Germans we jiggered. A pilot, no doubt."

"Were you a pilot, sir?" Hentges pressed.

Jack didn't answer. He just chuckled and said: "Alright, men. Stash your paratrooper helmets, okay? Put on those Kraut coal-scuttles. Schmidt, I want you driving the lead truck. I'll ride shot-gun. Since you speak perfect German and all, yer gonna talk our way past the front gate—tell 'em were the first contingent of Luftwaffe pilots to fly out the jets." Jack clapped the young corporal on the shoulder. *"Jawohl?"*

"M-Me?" Schmidt muttered, a little unnerved.

"That's right." Jack unholstered his High-Standard silencer-pistol and cocked it. "You speak pretty good German, old son. So yer the man for the job. But don't you worry none, I'll be sittin' right next to you. I'll tell ya what to say."

"O-kay," Schmidt replied tentatively.

"Then what?" Davis quarried.

"Once we're in, we'll split up. Your gang will head over to the SS-barracks and neutralize it—just like we planned. I don't care how you do it, but do it quickly. Then once yer done with that, rendezvous with my group at the aircraft lift. Understand?"

Davis nodded. "Yes, sir."

"In the meantime," Jack elaborated,"Hentges, me, Schmidt, and the rest of my group will head over to the final assembly bunker and set the charges and blow it to kingdom come."

"What if there's a snafu and we can't get in? Then what?"

Jack simpered. "Oh, we'll get in, Davis. Don't you fret about that. I have confidence in young Schmidt here. He'll speak some of that fancy German lingo he knows and get us in, no problem."

Schmidt grimaced. "Uh, right? Fancy German. Got it, sir."

Davis's eyes widened, the sergeant a bit leery. "Okay, sir. Whatever you say. We'll be ready for anything and everything—I guess."

"That's the spirit."

"So when the charges are set and we blow the place, sir—if we get that far," Justice interjected querulously "What about getting out of there? When things get all topsy-turvy that place is gonna be a hell on earth and crawling with angry Krauts."

"Just the way we came in, Sarge. With these trucks, or any other transport we can muster. Once we set off the charges and destroy those jets, and their assembly bunkers, we'll make our exit with covering fire, of course, protecting each other's tails as best we can. But it's gonna be kinda every man for himself, you see? The tough way out. Get back to the rendezvous point at Saalfeld as best you can and wait for the Lockheed pick up plane. Okay?"

Justice shook his head, sighing. "As best we can? Jeez."

"It's what we trained fer, Sarge. No surprises here, right?"

"Right," Hassler cut in. "We'll give those fucking Nazis a good going over." He fingered the bolt of his grease-gun. "O.S.S. style!"

"Alright now," Jack said with a wave. "Let's move out."

THE OPEL-BLITZ trucks rumbled past the main gate of the Walpersberg facility as sleepy-eyed SS-guards waved them through. Colonel McKavitt sat in the back of the last truck with Sergeant Major Boggs and Lieutenant Gunston, arms folded over his chest, legs crossed. He appeared to be unworried about the coming labor, his face stolid and impassive. McKavitt had no qualms about doing manual labor. In fact, he was looking forward it. Although some in the camp suggested he was a snobby upper-class officer who hated hard work, he really was a man who liked to work with his hands. His protestations were mainly about adhering to proper P.O.W. protocol, not about avoiding work. He wanted the Germans to respect the "rules of war," make them treat U.S. officers with some dignity.

"Well, sir," said Boggs. "Guess you'll be in the there with the rest of us today, huh? Working like a goddamn slave."

"Yeah," McKavitt replied. "But it won't be too bad, I think."

"You think?" Boggs chuckled. "Well, wait until you get in there, sir, you'll change your mind. It's hard, fucking work digging out those tunnels with a pick and shovel. Every muscle will be aching like hell by the time you're done. Those SS-goons will make damn sure of that."

"The Colonel will just be overseeing, Sergeant," Gunston interjected defensively. "He won't have to do any manual labor, von Warnstadt gave his word."

Boggs grinned. "Sure he did. But he's not here, is he, sir? That SS-Major doesn't give a fuck about what the Kommandant says. He'll make the Colonel do whatever he damn-well pleases."

"You think so, huh?"

"I know so."

"I'll work if I have to," McKavitt weighed in. "I'm not above it. It'll set a good example for the men, Lieutenant."

"Why the sudden change, sir? And what about—"

"And what about the Geneva Convention?" McKavitt cut in. "It's a moot point now. The Sergeant Major is right. The SS doesn't give a damn about all that. Dietrich will do whatever he wants regardless of what von Warnstadt says. Regardless of what the Geneva Convention says."

"Really? But..."

"It's the sad truth, Lieutenant. But there you have it. The rules of war are out. It's all about survival now. Do whatever it takes to survive and get back home, I say. And in one piece."

"So you'll let that SS bastard have his way then?" Gunston said with a pained look on his face. "Make you work?"

"Yeah. That's about the size of it, Lieutenant."

Gunston sighed disapprovingly.

"Do you think Dietrich will ride you hard, sir?" Boggs asked.

"He might. But I figure if I play along with him, humor him, he'll lay off of me. He's a son-of-a-bitch but he's not stupid. He'll leave me alone once he sees I'm willing to cooperate."

"Maybe, Colonel. But he claims you're Jewish. The Nazis hate the Jews, remember? Or have you forgotten?"

"I remember." McKavitt sat forward and pushed his crush cap off his brow, exhaling anxiously. "That's the part that worries me. I don't know how far Dietrich is willing to push that issue. I think he knows his claim is pretty thin but he might be willing to act out on it if he gets his nerve up. Which doesn't seem to be too difficult."

"You better play it cool, sir," Boggs advised. "Don't provoke him in any way. Humor him, just like you said."

"I plan to, Sergeant. I'm not stupid either. I know when to be-have myself. My life depends on it now. I'll play it cool, all right."

"Smart man." Boggs nodded. "No sense in getting killed now. This war's not long for ending, I'll bet."

"Right you are, Sergeant. Germany's finished."

The truck halted, jostling the men to stiff attention. Shortly, the tailgate fell open, and the Americans heard the familiar and loath-some voices of SS-guards barking out commands.

"Raus! Raus!" they shouted, the barrels of their MP-40 machine pistols gesturing threateningly. *"Komm raus ihr, Schweine!"*

McKavitt and the rest of the men leapt from the back of the truck onto the frozen ground, grimacing at the stiff breeze, hands jammed in their pockets. Hauptmann Becker promptly appeared and handed off the P.O.W. roster to the SS-Lieutenant in charge of the work detail. The SS-Lieutenant took hold of the roster, saluted, then motioned with a stiff arm, directing the Americans to the bunkers as several SS-guards stepped over and rudely shoved the P.O.W.'s into a loose formation. Becker returned the salute and re-boarded a truck, ready to return to Stalag Luft V. Then the Opel-Blitz trucks duly turned about and headed back to the main gate of the facility, their worn-out, six-cylinder engines rumbling laborious-ly. Dietrich soon materialized, his dirty, snow-caked Kübelwagen braking to a whining halt. He bounded from the back seat and stalked up to the SS-Lieutenant, his eyes beaming blue and hateful. When those ice-blue eyeballs fell upon Colonel McKavitt's slender frame, they flared wickedly.

"Colonel McKavitt!" he shouted, waving, gesturing with a hooked forefinger. "Come over here. I have a special task for you."

McKavitt sighed wearily and walked over, slowly, his chin yet held high. He came to a stiff halt in front of Dietrich, then saluted crisply, much to the surprise of everyone, Dietrich included. "Sir," he said. "Colonel David M. McKavitt, reporting as ordered."

Dietrich smiled amusedly, his hand touching the brim of his peaked cap laxly in reply. "Well, now, Colonel. That's more like it. I am very pleasantly surprised by your sudden obedience. Hah! But it won't help you now."

"I'll not fight it anymore, Dietrich. You win. What will you have of me, huh? What rotten little task do you have in mind for me?"

Dietrich chuckled. "You will be working in the enlisted man's latrine today, Colonel. Emptying piss-pots and shitters. A loathsome task—and a very smelly one, too." Dietrich pointed to a pile of shovels and pick-axes. "Take one of those shovels there, and then pick three men to accompany you on this *especial* detail."

McKavitt nodded, not even blinking an eye, walked over, picked up a shovel, and propped it on his shoulder. He turned around and looked back at the assembled men who were all watching intently. The American Colonel knew everyone was wondering what he might do or say, so he played it all very coolly, just like he said would. He calmly pointed to three men, Sergeant Major Boggs one of them. The three men picked up a shovel and shuffled over to McKavitt and stood next to him.

"Thanks a-fucking-lot, sir," Boggs muttered in a low voice.

"Don't mention it, Sergeant," McKavitt said with a little smirk.

"Very good, Colonel. Excellent," Dietrich declared approvingly. He turned to one his subordinates, a robust-looking Oberscharführer (Staff Sergeant), and ordered him to escort the four Americans to the latrines along with a four-man squad of SS-guards, each man armed with a menacingly looking automatic machine pistol.

McKavitt, Boggs, and the other two men, who were both corporals, and whose names where Farrell and Dunn, trudged across the snow-covered compound heading for the enlisted man's latrine, ragtag shovels propped on their shoulders, grim looks on their faces. Dietrich nodded elatedly as the apparently cowed Colonel marched off with his men on his way to do some demeaning manual labor. But Dietrich was not fooled. He knew the American colonel was up to something, he knew Colonel McKavitt was just humoring him. Once he checked in with the Herr Multhopp and the chief Messerschmitt engineer, Herr Bölkow, he would address McKavitt's suspicious behavior. No Jew-blooded schwein was going to fool him!

"OKAY, SCHMIDT, it's showtime," said Jack as he donned the Luftwaffe flight cap. "Just act calm and don't mince words with these dang Krauts. Got that?"

"Yes, sir. I got it," Corporal Schmidt replied, easing the big Opel-Blitz up to the checkpoint barricade blocking the entrance.

"Keep it simple. Tell 'em we're with JG-2 and here to fly the jets out. Don't get too wordy, okay? I know you can speak that High German and all, but these dickheads ain't about all that, understand?"

"Right. I'll keep it simple. Don't worry."

"Good." Jack nodded. "Okay. Get ready."

The Opel-Blitz whined to a stop and Schmidt rolled down the window. One of the four SS-guards approached the truck, his rifle slung over a shoulder, his greatcoat collar turned up against the elements. He was a tall, grim-faced, middle-aged man with a thin mustache. Schmidt cleared his throat and uttered in German: *"Morning. We're with JG-2... here to fly the—"*

"Your papers, please," the guard demanded curtly.

"P-Papers?" Schmidt gulped, his heart pounding. *"Oh, uh...papers."* Damn, he thought. No one said anything about papers!

Jack readily shoved a folded piece of paper into Schmidt hands, and then clapped him on the shoulder, saying in German: *"Ach! We almost forgot about that."* He smiled glibly, thumping the goggles perched on the brow of the German flight cap as if to give credence to his words. Schmidt handed the guard the clearence papers.

"You Luftwaffe gentlemen are a bit early, aren't you?" said the grim-faced guard, glancing at the paperwork. *"Thought you people weren't due in until 7 o'clock?"*

"Yes, we got an early start. Weather might turn bad later."

"Right." The SS-guard gestured to one of his comrades. *"Okay, Müller. Their paperwork checks out. Let them through."*

He handed the paperwork back to Schmidt, then motioned with a stiff arm, directing the two trucks through the checkpoint. By that time Jack had lit a cigarette and was puffing contently. He rolled the passenger side window down and waved a salute to one the other SS-guards, grinning jovially.

"Toller Tag zum Fliegen, ja?" he uttered in precise German.

Schmidt gassed the truck and motored through the checkpoint, his face glistening with sweat, his heart still pounding. "Jeez! I thought you said not to mince words these people, sir?" He grumbled, wheeling the big blue-gray Opel-Blitz around a curve and up the steep grade. "What was that all about, huh? I mean..."

"Couldn't resist it, Schmidt." Jack winked, exhaling smokily.

"I didn't know you could speak German?"

"There's a lot you don't know about me, Schmidt."

"And those papers? Where? How did you—"

"It's like I said earlier, Schmidt, old son. I know a little something about air forces and aircraft and all that stuff."

"So, were you a pilot or something before joining the O.S.S.?"

Jack nodded. "Yup. A pilot, or something."

"Nice. What did you fly? Were you a—"

"Keep yer eyes on the road, okay?" Jack interrupted. "No time for small talk right now. We gotta a job to do, Corporal."

"Right."

Jack took a long, contemplative drag from the cigarette, then tossed the butt out the window. "Maybe I'll tell ya about it one day, Corporal—if we survive all this."

Schmidt nodded, his hands on the wheel, his eyes on the road. The Captain was right, he thought. This was no time for small talk. They had a mission to complete and everyone had to have their head screwed on right. H-hour had finally arrived!

The two trucks rumbled up the steep grade slowly making their way up the gravel road that led to the main gate of the facility. Schmidt was still quite anxious, worrying about repeating that last little episode, once again at the main gate. But his worries were all for naught. For when they approached the gate brimming with more SS-guards, he was rather amazed when they promptly opened the barbed-wire gate and let them pass—without stopping them. He breathed a momentary sigh of relief as he steered the truck toward the facility bunkers, Jack sitting next to him garbed in a leather flight cap and goggles, looking very much like a German pilot, complete with a leather flying jerkin and matching gloves. He really looked like the classic Luftwaffe fighter pilot, he had to admit. Captain Daemon was indeed a convincing actor.

Before they'd proceeded to the SS-checkpoint, Jack had put on the rest of the Luftwaffe flight suit (sans leather flying boots) which were too small for his large feet; he still wore his size-twelve Cochran jump boots. But somehow, they looked okay with that jacked-up German getup. He surely looked the part, there was no doubt about it. Captain Daemon was a Luftwaffe pilot for all intent and purposes this day.

Once the two trucks had made it to the main road leading to the construction bunkers, the second truck with Sergeants Davis and Hassler and half of the group veered off, heading for the SS-barracks. Jack watched it in the truck's side mirror as it turned sharply and motored down the snowy, gravel road, thinking there were some very brave men aboard that German truck. He wondered if he'd ever see any of them again. Well, it didn't matter now. He knew his own survival was in question as was every man's on this most dangerous of all operations. Then he thought of Rose. That dear, sweet little gal of his. Would he ever see her again, he wondered? Would she weep for him when he was dead and gone? Would she even shed one tear for old Jack Knight?

NOT HUNGRY, Mrs. McKavitt?" said the kindly hospital steward.

"No," Rose replied absently, staring off into space, thinking.

"Shall I clear away these plates then, if you're finished?"

"Yes, go ahead. I'm finished."

The young steward stacked the plates in a neat pile, carefully placing the silverware in between them. In a few seconds, he had it cleared away and was turning for the door, when Rose stopped him.

"Sir? Do you have a cigarette, by chance?" she asked, suddenly snapping out of her thoughtful reverie.

"Uh, yes, I do," replied the steward, setting down the stack of dishes on a nearby table, then reached into his breast pocket for his pack of Players. He shook one loose and offered it to Rose, proffering the pack and the protruding cigarette. Rose took two cigarettes.

"You don't mind if I take two, do you? One for later?"

"Oh, no. Not a'tall. Take as many as ye like. I got plenty."

"Thank you, you're very kind, sir."

"My pleasure, ma'am. Need a light?"

214

"That would be perfect."

"Right-o." The steward flicked his lighter and lit the cigarette.

"The doctor says I ought not smoke while I'm pregnant," Rose said puffing the Players once it was good and lit.

"Aye. He might be right 'bout that, methinks."

"But one or two here and there can't be too harmful, no?"

"Probably not." The steward smiled and picked up the dishes.

"Thank you... what's your name, by the way?"

"Stewart—Ian Stewart, ma'am."

"Thank you, Ian. Thanks for the cigarettes."

"Yes, ma'am. You're quite welcome."

Ian Stewart, the hospital steward, trudged off with dishes as Rose sat there in her wheelchair and smoked the cigarette. She was feeling much better of late but still didn't have much of an appetite. The hospital food was actually quite good but she could never bring herself to eat very much of it. She was too worried about things these days to have a decent appetite. Rose worried about her unborn baby, she worried about her husband, and lately, she worried about Jack. By now, she no longer questioned her thoughts of him. He was much a part of her now as David was, or so it seemed. Even though Jack had lied to her about who he was, she knew he hadn't lied maliciously; he'd only been trying to keep his identity a secret. And Rose figured he might've told her who he really was one day —if they'd had stayed married. But that day had never come. Jack was shot down and duly captured by the Japanese. So she moved on and married another, and Jack and his terrible little secret didn't matter to her anymore.

And yet, his sudden reappearance seemed to have rekindled fond thoughts of him. It wasn't thoughts of lost love or yearning, she was quite sure of that. But it was thoughts of concern and worry for the man himself. Jack was still a man who deserved a certain degree of affection. Or was it pity? Did she feel sorry for him, she wondered? Did she really feel sad for him and everything that had befallen him? She couldn't decide. But she knew she still felt something for him. It surely wasn't love and it definitely wasn't hate. It was something in between. The kindly fondness of an old friend? Rose reasoned. Yes! Jack seemed like a long, lost friend to her now. Someone who had occupied a certain time and place in her life, someone who had been very close to her, and someone who she had confided in for a short while. A best friend.

"Hello, Mrs. McKavitt," she heard a familiar voice echoing outside her bemused thoughts. "How are you doing?"

She turned her head and saw who it was apprising her.

"Ah, Major Hickok." Rose nodded. "I'm fine. And you?"

"Busy as ever." Major Hickok removed his cap and sat down in a chair next to Rose's wheelchair. "I got word you contacted Supreme Allied Headquarters in Portsmouth. You requested some information about a—Nicklaus Daemon? Is that right?"

"Yes!" Rose doused the half-smoked cigarette in a cold cup of tea and sat forward. "Do you know anything about him?"

"Well, a little. He's an officer in the O.S.S., Mrs McKavitt. A Captain, to be precise."

"The O.S.S.?"

"Office of Strategic Services: an agency of the Joint Chiefs of Staff that coordinates espionage and activities behind enemy lines. It conducts multiple activities and missions, including intelligence by spying, performing acts of sabotage, waging propaganda, organizing and coordinating anti-Nazi resistance groups in Europe."

"Oh. Like the secret service?"

"Something like that."

"And Captain Daemon is an officer in this—O.S.S.?"

"Yes, ma'am. But that's all I really know. They're a bit secretive over at the O.S.S. They wouldn't tell me anything about him. I think they were a little unnerved I even asked about him."

"Is Jack—I mean Captain Daemon—is he a commando?"

"Sort of." Major Hickok gazed at Rose with a suspicious eye. "You said 'Jack'. Does he go by another name? Do you know him?"

"Well, I once knew him... a long time ago."

Major Hickok rummaged through the dusty recesses of his mind and recalled Roses's life history. As an Army Intelligence officer it was his job to pull up everything and anything on anyone when he began an investigation, whoever it was—the enemy, a general, even the wife of an Air Corps group commander. He remembered reading about her love affair with an American fighter ace back in '42, when she was living in Australia, before she married Colonel David McKavitt.

What was that fellow's name, he asked himself? John J...

"Jack Knight is his name, Major. Or *was* his name."

"You mean, John J. Knight, the Air Corps fighter ace?"

"Yes, that was his full name—then."

"And you think this Captain Daemon fellow is the same man?"

"I don't think so, I know so."

"Hmm, that's pretty, uh... far-fetched, don't you think?"

"No. Jack Knight and Captain Daemon are the same man."

"Well, according to what I read about John J. Knight, or Jack, as you call him—he got shot down in March '43, during the Battle of the Bismarck Sea. He was captured by the Japanese and then sent to one of their prison camps, somewhere in the Home Islands, I believe. And no one's ever heard of him since—as far as I know."

"As far as you know... well, he escaped that Japanese camp."

"Did he?" Major Hickok wanted to laugh. Instead, he sat upright and rasped his chin. "Heck, that's news to me, then."

"He changed his name again and joined this O.S.S."

"Changed his name—*again*—you say?"

"Aye. Before that, he was known as Sergeant James Castillo."

"Huh, interesting. Very interesting."

"I'm surprised, Major Hickok. As an Air Corps Intelligence officer, I thought you would have known about all this?"

Major Hickok's lips thinned resentfully. "Well, we—Intelligence, I mean—don't know everything, Mrs. McKavitt, obviously. And when it comes to the O.S.S., we know next to nothing."

"So it seems."

"If what you say is true, then there's been some sort of cover up regarding this Captain Daemon fellow, or John J. Knight, or... what was that other name you called him?"

"James Castillo."

"Yes—James Castillo." Major Hickok sighed. "Someone has gone through a lot of trouble to keep this guy a secret. Perhaps General Donovan himself, the director of the O.S.S. The O.S.S. is very secretive about who they recruit. And they'll take anybody and everybody, no matter how checkered their past is. Thugs, criminals, civilians, dishonorably discharged military men—anybody."

"Even ex-fighter pilots with phony names, aye?"

"Yes, even ex-fighter pilots with phony names."

"You said the director of the O.S.S. General Donovan might be behind the cover up? Maybe... but I know of someone who might be even more of culprit than General Donovan."

"Oh, yeah? Who might that be?"

"Colonel Thaddeus Truscott."

"*Colonel* Thaddeus Truscott? You mean Brigadier General Thaddeus Truscott, Chief of Staff, 5th Air Force, Southwest Asia."

"Yes, *him,* especially."

"Aha! That's right," Major Hickok's brain kindled warily. "Truscott was Jack Knight's group commander at one time, right? The 35th Fighter Group, wasn't it?"

"I think so."

Major Hickok stroked his chin, nodding. "So you think General Truscott is behind a cover up, eh? You think he and General Donovan got together and cooked up this *Captain Daemon* fellow and then turned him loose on the Nazis? Well, stranger things have happened concerning the O.S.S."

"So you believe me, Major?"

Major Hickok got up and donned his service cap. "Let's just say you've sparked my interest a great deal, Mrs. McKavitt. Now I want to know more about this Jack Knight (Captain Daemon), and what General Truscott's involvement is in all of this, as well as General Donovan's involvement. Something doesn't seem right about it all."

"Let me know what you find out, okay, Major?"

"I most certainly will." Major Hickok waved. "Bye, now."

"G'day, Major." Rose reached for the cigarette, then looked for a light. A moment later, she was puffing contently and looking thoughtful. Seems she knew more than Air Corps Intelligence did.

CHAPTER 13

HANS MULTHOPP arose from his small uncomfortable metal-framed bed and put on his glasses. He glared at the clock on the nightstand with sticky eyes and groaned; he had overslept by half an hour! He got up swiftly and put on his pants, then grabbed a shirt from the metal locker that served as his wardrobe cabinet. Everything was metal or concrete in this place, he lamented. It was a cold, draconian environment, insentient and stale. Nothing like the warmth and woodiness of the Aeronautical Research Institute. This facility was typical of all Nazi-built installations: cold, grim and spartan; it was built for function not fanfare—an excellent example of Herr Hitler's true architectural sensibilities.

Multhopp buttoned up his shirt and put on his shoes, then combed his wavy locks into some kind of order. He seized the white lab coat hanging on the coat rack and threw it over his shoulders. Now he was ready to meet the day, albeit a half-hour behind schedule. He had actually slept soundly for a change, not waking up once during his six-hour slumber. A true rarity for him, he realized. The two snifters of cognac had really helped, but they had caused him to oversleep. No matter, he thought, no one will notice. Amidst the multitude of Messerschmitt engineers, he was hardly ever noticed much less acknowledged. With the Me-262 as the standard jet fighter plane of the Third Reich, they scarcely considered his swept-wing contraptions a match. But he knew better. His Ta-183 *"Huckebein"* was a first-rate flying machine, a state-of-the-art design concept. He couldn't wait for its official debut.

Herr Multhopp exited the concrete cubicle and scurried down the long tubular corridor on his way to the facility office. It was actually a small staff room equipped with a coffeepot and a pastry dispenser, the latter none too appetizing; they were remarkably stale and tasteless and he abstained from eating them. He just wanted a hot cup of coffee to wake himself up. After he had completed his preliminary checks and services on the Ta-183, he could then adjourn to the facility cafeteria and have a proper breakfast. Then much later when the day's work had been done and his prize jet fighter had been flown out, he could descend the Walpersberg's snowy slopes and enjoy a celebratory meal in the Kahla Hofbrau below. He might even order himself a fine bottle of vintage Riesling and drink the whole thing by himself! Hans Multhopp was feeling quite giddy today, more so than ever before. Today would mark the official debut of his much-anticipated jet fighter plane. Today, he would see it take to the air and make its maiden flight—already gunned-up and ready for war. He was quite proud of that fact. Indeed, none of the Me-262's flying out today were equipped with guns. They would be armed once they arrived at Lechfeld Airbase, then equipped with radios. Multhopp chortled softly, thinking to himself: My prize little *Huckebein* is already brimming with guns and armed to the teeth. All ready for war! I just hope the Luftwaffe sent over an experienced enough pilot to fly it. I don't want some idiot crashing it and destroying all my hard work and planning.

Multhopp entered the staff room, and standing by the coffeepot, a steaming cup already in his hand, he saw Sturmbannführer Dietrich. Dietrich glanced at his wristwatch and glowered.

"Are you just arriving, Herr Multhopp?" he rasped.

"Unfortunately. Overslept a wee bit," Multhopp explained.

"Well, no matter, I suppose." Dietrich took a swallow of coffee and examined the pastries in the pastry dispenser. He snorted distastefully, seeing nothing he liked, and then sat down at the small-squared table, crossing his legs and leaning back in the chair. "The first jet doesn't depart for at least another hour yet. And I just got word from the main gate that the first contingent of pilots has already arrived."

"The first Me-262 flies out at 8 o'clock?"

"That's right. Weather permitting, of course."

"And what is the forecast for today?"

"Overcast and cloudy, with snow flurries later this afternoon."

"Nah-ja, not the best flying weather, but good enough."

"Is your prototype ready, Herr Multhopp?"

"It is. My technicians are making the final checks as we speak. Once it is refueled and the engine's run-up, it'll be ready for flight."

"Good. Because it will be second-in-line this morning."

"Oh? I thought it was scheduled to fly out last? Behind the Me-262's. Why the sudden schedule change?"

"Reichsmarschall Goering, that's why."

"Hmm? What do you mean?"

"He will be at Lechfeld this morning. He wants to see your jet firsthand, so I've been told. It was supposed to be first, but Herr Bölkow raised such a stink about it, I moved it to second."

"Goering wants to see my jet first?" Multhopp beamed.

"That's right." Dietrich nodded and took another sip. "When I told Herr Bölkow that, he pitched a little fit. *Gott!* I don't know why you engineering types have to be so damned temperamental all of the time. What difference does it really make, first or second?"

"None to me." Multhopp seized a cup and poured himself some coffee. "I'm just excited that Goring himself has come out to see my little *Huckebein* make its official debut."

"And I hope he's not disappointed, Herr Multhopp. Because the folks at Messerschmitt don't seem to be too enamored with it."

"They're just jealous, that's all. They see it as serious competition, something that might capture the Führer's interest." Multhopp adjusted his glasses "He initially thought very little of the Me-262, you know? He wanted to make it into a bomber not a fighter. Only after much persuasion was it allowed to be produced as a fighter."

"Is that so?" Dietrich replied rather carelessly. "Well, so far it has proved to be very effective, I hear. The American fighters facing it on a daily basis seem to be at a loss as how to deal with it."

"True. But once my jet fighter becomes operational, they'll be at a total loss. They have nothing in their current arsenal that even comes close. It'll be a turkey shoot for our brave Luftwaffe pilots."

"I'm glad you're so confident. I hope you're right."

"I just hope the Luftwaffe sent over some capable pilots. I don't want my prototype in the hands of some incompetent tyro."

"They're all experienced pilots, Herr Multhopp. From Stab III and 10./Erg. JG-2. That's the Richthofen Geschwader's reserve training and replacement wing. All very capable men. There's even a high-scoring ace among their ranks, I heard."

"Good, glad to hear it." Herr Multhopp took a hearty gulp of coffee and set the cup down. "Well, I must be on my way now, Herr Sturmbannführer. I must get to the workshop and check on my machine, make sure she's ready for flight. I wouldn't want to disappoint the Reichsmarschall this fine winter morning."

Hans Multhopp turned on a heel and strode out of the staff room, slamming the door behind him. Dietrich chuckled and got up, finished off the last dregs of coffee, and donned his peaked cap. He checked his Walther sidearm, making sure it was ready, then turned for the door. It was time now to pay someone a little visit, see how he was liking his newly assigned duties, however malodorous and loathsome they might be. Dietrich was not convinced by McKavitt's sudden cooperation.

"THIS IS FUCKING bullshit!" Sergeant Major Boggs rumbled bitterly. "Cleaning out latrines? I haven't done this since boot camp."

"Just keep shoveling, Sergeant," Colonel McKavitt urged. "We'll get through it soon enough."

"Dietrich, that lousy son-of-a-bitch! He's a real bastard, making you, of all people, do something like this."

"That, he is," McKavitt had to agree.

"I mean, forcing me or Farrell or Dunn here... that's one thing. But you, sir? A high-ranking officer—a Medal of Honor winner? That's goddamned dirty, sir. Downright despicable!"

"Don't make such a big deal about it, Boggs. You make it sound like I'm royalty or something. I'm just a guy like the rest of you men. Just because I wear these eagles on my collar doesn't make me exempt from the unpleasantness of everyday life."

"Yeah, well, you're a better man than I, sir, for saying so. I can't believe you're being so cool about it. If I was a West Point graduate and a Medal of Honor winner, I'd be hopping mad."

"Well, I'm not overjoyed about it, Sergeant. That's for damn sure. But I've got to do it or face graver consequences."

"Yeah," Corporal Dunn chimed in as he shoveled a load of shit into a bucket. "That Dietrich character's got an itchy finger. I believe he'd gun you down if you didn't do what he said."

"You're right, Corporal," McKavitt replied. "I thought maybe he was bluffing at first, or just acting like a hothead. But I really think he'd shoot me now if the notion suddenly struck him."

"He's a cold-blooded cocksucker," Boggs elaborated hatefully. "If he's still around when this war is over, he will hang for sure. And I'd like to be around to see it when it happens... see that bloody bastard choke on his own spit... watch his fucking eyes pop out of that little blond pinhead—"

"Halts Maul!" a guard barked, telling them to shut up, gesturing with his machine pistol. *"Sei ruhig! Sag nichts mehr!"*

Boggs growled, glaring at the guard a moment with hateful eyes, then went back to shoveling. McKavitt and the other two men resumed their onerous task without further comment. Yet, the Sergeant Major went on grumbling to himself, thinking what a bastard Dietrich was for making them shovel shit all morning, and worst of all, make Colonel McKavitt do it. Boggs didn't think too much of McKavitt when he first arrived at the camp. But after a short time, the West Point Colonel kind of grew on him. The man was an upstanding officer and one with an impressive war record. He had fought in the Battle of Britain as a Spitfire pilot, then fought in the Pacific, racking up an impressive score. He eventually won the Medal of Honor and could have easily retired to a comfy, stateside air base afterwards, spending the rest of the war as an instructor or a staff officer. But nothing doing. He petitioned the Air Corps General Staff for another combat posting and got it after much begging and finagling. He was ordered off to the E.T.O. and the 8th Air Force and took command of a front line fighter group. With a pretty little Aussie wife and that pretty little gold medal, Colonel David McKavitt could have justifiedly called it quits and rested on his laurels and no one would have ever begrudged him for doing so. Now, he was just a poor, pathetic P.O.W. serving out his time in a German prison camp, suffering ungodly privations and doing degrading manual labor. It must have been a rude slap in the face for the handsome Air Corps Colonel.

"Well, now, Colonel," the grating voice of Sturmbannführer Dietrich suddenly sounded in the prisoner's ears. "Having fun yet?"

The four Americans paused their work a moment and looked up at the tall SS-Major, Boggs scowling bitterly, Dunn and Farrell evincing tight-lipped frowns. McKavitt was grinning.

"Oh, yeah. Nothing like shoveling a little shit in the morning, *mein Herr,"* he quipped. "Gets the blood pumping good and hot."

"I'm glad you're so excited about it, Colonel. But it makes me very suspicious. I can't believe you'd cower so meekly now."

"Cower?" McKavitt chuckled. "No, no. I'm not cowering, Dietrich. I'm just cooperating, that's all."

"Are you?" Dietrich scoffed. "You're just trying to play me for a fool, Colonel. Humor me, play along with me, thinking I'll leave you alone if you comply with my orders. Nah, nah! I know what you're up to. You can't fool me that easily."

Boggs cut in. "Why don't you just lay off—"

"Stand down, Sergeant," McKavitt commanded, his hand raised like a stop sign. "I can handle myself. I don't need your help."

"But, sir. This S.O.B. is just—"

"Pipe down, Boggs! I can deal with this asshole myself."

"Asshole?" Dietrich bristled, his eyes suddenly enraged slits "I am familiar with the term, Colonel. We have a similar word in German, and it means the same thing." Dietrich stepped down into the fetid drainage ditch where the four men were standing, and stood face-to-face with Colonel McKavitt, his jaw pulsing vindictively.

"Then you know exactly what I mean, Dietrich." McKavitt was smiling smugly when he said that.

"An asshole, am I?" Dietrich returned hotly. He drew his Walther sidearm and raised it to McKavitt's face. "Let me show you what an asshole is capable of, Colonel." He cocked the bolt and pressed the barrel against McKavitt's cheek, sneering venomously.

"That old routine again?" McKavitt rejoined. "So you'd gun me down without a chance to defend myself, eh?" He sucked his teeth mockingly. "How cowardly and typical of your kind. I was wrong to call you an asshole. You're just a yellow-bellied bastard, that's all."

Dietrich huffed, suppressing the urge to outright shoot the Colonel in the face, and instead, reared back and pistol-whipped him across the cheek, bloodying his nose, knocking him down. McKavitt fell backwards into the ditch landing flat on his back in a pile of shit and mud, his leather jacket squelching sickeningly. Boggs reacted instinctively, wielding his shovel like a baseball bat, and whacked the SS-Major across the shoulders, knocking him sideways into the ditch wall.

"Nazi son-of-a-bitch!" Boggs raged.

The guards raised their machine pistols ready to shoot the Sergeant Major where he stood but were quickly stopped by Dietrich's halting hand. He jumped up and turned to face Boggs.

Nein!Nein! he shouted to the guards. *"Verdammter Amerikaner! Ach! Du bist ein toter Mann!"* Dietrich promptly popped off three rounds into Bogg's chest, retaliating in a furious spate of rage. Boggs toppled over in a blood-spurting heap, clutching his chest, moaning painfully. Once he settled into the reeking muck in a groaning, writhing state, Dietrich pumped three more rounds into him, shooting him in the head twice. McKavitt was up by then and he tried to assail Dietrich from behind, only one of the guards fired a quick burst preventing him from doing so, just narrowly missing his feet. Smoke, mud, and blood went everywhere. McKavitt stopped dead in his tracks, hands raised.

Dunn and Farrell dropped their shovels and raised their hands as more SS-guards appeared on the scene, weapons drawn. Dietrich holstered his sidearm and hopped up out of the drainage ditch, shaking his head detestably. He flicked some mud from his fingers.

"Nah-ja," he quipped coolly. "Nothing like shoveling a little shit in the morning, eh? Gets the blood pumping good and hot."

Colonel McKavitt just stood there, hands raised, numb with shock, staring at Boggs' bloodied body, frowning dolefully, sighing lugubriously. "Boggs, you poor old son-of-a-gun," he finally said. "W-Why did you do it? Why? Damn!"

"A foolish act, Colonel. Very foolish."

"You bloody bastard!"

Dietrich smiled. He pointed to Boggs' prostrate body and ordered his men to carry it away. Two guards seized the dead body and obediently hauled it off. Then Dietrich hooked a finger at McKavitt and said: "Come with me, Colonel. I want to show you something. Show you where we dump useless lumps of flesh."

A guard shoved McKavitt from behind, and he numbly paced off behind Dietrich, his arms half-raised, his eyes misty with remorse.

CORPORAL SCHMIDT parked the Opel-Blitz truck next to two other trucks marked with SS insignia inside a concrete, garage-like structure. A noncom dressed in a field cap and fur-lined anorak approached the truck, shaking his head and muttering heated expletives. Seems Schmidt had parked the truck in the wrong place.

"You can't park there, damn you!" he was saying as he walked up. *"It's reserved for SS vehicles. Move this thing out of here!"*

Jack raised a halting finger, then drew his High Standard silencer. "Hang tight, Schmidt. I'll handle this, okay?" he said, then reached for the handle and opened the passenger door.

Schmidt nodded. "Yes, sir." He turned to Justice who was poking his head through the truck's small cab window, wanting to know what was going on. "Tell the men to hang back a moment."

"Will do," Justice replied.

Jack got out and met the SS-noncom halfway across the floor, the High Standard barely concealed in the dim light of the garage. He was smiling coolly when he approached the noncom, nodding animatedly, the Luftwaffe flight cap perched securely on his head.

"Ja, Ja, mein Herr," he replied, then rejoined glibly. *"So we're double-parked. Big deal!"* With that said, he plugged the noncom with two, quick, silenced rounds, cutting him down in mid-step.

The stunned noncom gasped as he collapsed to his knees, and then fell face-forward on the cold pavement, a red pool of blood swiftly spreading around him thereafter. Jack rapped his knuckles on the truck's tailgate as he looked around for more Germans.

"Alright, fellas," he said in a loud whisper. "C'mon out. The coast is clear—for the moment."

The tailgate dropped and Justice, Hentges, Hays, Carter, and the radioman Sparky Powell, quickly disembarked. Within a couple of seconds all seven men were crouched in a little huddle behind a stack of oil barrels, their M3 grease-guns locked and loaded.

"Okay, gents," said Jack. "Now listen carefully." He pulled out a neat, hand-drawn map of the REIMAHG production facility and spread it out evenly on the pavement. "We're *here...*" he pointed, "in this vehicle garage... and our first objective, is *here,* this assembly bunker right here. Ya git the picture, right?""

The men nodded affirmatively, listening carefully.

"It's about 200 yards from here," Jack went on, "and it's the primary assembly bunker, and the final stage of the assembly process. It's where the jets get fitted with avionic equipment. So we'll set our charges there first, okay?"

"Wasn't that the original plan, sir?" Hentges asked. "I mean, we were supposed to do all that in total darkness. But now...?" He glanced at his wristwatch; it was 06:50 hours and the dim light of dawn was just breaking over the horizon. "In broad daylight, sir?"

"Yeah, well, we're running a wee bit behind, Hentges," Jack replied, then shrugged. "We'll just have to make due, won't we?"

Hentges sighed. "Yes, sir. I guess we will."

"We should wait until dark, sir," Justice suggested. "Right now, every Kraut in the joint will be out and about. We'll be spotted—"

"If we wait 'til night, Sarge," Jack returned curtly, "then those jets will already be long gone. Our mission changed when that information got relayed to us. We gotta hammer those assembled jets now, *today,* before they're flown out for weapons fitting."

"Right." Justice frowned. "But it's going to be really tough moving around here in the daylight without being seen."

"Yup, it sure is. But we can do it if we're careful, Sarge. Besides, once Sergeant Davis and his bunch get going on that SS-barracks, all hell is gonna break loose anyway. But it'll create mass confusion, and that'll be our cover, see? Once the Krauts are running around wondering what the hell's going on, we'll be setting charges and destroying those jets. And they'll hardly be the wiser."

"Okay, sir. Whatever you say."

"That's the spirit." Jack scooped up the map, folded it neatly, and stuffed it in his jacket pocket. "Remember, I'm still in this Luftwaffe get-up. I can still dupe the Germans into thinking I'm one of their own. Just follow my lead, men. You can't go wrong."

The men nodded, albeit reluctantly.

"All-righty then, let's move out."

The seven men rose from the impromptu little huddle and scurried out of the garage, following Jack in a crouching, single-file line, following him out into the open, ducking behind crates, barrels, and various vehicles of all sorts and kinds as they went.

Within minutes, they were in sight of the assembly bunker.

They'd only seen one or two Germans as they made their way across the facility compound, all of them civilians in coveralls or white lab coats. They only saw one SS-guard along the way. It seems the guards stayed indoors due to the cold up here on the facility compound. Or perhaps there weren't that many just as Colonel Bruce had predicted? It was still early in the morning and the SS-guards were scarcely getting ready for the day while the others were probably impatiently waiting for their reliefs to arrive. It was really the perfect time to infiltrate the facility, Jack surmised. They would catch the Germans between the proverbial "shift-change," and it would be their undoing.

When they were a mere ten yards from the main entrance of the assembly bunker (a large steel door) laying underneath a long, flat-bed trailer, hiding, observing the sparse activity, Jack motioned to Sergeant Justice.

"Alright, Sarge, hang tight a moment with the men. I'm going in there and see what's what, playing the part of a hotshot Luftwaffe ace. Wait for my signal, okay?"

"And what signal will that be, sir?" Justice replied caustically.

"Dunno yet. But you'll know it when you hear it."

"Right." Justice frowned, shaking his head.

Jack stashed his grease-gun and hopped up, his High Standard silencer tucked snugly in the holster of the German pistol belt. He paced over to the personal entrance beside the large steel door, looking very much like a swaggering Luftwaffe fighter pilot in a leather flight jerkin and fleece-lined flight cap, the baggy, blue-gray, two-piece flying suit fitting him to near perfection. He certainly evinced the proper image of a German airman ready to take to the skies in a world-beating jet fighter. And his German was better than average, good enough for short, concise phrases. Jack also knew the Luftwaffe uniform he wore displayed the rank of a Major, high enough to order noncoms and junior officers around. He hoped it would all be enough to get him past the Krauts guarding the place. He calmly lit a cigarette as he walked up to the entrance trying to look as cool as possible, paused at the door, took a deep drag, exhaled, and then jerked the door open and went inside.

"Guten Morgan, mein Herren," he said, once inside the bunker. *"I'm Major... um—Wissemann. Major Wissemann, Stab III, JG-2,*

here to fly the Me-262's to... uh, bla, bla, bla," he said firmly, only that last part muttered under his breath. He didn't know where the jets were being flown to exactly so he trailed off quietly hoping no one would notice. And as it appeared, no one did.

A couple of engineers looked up, one of them glancing at his pocket watch noting the early hour, frowning, shaking his head. *"Gott! You're an hour early, Herr Major,"* he grumbled. *"Why, the first jet was just off-loaded only moments ago, and is about to be fueled up. The second is on its way up now."*

"No problem. I can wait. Just checking in that's all."

Jack smiled inwardly, thinking his German was really getting good. All those quiet lonely nights at Camp X had finally paid off. Whilst the other recruits had spent their nights drinking and playing cards, he'd studied the Danish and German languages, learning plenty of useful words and phrases. He'd kept it a little secret hoping to use it one day for something worthwhile. Now that day had finally come and he would make full use of it.

Jack looked around, trying to suss out the situation and the personnel inside the assembly bunker. He saw one SS-guard, a big man armed with a Schmeisser MP-40, and nine mechanics besides four engineers in lab coats. Fourteen people in all. He also saw, for the first time, a German jet—a Messerschmitt Me-262, to be precise. He was quietly awed by what he saw. The twin-engined fighter-jet looked neatly streamlined and agile with its slender, near-pointed nose and swept-back wings, parked on its stout tricycle undercarriage, looking mean and stoic; ominous-looking may have been a better way to describe it.

Two mechanics hovered over the cockpit, standing on a tall, four-wheeled metal scaffolding, making some final adjustments to the cockpit. Behind that two-engined jet wonder, Jack saw a dozen more parked behind it, everyone of them gleaming with metallic newness, their two-toned camouflage paint jobs glimmering in the artificial lighting of the assembly bunker. It was a chilling sight to see all those new jets lined up and ready to go.

And they were a sight for sore eyes, Jack's pining aviator eyes. What a thrill it must be to fly one, he thought. To soar once more on slender wings and skip the light fandago... Jack! Snap out of it! No, no. They must never ever take flight. They must be destroyed!

SERGEANT DAVIS led his eight-man team from the Opel-Blitz truck into the enclosed compound of the SS-barracks. They were armed with hand grenades and sub-machine guns; they were also armed with one Browning .30-caliber machine gun, which Tech Corporals Ricci and Foster set up on a tripod 30 yards from the front entrance, underneath a parked truck. Davis and Hassler would assail the two-story barracks from the back door along with Corporals Ames, Sims, and Russell, with Sergeant Bryant, the group's medical corpsman, waiting in wings in case anyone got wounded. Howbeit, he knew he wouldn't be able to do much if someone was mortally wounded. And also knew if anyone got left behind due to serious injuries, they would be at the mercy of the SS, which according to Colonel Bruce, had no mercy. Surprise would be the deciding factor in neutralizing the barracks full of SS-troopers, who were hopefully still in the throes of sleep and laxity. But once the shooting started the whole facility would be on high alert. Every German within a mile of the place would converge on the Walpersberg, and with a vengeance, too. Bryant chagrined warily, it remained to be seen how many men of O.G. NEMESIS would actually survive this crack--brained operation. The odds were not in their favor.

Davis and Hassler crept up to the back door and peered through a side window, trying to see inside the barracks. Davis glimpsed through the dirty glass concealed by the shadows, and saw about fifty men in various states of undress, some in long johns, some in shirttails, some still languishing in bed. Only one or two were actually fully dressed. And nowhere did he see weapons of any kind. They were either in an adjoining room or most likely in a nearby armory, ready to be issued at a moment's notice. Davis also noticed two stairwells on each end of the barracks, each one leading to the upper floor. Davis quickly devised a plan of attack.

"Okay, men, listen up," he said in a low voice. "Looks like the Germans are still getting ready for the day. This will be our one and only chance to take these guys out. Sergeant Hassler, Russell, and myself will toss grenades and hose these fuckers down with machine gun fire. Ames and Sims... I want you two on the near stairwells. When the shooting starts, they're gonna come piling down those steps mad as hell. Shoot them up when they start coming down. The rest will sure enough start pouring out the front door when they realize what's going on. Ricci and Foster will take care of them. Keep your wits about you, gentlemen. It's gonna get noisy and smoky in there, bullets will be flying in every direction. Confusion will reign. But just remember your training and reload your magazines with careful coordination."

"Sure, man," Hassler chimed in. "That's easier said than done."

"Don't be a wiseacre, Hassler," Davis rejoined. "You know what it's like when the shooting starts and things get hot."

"Sure." Hassler grinned. "But sometimes it ain't that easy."

"Whatever." Davis signaled. "Okay—let's do it!"

Davis grabbed a Mk. 2 "frag" grenade from the canvas pouch slung around his neck and pulled the pin. Each man did the same thing, then they rose from their crouch and moved to the door. Davis gave a nod and reached for the door handle, and slowly turned it, which surprisingly, was unlocked. He released the fuse lever, counted to three, then tossed the grenade in. Three more grenades thudded to the floor a second later. Shortly, four concussive blasts rocked the innards of the barracks accompanied by shrill shrieks of pain and misery. Sergeant Davis burst through the door, his grease-gun spouting a steady stream of .45-caliber bullets, Hassler and Russell right behind him, both of their guns flaring hotly. They caught the Germans totally unawares, gunning them down where they stood, cutting them down in spewing bloody heaps, spinning them around, cutting them down ruthlessly. It was a blood-red scene of mayhem and murder. Not one German was able to escape the wrath of four fire-breathing grease-guns. And just like Davis predicted, the Krauts came bounding down the four stairwells half-dressed and mad as hell. Only three were armed. Two were cut down before they had a chance to return fire. One SS-man did manage to get off a volley; he caught Corporal Ames in the chest as he tried to reload his grease-gun. The young noncom pitched over in a gasping cry, dropping his weapon and falling to the ground, landing on top of a pile of dead Germans. A second later, he was dead; the first casualty of the operation. Hassler spun around and hammered the German, killing him with a ten-round volley, then pulled the pin of another grenade and tossed it up the stairwell. An echoing blast erupted a second later.

At the other end of the barracks, SS-men were bouncing down the stairs and running out the front door, only to be mowed down by Foster and Ricci, who had their machine gun perfectly sighted on the front entrance. Twenty more Germans bit the dust before they halted their confused departure. And by that time, Davis and Russell had made their way across the barracks floor and were shooting them from behind, spilling their blood and guts all over the place. It was a heinous scene of pure slaughter. The dozy SS-men never had a chance to defend themselves and well over a hundred lay dead or dying on the floor and up and down the four stairwells. Bryant crouched outside the back door grimacing with every shot and explosion as he waited for the call of "Medic!" But no one called. So far, no one had been wounded.

"Okay, men!" Sergeant Davis shouted. "Let's get upstairs and finish off these Krauts! We've only killed about a hundred. There's still plenty more up there, I'm sure."

"Yeah!" Hassler replied slapping home a fresh magazine, reloading his grease-gun. "Let's keep it going. They're onto us now."

Russell paused a moment, standing over Ames' bloody and prostrate body, lamenting his fate. "Sorry, old buddy. Sorry it had to end this way. But... I'll be seeing you on the other side soon enough. Don't you worry, old friend."

Russell reloaded and darted up the blood-spattered stairwell grunting all the way. Soon, gunfire crackled again, followed by muffled explosions and bloodcurdling cries as he, Davis, and Hassler continued their murderous work, killing one SS-man after another. Soon, that homicidal tumult was followed by another noise, the shrill sound of alarms. The facility was now on alert! It was just a matter of time before every German in the facility realized what was going on. Meanwhile, Jack was playing his part to a tee...

"Ja, Ja, mein Herr," said Jack to the first engineer, the cigarette burning between his lips. "I know how to fly one of these things."

"I hope so. They're very finicky machines, Major. Not at all like your Bf-109's of FW-190's. Much faster. Very complicated."

The SS-guard got curious and walked over, eyeing Jack suspiciously, yet his MP-40 machine pistol still slung over his shoulder.

"You are a Luftwaffe pilot?" He asked, glaring at Jack with

probing eyes, looking him over from head to toe.

"Well, the next best thing, *Junge,*" Jack quipped, winking.

Suddenly, the facility alarm began blaring, perking up every-one's ears. The guard turned to look away as Jack drew his silencer.

"Hmm?" the guard grunted. *"Was zum Teufel?"*

"Ja, Ja," Jack replied, and triggered two silenced rounds into the guard's chest. "All hell is breaking loose, my friend."

The guard crumpled to the floor, blood spurting from his mouth, a stunned look in his eyes. As he fell down, the engineers gasped and cowered into a meek little cluster, muttering fearfully, incredu-lous looks on their faces. Jack waved the silencer and ordered them to lay on the floor, face down, arms and legs spread out.

But they hesitated.

"Los, mein Herren!" Jack barked, pointing the pistol directly at one of the engineers, aiming to shoot him if he did not comply. They duly complied and flopped to the floor, laying face down, muttering anxiously. At the same time, one of the mechanics on the scaffold-ing boldly challenged Jack, shouting at him, throwing a heavy iron wrench at him. Jack ducked, the wrench missed, and the silencer blipped again, hitting the mechanic in the shoulder, knocking him off the scaffolding. He fell head-over-heels to the cold concrete and hit with a bone-breaking thud, then laid there groaning painfully, clutching his bloodied shoulder.

"Hände Hoch!'" Jack growled, ordering everyone to raise their hands high, then told them to lay down on the floor. *"Hinlegen!"*

They all complied, fearfully, worried Jack might shoot them, too. When they had all laid down, Jack popped his head out the per-sonnel door and whistled. Justice and the rest of the men readily hopped up and dashed inside the bunker, panting anxiously, their ears ringing with the sounds of sirens, knowing that time was of the essence now.

"All right, Hentges—Schmidt," Jack snapped. "Get busy! Start setting those charges. We ain't got much time. Snap it up now!"

"Yes, sir," Boomer Hentges replied, removing the demolition kit from his shoulders, and opened it up.

Schmidt did the same, and soon, both men began rigging up half-pound blocks of TNT to the jets themselves whilst the German engineers and mechanics watched in abject horror. Then Corporals

Hays and Carter duly herded them into an adjoining room (a utility room) and locked them in at Jack's curt command. In the meantime, Sergeant Justice stood guard at the door ready for the coming onslaught. Soon enough, more SS-guards would appear on the scene armed to the teeth. He hoped they could get the charges set before then because he had no illusions about holding off an entire battalion of pissed-off SS-men with just a handful of grease-guns and a few hand grenades. "Hurry it up, you guys!" Justice shouted.

HE STOOD AT THE top of aircraft lift near the mountaintop runway waiting for his prized jet fighter, watching the mechanics and technicians prep the Me-262 for flight. Herr Multhopp was cloaked in a hound's-tooth overcoat, leather gloves, and an old homburg. Although the temperature wasn't all that cold, the wind atop the Walpersberg could be frigid and biting this time of year. But he hardly noticed it. The warmth of pure elation warmed his middle-aged bones today. His Ta-183 prototype, his precious little *"Huckebein,"* was finally making its debut. Today it would fly out and set a new standard for jet-propelled aviation; today it would set a new precedent for all jet fighters to come. The future of jet technology rested on the mighty, swept-back wings of the Focke-Wulf Ta-183 air superiority fighter, albeit just wooden wings. Once Goering and his RLM. cronies saw it winging in over Lechfeld Air Base, they would be awed to the point of adulation. The Luftwaffe's newest jet fighter would save them from the Führer's wrath and turn the tide of the air war. The brave airman of Germany's onetime invincible air force would once again rule the skies over Europe.

"Gott! What's taking so long?" Multhopp grumbled, nudging one of the maintenance techs working the lift. "What's the holdup?"

"Nothing. The lift is just a slow-going piece of machinery, Herr Multhopp," replied the maintenance tech matter-of-factly. "It wasn't designed to haul three-ton jet fighters up the side of a mountain."

"Well, it was built for just this task, I believe," Herr Multhopp returned sharply. "The engineers who designed it knew what—"

"Ach! Engineers!" the tech rumbled bitterly "They're all the same. Just a bunch of over-wrought pinheads."

Multhopp's brow arched peevishly. *"I'm* an engineer."

The man nodded. "Case and point, *mein Herr.*"

"Your insolence has been duly noted, sir."

"Whatever."

The tech lit a cigarette, and then made an adjustment to the winch motor. The winch clanked and clanged and sped up just a hair, hauling the 3-ton jet plane up the mountainside and along the railed ramp at a slow but steady pace.

"Can't that thing go any faster?" Multhopp queried hotly.

"No. The winch is at full-speed now," the tech informed him, puffing his cigarette luxuriously. "Oh, don't you worry. It'll be up in a couple of minutes. Then we can offload it."

"Idiot!" Herr Multhopp muttered under his breath.

He walked over to the five-foot guardrail and peered down the side of the mountain, seeing his tarp-covered fighter jet slowly rising from the hazy gloom below. Although it was securely chained to the steel aircraft lift, it shook and shimmied with every turn of the winch. Multhopp bit at his nether lip, angst swelling up in his gut, his heart rate rising exponentially. He watched in sheer anxiety as the winch slowly reeled his jet fighter plane up the mountainside. The thought of his precious work of art being bashed to little pieces, his hopes and dreams being smashed to smithereens along with it, was just too much to bear at the moment. His masterpiece mustn't perish so haphazardly.

"Just a few more meters, Herr Multhopp," the surly tech assured the anxious engineer. "And we'll have it up and secured."

"Then it must be refueled, and fitted with the take-off rockets. Another laborious process, I'm sure."

"Well, Rome wasn't built in a day, *mein Herr.*"

"And I don't have a thousand years to wait around, either."

After a few minutes, the aircraft lift carrying Herr Multhopp's jet fighter plane reached the top of the mountain and the concrete docking platform. Once the lift was secured and the winch locked into place, the techs removed the anchoring chains. Then the front wheel of the Ta-183 was hitched to a powerful diesel-powered tractor and towed over to a fuel-pumping bowser, where its six fuselage-mounted fuel cells were topped off with 500 liters of high-octane J-2 aviation fuel. The jet's six fuel cells could hold up to 1,500 liters of fuel but it would only need a 1,000 for today's flight.

Suddenly, the operations hut's alarm klaxon blared loudly; every man stopped to listen. Herr Multhopp jerked his head in the direction of the bright red pulsating light affixed to the front door of the hut, his mouth agape, his head cocked perplexedly. Then the hut's wall-mounted telephone rang.

"What's going on, I wonder?" he said to the maintenance tech.

The tech shrugged. "Don't know? Perhaps it's just a drill."

"No! Not at this hour. Not while we're in the middle of fueling and prepping the jets for flight."

Herr Bölkow hurried over to the hut and answered the telephone. He came back a moment later with a disturbed look on his paled face. *"Lieber Gott!"* he exclaimed. "We're under attack!"

"What?" Multhopp replied, his eyes flaring widely.

"We're under attack! That was Sturmbannführer Dietrich on the phone. The facility is being assaulted by American c-commandos," Bölkow said. "The SS-barracks is being shot up as we speak!"

Multhopp gasped. "Good Heavens! Are you serious?"

"Quite! Dietrich said they're here to blow up the facility, destroy our jet aircraft—kill us all!"

"Scheisse!" Multhopp cursed. "And today of all the days."

He scampered over to the fuel-bowser where he urged the attendants to hurry up the refueling process. Everywhere on the mountaintop airstrip men began running to-and-fro in a confused rabble. Suddenly, the important work of readying the jets for the flight to Lechfeld didn't seem so important. Only their safety seemed to matter now. But Multhopp wasn't so easily distracted from the job at hand. He kept at the attendants and technicians, barking orders at them, ordering them to hurry up, even lending a hand himself with the takeoff rockets. And before long, his sleek-looking Ta-183 jet-fighter was ready for flight. Now he just needed a pilot.

The Me-262 jet sat at the end of the runway, its twin turbojets whining with accumulating power as the mechanics revved them up, warming them for the flight. In just a few minutes it would be ready for takeoff. The takeoff-assist rockets were in place and it was ready for flight. So where were those damn Luftwaffe pilots?

CHAPTER 14

STURMBANNFÜHRER Emil Dietrich hung up the telephone handset and turned to face Colonel McKavitt, who was standing behind him amidst two beefy-looking guards, his nose still smarting and oozing blood. Dietrich sneered, regarding the American Colonel with an evil glare.

"Seems your countrymen have decided to destroy our quaint little facility, Colonel," Dietrich rasped. "A bold but stupid idea."

"I hope they accomplish the job, Dietrich," McKavitt retorted.

"They might disrupt the flow of production, but they won't destroy this facility, that's for certain. Not on my watch."

"Well, if they fail, they'll just send in another team, and then another." McKavitt smirked. "Or maybe the 8th Air Force will just bomb this place to kingdom come."

"It will do them no good, Colonel. This place is impervious to Allied bombers. Our bunkers are too strong and well-built. Nothing can penetrate their thick concrete ceilings and walls."

"Maybe that why they sent in a commando team."

"And that will do them no good, either!" Dietrich picked up the handset and dialed a number. "When the rest of my men arrive from Berga, it will be all over for them." The dispatch operator came on the line and Dietrich had him patch a call through to the work camp at Berga—the evacuation site along the Elster River. A short moment later Dietrich was talking to his second-in-command Hauptsturmführer Gottfried Hengl, who was a Captain in the Waffen SS.

"Hengl..." said Dietrich into the handset. "Close down operations over there. Gather up all your men and heavy armaments and come here to the facility—immediately. We are under attack!"

"Jawohl, Herr Sturmbannführer," Hengl obeyed.

Dietrich hung up the handset. "Now, where were we? Ah, yes. I was going to show you something. Something interesting."

McKavitt scoffed. "Interesting? Huh, I doubt that."

"Oh, you'll find it *very* interesting, Colonel. Indeed, you will."

Dietrich motioned to the guards. One nudged McKavitt roughly, then all four men marched off down the corridor. A moment later, they were inside a large warehouse next to a railway spur. The SS-Major led McKavitt to a parked boxcar and opened its sliding door.

McKavitt gasped when he saw contents of that boxcar. He saw the heaped naked bodies of at least a thousand dead men. The decaying bodies were stacked one on top of the other, all the way to the ceiling of the boxcar. The stench was dreadful. The stunned Air Corps Colonel almost wretched feeling bile rise up into his throat.

"G-Good God!" he exclaimed, covering his mouth and nose with a trembling hand. "You people are absolutely evil!"

Dietrich smiled. "They're the dregs of our labor force, Colonel. Jews, mostly. Poor Polish peasants, and a few Americans, too,"

"You fucking bastard!" McKavitt spouted. "You'll hang for this, Dietrich. You and all your sick, demented SS-cronies."

Dietrich chuckled. "Sick, are we? Demented you say? No, no more than your own people, Colonel. You fire-bomb our cities to the ground, killing thousands upon thousands of innocent civilians; burning poor little boys and girls to a crisp; maiming and displacing thousands of decent German families. Good people, all of them. Dear, guiltless souls."

"Yeah, well, war is hell, isn't, Dietrich?" McKavitt returned.

"Indeed, it is." Dietrich seized the boxcar's door and slammed it shut. "And hell is where you're going to spend eternity, Colonel."

"And you'll be right down there with me, you rotten bastard."

"But not anytime soon, my dear Colonel." Dietrich drew his Walther, cocked it, then placed the barrel right above McKavitt's nose. "You'll get to meet the devil first, I daresay. Tell him what a wonderful man you are for slaughtering thousands of innocent German citizens—"

A burst of rifle fire suddenly erupted from the shadows of the warehouse, hitting one of the SS-guards, killing him instantly. Dietrich spun around to see a trio of olive-drab attired men dashing toward him, their guns flaring hotly. McKavitt instinctively flopped to the ground as the other SS-guard returned fire. He missed and was promptly dispatched, the force of a well-aimed .30-caliber rifle shot knocking him backwards onto the ground. Dietrich popped off a couple of rounds as he dashed away from the scene, ducking behind the boxcar as he ran. A second later, he was gone. McKavitt was hefted up from the ground by two strong arms. When he was standing upright once again, he said:

"Who the hell are you guys?"

"We're with the O.S.S., Colonel," said one of the men. "A special recon team sent ahead of the attacking operations group."

"The O.S.S.?"

"Yes, sir." The man nodded keenly. "All that commotion you've heard is Operations Group NEMESIS—sent here to destroy this facility. We're the three-man Jedburgh team sent ahead of them."

"I see."

"I'm Staff Sergeant McDonald," he pointed. "And these are my two buddies, Corporals Landers and Edwards."

"Nice to meet you, gentlemen. I'm Colonel David McKavitt."

"Yes, we know." Edwards smiled.

"We've been trying to find you, Colonel," explained Sergeant McDonald, "and we could have done it sooner if our radio hadn't crapped out on us all of a sudden."

"Yeah," Edwards elaborated. "Damn thing must have shorted out or something. Couldn't send or receive any messages."

"You were trying to find *me,* you said?" McKavitt queried.

"Yes, sir," McDonald replied. "Before our radio quit, we received a transmission that you would be here in the facility."

"And how did your people know that?"

"Our headquarters got a call from British Intelligence, Colonel. Seems one of their field agents received a clandestine transmission from a Group Captain named Hawker, a senior P.O.W. in your camp, I believe?"

"Hawker?" McKavitt's puzzled look turned into a smile. "Well, that old Limey sun-of-a-gun! Yeah, he knew I was here, all right."

"He said you might be in danger of losing your life. He said the SS had singled you out for a work detachment—and because of your Jewish background—was a death sentence, for certain."

"It certainly was." McKavitt sighed wearily, stroking the back of his neck. "And you guys got here just in the nick of time. That SS-Major was about to add me to his list of murdered prisoners."

"Glad to be of service, sir," McDonald said with a stiff nod. "Now we gotta get you out of this goddamn place in one piece."

"Right," McKavitt agreed. He picked up one of the MP-40's laying on the ground and cocked it. "C'mon. I'll show you around."

"OKAY, DAVIS," said Sergeant Hank Hassler. "The barracks is clear. All the Krauts are dead."

"Good," Davis replied, reloading his grease-gun. "But this ain't six hundred SS-guards, Hassler. I count maybe... two hundred?"

"One hundred and ninety-six—counting the ones Ricci and Foster waxed as they tried to run out the front door."

"You counted them all?" Davis eyes widened incredulously.

"Yeah. I'm good at adding numbers."

"So where are the other four-hundred-plus guards, I wonder?"

"Not here, that's for damn sure. Fucking intelligence staffers!" Hassler spat." They never get it right!"

"So who'd we lose? Any casualties?"

"Ames got it," Bryant interjected. "Poor devil. Nothing I could do for him. He died instantly after he got hit."

Russell nodded. "Too bad for him. He was a good guy."

"Any other casualties?" Davis asked.

"Nope. You guys blew through this place like gangbusters. The Krauts never had a chance. I'm amazed only Ames got tapped."

"Well, we've still got a hell of a fight on our hands, gentlemen. There's still a bunch Krauts around here somewhere. And they know we're here by now. This is where it gets real interesting."

"Yeah. Real interesting."

Davis whistled, rallying the rest of the men together.

Ricci and Foster dismantled their tripod and joined the huddled group inside the barracks, Russell standing guard as Sergeant Davis quickly briefed them on the next phase of their assault.

"Listen up," he said. "Let's mount up and get over to the aircraft lift and link up with Captain Daemon's team. I'm sure they're going to need our help now that the whole place is on high alert."

"What about the other SS-Krauts, Davis?" Hassler asked.

"They're around here somewhere, Hank. I'm sure we'll bump into them at any moment. So we need not go looking for them. They'll find us, sure enough."

"Maybe they're off-site, Sergeant," said Tech-5 Ricci. "There is another work camp nearby—that, according to Colonel Bruce."

"I hope the hell so, Ricci. That would be a godsend."

"So do I," Bryant interjected. "We really don't have the fire-power to handle four hundred pissed-off SS-troops."

"That's a fight we're going to avoid, if we can." Sergeant Davis gestured to the back door. "All right. Let's move out. Let's get over to the aircraft lift, posthaste. I'm sure Captain Daemon and his team are going to need our help right about now."

The seven-man team bounded out the back door and clambered aboard the parked Opel-Blitz, alarm bells ringing in their ears. The whole place was on high-alert and every German knew of their presence now and what was going on. Soon, the facility would be crawling with angry SS-men and any reinforcements they could muster.

As Tech Sergeant Frank Davis sat in the passenger seat of the Luftwaffe truck, thinking. He had no more illusions of surviving the operation at that point. Intelligence had dropped the ball, somehow, failing to realize only two hundred Germans were housed in that barracks—not six hundred. It was a critical miscue on their part but one that turned out to be okay in the long run.

Surprise had been the deciding factor in neutralizing the barracks. However, attacking a barracks housing six hundred SS-troops, in broad daylight, was not something Sergeant Davis had been looking forward to. Eight men armed with only sub-machine guns and grenades was just plain suicide. Yet, it had all worked out, somehow. The gods of war had been forgiving—so far. But Davis knew what lay ahead; nothing but deadly close combat and savage hand-to-hand fighting, and no amount of luck could save him and his men from their impending fate. It seemed as if the devil himself was waiting for them.

SERGEANT HENTGES and Corporal Schmidt had set all the half-pound TNT charges, rigging them with blasting caps; they had spooled out enough firing wire to connect them all to a hand-held blasting machine. It had been a nerve-racking job doing all of that under the pressure of time and blaring alarm bells. But the job was almost done, and they had all the jets wired with explosive charges. Now they just had to get a detonating wire spooled out of the assembly bunker and to a safe place so they could detonate the charges with the blasting machine.

"Okay, Captain," said Hentges, "we're about done here. We need to get clear of this place now so we can detonate the charges."

"Right," Jack replied with a nod. "What's it looking like, Sarge?" he asked Justice, who was still standing guard at the door.

He peered out the door. "Clear, looks like. For now, anyway."

"Good," Jack said. "Let's run some wire out the door then, underneath that flatbed trailer, then rig up the blasting machine. That ought to put us well-clear of this bunker when those charges go off."

"We only need to get outside these walls, sir, really," Hentges explained, spooling out some wire. "The resulting explosions won't hurt these concrete walls and ceiling very much. They're too damn thick. We'd be okay if we stood right outside. They're rock-solid."

"But everything else inside this bunker will be blown to hell and back, right, Hentges?"

"Yes, sir. Everything inside of here will be totally destroyed."

"Sweet. That's all I needed to hear."

Jack joined Justice at the door, then opened it a crack and looked out. He saw no one outside. He drew his silencer and stepped out, Justice and the rest of the men skulking behind him.

"What about all those mechanics and engineers locked in that utility closet, sir?" Schmidt asked.

"What about 'em?" Jack replied as he dashed over to the trailer.

"We're just going to leave them in there, sir? I mean... just let them die like that?"

"Yup," Jack replied laconically. "Just like that, Schmidt."

"They're all part of the works," Justice threw in.

"Jesus, that's cold-blooded."

"That's war, son. Ruthless and cold-blooded."

The seven men took up defensive positions underneath and around the unhitched flatbed trailer. And as they did so, frenetic gunfire suddenly erupted from a previously unseen pillbox (three SS-men manning a MG-42 machine gun). Carter convulsed jerkily as the second volley caught him in the backside and rib cage, ripping him open and spilling his blood and guts all over the snow-covered ground just as he tried to duck under the flatbed trailer. He gasped, collapsed, and then promptly expired face down in the dirty snow. A pool of dark-red swiftly spread around his lifeless form. Jack grabbed his stashed grease-gun and returned fire, shooting in the general direction of the gunfire. There was an immediate retort of twenty 7.92-millimeter rounds that kicked up the earth and ricocheted noisily off the metal frame of the trailer. Jack and the rest of the men cowed helplessly in the snow, cursing.

"I'll be damned!" Jack imprecated. "Those Krauts have got us zeroed in—that meat-grinder will tear us to shreds, for sure."

"Shit!" Justice cursed bitterly. "They got Carter. Poor kid's stiffer than a frozen side of beef already."

Another vicious salvo ricocheted off the sides of the flatbed trailer, ripping up ice and snow in front. A spate of gunfire responded in kind as each man let loose a burst, aiming for the flashes of fire coming from the concrete pillbox. In the meantime, Hentges and Schmidt tested the circuit with a galvanometer. The reading was positive—the circuit was good! Next, they rigged up the ten-cap blasting machine, screwing down the spliced wire leads to terminals, making sure the firing wires touched only the terminals and not the metal of the blasting machine itself. Hentges inserted the handle into the blasting machine, looked left, then right, then yelled:

"Fire in the hole! Fire in the hole!"

He gave the hand-held blasting machine a quick twist and detonated the charges inside the assembly bunker. There was a series of muffled explosions; the personnel door blew off amid swirling smoke and debris; the large iron door buckled but remained intact; two cracks appeared in one of the concrete walls but it also held firm. All gunfire ceased for a moment as the men of O.G. NEMESIS gazed upon their destructive handy work. The German gunners had ceased firing, too, wondering what had just happened, seeing black smoke billowing out the doorway of the assembly bunker.

"Hot-damn!" Jack rejoiced excitedly, his blue eyes agog with glee. "Mission accomplished! Good job, Hentges—good job, Schmidt."

"Thank you, sir," Hentges replied, then ducked his head down in the snow as another volley of machine gunfire marched up the ground in front him. The Germans had recovered from their wonderment, cutting loose another savage fusillade. Sergeant Justice returned fire with the B.A.R., hitting the concrete pillbox, punching out little davits of concrete, making the Germans ceasefire for a just a moment.

"We gotta get out from under that goddamn Kraut machine gun, sir!" he shouted to Jack. "Or we're all dead meat, too!"

"Ya got that right, Sarge," Jack replied irritably, huffing. "And before more Germans show up."

"What do you intend to do, sir?" Justice asked as he fired off another burst from his B.A.R.

"Knock out that dang machine gun!" Jack reached into his grenade pouch and pulled out two grenades. "Okay, gents, I'm gonna need a helluva lot of suppressive fire. When I take off, start hammering that pillbox with everything you got, ya hear?"

"What? Are you crazy?" Hentges spouted. "That machine gun will cut you to pieces before you even get five paces from here."

"Got a better idea, Hentges?" Jack replied, glaring, then cocked his grease-gun. "Okay, start shooting, gents. And keep it coming!"

Jack pulled the pin of one grenade, stood up halfway, and then lobbed it at the pillbox. The next instant he was running across the open terrain, his grease-gun tucked in his right arm rattling away, the second grenade firmly grasped in his left hand. The men laid down a withering barrage of suppressive fire as he ran toward the pillbox, careful not to hit him as he darted left and right, trying to confuse the aim of the German gunners. The grenade exploded right outside of the pillbox's loophole, causing the gunners to halt their fire for just a moment, giving Jack precious extra seconds in which to brave the snowy terrain. In fact, it was a magnificent throw! If it had been a runner trying to round third base and run all the way to home, he would have been easily cut down and tagged out. As Jack got closer, and the smoke cleared, the machine gun open fired once again. He continued to dodge left and right, the suppressive fire getting sparser and sparser as he got nearer to the pillbox, the men fearful of hitting him instead of the pillbox. They watched in utter amazement as he made his mad dash, some thinking he was insanely heroic, others thinking he was insanely stupid.

Then when he was just ten yards from the pillbox, he was suddenly struck by a single round (not a fatal wound) but one that put him on serious notice, causing him to stumble and fall. The bullet had hit him on his right hand, grazing his knuckles and ripping open his glove. He was surprised more than anything else, his vain sense of invincibility suddenly shattered by that lone bullet. And then that little voice inside his head promptly reminded him: *Hell, Jack. You ain't gonna live forever. Your time has come. It's time to meet your maker, pardner.*

"Naw," Jack protested. "I ain't finished yet, not by a long shot!"

A TELEPHONE CALL from the barracks confirmed Dietrich's worst fears. The American commandos had essentially eliminated his primary guard force. All that remained were the guards still on duty—about a hundred men in all. Some of those men had just come on duty when the work detachment of P.O.W.'s arrived and were still somewhat fresh. However, the rest of the guards were quite tired and due for a relief. Most of them had started their watch the night before, each one of them pulling a typical eight-hour shift.

But Dietrich wasn't worried. He knew most of his men were elite, hard-boiled types, tough men used to long hours of duty. A few extra hours wouldn't affect them. In fact, a pitched battle with American commandos would be just what they needed at this hour. SS-men were not well-suited for idle times or too much rest. They craved action and the thrill of combat... and today, they would finally see some action.

"What's the situation, *Herr Sturmbannführer," Rottenführer* Wenzel asked. "What's going on, sir?"

"The American commandos have killed most of our men, storming the barracks with bombs and bullets. But never fear, my dear Wenzel. Hauptsturmführer Hengl will be here shortly with the rest of the battalion, then we'll crush these dirty American *Schweine!*"

"How many commandos are there, you think?"

"Maybe forty or fifty, at the most? Nothing we can't handle."

"Hmm, I hope you're right."

Both men were standing in the duty-shack near the main gate. Dietrich had made good his escape and had already rallied most of his men. They'd quickly responded and rounded up the American P.O.W.'s and all the other prisoners, most of them Poles and Czechs, a few Russians, and locked them up in a barbed-wire stockade. Now the guards were free to retaliate; now they could do what they did best: kill the enemy.

The duty-shack telephone rang. Dietrich picked it up instantly.

"Yes?" he said into the mouthpiece.

"The main assembly bunker has just been blown up, *Herr Sturmbannführer*—destroyed!" explained the frantic guard.

"What?" Dietrich exclaimed. *"All* the jets were destroyed?"

"All except the three already atop the Walpersberg."

"Only three left out of sixteen jet fighters?" Dietrich queried.

"That's right, sir. Only three left—so far."

"Verdammt! Was Herr Multhopp's jet—"

"No, sir. His jet is still on the tarmac, waiting for a pilot."

Dietrich glanced at the clock on the wall. "Where are those goddamned Luftwaffe pilots?" he growled. "They arrived a while ago! I received official word from the front gate that they were here. "

"Perhaps they were delayed?"

"Perhaps." Dietrich sighed, then ordered: "All right, get a platoon of men up there immediately. Protect those jets and the runway, too. The Americans might try to destroy it as well."

"Verstanden, Herr Sturmbannführer—"

"Protect those jets at all cost, Feldwebel! Do not allow them to be destroyed. They are all that remain of our production run. And one of them is a brand-new prototype—perhaps the Reich's last chance for regaining air supremacy. Protect it with your life!"

"Jawohl, Herr Sturmbannführer!"

Dietrich hung up the telephone. He gestured to Wenzel.

"C'mon, Wenzel," he said. "We must rally the men and get to the mountaintop. We must stop the Americans before they do any more damage." He darted out the door, Wenzel right on his heels.

A moment later, they were racing for the mountaintop runway in Dietrich's Kübelwagen, sixty men coming up behind in a truck, every one of them armed with an MP-40, everyone of them grim-faced and ready for action. The fate of the Reich and the Luftwaffe itself rested on their tired but broad shoulders. They knew what was coming, and they were looking forward to it. A hard-fought battle with elite American commandos—a do or die battle.

THE THREE MEN skulked along the fringe of the walkway leading back to the main compound, all three armed and ready for anything and everything. The facility alarm was still going off and they could hear the sounds of gunfire in the near distance. The place was definitely under a brutal siege. Colonel McKavitt followed the three O.S.S. men closely glad to be free, finally. At least for the time being, ayway.

"We've got to get you to the rendezvous point at Saalfeld, sir," said Staff Sergeant McDonald to Colonel McKavitt. "A Lockheed C-40 transport plane will be landing their just after dusk."

"They sent an airplane just for me, Sergeant?" McKavitt questioned, surprised by McDonald's statement.

"Well, sir, it's really for the operational group. Not just you."

"How many men are in the operational group, Sergeant?"

"Fifteen—plus two officers."

Colonel McKavitt's eyes blinked incredulously. He knew a Lockheed C-40 could only carry about eight or nine men, not counting the pilot and co-pilot. Maybe ten could be crammed in if necessary. But not more than that. McKavitt reluctantly realized the O.S.S. High Command had counted on heavy casualties.

"What the E.T.A., Sergeant—exactly."

"Nineteen-hundred hours."

"Well, we have plenty of time then."

"Uh, what do you mean by that, sir?"

"I've got to do my part, that's what I mean."

"Your part, sir?" Corporal Landers chimed in.

"Before that SS-officer led me to that warehouse and boxcar, Corporal, he called one of his junior officers—requesting some back-up. A whole hell of a lot more SS-troops are going to arrive within the hour."

"You mean the SS-battalion at Berga?"

"Precisely. About five hundred men, I think?"

"Look, sir," McDonald interjected. "Our orders are to evacuate you to a safe house in Saalfeld—get you out of harm's way."

"Yeah, well, I can understand your superior's concern for my well-being, Sergeant. But my main concern is for my men. I've got to free some of them if I can. I can't let them rot here in this godforsaken place." McKavitt cocked the MP-40 for effect.

"Free them?" McDonald scoffed dubiously. "That's three-hundred-plus men! And where are they going to sit, sir? On the wings and fuselage of that little Lockheed—"

"Don't be a wise guy, Sergeant," McKavitt rejoined. "We have a contingency plan in effect. In the event of a major escape, the P.O.W.'s have special orders as where to go. We've got safe houses too, Sergeant."

"For three hundred and... and..."

"Three hundred and fifty, Sergeant." McKavitt clarified, then sighed lugubriously, thinking about poor Sergeant Major Boggs. "Well, three hundred and forty-nine, actually."

"Whatever the number, sir, that's still a lot of men to manage in one breakout. Not all of them will be successful, I guarantee you."

"You're probably right, Sergeant. Not all of them will make it to freedom. Not even half will make it, I daresay. But so long as one gets out and makes it home, that'll be a success for us."

"Yeah. That *one* is you, sir," Corporal Edwards reiterated.

"That's right," said McDonald. "Our orders are to get you out of here alive and to a safe house, then to the Lockheed transport plane. Those orders came down from 8th Air Force General Staff, Colonel, not just the O.S.S. From General Doolittle himself, sir!"

"Really?" McKavitt grinned. "I'm touched. I thought he'd forgotten about me." He shook his head. "Well, it doesn't matter what your orders are, Sergeant, or where they came from. I've still got a responsibility to my men. I've got to help them any way I can."

McDonald huffed, staring at his comrades with annoyed eyes. Edwards shrugged his shoulders noncommittally. Corporal Lander's smile was tight-lipped; he kind of liked the Colonel's hell-for-leather attitude. He truly was the Medal of Honor winner he'd read about in so many O.S.S and Air Corps intelligence reports. Fearless, daring, strong-willed, and righteous to the core. Nothing less for Colonel David M. McKavitt, U.S.A.A.C. An honorable man, indeed.

"C'mon, gentlemen," McKavitt said, leading the way now. "Let's get back to the P.O.W. stockade, see what kind of mischief we can get into. I figure we've got about forty-five minutes before those SS reinforcements arrive. Let's see how many prisoners we can free 'til then."

"Sir, I must insist!" McDonald pressed. "We should get out of here while getting is good. Before all hell really breaks loose!"

"Yeah, Colonel," Corporal Landers agreed. "You don't have to be the hero now. You already have our respect. We know you're a Medal of Honor winner and all. You don't have to impress us, sir."

"Who said anything about being a hero, Corporal?" Colonel McKavitt returned curtly. "I'm just doing my duty, that's all."

JACK GOT UP from the frosty ground as yet another volley of bullets struck nearby. His hand was oozing blood, and it hurt like hell, but it seemed to be okay, otherwise. His poor right hand, he lamented. How many times had they been shot? Once by a Japanese ace, once by a German Navy captain, and now by a Kraut MG-42. He was just plain lucky, he guessed, that it had never been shot off completely. Gawd! One more Purple Heart wouldn't make a damn bit of difference to him. He'd rather win the Medal of Honor posthumously than get one more of those medals. He dashed forward, his grease-gun rattling.

More German bullets chewed up the snow and ground around him but none hit him. And in a few more steps, he was on the pillbox's apron. He yanked the cotter pin from the grenade with his teeth, counted to three, and then tossed it through the loophole. He ducked to one side of the pillbox after he tossed the grenade, taking cover from the blast. A second later, a muffled explosion complete with shrieks of pain and misery emanated from the innards of the pillbox. A faint black cloud drifted out from the loophole... followed by utter silence. No more gunfire. He had killed the machine gun crew. Jack had done it, he'd knocked out the German machine gun!

"Okay, fellers!" he yelled. "Up and at 'em! Coast is clear!"

The men got up, one by one, crawling from underneath the flatbed trailer. They quickly reassembled near the pillbox. Jack was just catching his breath as they all gathered around, him eyeing his bleeding hand, the men eyeing the smoldering pillbox.

"Good job, sir!" Corporal Schmidt was the first say.

"Yeah, that was something else, Captain," Powell, added.

"You think?" Jack was gazing at his bloody hand and thinking how that bullet could have easily hit him somewhere else, like his heart or his head. "Well, it wasn't a clean getaway, I tell ya what. Those Krauts tagged me, alright. Could've outright killed me if they'd aimed a little better." Jack reached into his pant's pocket and pulled out a handkerchief and began wrapping his right hand with it.

"How bad is it, sir?" Justice asked.

"Just a scratch, Sarge. Nothing that'll slow me down."

Jack's hand hurt badly, but he didn't want them to know that. The German bullet had reopened an old war wound, the one Nishizawa had given him on his last day or aerial combat. His hand had never really healed properly, and it was always stiff and ungainly. Jack was lucky he was left-handed, though, so most hand-held tasks were manageable. But his right hand was his "stick-hand," the one he used to operate the control column of an airplane. If he ever wanted to fly again, he'd have a difficult time doing it. Would he ever fly again, he wondered? Would he ever climb into the cockpit of a fast fighter plane again?

"Okay," said Justice, reloading his B.A.R. "What's next?"

"I only counted thirteen jets inside that assembly bunker, so I reckon there's gotta be three more around here somewhere."

"You mean... we're not done yet, sir?" Hentges interjected.

"We came to destroy the assembly bunkers and *all* the jets, Hentges. That was the mission. And I aim to finish what I started."

Justice looked up and gazed at the ominous-looking hilltop that was the Walpersberg. Although it was slightly obscured by the morning fog, he could just see the aircraft lift going up the mountainside, slowly, and the telltale signs of a Me-262 tail assembly sticking out from underneath a protective tarp, its blocky, black swastika stenciled on the tailplane. He whipped out his binoculars and got a better look.

"Look—there," he said, pointing, gazing through the binoculars. "There's one of the missing jets. It's being elevated to the mountaintop runway. And I bet there's two more up there already."

Jack motioned. "Lemme have a look, Sarge."

Justice handed over the binoculars. Jack placed them on his eyes and gazed up at the mountainside. "Yup, yer right, Sarge. That's a Me-262 alright. And where there's one there'll be two more."

"So how in the hell do we get up there, sir," Sparky Powell inquired. "On that aircraft lift?"

"Maybe." Jack pulled out his little map and looked at it a moment, trying to see if there was another way onto the mountaintop besides the aircraft lift. "Well, there seems to be a small tunnel entrance next to the loading platform of the lift. I bet that's the personnel entrance for the mountaintop runway. I think there might be a trolley or something similar in there, or maybe a service elevator of some kind."

"You *think*—sir?" Justice queried, tacking on 'sir' as just a buffer for his own simmering animosity. He was still annoyed with Jack but he didn't want to berate him while his hand was hurt and bleeding, and when he was fresh from a shootout with the Germans. By this time he had gotten accustomed to Jack's free-for-all style of leadership. The Captain was certainly foolhardy, and very lucky. Perhaps he had some special connection with serendipity or kismet? Well, whatever it was, he was one fortunate bastard, Justice had to admit reluctantly.

"An educated guess, Sarge," Jack rejoined. "The Germans are a smart bunch of people—downright clever, they are. There'll be some sort of automated trolley or elevator rigged up in there, I can guarantee it."

"That's all the intelligence we have on this damn place, sir?" Hentges asked disbelievingly. "That little map of yours?"

"Yup." Jack refolded the map and tucked into his breast pocket. "The three-man Jedburgh team was supposed to transmit again after their initial report, fill us in on the finer details of this facility. But they never radioed back with a reconnaissance report. So my little map is all we got, Hentges. Better than nothing, eh?"

Hentges sighed. "I suppose."

Jack glanced at his watch.

"I reckon Sergeant Davis and his bunch ought to be done with their work by now," he said, "based on the commotion the alarms have been making. We gotta link up with them at the aircraft lift now. We're definitely gonna need their firepower."

OPEL-BLITZ groaned to a dead stop as Sergeant Hassler stomped on the brakes. Tech Sergeant Davis threw open the door and got out just as the other men bounded from the rear of the truck. And as they assembled in a line formation and headed over to the loading area of the aircraft lift, skirting other parked vehicles and small buildings, an echoing volley of machine gun fire suddenly erupted. Ricci was hit instantly. The rest of the men alertly took cover.

"All right, men," Davis shouted, "here's where it gets dicey!"

Corpsman Melvin Bryant dutifully retrieved Ricci's limp body, dragging it behind a stack of wooden crates and sought to give some sort of first-aid, thinking he still might be alive. But Bryant was sadly disappointed. Ricci was already long gone from this world. He took one of Ricci's dog tags from around his neck and put it in his jacket pocket. Now he had two to bring back. He wondered though, who would collect his dog tag when his time came. Who would survive this goddamned fool's errand and live to tell about it?

"Set up that machine gun, Foster," Davis ordered. "Sims, you take Ricci's place. See if you two can get some suppressive gunfire on that goddamn meat-grinder."

"Will do, Sergeant," Foster obeyed. He began setting up the .30-caliber machine gun while Sims broke out a belt of ammo.

"Maybe we can out-flank that Kraut machine gun, Frank," said Hassler, crouched shoulder to shoulder with Sergeant Davis.

Davis pulled out his binoculars and scanned the terrain ahead. He saw a sand-bagged machine gun emplacement and about ten Germans. Three were manning the MG-42 machine gun and seven others were spread out around the loading station, taking cover behind a low brick wall. The lift was going up as the powered-winch was still in operation. Davis could see one maintenance tech in coveralls manning the controls. The Me-262 on the lift was about three-quarters up the mountainside and was steadily moving upward.

"All right, Hank," Davis replied. "Take Corporal Russell with you. Hustle around the left side of that gun emplacement and lob some grenades at it. We'll keep the Krauts busy—laying down suppressive fire. Got it?"

"Got it." Hassler pointed. "Okay, Russell—you're with me."

Russell nodded, slapping home a fresh magazine.

Once Foster and Sims had the .30-caliber machine gun set up, they began firing, Foster at the trigger, Sims feeding the ammo. A withering salvo of gunfire began to rain down on the Germans along with small arms fire from Sergeant Davis and the rest of the men. The Germans were hard-pressed to return fire and cowered fearfully between token retorts of gunfire. In the meantime, Hassler and Russell skulked around the left side of the machine gun emplacement, moving forward carefully and slowly, gradually gaining ground, darting from one makeshift defilade to the next, hiding behind parked vehicles, ducking behind stacks of crates, taking cover behind oil barrels, dashing left and right to confuse the enemy's aim, until they were less than thirty yards from the machine gun.

Hassler seized a grenade from his pouch and pulled the pin.

"Okay," he said to Russell, "Here goes!" He threw the grenade.

The grenade landed shy of the sandbags and exploded, ripping open some of them and partially collapsing the emplacement. An guard was killed, and another was wounded. But the MG-42 wasn't destroyed. And when the Germans realized they were being outflanked on the left side, they redirected their gunfire onto Hassler's and Russell's position. A storm of steel soon pummeled their area.

"That got their attention!" Russell exclaimed just as a pair of German "potato-masher" grenades came sailing through the air and landed next to them. Hassler alertly snatched one up and threw it back toward the Germans. Russell grabbed the other, and at the very moment he cocked his arm back to fling it, it exploded, taking off his right arm at the elbow and the right half of his face. Bits of shrapnel pelted Hassler, bloodying his shoulder and neck and bursting an eardrum as well. Russell screamed and collapsed to his knees, muttered something indiscernible, then expired after flopping over face down in the snow.

"J-Jesus Christ!" Hassler said with a sickened grimace, gazing at Russell's prostrate body, seeing his charred elbow socket smoldering and leaking blood. Hassler fingered his neck and shoulder, feeling the blood oozing out with each heartbeat, and figured his time in this world was just about up, too. He nodded, his ears ringing horribly, and smiled.

"Time to take out that machine gun, Hank," he said to himself.

And just as he was about to get up and storm that machine gun single-handedly, Corpsman Melvin Bryant was on him, holding him down by the shoulders, easing him to the snowy ground below.

"Easy now, Sergeant," said Bryant. "I gotcha. I'll have you patched up in a jiffy." He opened his medical kit and began administering first aid, opening a pack of sulfur, dusting Hassler's wounds.

"T-Thanks, Mel," Hassler replied, scarcely understanding Bryant's consoling words due to his ringing eardrums.

Meanwhile, Sergeant Davis and the rest of the men had moved forward and frontally assaulted the machine gun emplacement, finally silencing the SS-gunners, killing them whilst their remaining six comrades retreated into the tunnel leading to the personnel entrance. The tech working the controls of the winch went with them, leaving the winch on automatic which finally raised the shackled Me-262 to the peak of the mountainside. But once Davis got to the control booth of the winch, he shut it off. Then he tossed an H.E. grenade onto it and disabled it for good. The winch was certainly toast, but the German jet was atop the mountain now, stopped just shy of the docking platform, hanging in the breeze, stuck in limbo, unable to be off-loaded.

"Okay, men," Davis said. "Let's hope Captain Daemon's group shows up soon. In the meantime, we've got to get into that tunnel and flush out those Krauts. Reposition that machine gun!"

Foster and Sims obediently moved the .30-caliber and trained the barrel on the tunnel entrance while Davis carefully reconnoitered it, creeping up the left side, peering inside. He saw a concrete chamber dimly lit with wall-mounted electric light bulbs and the sliding metal doors of an electric service elevator. He didn't see or hear anything of the SS-guards who had just recently retreated into the chamber. And judging by the whirring sounds of the elevator, he figured they were already on their way up to the mountaintop. Davis lit a cigarette and went inside, looking around, taking a breather.

Outside, Corpsman Bryant was finishing up his work on Sergeant Hassler, who was up and on his feet now, breathing laboriously but still very much alive and able to carry on. He was ready for more action. Suddenly, the sounds of approaching vehicles sounded in their ears. Hell! Here come Krauts now, thought Bryant.

CHAPTER 15

B RIGADIER GENERAL Thaddeus Huxley Truscott, III, got up from his desk and donned his service cap. He was finished with his paperwork, finally, and now it was time to adjourn to the Officer's Club for a couple of drinks and a hearty meal. It had been another long day. Being the 5th Air Force Chief of Staff was a tough job sometimes, tougher than being a group commander. But Truscott was made of sterner stuff and he was up to the task. The war against Japan was going famously and American forces were pushing the Japanese back on all fronts. It was just a matter of time before the Japan capitulated. The fighters and bombers of the 5th Air Force were ranging far and wide these days, destroying the once mighty Japanese Navy and its air force, ship by ship, plane by plane. The Japanese Army was being systematically crushed as well, and its outdated fighters were routinely blasted from the sky.

Truscott could take comfort in the fact that he'd had a hand in that destruction. He'd helped destroy the Japanese war machine and the rewards of that destruction had been forthcoming in the form of promotions and decorations. He'd recently been awarded the Distinguished Service Medal by General MacArthur for all his hard work and perseverance. And soon, he might even see a second star grace his shoulder boards; General Kenny had hinted several times over the past few months that a promotion to Major General might be in his near future. That made Truscott smile. Going from Lt. Colonel to Major General in just four years time was quite remarkable if not unheard of. For nearly twenty-eight years now, he had served faithfully and honorable.

"General?" He heard his aide Staff Sergeant Stabler calling him.

"Yes, what is it, Sergeant?" Truscott replied, stepping into the antechamber where Stabler was standing by his desk.

"General Kenney just called. Says he wants you to stop by his office before you go over to the Officer's Club.

Truscott glanced at his watch. "At this hour?"

"Yes, sir."

"Well... That's unusual."

"He said it's urgent and that you should come over right away."

"Really?" Truscott's brow narrowed.

"Yes, sir." Stabler nodded. "That's what he said." Stabler cleared his throat. "Apparently, he got a teletype from London about an hour ago... something concerning you."

"A teletype? From London?" Truscott's eyes widened. "About me? What about? Did he say?"

"No, sir."

"Hmm." Truscott stroked his chin, wondering what it could be.

"Maybe it's about that promotion, sir?" Stabler suggested.

Truscott's eyes kindled. "Yes! That's what it is. General Kenney is going to promote me—to Major General. That's what it's all about." Truscott nodded spiritedly. "It must be!"

"What else could it be, sir?"

"Nothing!" Truscott waved. "Okay, I'm off. See you later."

Stabler saluted. "Congratulations in advance, sir."

"Thank you, Stabler."

Truscott slammed out of the antechamber and bounded down the steps of the operations building, and then headed over to General Kenney's office, which was in the Amp Building, corner of Queen and Edward Street. The prospect of another promotion certainly quickened his steps, making him giddy even. His heart was fluttering, too, at the prospect of receiving a higher commission, and at the behest of General Kenney himself. That was the greatest honor any officer could receive in this man's Air Corps. "Old bust 'em up George," as he was better known in the Pacific Theater, had recommended him for a promotion. It didn't get any better than this. Or did it? Maybe General Kenney's going to pin the Medal of Honor on me, Truscott thought.

"Hell yes, there is a God!"

Within a few short minutes, Truscott was standing in the anteroom of General Kenney's office. He gave his name to the female Army secretary on duty, a cute W.A.A.C. with bright eyes and the collar tabs of a 1st Lieutenant. It was a formality, really. For she knew General Truscott well enough by now, by his many office visits, and by his constant doting comments. She was quite a looker and Truscott was always very sweet on her.

"Go right in, General," she said with a big toothy grin. "He's been expecting you."

"Thank you, Beryl. Er, uh... Lieutenant Stevenson," Truscott replied, taking off his cap and smoothing back his graying hair.

He jerked the door open forcefully, as was his usual way, and entered the office. General Kenney was sitting behind his desk, smoking a cigarette, poring over a typed document. He looked up when Truscott came in, his thoughtful expression quickly switching to one of grim alertness. He laid down the document and gestured to an empty chair.

"Have a seat, Thad," he said. "This won't take long."

"Thank you, George." Truscott sat down and crossed his legs.

George C. Kenney was a 3-star general and commander of the Far East Air Force (F.E.A.F.), which included the 5th, 13th, and 7th Air Forces. Kenney initially enlisted as a flying cadet in the Aviation Section, U.S. Signal Corps in 1917, and then served on the Western Front with the 91st Aero Squadron. He was awarded the Silver Star, and the Distinguished Service Cross for actions in which he fought off six German fighters and shot down two. After the war ended, he participated in the Occupation of the Rhineland.

Returning to the United States, he flew reconnaissance missions along the border between the U.S. and Mexico during the Mexican Revolution. Eventually commissioned into the Regular Army in 1920, he attended the Air Corps Tactical School, and later became an instructor there. He was responsible for the acceptance of the Martin NBS-1 bombers built by Curtis, and test flew them. He also developed some techniques for mounting .30-caliber machine guns on the wings of a D.H.4 two-seater. In July 1942, he assumed command of the Allied Air Forces and 5th Air Force in the Southwest Pacific Area. Under Genral Kenney's command, the 5th Air Force developed innovative command structures, weapons, and tactics that reflected his orientation towards attack aviation. The new weapons and tactics won perhaps his greatest victory: the Battle of the Bismarck Sea in March 1943. The same battle in which Captain John J. Knight had been shot down and was later captured by the Japanese.

"I received this teletype from London an hour ago," General Kenney began, "And I am stunned by what it says."

Truscott uncrossed his legs. "Hmm?" he grunted. "What do you mean by... 'stunned by what it says'?"

"Well, to come straight to the point, Thad, it says that you knew about Captain John J. Knight's true identity."

Truscott laughed nervously. "W-What?"

"You heard me." Kenney leaned forward. "You knew Knight was a phony and a noncom impersonating an officer. You knew he had taken another man's identity (a dead man's identity) no less. Sergeant James Castillo was his real name, a man from West Texas, a man gone A.W.O.L. from his unit, the same man involved in a fatal car accident five years ago, the same accident in which Castillo assumed the identity of the real John J. Knight, a graduate of U.C.L.A. and a pilot cadet stationed at Kelly Field, San Antonio."

Truscott began sweating. "Well, uh... I um—"

"Furthermore," General Kenney pressed on, "You nurtured his career and built him up in the press, touting him as the first man to break Rickenbacker's Great War record of 26 kills. All the while knowing of his sordid past, and... illegal entry into the ranks of the Air Corps—the officer corps, mind you—and keeping it all a great big secret, Thad."

"That's ridiculous, George. Who cooked up this lie?"

"It's not ridiculous, and it's not a lie, and you know it."

"Let me see that!" Truscott demanded. "Who is making these outlandish accusations, god-damn it! I want to know."

"Here, take a look." Kenney handed Truscott the single-page document, stubbed out his cigarette, then leaned back in his chair. "It's all there in black and white. Countersigned by an Air Corps intelligence officer of the 8th Air Force. Read it and see."

"Yes, I'll read it all right!"

Truscott snatched the document out of Kenney's hand and sank back in his chair, scowling, muttering muted expletives.

He leaned forward, scowling bitterly, and read:

CLASSIFIED

(URGENT)

LONDON, 0730, 12 JANUARY 1945

FROM: MAJOR G.E. HICOCK (S-2) 479TH FG, 65th FW,
      VIII Fighter Command, 8TH Air Force.

TO: (EYES ONLY) GENERAL GEORGE C. KENNEY, (FEAF)
    SOUTHWEST PACIFIC AREA, BRISBANE, AUSTRALIA

CONCERNING: Capt. Nicklaus DAEMON (O.S.S.) a.k.a. (Capt.
            John J.KNIGHT) a.k.a.(Sgt.James CASTILLO)

General Kenney,

    It has come to my attention through careful investiga-
tion and examination of Air Corps records,that the OSS
officer known as Capt. Nicklaus Daemon is actually John
J. Knight (Jack),who beforehand was a sergeant known as
James Castillo. This information was inferred to me by
Knight's (Castillo) ex-wife, Rose McKavitt, presently
married to Col. David M. McKavitt, a 8th Air Force airman currently imprisoned in Germany. According to Mrs.
McKavitt, General Truscott, then a Colonel, knew about
Knight's true identity long before he became an acclaimed air ace, long before he challenged Rickenbacker's war record. Truscott purposely obfuscated the facts
and hid the truth about "Jack Knight" from the Air Corps
and the American public, and the press, claiming he did
it for the greater good of the country and for the war
effort. This cannot be overlooked by the Air Corps and
General Staff. A great falsehood has been perpetrated
and the guilty parties must be brought to justice. An
official investigation has been ordered by General Marshall and inquiries and hearings will commence shortly.

                              Sincerely Submitted
                          Maj. G.E. Hickok, (S-2)
                             Intelligence, 8th AF
                               479th FG,65th FW
                             Wattisham, England

When General Truscott finished reading the teletype, he laid it on General Kenney's desk, shaking his head, snorting implacably.

"So what," was his only answer.

"So what?" General Kenney replied, nonplussed.

"So what if I knew about Knight's past, hmm? So what if I promoted his career and built him up with the public and the press? The man was a first-class pilot and marksman. He was blasting the Japs out of the sky when no one else was, setting an example for those to follow. By the time I discovered his true identity, and the way he came about it, he was already a household name. He was all over the newspapers and newsreels if you recall? Well on his way to becoming an ace."

"True, but——"

"So I just went with it, George," Truscott waxed on. "I overlooked it and let it develop into something worthwhile."

"Something worthwhile? And what would that be?"

"George, It would have been very embarrassing for the Air Corps and the war effort, and for you, I have to say, not to mention myself and the rest of the General Staff. If Knight's story would've gone public at the height of his fame, then it would have been a messy and awkward backlash, staining the reputation of our great air service and its illustrious officer corps. The press would've had a field day with it. I just couldn't let that happen. Not at that time. Too much was at state."

"So you admit to the claims stated in that document?"

"I admit to encouraging a man's career. I admit to giving our armed forces a boost to its morale when it was at an all-time low. I acknowledge the fact that a man with humble beginnings can aspire to great things despite the credentialism and prejudice that besets our military establishment and our society. Sometimes these things have to be overlooked in order to succeed, especially during wartime. Sometimes men of lesser character and questionable background must be given a genuine chance to lead the way, especially those with exceptional skills."

General Kenney sat back in his chair and thought about that for a moment. In a strange way, Truscott was right. Exposing Knight at the height of his fame would have been an ugly scene, one that would have tainted the Air Corps waning reputation at that time.

Such a bombshell would have caused an ungodly uproar, something the service might not survive not to mention certain high-ranking officer's careers, his specifically. Truscott was correct in his efforts to promote a man's military exploits but wrong in trying to keep his past a secret. Such a thing should've been brought forth and dealt with at that time not kept hidden until it was too forgone and too damaging to reveal. Exposing John J. Knight's true self would have been an awkward and uncomfortable situation, one the high command or the government would not have tolerated, one that would have enacted serious repercussions. Truscott had not only saved face for himself but for the Air Corps, too, and perhaps the country as well. At a time when the Japanese were winning victory after victory, incurring one defeat after another, Jack Knight came soaring through the sky in his twin-tailed fighter scoring a multitude of aerial kills, defeating the enemies of the nation, winning honor for himself, and winning honor for his country. It was an odd duality of situations and events back then, but also a thing of necessity.

The "Texas Tornado" had blown through the Pacific Theater like an unstoppable typhoon, laying waste to the enemies of the good god-fearing people of the United States of America, giving them hope and promise for the future. As dirty and disreputable as Knight's past was, his salient fame and future represented the path the United States wanted to take—the path to total victory—no matter how it was achieved or who had to die in the process. Knight represented that image more than anyone else. Not all of America's heroes were clean-cut West Point graduates like Colonel David 'Mack' McKavitt. It was unbelievable, but sometimes they were just plain old homespun rakehells like Captain Jack Knight.

AS JACK and the rest of his little group emerged from the cover of two parked trucks, they heard the familiar sound of an American .30-caliber machine gun rattling away. And when they got closer to the sound, they saw the infamous field-gray uniforms of some fifty-plus SS-guards swarming around it and the loading area of the aircraft lift. And from what Jack could see, Sergeant Davis and his men had apparently taken and secured the aircraft lift and set up a defensive position. Two platoons of SS-guards were savagely assaulting them, coming at them from all sides. They wouldn't last long, he knew; he and his men would have to intervene swiftly or Davis and his group would soon be dead.

"Alright, fellers," said Jack. "We gotta git those dang Krauts off of Sergeant Davis and his bunch, and real quick-like."

"Okay, Captain," Justice replied, slapping a fresh clip in his B.A.R. "Just say when and where. I'm ready to kill some Krauts."

Jack grinned. "Okay, Sarge." He pointed. "Take Schmidt and Powell, and shuffle off to the left, over to that stack of crates, and wait fer my signal. Hays, Hentges, and myself will go up the right side, over to that little hut, and git set up. When we start firing—that's the signal—you, Powell, and Schmidt let 'em have it, okay? If'n we can outflank these bastards, maybe we can draw them off of Davis' position."

"Right." Justice nodded grimly.

Jack paused and looked each man in the eye.

"This is where we earn our pay, gents," he said. "This is what we signed up for. Make yer Ma and Pa proud. Make me proud, too. 'Cause you fellers are the best bunch of guys I've ever served with, no lying. If'n we all die, we die with our boots on, finger on the trigger, a sneer on our lips. Good luck. I'll see ya'll on the other side."

Justice couldn't help but smile. He had not liked Jack too much a few days ago. But that had all changed now. He had developed a queer sense of respect and admiration for the tough-talking Texan. Captain Daemon was right when he'd said he was not like any officer Justice ever served under. He possessed raw courage and the spirit of the devil himself; he was a man possessed with an unflinching approach to duty and a fearless killer to boot. He was unbelievable lucky, too, something Sergeant Justice had seen firsthand. Maybe Daemon was a madman, Justice thought. Maybe he was a first-rate lunatic. But lunatic or not, Captain Daemon was the man he'd follow anywhere now.

"Let's git to it," Jack ordered.

Justice, Powell and Schmidt peeled off smartly, scurrying over to the stacked crates, crouching as they went. Jack, Hentges and Hays, scampered over to the little concrete hut, which was actually a small power station for the elevator and aircraft lift. They hid under the lee of the hut's tiny gables, watching their quarry through squinted eyes. Jack stood at the head of that hidden queue of men, his left hand clutching a grenade, his arm poised and ready to throw, his jaw clamped shut, his heart drubbing steadily. He pulled the pin, leaned back, and threw.

"Open fire!" he shouted. "Shoot 'em up, men!"

Hays and Hentges opened fire on the Krauts, catching them totally unawares as they crouched behind their makeshift defilade of crates and parked vehicles. The grenade exploded near an idling Kübelwagen, killing the driver and wounding the officer crouching next it. And after Jack had tossed the grenade, he too, was blasting away with his grease- gun, gunning down three more SS-men as they tried to turn around and return fire. Justice and Powell had gotten into the act by then, hammering the stunned Germans from the other side, killing off a few more before they could take cover. But where could they go? Where could they hide? Because as soon as Davis and his men realized what was happening, they too opened fire, the .30-caliber machine gun cutting down a swath of SS-guards like a scythe cutting down stalks of wheat.

A few more grenades landed amidst the scrambling Krauts, scattering their guts and blood all over the dirty snow. And soon, they were dashing off, one by one, retreating back whence they came, almost half their numbers killed or wounded, their egos seriously bruised; it wasn't every day that elite SS-troops (be they just simple prison guards in this case) were forced to retreat, and then, begrudgingly, had to regroup further away. The officer wounded by the grenade blast was back on his feet, and miraculously, was returning fire with his pistol. He managed to tag Corporal Sims in the chest as he stood up to fetch another belt of ammo, stopping him where he stood. Bloodied and gasping for breath, he fell backwards into the sandbags and expired a second later. Foster dropped back, leaving the .30-caliber gun for lack of ammunition.

The SS-officer rallied his troops, and they slowly began to creep around the concrete hut trying to outflank Jack's position with their still superior numbers. A protracted firefight soon developed as both sides exchanged round after round, volley after volley. A few more Germans went down, but so did Corporal Hays, the young footballer from Georgia. He got hit when Jack ordered everyone to abandon their positions by the hut, flee to safer ground, ultimately linking up with Davis' beleaguered men. Hays lay there moaning and groaning, bleeding out on the icy ground as the fight went on around him. Corpsman Bryant watched helplessly, unable to get to him because of the gunfire. A minute later, Hays was silent and unmoving. Dead.

"YOU'RE WOUNDED, Herr Sturmbannführer!" exclaimed the SS-staff sergeant as he gazed at Dietrich's blood-stained tunic.

"A minor wound," Dietrich replied nervelessly. "Nothing that will slow me down, I assure you."

The SS-staff sergeant wasn't so sure about that. The left side of Dietrich's face was badly charred and his hair was singed. He had several blood spots on his tunic and arm sleeve where searing shrapnel had penetrated. His left hand was bleeding and twitching and blackened with powder stains. But he didn't seem to mind. If he was in pain, he did not show it. The SS-staff sergeant really wasn't surprised. Sturmbannführer Emil Dietrich was a tough soldier, the toughest there was, one decorated many times for his heroics on the Russian Front.

He had every medal the Third Reich could give, including its highest, the Knight's Cross with Swords and Oak Leaves. Dietrich had also earned umpteen wound badges over the course of his five-year combat career, first being wounded in the invasion of Poland, then again during the Battle of France in 1940. Two years later, he was seriously wounded during the siege of Stalingrad, and spent the next ten months in a hospital bed with a broken hip and two broken legs, when a building collapsed on him after a Russian T-34 tank shelled it.

Dietrich was lucky he survived, for no one else in his platoon had; he seemed indestructible. Indeed, more so than his old friend and driver Rottenführer Wenzel, who was now lying dead on the frozen earth. Wenzel had been with him since the beginning of the war and had suffered nearly as many wounds as Dietrich had—one that almost left him totally lame. After their last tour of duty, which saw them fighting at the Battle of Kursk, the greatest tank battle the war had yet seen, they were both wounded when their Tiger tank was knocked out by four Russian tanks. Then after a long convalescence, they were both retired from combat duty and permanently assigned to the *Totenkopfverbände Divsion* (the Death's Head Division), where they oversaw the transfer and deportation of Jews and other prisoners of war. It wasn't the most glamorous work but not the most dangerous either. Dietrich delved into his new duties with the same fervor and élan he had exhibited whilst in Waffen-SS. Needless to say, he always enjoyed his work.

"I'm afraid Wenzel is dead, sir," the SS-sergeant reported.

"Yes, I know," Dietrich replied, apparently unmoved by his old friend's death. Outwardly, he showed no signs of remorse, but inwardly, he was deeply saddened. Although he and Wenzel had almost been twenty years apart in age, and segregated by the levels of the rank-and-file and the officer corps, they had bonded affably and become good friends over the course of the war. Wenzel had fought in the Great War as a teen-aged infantryman and had won the Iron Cross, 1st Class during the Marne-Reims Offensive of June 1918. And he had fought in nearly every campaign the Waffen-SS had ever participated in and had earned plenty of medals, and plenty of war wounds. Now he lay dead in a virtually unknown production facility far from the tumult of the frontlines. Not the most honorable of places to die, Dietrich lamented. A hero's death should occur on a great battlefield not in some indiscriminate place deep inside the homeland. But, alas, Germany itself had become a battleground these days, and would surely see its borders invaded in the near future. He had no doubt about that; this little commando raid was just the beginning. Hopefully, not the beginning of the end.

"Once we dispatch these Ami commandos," he said. "We'll have a proper burial for Wenzel. One befitting a hero of the Reich."

The sergeant nodded glumly. There would be a burial for more than just one man, he thought. Dead bodies were everywhere.

"How many men are left?" Dietrich asked.

"Thirty-eight, counting you and I, sir."

"Hmm... Then we must wait for Hauptsturmführer Hengl's troops to arrive," Dietrich said, wiping the blood from his partially charred face with a handkerchief. "The Americans can't go anywhere right now. We have them boxed in. They may possess the high ground and a somewhat fortified position, but we will soon have half-tracks and armored cars to assault them with."

"Half-tracks and armored cars?" The staff sergeant returned, a bit nonplussed. "If we mount a full-scale assault with those things, sir, the infrastructure of the facility might be compromised. The destruction may render this place inoperable. I don't think the Reichsmarschall—"

"I don't give a damn what Reichsmarschall Goering thinks!" Dietrich snarled. "We must crush these Ami bastards, here and now!"

COLONEL MCKAVITT and the three O.S.S. men crept up to the corner of a building, the echos of nearby gunfire sounding in their ears. O.G. NEMISIS was certainly the cause of it, he realized. Those guys were really giving it to the Krauts, lock, stock and barrel. He also realized that if the SS-battalion from Berga arrived any time soon, those men would surely be overwhelmed and killed. He needed to let them know what was coming, but he also needed to free his fellow P.O.W.'s. Then McKavitt realized something else. A gang of recently liberated prisoners would make an excellent group of reinforcements. If he could get to the holding pens and free some of them, arm them, they might be able to overpower the SS-guards besieging the O.S.S. group before the SS-battalion arrived. Better yet, stop them at the gates before they ever entered the facility. Perhaps some kind of defense could be mounted with a few machine guns and some determined P.O.W.'s. It was a madcap idea, he knew, but one that just might work.

"Hey, Sergeant McDonald," he said as he paused at the corner, "is there an armory or munitions dump around he somewhere?"

"Yes, sir." McDonald nodded. "There's an armory next to the duty-shack near the main gate. What do you have in mind, sir?"

"If we can overpower the Krauts guarding the P.O.W.'s, which there aren't many of at this hour, maybe we can free some of my men and arm them." McKavitt nodded. "I'm sure there's still quite a few rifles and machine guns in that armory. We can use them to hold off that SS-battalion at the gates of this stinking place."

McDonald gazed at his two comrades, glaring, shaking his head. He sighed heavily and turned back to McKavitt, saying:

"Sir, that's a risky plan. That SS-battalion will be armed to the teeth. And if I know the SS, and I know them well, they'll be accompanied by a few more men—a tank brigade or regiment even."

"That might well be true, Sergeant," McKavitt returned. "But we have to do something. We can't let your men perish so helplessly, nor abandon my men, either. We've got to warn them and help them and a band of armed and angry P.O.W.'s might be their ticket out of here. We have to do something. We've got to try at least."

"We should stick to the original plan, sir, get you out of here while we still can. Rallying a bunch of war-weary P.O.W.'s against an elite SS-battalion is just nuts. It's downright stupid, sir. They'll be massacred, for sure. No doubt about it!"

"I'm not leaving without trying to do something. You can forget that. I'm going to do what I can for what it's worth."

"For what it's worth? You'll be killed, sir."

"That's a chance I'm willing to take, Sergeant."

The three O.S.S. men exchanged inexorable glances.

"You sure are a hard-charger, sir," Corporal Landers spoke up.

"Yeah, I suppose so. It's what's gotten me through this war, Corporal. Against the Japanese, and against the Germans." McKavitt nodded stolidly and added: "A famous French ace once said: 'If one hasn't given his all, then he has given nothing.'"

McDonald and his two comrades were at a loss for words. They just stood there in silence and contemplated that for a moment.

"C'mon, gentlemen," said McKavitt, slapping the magazine of the MP-40. "Let's get over to the holding pens and see what we can do. We don't have a lot of time." With that said, the determined Colonel darted from behind the corner of that windy building and dashed across the snow-covered ground to the cover of another. The three O.S.S. men followed closely, crouching and staying low as they could. McKavitt eventually led them back down the hillside to where the holding pens were, and hid behind a truck near the main gate. Just across from the pens were the armory and the duty hut.

From where McKavitt was hiding, he could see the P.O.W's standing around inside a large holding pen, and the few SS-guards guarding them; twelve guards in all. Nine were spread out evenly around the front perimeter of the barbwire fence. There were two guards manning a MG-42 machine gun up in a watchtower, overlooking the holding pen and front gate. And there appeared to be only one guard inside the duty shack at the moment. There was no one guarding the armory.

McKavitt quickly devised a plan.

"Okay, men," he said in a hushed voice. "Here's what we're going to do... First, we're going to take out those two Krauts up in that watchtower. Take them out before they can fire that machine gun."

"Ah-huh. And how do we do that, sir?" McDonald asked.

McKavitt turned to Edwards and Landers and gestured. "Which one of you guys shot that SS-guard right before Dietrich was about to plug me, huh? Which one of you is the sharpshooter?"

Edwards grinned. "That would be me, sir. I'm the one who shot the guard standing next to you."

"That was a hell of a shot, Edwards."

"Thank you, sir."

"Can you do it again?" McKavitt asked. "Can you hit those two guards up in that tower—from here?"

Edwards looked up at the tower. "Yeah, I think so."

"Good." McKavitt winked. "Don't miss, okay?"

"I won't, sir. I'll get them."

"Got any hand grenades, Landers?" McKavitt asked.

"Yes, sir. I do." He reached into his canvas pouch and pulled one out. "Where do you want me to throw it?"

McKavitt pointed. "Way the hell over there—on the other side of the fence, Landers. As far as you can throw it."

"Hmm? Why there, sir?"

"To create a diversion, that's why," Colonel McKavitt explained. "Once that thing goes off, all those nervy SS-guards are going to turn in that direction and wonder what the hell is going on. That's when you pop the two guards in the tower, Edwards. Right after that, Sergeant McDonald and I are going to dash over to the duty hut and toss a grenade inside. Then you and Landers start shooting up the guards one by one as they try to turn tail or return fire. By that time, McDonald and I will be at armory's doorstep ready to give supporting fire."

McDonald frowned. "Sir, with all those rounds going off everywhere, aren't you worried a few might hit the P.O.W.'s?"

"That's a chance I'll have to take," McKavitt answered.

"Really? I mean—"

"Look, Sergeant, once the shooting starts they'll most likely hit the deck and take cover on the ground. After so many months and years in a prison camp, they're a bit skiddish. They know when to get the hell out of harm's way, and in one great big hurry, too. So don't worry about them, okay? Those men know how to survive."

"Okay, sir. Whatever you say."

McKavitt glanced at his watch and then motioned to Edwards. "Go ahead and get set, Corporal—sight in one of those guards, and as soon as the grenade goes off, let him have it. Don't miss."

"Yes, sir. I'll get him." Edwards took the sling of his M1 carbine and wrapped it around his forearm, then took up a kneeling position behind the front fender of the truck, then took careful aim.

In the meantime, Landers readied the grenade, pulling the pin, setting himself up for a long throw. When Edwards and Landers were set and ready, McKavitt gave the signal.

Landers flung the grenade as hard and as far as he could—about 50 yards—and saw it land well on the other side of the tall barbed wire fence surrounding the facility, right in the middle of the road leading to the main gate. A second later, it exploded with a resounding blast. Every man jumped with a start, the P.O.W.'s flinging themselves to the ground, the SS-guards jerking to stiff attention, lurching towards the direction of the explosion—just as McKavitt said they would. Two shots were promptly fired, the first hitting one of the guards in the tower, upending him and causing him to fall out, the second shot hitting the other guard in the shoulder, spinning him off to the floor of the tower, not dead but seriously wounded.

McKavitt and McDonald were already dashing for the duty hut as all of that happened, McKavitt hammering a guard with the MP-40 as he stepped out of the opened door, McDonald rolling a grenade into the hut like a bowling ball. The guard doubled over, shot near to death, and then felt a concussive blast go off behind him, which catapulted him bodily across the snow-covered ground, head over heels. And by that time, McKavitt and McDonald were already at the armory's doorstep, turning about to give Landers and Edwards supportive fire. Two guards had been dropped by the time McKavitt turned his attention to them, Landers and Edwards each killing one. The remaining SS-guards turned tail and ran for the cover of the tower's tall, tree-like supports, but found little cover behind them. Two more fell to Edward's sharpshooting eye, four to McDonald's grease-gun. The last guard threw down his gun and surrendered, jerking his arms up high thereafter. As he stepped out from behind the tower's supports a shot rang out and hit him in the chest, right where his heart was. He fell backwards and landed flat on his backside, shot deader than a Thanksgiving turkey.

"Fucking SS!" Corporal Edwards was heard to say as he stepped from behind the Opel-Blitz truck. "I accept no form of surrender from those goddamn bastards."

McKavitt held back a smirk, gazing at the young O.S.S. noncom with somewhat amazed eyes, not thinking Edwards to be the cold-blooded killer that he was. And when the smoke finally cleared, some three-hundred-plus P.O.W.'s were standing on their feet, cheering, clapping, whistling, profoundly awed by the gunplay they'd just witnessed.

McDonald was awed, too. He couldn't believe the whole thing had gone down without one American casualty. And it all happened just as McKavitt said it would happen. Not one P.O.W. was hit and the SS-guards reacted just as he said they would. It was something short of a miracle, he thought. That son-of-a-bitch of an Air Corps Colonel knew exactly what he was doing the whole time. Maybe that's why he's a winner of the Medal of Honor. A fighter plane or not, this guy's a hard-charger, just like Corporal Landers had said.

"Okay, gentlemen," McKavitt declared, gesturing to the P.O.W.'s. "We'll have you guys out in a jiffy. Hang tight a moment while I find the keys to the holding pen."

He turned and went inside the duty hut, sidestepping a dead SS-guard that was laying on the floor. McKavitt suddenly realized, two Germans had been inside the duty hut, not one. Nevertheless, Mc-Donald's grenade had dispatched him along with the other, killing him where he stood as gazed out a side window, his piping hot cup of coffee now spilt all over the cold floor along with his blood. Even without the knowledge of that extra German, Colonel McKavitt's plan had worked out like a charm. A testament to his keen knowledge of warfare.

McKavitt swiftly found the keys to the holding pen and then freed his men, unlocking the iron padlocks, throwing the gates open, feeling a hundred-plus glad hands on his shoulders, seeing big smiles on the once grim-faced P.O.W.'s. And within a few minutes, many of them were arming themselves with German weapons, ready to fight again.

"Alright, men," McKavitt said. "Get ready for the fight of your lives. Some of us have to get over to the aircraft lift and help out our O.S.S. buddies. The rest of you have to stay here and get ready for the SS-battalion that's surely on its way over here."

There were a few grumbles amidst the cries of growing fervor.

"We're all airmen," McKavitt bellowed. "But we can still fight without our wings. We can show these Nazi bastards just what the U.S. Air Corps is capable of—in the air—and on the ground!"

With that stated, Colonel McKavitt rounded up his senior non-coms and filled them in on what was happening, telling them of the O.S.S. group, telling them of the impending arrival of the SS-battalion from Berga. The senior N.C.O.'s soon had the men organized into small groups, most of them armed with German machine pistols and rifles from the armory. There wasn't near enough to go around to arm every man individually. But those men unarmed set themselves to bolstering the front gate's defenses. They parked the truck right in front of the entrance, blocking it, then manned the MG-42 in the tower, two airmen on the gun itself, two others standing watch with German field glasses.

As all of that was happening, McKavitt took the three O.S.S. men and fifty P.O.W.'s, all armed with Mauser carbines, and headed over to the aircraft lift. There were shots still going off; he knew O.G. NEMESIS was still under attack by Dietrich's men. He knew they needed help, and they needed it fast. Time was running out on the whole operation, and the devil himself was on its way over to the Walpersberg in the form of a grinning death's head battalion—the infamous Waffen SS. No form of mercy would be given by those diabolical characters, McKavitt knew. He was hoping for another miracle. Would the gods of war see fit to bestow another one today? Would his courageous efforts be wasted on a fight that seemed doomed from the start? Was all of this for naught? What did fate have in store? Only the devil knew.

JACK RELOADED his grease-gun, slapping home a fresh 30-round magazine, and then fired off a six-round volley. German soldiers cowered fearfully behind a shot-up Stöwer 4x4 as the rounds ricocheted off the fenders and hood, sparking dully and clanging noisily. And once they had recovered from the volley, they returned fire in kind, causing Jack to duck down and take cover. Back and forth it went for so many minutes, each side retaliating sporadically, almost in a token manner.

"What now!" Justice hollered from his crouched position behind a stack of sandbags. "The Krauts have got us hemmed in good!"

Jack nodded knowingly. Indeed, what now, he thought? How could they get out from under this grim situation? Colonel Bruce's plan had not figured this situation into his plan of attack—the remnants of O.G. NEMESIS boxed in and cut off from any outside help. He needed some kind of miracle, and he needed it right now.

"Hang tight, Sarge!" Knight yelled back. "I'm thinkin' on it."

"Well, you better think fast, sir! Those Krauts are bound to be reinforced any minute now. We can't hold them off forever."

Davis had to agree. "What's the plan, Captain? Where do we go from here? We gotta do something. This place is surely going to be crawling with every Kraut outfit within ten miles of this place."

Jack, who was standing next to Sergeant Davis, smiled crookedly as an idea blossomed in his brain. "Yer going to lead the men back to that truck over yonder," he pointed, "back where you came from, while me and Sergeant Justice hold off the Krauts with that German meat-grinder and his B.A.R. We'll toss over a few grenades here and there, too, to keep 'em real busy. That outta give you guys plenty of time to get over there and then high-tale it out of here."

"And what about you and Justice, sir?" Davis replied, "What are you two going to do? Stay back and get slaughtered? Once the Krauts figure out what's happening, they're going to storm this position and murder you guys like there's no tomorrow."

"Nah," Jack returned coolly. "Once you guys are in the clear, Justice and I are gonna hotfoot it over to that elevator and go to the top of the mountain. There's still three jets up there we haven't knocked out." He smiled. "I came here to do a job, Sergeant, and I aim to finish it. And I cain't leave until it's all over and done with."

"Ah, Jeez!" Davis scoffed. "Spare me the hero bullshit, will you, sir? It's time to bug out, now—all of us—or we're all going to deader than a Christmas goose on Christmas day. There's at least six guards up there, that I know of, and probably a few more. You might kill one or two but the rest will get you. Then the others will come up after you and really grind your blood and guts into snow. You'll die a horrible death, sir. The SS is fucking merciless!"

"I know, Sergeant," Jack replied. "But I never planned on leaving here alive in the first place. This is Jack Knight's last stand. This is where he gets to meet his maker—or dance with the devil—whichever one is his fate. But either way, he's dying today."

Davis's brow narrowed. "Who the heck is *Jack Knight?* What are you talking about, sir?"

Jack shook his head. "Nothing. Nobody. It's a long story. One we ain't got time to chew the fat over." He clapped Davis on the shoulder. "Alright now, tell the fellas to get ready to fall back. In the meantime, I'll inform Justice of our plan. Then we'll start layin' down some heavy firepower so you and the men can git outta here."

"You're crazy, you know that, sir?"

"Yeah, I know. Crazier than a wild Injun."

Jack scurried away, crouching behind the cover of the low brick wall as he went, heading over to Justice's position. Sergeant Hassler, who had been standing nearby and had heard Jack's strange affirmation, knelt down next to Davis and sighed wearily.

"That guy is one strange character," he said to Davis. "A real piece of work, he is. I wonder what his story is?"

"Who the hell knows?" Davis replied. "We've all got a good one, I guess. That's why we joined the O.S.S. Right?"

"Yeah, I guess so."

Jack reached Justice's position after a series of tentative steps, drawing fire from the SS-men who saw him scampering behind the wall, causing him to pause his progress here and there. The Germans seemed to getting bolder by the second. Jack realized they would soon come storming over and attempt an all out assault. He and Justice had to get set and ready before that happened.

"Listen up, Sarge," Jack said as he hunkered down near the ex-Marine's side. "Here's what we're gonna do." Jack quickly explained the details of his proposed plan to Sergeant Justice in a breathless dialogue steeped with plenty of his trademark West Texas twang. Justice wanted to protest, make a fuss about it, but instead, he just grinned, half-laughing, half-grumbling, then nodded.

"Sure, Captain," he said. "Whatever you say."

"We're gonna lay down so much hellfire, Sarge, these Krauts are gonna think they died and went to hell," Jack quipped. "Then we're gonna get our tail-ends up the mountainside and finish this."

Jack laid his grease-gun own and seized a belt of 7.92-millimeter bullets from a German ammo box and darted over to the MG-42. He handily loaded the Kraut machine gun and then cocked it, getting it ready for some bloody work. Justice reloaded his B.A.R. and took up a position, kneeling near Jack, and readied himself for the all-out gunfight. Once Jack was set, he took aim, and fired.

That was the signal for Davis and the rest of the men. They peeled off one by one, quietly scurrying away as Jack and Justice laid down a hellish stream of gunfire, one so intense that the Germans had no choice but to stay right where they were or risk getting shot and killed. It was a beastly display of firepower and it gave the men plenty of time to make their getaway. But one man stayed, defying Sergeant Davis' direct order to pull out. He was not going to be left out and miss the greatest firefight of his entire career.

"Here, sir, let me help you with that thing," said Sergeant Hank Hassler, a pair of ammo belts draped around his shoulders, a third clenched in his blood-stained hands.

"Hassler?" Jack said, blasting off a burst. "What the heck are you doin' here? Yer were supposed to fall back with the others."

"Nothing doing, sir," Hassler protested as he grabbed hold of Jack's empty belt of ammo and fed it more steadily into the bolt. "I'm not going anywhere while there's still some fun to be had."

Justice shook his head, more amused than disgusted. How in the world had he ended up with the two most fanatical soldiers in all the O.S.S., he wanted to know? How had he allowed himself to be taken in by their reckless bravado and hellbent heroics? Suddenly, visions of Guadalcanal began to replay themselves in his mind, visions of swarming Japanese soldiers surging ahead in a ludicrous banzai charge complete with war cries and bayonets. Well, these ain't the stinking Japs we're fighting today, he said to himself. These are the Germans, the elite Waffen SS, merciless bastards. O Lord help us!

Meanwhile, Sergeant Frank Davis, Corpsman Bryant, Sparky Powell, Sergeant Hentges, Corporal Schmidt, and Foster, made their getaway, dashing back to the Opel-Blitz in which they'd arrived.

CHAPTER 16

HANS MULTHOPP gasped frightfully as he stared down the windswept mountainside. *"Lieber Gott!* What on earth is going on down there?" He heard machine gun fire and explosions going off with some unsettling frequency. A full-scale battle was raging down below and it made him very anxious. His anxiety didn't concern his personal safety, but the safety of his jet fighter, his precious little *"Huckebein,"* the Focke-Wulf Ta-183.

"A fanatical band of American commandos has infiltrated our defenses," explained the SS-corporal standing beside him. "But they will soon be crushed once our reinforcements arrive."

"And when will that be?" Multhopp asked.

"Within a half-hour, I should think?"

"A half-hour?" a voice rumbled behind them. It was the chief engineer from the Messerschmitt company, Herr Bölkow The same man who had berated Herr Multhopp and his jet fighter only days ago. He stalked up and gazed over the guardrail and shook his head. "No!" he exclaimed. "That will not be soon enough. Those commandos will come up here soon and continue their bloody work."

"We are prepared for them, sir," replied the SS-corporal.

"I hope you are. Beforehand, my jet fighter will most assuredly leave this mountaintop facility with or without a Luftwaffe pilot."

Herr Multhopp's brow arched perplexedly. "Oh? And how will that happen? Will you fly that jet fighter out of here yourself?"

"No, you idiot!" Herr Bölkow snapped. "One of my men is a qualified pilot. He will fly it."

"You mean Anton Kuppinger?" Herr Multhopp questioned.

"*Ja!* He is a licensed test pilot—with over fifty hours on the Me-262." Herr Bölkow sneered. "More so than any current Luftwaffe pilot, I daresay. He is preparing to fly out as we speak."

"Oh," Herr Multhopp replied, nonplussed.

"And who will fly your machine out when the time comes?" the SS-corporal asked Herr Multhopp.

Herr Multhopp pushed his glasses up the bridge of his nose and cleared his throat awkwardly. "Um... I-I will, of course."

"You?" Herr Bölkow burst out laughing. "Oh my, that's rich! Hilarious! Are you even qualified to fly, Herr Multhopp?"

"I am. I designed and built my machine, and I can fly it, too. My pilot's license is as current as any man's on this mountaintop."

"*Quatsch!*" Herr Bölkow scoffed. "That contraption you call a fighter plane is a deathtrap, Herr Multhopp. You will kill yourself in that thing. Of that, I am sure."

"I think not, sir. It is the easiest plane in the world to fly."

Herr Multhopp wasn't bragging when he said that. According to the test pilot at Rechlin who flew the Ta-183 on its maiden flight, he said it was the most delightful plane he'd ever flown. It was light on the controls and exceedingly responsive to the pilot's every whim. He had no doubt in his mind he could fly it. His only worry was taking off from the Walpersberg's shortened runway. But the takeoff-assist rockets would solve that problem. The only trouble was, he'd never used such devices before. He was a little bit apprehensive.

"Well, good luck with that, Herr Multhopp," Herr Bölkow intoned rather spiteful. "You're will need it." He about-faced and stalked off, laughing, shaking his head.

"Can you really fly your own machine, sir?" asked the SS-corporal, a concerned look on his face.

"Of course I can." Herr Multhopp nodded. "Nothing to it."

He paced off smartly, leaving the SS-corporal standing slack-jawed at the guardrail heading for the operations hut, determined to fly his jet off the Walpersberg himself. The only way to get anything done properly, he told himself, was to do it yourself. Something he'd always been accustomed to doing, and this situation would be no different from the rest.

At the far end of the runway, a Me-262 stood on its tricycle landing gear, its twin Jumo engines still whining with subdued power. It was fully warmed-up now and ready for flight, perhaps even running a little hot at this point. The Luftwaffe pilots had never shown up, so, the Messerschmitt engineers decided that one of them would fly it to Lechfeld themselves. Though the temperature was well below freezing that day, the risk of the twin-turbojet engines overheating was still very high. If the Me-262 did not takeoff within the next ten minutes, there would be a danger of engine damage, or worse, an engine fire The J-2 aviation fuel used by the Jumo turbojets was highly combustible, and the danger of a volatile engine fire was always a serious prospect in the takeoff procedure. The engines had to be run up slowly as to not overheat them or cause them to catch fire. Sometimes, they just blew up. This was the one thing that irked Luftwaffe pilots the most. The Me-262 could not get airborne in a hurry during an interception alert. It was an agonizing several minutes for a pilot sitting in the cockpit of a Me-262, sitting on the runway, carefully easing the throttles up to full power, watching the temperature gauges steadily rise to the red zone.

Herr Multhopp entered the operations hut and announced his intentions to his fellow engineers, much to their astonishment.

"What?" said one, gasping. *"You* are going to fly it?"

"That's right," Herr Multhopp replied confidently. "Those commandos will be up here any minute. They will attempt to destroy our prized jet fighter. We cannot let that happen. We must—I must —fly the Ta-183 to Lechfeld myself, or all of our hard work and labor will have been wasted. Help me get into my flight suit, will you? We must hurry or all will be lost."

The Focke-Wulf engineers glared at one another, eyes aghast with disbelief, jaws limp with doubt. They could hardly believe what Herr Multhopp was proposing to do: fly a basically untested fighter jet off a short mountaintop runway under the pressure of an imminent Allied attack. It was a bold thing to do if not foolhardy. But there was really no other alternative. It had to be done, and it had to be done immediately.

"C'mon, you slugs!" Herr Multhopp barked. "Move with some purpose, *ja?* Let's get to the Ta-183 and prep it for flight."

The engineers bolted into action. Time was of the essence now.

STURMBANNFÜHRER Emil Dietrich gazed through his field glasses and studied the American's defensive position. He could only see gunfire coming from one place—the sandbagged MG-42. And from what he could see, only three men seemed to be manning the gun. The other positions that had only moments ago been so alive with gunfire, were now strangely silent. Dietrich suspected some of the Americans must have either been killed off or had retreated—most likely the latter. That would explain the sudden and heavy gunfire coming from the machine gun. The three Americans were laying down a heavy barrage of fire so their fellow comrades could make a hasty retreat, withdrawing to safer ground. Or more likely, attempting to flee the facility altogether.

"How many men do we have left now, Oberscharführer?" Dietrich asked the SS-staff sergeant kneeling nearby.

"Thirty-five, sir."

"Aha." Dietrich nodded, gesturing with his Walther. "Plenty of men to storm that machine gun, I'd say."

"Will we not wait for Hengl's men, sir? Our reinforcements?"

"No. We will attack now. We can't wait any longer. We must dispatch those *Amis* right now. They're considerably thinned out."

"So I see."

"All right, let's get ready."

"Yes, sir. How shall we proceed with the assault?"

"Take a squad of men and try to outflank the left side," said Dietrich. "I'll lead another squad and try to outflank the right side. The rest of the men will give supporting fire from the center. A bombardment of hand grenades ought to add to the mayhem coming from the center. If we time this right, Oberscharführer, we can overwhelm the Americans without heavy casualties."

"Hmm. I hope you're right about that."

"Okay, pass the word then. Get your men into position. We'll make our assault in five minutes." Dietrich glanced at his wristwatch. "At zero-nine-forty-five, we go, Oberscharführer."

The sergeant nodded. He turned to one of his subordinates, a private, and gave him orders to notify all the men of the assault. The private then crawled away and began telling the men to get ready.

Within a couple of minutes, all the SS-men were informed of the assault and were shuffling into position. Ten men would accompany Dietrich and assault the right side, whilst the SS-staff sergeant and his eight men would assault the left. The remaining fifteen men took up defensive positions near the center, facing the Americans and the MG-42 machine gun, ready to lob some grenades and give their comrades supporting fire. When the first hand grenades were thrown, that's when the attack would commence.

Dietrich crouched on one knee, a fully loaded MP-40 machine pistol in his bloody and charred hands, his Walther sidearm tucked firmly in his holster armed with eight 9-millimeter rounds. In turn, each man behind him was also armed with an MP-40 and some form of sidearm or grenade. About fifty yards away, the SS-staff sergeant and his men waited on bent knees and were similar armed to the teeth. All were ready for the two-pronged attack. Then, at exactly 09:45 hours, the first grenades were tossed followed by a blistering barrage of machine pistol gunfire. The fusillade of fire was a frightening spectacle to behold.

"ANGRIFF!" Dietrich shouted as he leaped up and dashed across open ground, his MP-40 rattling off a fiery burst, his men spilling out behind him. The SS-staff sergeant and his men were up and running too, spreading out over the snowy ground and running hard for the sandbag fortification and its barking machine gun. Several were hit and instantly killed as the stream of bullets from the MG-42 found them. The others just kept on coming, running and returning fire with their machine pistols. Dietrich's assault drew a similar salvo of fire as the American firing the big B.A.R. cut loose with a wicked series of bursts, the distinctive bark of that .30-caliber automatic rifle echoing stridently as it also found its mark. Two SS-men were hit and killed, a third was wounded in the arm, and he fell limp and bleeding on the snow, his comrades leaping over his prostrate body screaming and hollering their curses as they charged on ahead.

Fiery gunfire crisscrossed the snowy turf as both sides discharged their weapons, the Germans getting ever closer to their proposed destination, their ranks thinning alarmingly as they went, the Americans keeping the pressure on them with a savage volley of machine gun fire. And before long, the SS-men were within arm's reach of their quarry...

"HERE THEY COME!" Sergeant Justice shouted as he emptied his clip into a trio of storming SS-men. "Get ready to vacate this position and fall back to the tunnel."

Hank Hassler let go of the ammo belt and drew his 7-inch commando dagger from the leather sheath fixed to his belt and growled.

"Let 'em come," he rejoined. "I'll cut those bastards to pieces!"

"Okay, fellers," Jack declared as he finished the last belt of 7.92-millimeter ammo, sending a few more Krauts off to Valhalla. "It's been nice knowing ya!"

He drew his High Standard silencer and turned away for the tunnel entrance and elevator, leaping over a pile of fallen sandbags running as fast as his tired legs could carry him. Sergeant Justice was right behind him his B.A.R. firmly clenched in his cold and clammy hands, running as fast as he could go. But Hassler was not running with them. He had decided to stay and fight it out with the Germans, having no desire to take off running in his weak and wounded state. This would be his last stand, his last battle—his last hoorah.

A moment later, the SS-men were piling into the sandbag fortification, their machine pistols rattling savagely, their mouths spewing hateful curses. Hassler slashed one across the throat as he came at him, then felt a burst of gunfire burning through his backside as another SS-shot him from behind. Hassler grunted painfully as those bullets tore through him and stole his breath, spilled his blood, then stopped his heart. Yet, in one last ditch effort, scarcely clinging to the final threads of his life, he plunged the dagger into the neck of another SS-man and stabbed him to death. Both men pitched over in stiff heaps and expired a second later, one on top of the other, Hassler still holding his dagger, the German staring blankly at the sky. Sergeant Hassler was dead, finally, but so were two more SS-men.

By that time, Jack and Sergeant Justice were at the tunnel entrance, and Dietrich and his remaining men were close behind them. Justice paused at the entrance and reloaded his B.A.R. He would hold off the Germans so his C.O. could get into the elevator and go up to the top and finish the mission finally.

"Okay, sir," he said, half-laughing. "I'll see you when I see you —in hell, I reckon?"

"Yup. See ya there, Sarge." Jack waved a little salute and darted into the tunnel entrance and to the elevator's double-doors.

Sergeant Justice shook his head grimly. "I knew that sorry son-of-a-bitch would get me killed one day. I just knew it. Oh, well, Bob," he said to himself. "How long do you want to live, anyway?"

A double-burst from the B.A.R. took out two more Krauts as they approached Justice. Then he felt the vicious sting of a 9-millimeter slug slam into his shoulder, then into his chest, then lastly into his skull, his dimming red eyes scarcely seeing the man who'd shot him. Those fading, bloodshot orbs saw a blond and slender, half-burnt, half-monster of a man in a bloody SS-uniform, the barrel of his smoking sidearm pointed directly at him. Then he saw nothing. And somewhere in the recesses of his dying mind, he heard the opening chords of the Marine Corps Hymn... and he knew he was homeward bound, finally.

The SS-officer, Emil Dietrich, reloaded his Walther sidearm as he stepped over Justice's dead body. Then he went inside the tunnel entrance, one of his remaining men still at his side, and looked around quietly. He saw no one. He did see that the elevator was on its way down, its green and red service lights blinking in the downward position. Suddenly, a muffled double-blip sounded from a darkened recess of the tunnel entrance. The SS-man gasped and doubled over as a pair of .22-caliber silenced rounds tore through him, then fell to the ground, dead. Dietrich spun around and triggered a round from his Walther, shooting into the shadows, then felt a searing hot bullet graze his rib cage as another silenced bullet erupted from the shadows. He grimaced and staggered, almost losing his balance.

"You dirty bastard!" he grated. "Why don't you come out of the shadows and fight me like a man!"

"I sure enough will," came the edgy, uttered drawl. "I'm outta bullets, anyway." That sly affirmation was accompanied by a left-hook so forceful that it knocked Dietrich to the ground. He lost his grip of the Walther and dropped it, then saw it go spinning off into the shadows as a size-twelve Cochran jump boot kicked it away. He shortly saw the man who'd kicked it, the lanky American officer who'd been manning the MG-42 only moments before. "C'mon, *mein Herr*. Let's rumble!"

Dietrich rasped his jaw where that wicked left-hook had landed and groaned, shaking his head jerkily, trying to shake off the cobwebs. He felt the taste of blood in his mouth as one of his back molars came loose. He got up slowly and spat, ejecting the molar in a spate of blood.

"So you want to fight, *ja?*" said Dietrich, raising his arms in a boxer's-like stance, clenching his fists tightly.

"Yeah!" Jack replied. "Let's see what yer made of Kraut."

Dietrich threw a right jab that missed, then felt a left uppercut strike his ribs, right where the bullet had grazed him. He gasped painfully and dropped to a knee, right as a booted foot kicked him across the face, busting his lip and bloodying his nose, knocking him flat on his back. Dietrich growled and hopped up. He wiped the dribbling blood from his ugly, burnt countenance with the sleeve of his uniform, and lunged forward, grappling Jack with clumsy arms.

"You wanna wrassle or you wanna to fight?" Jack quipped.

He shoved Dietrich backwards and threw another punch that narrowly missed. Dietrich retaliated with a right jab that hit Jack on his chin, snapping his head to one side. The lanky Texan grimaced and stepped back, then danced forward and landed a two-punch combination that made the SS-officer stagger backwards. Dietrich regrouped and fired off a quick salvo of fists that caught Jack in the mid-section, doubling him over, then felt a hard right hit him on the cheekbone as Jack answered in kind. By that time, the elevator had come down its double-doors sliding open with a metallic clang.

Jack reared back and landed a wicked haymaker that spun Dietrich off into the direction of the elevator, causing him to stumble badly. And just as he tried to regain his balance, he saw the American leap forward and tackle him, sending both men crashing into the elevator's back wall. As they both struggled upwards, clawing at each other's face, trying to choke one another, the elevator buckled mechanically, feeling the weight of two bodies on its steel hydraulic platform, and both doors promptly shut tight. At about that time, four of Dietrich's men arrived on the scene but they were too late to intervene. Up went the elevator, the sounds of a violent struggle going on inside of it, two men determined to kill one another with just their bare hands and their wits, two wounded men almost at the limit of their physical strength.

Jack pummeled Dietrich with a left and a right, then another left and another right. But his right hand was hurting so badly from his gunshot wound that it didn't have much effect on the bleeding and half-burnt SS-officer. Dietrich's ribs were hurting terribly where he had been grazed by the .22-caliber bullet, and his charred face was still stinging from the grenade blast, yet he fought on like a man possessed. But his strength was fading fast, too, and he knew it. There was nothing in that snug 8-by-10 foot box of an elevator to use as a weapon. Only bare hands and determination, the latter of which was quickly diminishing in both men with every heartbeat. Even so, both men fought on as the elevator progressively made its way up the 1,000-foot elevator shaft, punching, kicking, jabbing, pounding, biting even. At some point during the violent struggle, Jack realized the man he was fighting was the infamous Sturmbannführer Dietrich, commander of the SS Guard Battalion and a highly decorated officer, the man Colonel Bruce had warned him about, and the very man Jack had vowed to kill personally.

WHEN COLONEL McKavitt and his ragged band of P.O.W.'s finally arrived on the scene, the battle was already over. He did find a multitude of dead bodies everywhere, most of them German, and he found a few Americans among the dead, too. There were still a few SS-guards lingering about, five men who were just emerging from the tunnel entrance when the fifty-plus gang of prisoners including three O.S.S. men showed up. The five battle-wearied SS-men wisely threw down their weapons and surrendered when they saw the angry band of armed P.O.W.'s coming toward them. And shortly, after a quick interrogation, Colonel McKavitt learned of the pitched battle and the miraculous escape of one O.S.S. officer. The guards also told McKavitt that he was being pursued by their commander Sturmbannführer Dietrich, and that both men had gone up the elevator together, fighting each other furiously. McKavitt quickly formulated a plan of action.

"Okay, gentlemen," he said to the three O.S.S. men, "We're going up after them, see if we can help your officer out in some way. That Dietrich character is one nasty son-of-a-bitch, and he'll stop at nothing to accomplish his evil tasks."

"Well, Captain Daemon is an S.O.B himself, sir," said McDonald. "He'll be in perfect company with that bastard, I guarantee it."

"Hmm, he sounds like the devil himself," McKavitt replied.

"Oh, yeah. He's a devil all right, sir. No one meaner than him."

McKavitt turned to the throng of P.O.W.'s, gesturing.

"Okay, men" he said. "The rest of you police up these weapons and spare ammo. We're going to need all of it if we are to hold off the coming attack. In the meantime, Sergeant McDonald, myself, and his men are going to the top of the Walpersberg and see if we can find Dietrich and the O.S.S. officer. And when I find Dietrich, I gonna kill that goddamn bastard myself—if he's not already dead."

The men cheered lustfully at the sound of that gritty declaration. Then they all dutifully spread out and began picking up the leftover weaponry, prying MP-40's and Mauser carbines from cold dead German hands. Soon, they had a few more automatic machine pistols and rifles to share with their buddies, including an MG-42 machine gun and an American .30-caliber machine gun, sans the required ammo. Meanwhile, Colonel McKavitt and the three O.S.S. men made their way over to the tunnel entrance and elevator shaft, hoping to get up to the top and stop Dietrich and help the O.S.S. officer if they could. McKavitt had a personal score to settle with the monstrous SS-officer, avenging the death of Sergeant Major Boggs chief among the many slights and infractions perpetrated by the evil Sturmbannführer Dietrich. The Air Corps Colonel only hoped Dietrich would still be alive when he finally found him. Because this Captain Daemon fellow sounded like a hellish bastard himself, like someone he once knew a long time ago.

THE MESSERSCHMITT engineer Anton Kuppinger eased his slender frame into the Me-262 cockpit, attired in a padded fight suit and leather flight cap, ready to fly the twin-engined jet off the mountaintop. He was an accomplished test pilot as well as a mechanical engineer, and he probably knew better than anyone else how to fly a Me-262 jet fighter. And not far from him and his idling jet, Hans Multhopp was getting ready to climb into his prized jet fighter and fly it out as well. He was bedecked in a special pressurized flying suit, one especially designed for the high-flying Ta-183, designed by himself, no less. He was a good pilot, but nothing compared to the experienced Anton Kuppinger.

Multhopp felt a bit apprehensive, to say the least, having flown his prototype jet fighter only once before, several months ago at the Rechlin Test Facility in front of a small group of RLM onlookers that included Hermann Goering and Albert Speer, the latter the acclaimed architect and now new director of all German armament production. The test flight went well and Goering and Speer were suitably impressed. But the Ta-183 he was about to fly was a slightly different model than the one flown at Rechlin (much lighter and much faster) and armed to the teeth with four fully-loaded 30-millimeter cannons, the latter something Multhopp had insisted upon. Anything to get a leg up on his Messerschmitt competitors, he had told his small group of engineers. A flight-ready and fully armed Ta-183 would put the RLM staffers on notice, making them realize that his feisty little *"Huckebein"* was the fastest jet fighter in all the world, and the best armed.

"Okay, Herr Multhopp," said the Focke-Wulf flight mechanic. "She's all fueled up and ready for flying.

"E-Excellent," Herr Multhopp managed to say without sounding too nervous. "As soon as the Me-262 takes off, I will taxi the Ta-183 to the runway, and I will take off."

"Remember to go easy on the throttle during rev-up, sir," warned the flight mechanic. "And don't forget to toggle the takeoff-assist rockets once you've acquired maximum thrust."

"Ja, Ja, I'll remember."

"Because if you don't, well... You know what will happen."

"I-Indeed." Herr Multhopp gulped nervously.

With the HeS-011 turbojet whining in his ears, Herr Multhopp donned his flight cap, and then put a gloved hand on the removable entry ladder and clambered up to the cockpit. He glanced over the Ta-183 as he did this, quickly noticing the black German cross and swastika insignia painted on the fuselage and tail assembly. Somehow, that little crooked cross on the vertical stabilizer looked perfectly ominous and foreboding—sinister was a better description. It suddenly dawned on him that he'd designed and built a machine for Adolf Hitler and the Nazi regime, constructed a machine designed to shoot down American bombers and kill their airmen, and do it as swiftly and efficiently as possible; its four 30-millimeter cannons were downright murderous.

He threw a leg over the cockpit coaming and got into the cockpit, settling uneasily into the padded seat, feeling the bulky parachute pack pressing uncomfortably against his spine. It was a tight fit. He had not designed the cockpit of the Ta-183 to accommodate a pilot using the standard German parachute pack. Herr Multhopp and his team had been working on an ejection seat, of sorts, something far more functional and compact. However, the bureaucrats at RLM balked at the idea, saying it was too expensive and too time consuming to reconfigure the Ta-183's tiny cockpit. They wanted Herr Multhopp's speedy *Huckebein* rolling off the assembly lines no later than May 8th, and to hold up production for something as untried and untested as an ejection seat was unimportant at the time. The pilots would just have to make do were their exact words.

As the flight mechanic strapped him into the cockpit, two men suddenly came bursting through the wooden door of the steel-girded elevator shack, tumbling head over heels into the snow, grappling one another in a furious battle of fisticuffs. Herr Multhopp instantly recognized Sturmbannführer Dietrich's slender, blond-headed countenance and SS-uniform. The other man, dressed in a Luftwaffe uniform, he did not recognize. Was he one of the pilots tasked to fly the jets to Lechfeld Air Base? And why was Dietrich fighting with him? Ach! This is taking service rivalries a little too far, Multhopp thought. This is absurd! What on earth is going on here?

That "Luftwaffe pilot," none other than Captain Nicklaus Daemon of the O.S.S. (better known as Jack Knight) jumped up and slugged Dietrich across the jaw so hard that he literally broke it, knocking out two more teeth and sending the dazed SS-officer tumbling backwards into the snow almost knocked out unconscious. The SS-men who had fled Sergeant Davis's earlier assault quickly appeared on the scene, machine pistols drawn and ready, yet quite unprepared with what they found. There lay the infamous Sturmbannführer Dietrich on his backside, bloody and burned, and hovering over him, a Luftwaffe Major of questionable identity. And in their brief moment of indecision, Jack made his move. He calmly walked over to one of the SS-men and rattled off something in German, smirking, then struck like lightening.

Before anyone could react, he stripped the MP-40 from the dumbfounded German's hands and fired off a long volley that killed all six men where they stood. It was a lurid sight to behold, and one that put the entire mountaintop on notice. Herr Multhopp saw it, his engineers saw it, the Messerschmitt people saw it—and so did Anton Kuppinger. He wisely engaged the throttles of the twin Jumo turbojets and then released the Me-262's wheel brakes a moment later. The jet began rolling down the runway, slowly at first, but then more rapidly as it gained speed. When Kuppinger toggled the take-off-assist rockets, it lifted off the ground. That's when Jack realized what was going on. "Dang it!" he cursed. "That jet is gettin' away."

He saw it rise into the air, its rockets burning brightly, lifting the heavy twin-engined jet fighter into the atmosphere and off the top of the Walpersberg. Jack grit his teeth, annoyed with himself.

"S-So you h-have failed," he heard Dietrich's voice muttering in the background. "As I k-knew you w-would." He laughed weakly having just enough strength left to intone some bitter sarcasm.

Jack huffed, having had enough of the man's evil ways and caustic commentary. He turned and walked over to Dietrich, re-cocked the MP-40, aimed it straight at his face—and fired. Only one round came out, Jack having spent the other twenty-nine cartridges on the six SS-guards. But it was enough. Dietrich's head exploded in a ugly blob of blood and brains, and he was silenced forever, finally.

"Shut the hell up, you!" Jack quipped as he pulled the trigger, then threw the empty MP-40 on the ground. As he turned for the other jet which was now revving up on the hardstand, he saw the Me-262 disappear into the clouds above, heard its powerful engines swiftly carrying it away. Jack was irked to no end. He had not fulfilled all his mission objectives, and he was almost angry himself. Almost. Then an idea lit inside his devilish brain, an idea so preposterous, one so hair-brained, that it just might work. He drew his empty High Standard silencer, determined to commandeer that odd-looking jet plane, bluff his way into the cockpit, and chase down that Me-262 and destroy it somehow, perhaps by ramming it, if need be, sacrificing himself in the process. Well, he'd had no illusions of surviving this operation, anyway. If he had to die today what better way than in the cockpit of a fast jet fighter. It was his heaven-sent destiny. Or was it sent straight from hell?

Herr Multhopp glared at the man pacing toward him, suddenly having a sick feeling in the pit of his stomach. He saw the drawn pistol and the dead SS-men behind him, and he knew that this man meant business. Was he really a Luftwaffe pilot? How could a member of the German air force be so ruthless and so cold-blooded, gunning down seven fellow countrymen, even if they were from the hated SS? This man was not a Luftwaffe pilot, Multhopp adroitly deduced. He probably wasn't even German. So who was he, then? He was about to find out.

"Guten Morgen," said Jack as he halted in front of the idling Ta-183, staring at it with eyes full of wonder. *"Wie geht es Ihnen?"*

Herr Multhopp and his gathered engineers stared blankly at the lanky man in the Luftwaffe uniform not knowing what to say or do.

So, here is Germany's latest wonder weapon, eh? Jack said to himself. A snub-nosed little fighter with swept-back wings and a turbojet engine. Right nice looking thing, it is. Fast too, I bet!

Jack looked around at the assembled men gawking at him, noticing none of them were armed or looked the least bit threatening. He smiled and motioned to Herr Multhopp, waving the pistol, acting as if it was still fully loaded and that he intended to use it if had to.

"Komm raus, mein Herr," Jack ordered. *"Schnell!"*

Multhopp took a nervous little breath and pointed to himself.

"Yes, you! Come down from there. I will take it from here. I will fly this jet to where it needs to go," Jack said in near perfect German. He was really proud of himself; he'd learned to speak the language and was keen to use it whenever he could, especially in situations like this, and with people like this. Jack had a special admiration for aeronautical engineers. They designed and built the machines that enabled him to soar above clouds and be free of earthly restraints and restrictions. Jack never felt freer in all his life than time spent flying an airplane, be it prop-driven or jet-propelled. And today would be the highlight of his flying career; today he would soar higher than ever before; today he would pierce the heavens and touch the face of the gods.

Herr Multhopp removed his flight cap and stood up in the cockpit seat. He hesitated a moment, then got out, then climbed down the entry ladder, his heart beating madly in his chest, his face burning red-hot.

"Wait just a damn minute!" the flight mechanic protested. "Who in the hell do you think you are? You can't just waltz over here and take over! What is your name, damn you! Who are you?"

Jack grinned. "Some folks call me Captain Nicklaus Daemon of the O.S.S. Some folks know me as John J. Knight, the high-flying fighter ace. And a few people might know me as Sergeant James Castillo, a poor little old nobody from West Texas. Some have even called me the Devil himself. But you can call me—Jack. The greatest fighter pilot in all the world, and the luckiest man alive."

"You are an American fighter pilot?" Multhopp asked, glaring at the tall, swarthy man in the Luftwaffe jerkin and flying cap, noticing the cuts and bruises on his face and the blood on his hands. He also saw the jagged scar across the left side of his face and realized this man was definitely a war veteran. The name John J. Knight even sounded familiar to him. Somewhere in the past he had heard the name before. Where, he could not remember. But he knew it meant something, and he knew this man was an experienced pilot. He could just sense it.

"Jawohl, mein Herr," Jack drawled. "So if you'll excuse me for being so rude, I have a plane to catch." He put a booted foot on the first rung of the entry ladder and winked.

"Hold on a minute!" the mechanic protested. "You can't—"

"Nah, nah," Herr Multhopp intervened. "This man is a seasoned pilot and he will fly the Ta-183 to Lechfeld Air Base. Let him do his job, will you please?" He motioned to the mechanic. "Strap him in, Johann. This officer has my permission to fly my jet fighter."

The mechanic blinked incredulously wondering if his boss had totally lost his marbles. This man had just mercilessly slaughtered seven SS-men, including the much-hated Sturmbannführer Dietrich. Now he was going to be allowed to fly Herr Multhopp's acclaimed Ta-183 jet fighter? He wasn't even a real Luftwaffe pilot; he wasn't even German, for heaven's sake! This was madness! Unbelievable! Unprecedented! But it was happening. The man, whoever he was, was going to fly Herr Multhopp's prized little *Huckebein* today.

"Lechfeld Air Base, eh?" Jack replied staring at the sky. "Down south from here a piece?"

Herr Multhopp nodded. *"Ja.* There is a map in the cockpit. It is not far from here. You will find it quite easily, I'm sure."

"I surely will." Jack climbed a rung, paused, and then asked: "Say, *mein Herr?* What's your name, by the way?"

The bespectacled engineer jerked a nod. "Hans Multhopp, at your service... chief engineer and designer of this fine machine—the Ta-183A 'Huckebein' the fastest fighter plane ever built."

Jack smiled. "The *Huckebein,* eh? I like it. I like it a lot." Then he added, nodding keenly: "Nice to meet you, Hans. You've got a right nice little ship here. I'll take care of her, don't you worry."

Herr Multhopp unstrapped his parachute pack and offered it to Jack. "Here, you might need this—Jack."

Jack shook his head. "Don't need it. Not where I'm going."

The determined fighter pilot from West Texas climbed the remaining rungs of the ladder and got into the cockpit. The flight mechanic reluctantly strapped him in, thereafter, muttering implacably under his breath. Then he filled Jack in on all the takeoff procedures, warning him of over-accelerating the engine, and telling him about the takeoff rockets and where to toggle them. Jack glanced over the instrument panel noting the various gauges and dials and saw nothing unusual except that everything was written in German and was marked in metric units. Nothing he couldn't interpret or figure out. In fact, the Ta-183's cockpit and instrument panel seemed rather simplistic for such a modern jet aircraft. Nothing compared to his old mount the P-38 Lightning.

The mechanic kept rattling off in German and pointing out the various controls and gauges of the Ta-183, so much so, that Jack had to wave him off, saying: *"Ja, Ja, mein Herr!* I get it, I get it. I know how to fly a plane, okay? Hop off now. Let me git going, will ya?"

The mechanic climbed down, huffing and puffing, annoyed to no end. He hastily removed the entry ladder and then slapped the nose of the Ta-183, scowling bitterly. *"Los! Hau ab!"*

Everyone stepped back as Jack closed the bubble canopy. Then he eased the throttle up a few notches and pulled away from the hardstand, taxiing slowly to the end of the runway. He flashed the thumbs-up signal to Herr Multhopp as he went, grinning like a little kid on Christmas Day. Multhopp saw it and he returned the thumbs-up gesture, also grinning like a little kid, not the least bit worried that he had just handed over his greatest achievement to an enemy combatant. He knew the man was a great pilot, whoever he was.

Indeed. Whoever he was, American or German, pilot or soldier, devil or daredevil, he was truly an extraordinary man. There was no doubt in Hans Multhopp's mind at that moment. This Jack Knight fellow was the only man who could fly his wondrous little *Huckebein*. He was indeed a man of true genius, raw courage and common sense. Yes, Hans, such men really do exist, he told himself. The world is not just full of stupid fools. There are still a few men with some honor. Heroes still walk the earth. Some of them even fly!

COLONEL MCKAVITT and the three O.S.S. men exited the elevator, kicking open the door of the steel-girded shack that sheltered it and spilled out onto the snowy windswept mountaintop. McKavitt was amazed with what he saw. The Germans had basically built an airstrip on top of the Walpersberg, complete with hangars, hardstands and an operations hut. He also saw the bloodied bodies of seven SS-men lying in the snow, one of them in a very familiar uniform. He walked over to the dead body and swiftly recognized it as Dietrich's, the man he'd vowed to kill for murdering Sergeant Major Boggs. But somebody had beat him to it. The murderous SS-officer lay sprawled out in the snow, his head nearly blown off. Only the faintest remnants of blond hair and the distinctive collar tabs of a Waffen SS-Major let McKavitt know it was really Sturmbannführer Dietrich laying there before him.

Then the high-pitched whine of a turbojet engine caught his attention. He spun around and saw a queer looking airplane pulling up to the runway, apparently getting ready for takeoff. McKavitt didn't recognize the jet, thinking at first it was some kind of modified Me-262 design. But as he got a closer look, he realized this jet was one of the Nazis more advanced designs, not a Me-262 at all.

It only had one engine and it was smaller and more streamlined. It had a distinctive T-tail and narrow sweptback wings. The nose was had a bifurcated air intake, designed to induct air into its gas-guzzling turbojet engine. It was an odd-looking machine but nonetheless unique. McKavitt was awed as much as he was upset. This airplane was a quantum leap in jet design, and if the Nazis were producing something as advanced as this, then the airmen of the U.S. Air Corps were in for a really bad time. He started running.

"C'mon, Sergeant!" McKavitt said, re-cocking his MP-40, running faster. "We gotta stop that thing before it takes off!"

"Stop it?" Sergeant McDonald replied, mystified. "How are we going to to that, sir?"

"I don't know exactly. But we've got to try something!"

All three ran hard for the revving jet fighter, taking potshots at it as they ran. When they approached the huddled gang of German mechanics and engineers standing around watching the jet as it started it takeoff run, McKavitt paused and caught his breath. The Germans were glaring at him wide-eyed and angry, one man especially. It was Hans Multhopp, and he was incensed that someone was trying to shoot up his precious jet fighter.

"Gott!" he exclaimed. *"Was machs du? Verrückt kerl!"* The bespectacled engineer grabbed the barrel of McKavitt's machine pistol and forced it down, causing it to discharge into the ground.

"Goddamn you!" McKavitt cursed. He reared back and hit Multhopp with the butt of the gun, knocking him to the ground. The other engineers and mechanics rallied around Multhopp, protecting him, lunging at the Americans as the chief mechanic hefted Herr Multhopp up from the snowy ground, scowling evilly at McKavitt.

Corporal Edwards was on a bent knee, taking aim at the jet which was now rolling down the runway. Landers fired, slowly at first, then more quickly as the jet roared by, its takeoff-rockets lit and burning furiously, lifting it off the short-paved runway. As the Ta-183 zoomed by, Colonel McKavitt got a good look at the pilot sitting in the cockpit. He gasped unbelievably as the pilot waved back at him, evincing a churlish grin that McKavitt had seen so many times before in the past; a grin so unforgettable that McKavitt thought he was dreaming it now.

"My God, that looks like...but it can't be? How in the world?"

"Holy cow! That's Captain Daemon, sir," said Sergeant McDonald. "The officer I was telling you about? He's flying the plane!"

"What?" Landers held his fire a moment. "How in the—"

"Nah, Nah!" Multhopp interjected. "That is John J. Knight, the American fighter ace. I remember reading about him a long time ago. He was one of America's greatest aces. One of its first heroes."

"Jack Knight, here?" McKavitt uttered bewildered. "But how?"

CHAPTER 17

12 JANUARY 1945
FRIDAY, 1030 HOURS
ALEXANDRA'S MILITARY HOSPITAL

ROSE MCKAVITT sat upright in the wheelchair, leaning forward as she wheeled herself closer to the window. She had just finished her therapy and had adjourned to her usual spot in the recreation ward of the hospital. She really wanted another cigarette but had refrained from smoking one, thinking about her unborn baby. She actually had a whole pack of Players, compliments of Ian Stewart, the kindly hospital steward. But she realized she had to think about the future, thinking about bringing a healthy baby into this world, then raising it up properly, because her life was no longer her own to forsake on such vices like smoking and drinking. She had a family to think about now, not just her baby, but of husband David, too. Rose had to be strong and healthy when he returned whenever that was. She didn't dare think about him not returning at war's end; she had convinced herself that he would return, there could be no other outcome.

Her husband Colonel David M. McKavitt, a P.O.W. in Germany, would return once the hostilities were concluded. Rose sighed. And when would that be, she thought. When would the war be over? According to the newspapers that was still a long way off. The Germans were still fighting hard and not giving up. Every city and town was being defended like it was the last. Allied soldiers were still dying in unsettling numbers. But the war was slowly moving toward German territory. Soon, said the reporters of the press, the war would be fought on German soil. With three Allied armies advancing from the west and the Russians looming in the east, Germany's days were numbered. These were the last days of the Third Reich.

"Mrs. McKavitt," Rose heard a hospital nurse sounding in her ears, jarring her from her dispirited reverie. "You have visitors."

"Visitors?" Rose replied, turning head away from the window.

"Yes, ma'am. Two officers of the U. S. Army Air Corps."

Rose wheeled her wheelchair around. "The Air Corps?"

"Yes, ma'am. A General Warlick and a Major Hickok, here to visit you. Will you see them, ma'am? Are you feeling up to it?"

"A-Aye... I am," Rose replied. "Please, show them in"

"Right away, Mrs. McKavitt."

The nurse turned away and strode to the door. A moment later, the two Air Corps officers appeared, General Warlick puffing one of his odious coronas, his cap under his arm, Major Hickok clutching an envelope in his right hand. General Warlick paused in front of Rose, smiling, his ruddy complexion beaming playfully. The Major stopped beside him, bowing his head, a serious look on his face.

"Ah, General Warlick and Major Hickok," said Rose. "To what do I owe this auspicious pleasure, hmm?"

"Mrs. McKavitt," General Warlick rumbled. "How are you?"

"Fine, thank you. And you?"

"Doing well, better than I deserve."

"And you, Major Hickok. What brings you to Alexander's Military Hospital again so soon?"

"Morning, Mrs. McKavitt," replied Major Hickok, removing his cap and smoothing down his black hair. "Well, I have some interesting news to relay to you.... and this envelope to deliver."

"Oh? An envelope, you say?"

"Yes, ma'am. A letter, I believe. From a... Captain Nicklaus Daemon, O.S.S." Hickok presented the yellowed envelope to Rose.

Rose stiffened, then leaned forward and took the envelope from the Major's hand. She glanced at the writing on the front, reading the return address and postmark. She made a puzzled little face.

"Why, this is from... France? Isn't it?"

"Yes, ma'am. It is. From O.S.S. Headquarters, Paris, in fact."

"Is that where Jack—I mean—Captain Daemon is now?"

"Well, he was. But he's been sent on a mission to Germany, we think? The O.S.S. is not very forthcoming with information—"

"What Major Hickok is trying to say Mrs. McKavitt," General Warlick interjected gruffly. "Is those sons-of-bitches at the O.S.S.

won't give out any information. Their goings-on are classified and top secret, so they say. It's all a load of bullshit if you ask me."

"But they sent this envelope," Major Hickok explained. "My intelligence people intercepted it when they saw your name typed on it. Since we last spoke, Mrs. McKavitt, I've investigated your ex-husband John J. Knight. I've also checked up on General Truscott, too. Seems what you told me was all true. There was a cover-up. Truscott hid the fact that 'Sergeant James Castillo' took John J. Knight's identity after a fatal car crash in Texas, then passed himself off as an officer and completed his advanced flight training at Kelly Field. He was then sent to the Pacific Theater, thereafter, to the 35th Fighter Group, to be exact, and the rest is history, as they say."

"Yes, Major," Rose replied. "I sort of knew about all that already. What I want to know is: how did Jack—Captain Daemon—get into the Army again, the O.S.S., specifically? How was he allowed to serve again when his past was so out in the open? Didn't the Army and the Air Corps know about him when he returned from that Japanese P.O.W. camp? Would he have been dealt with then? I mean, really, air hero or not, Jack stole someone's identity then passed himself off as an officer. Isn't that against Army regulations? Shouldn't he punished, or arrested, or something?"

"Yes, he should have," General Warlick answered, his corona waving about insistently. "As it turns out Mrs. McKavitt, General Truscott once again hid Jack's identity after he miraculously returned from that Japanese prison camp, stealing a Jap Zero fighter and flying it all the way to Saipan, no less—that's where our Navy was at that time. Right gutsy of him, I'd say. But still not exonerating enough for Truscott to do what he did, afterwards."

"What did he do, General?"

"He hid the fact that Jack had returned. The Air Corps was never the wiser as it turned out."

"And how was that even possible?"

"Because when Jack was fished out of the sea by an American destroyer, after being shot down," Major Hickok threw in, "he was wearing a Japanese uniform and had no dog tags. Because of that and his swarthy appearance, they assumed him to be a Jap officer. Then he was sent to the Navy Hospital at Pearl Harbor for treatment of his wounds."

"His wounds?"

"Yes, ma'am. He'd been shot in the shoulder, not a serious wound, but a wound nonetheless. He also suffered a terrible concussion when he crashed into the sea, breaking his arm as well. Banged up his face badly, too, I understand. And on top of all that, he was suffering from amnesia."

"Amnesia?"

"That's right. When he hit his head on the dash panel of that Jap Zero, he blacked out and lost his memory for a while. He had no clue as to who he was. And neither did the doctors at Navy Hospital. He was being held as an enemy combatant until his identity could be verified. He finally did snap out of it, though."

"And that's when Truscott showed up, aye?" Rose surmised.

"Precisely." Major Hickok nodded. "In fear of his sordid involvement in Jack's big charade, Truscott had him transferred to the O.S.S. where he could be trained as a secret agent and given a new identity. It seems General Donovan and Truscott are old friends. Anyway, to keep his name clear of any shenanigans, Truscott kept Jack's return on the quiet, taking custody of him and keeping his name out of the reports somehow until he had him packed off to the O.S.S. where he could disappear once again."

"I wouldn't put it past Truscott, that old bastard."

"Well, as it turns out, Jack is an exemplary agent, indestructible as fate would have it. When he got to France for his next mission, he sent you this. It's a letter, and there's a copy of his last-will-and-testament in it, too. He lists you as the—"

"You opened my mail, Major?" Rose rejoined.

"Well, yes, I did. As an Air Corps Intelligence officer, it's—"

"Oh, spare us the fucking bullshit, Major," General Warlick interrupted crudely. "We know it's your job to do that. Just get on with the explanation already, okay?"

"Uh, yes, sir." Hickok cleared his throat. "Captain Daemon (Jack), lists you as the recipient of his Army life insurance, ma'am."

"What?" Rose gasped, stunned.

"That's right, Mrs. McKavitt," General Warlick interceded. "If Captain Daemon—Jack Knight, I mean—gets killed in action, you'll be the recipient of $10, 00 dollars."

"$10, 00 dollars?" Rose's eye's widened, then misted over.

"Yes, ma'am," Major Hickok affirmed. "Since Jack has no next of kin, no family, no brothers, no sisters, he listed you as the life insurance policy's recipient. Payable only to you, his ex-wife."

"But, but... I was never really his ex-wife, Major. I had the marriage annulled a month after he was shot down and captured. After I learnt the ugly truth about him from General Truscott. How—what, I mean..." Rose trailed off there, tears starting to fill her eyes.

"That doesn't really matter according to the U.S. Army Personnel Department. You're still listed as his legal wife. The records were never updated, apparently. Even after you got remarried."

"So am I bigamist according to U.S. Army Personnel?"

"Technically," General Warlick imparted. "But it won't affect the outcome of the life insurance payments... the *income* is what's important." He smirked, realizing he'd made a clever joke.

Major Hickok rolled his eyes. "The policy was written before anyone knew the truth, Mrs. McKavitt. I suspect Jack knew about Army Personnel's little gaff, that's why he had it made out to you. I guess he felt he was still married to you. Well, on paper, anyway."

Rose's tears were in full spate now. She tried to hide her face with her hands, but she couldn't hide the fact she was upset, deeply moved was a better description. Now she felt terrible for rejecting Jack. He'd come to her that day and apologized for all he had done. But Rose was still hurt, and wouldn't accept his apology, or the roses he'd brought her. She left them to lay there in the dust of the windowsill, in the settling dust of a grand apology, in the wake of a terrible lie, one that had left them both feeling dejected and hurt. But Jack hadn't given up, she realized. He had gone on and marked her down as his own, still his wife, and the recipient of quite a healthy sum of money (if he died in combat), money that would be badly needed in the coming months. It was really too much for her, and she sobbed uncontrollably, hands over her face, her head bent low, tears streaming down her reddening face.

"If it's any conciliation, Mrs. McKavitt," said General Warlick. "The War Department has ordered a full investigation into all of this. General Truscott's commanding officer has been notified, so has General MacArthur and General Marshall. They'll get it sorted out eventually, rest assured. Jack's past will no longer haunt you, ma'am." The General puffed his corona gesturing placatingly.

Rose kept on crying, barely hearing any of that.

"All right, Major," said General Warlick, shaking his head. "Let's go. She's in no condition to hear anymore. Let's get back to the base and proceed with our special interdiction mission. We're done here."

"Yes, sir." Major Hickok donned his cap. "Goodbye, Mrs. McKavitt. We'll be back again, I'm sure." He waved.

Rose cried even louder, totally distraught now.

"Jesus H. Christ!" General Warlick imprecated bitterly as he and Major Hickok walked away. "Some women just can't handle the truth. My wife's the same goddamn way."

"Yeah," Hickok replied. "And what an awful truth to bear."

SERGEANT DAVIS and the rest of his men motored down the slushy roadway heading for the west gate of the REIMAHG facility. It was a secondary entrance into the facility, mainly used for maintenance and supply vehicles—a kind of service entrance for the Walpersberg complex. It would be sparsely guarded at this hour, Davis hoped. With all the alarms going off and the whole place on high alert, he was banking on the fact that there would be very few or no guards at all manning the west gate. He was sadly mistaken. For when the Opel-Blitz truck finally reached the gate, a squad of SS-guards were waiting for him and his men. The guards immediately opened fire when the 3-ton truck came rumbling toward the barbwire and wood-framed gate, blasting it with their MP-40 machine pistols and their Mauser carbines. A half-track equipped with a MG-42 also contributed to the gunfire.

"Goddamn it!" Sergeant Davis cursed as gassed the truck, intending to crash straight through the gate. "Hang on, gents! We're busting out of this stinking place!"

As he steered the 3-ton truck on a direct path towards the gate, a blistering volley of 7.92-millimeter rounds came smashing through the windshield, shattering it, killing Sparky Powell instantly, who was sitting next to him and wounding Sergeant Davis in the shoulder. Davis lost control of the truck when the front-left tire burst after being hit, causing the 3-ton Opel-Blitz to skid sideways and then flip over onto its side, crashing with a bone-jarring thud. Dazed and badly shaken by the upending crash, Corpsman Melvin Bryant, Sergeant Hentges, Corporal Schmidt, and Tech-5 Foster emerged from the back of the truck slowly, their grease-guns flaring in retort.

The eight SS-guards were killed in the ensuing firefight but not before Davis and Foster were shot dead; Frank Davis died shortly after he crawled from the cab of the wrecked truck, getting hit multiple times in the chest and arms whilst he tried to scramble for cover. Foster got it thereafter when a grenade went off nearby him, the searing shrapnel punching through his young, twenty-year-old body multiple times. And when the smoke finally cleared, only Hentges, Schmidt and Bryant remained. The three men swiftly mounted the six-ton German half-track and smashed through the west gate and then headed south for the rendezvous point at Saalfeld. The Lockheed C-40 transport plane was due to land at dusk, and they wanted to make damn sure they were there when it arrived. No one had to tell them twice what would happen to them if they didn't make it on time. Their job was done—finally.

HAUPTMANN HENGL got an unpleasant surprise when he and his men finally arrived at the gates of the REIMAHG facility. As his small convoy of three heavy armored cars and four six-ton half-tracks approached the gates via the main road, a withering salvo of machine gun fire and small arms fire assaulted them. An Opel-Blitz truck blocked the main entrance into the facility, forcing his battalion to dismount and take cover in the shoulders and ditches of the road. He ordered the armored car commanders to blast the truck out of the way with their 50-millimeter guns, but they only set it afire, inadvertently creating an impassable flaming burning roadblock.

McKavitt had descended the mountaintop by then, returning to the front gate after witnessing a very strange event. The man in the odd-looking jet fighter was unquestionably Jack Knight, he had no doubts about that. How he had escaped from that Jap P.O.W. camp was a mystery to him. But he didn't have time to contemplate it.

At the moment, he had to lead a life or death defense with a ragtag force of American, Russian, Poles and Czechs. Armed only with light machine pistols and rifles and one MG-42, the P.O.W.'s fought the assaulting SS-battalion with the verve and tenacity of a seasoned combat unit, even though most of them were just simple airmen.

"We can't hold them off forever, sir," Sergeant McDonald said to Colonel McKavitt as he crouched behind a pile of debris. "They're bound to break through. We should retreat to—"

"Retreat to where, Sergeant? We're boxed up in here like dogs in a dog pound. There's no place we can go where the Krauts won't find us. We have to stand and fight, right here and now."

"We could retreat through the west gate, Colonel," Landers suggested. "Then make our way to Saalfeld and rendezvous with the transport plane."

"Nothing doing, Corporal," McKavitt replied. "I'm staying here with these men and fight it out with the Germans."

"That's fucking insane, sir!" McDonald shot back. "We'll all be killed, massacred, slaughtered! Those Krauts over there aren't just plain old Waffen SS. They're part of the *Totenkopfverbände Division*—that's the Death's Head Division, in plain English. They're bloody merciless killers and they'll stop at nothing to wipe us out."

"C'mon, sir," Landers urged. "Let's get the hell out of here,"

"No!" McKavitt snapped. "I've made my decision, gentlemen. We stand and fight. Retreat if want to—but I'm staying."

Sergeant McDonald grit his teeth. This officer was one gung-ho son-of-a-bitch, and a real pain in the ass, too! McDonald's job had not only been to reconnoiter the REIMAHG facility for O.G. NEMESIS, but to find and extricate Colonel David McKavitt, the pride of the 8th Air Force and a Medal of Honor winner. When R.A.F. Group Captain Hawker had notified a British intelligence agent inside Germany, via a homemade transmitter, that McKavitt had been singled out by the SS for being Jewish and was sent to the Walpersberg for laborious work details, the Brits contacted the U.S. Air Corps, who in turn contacted the O.S.S., and a rescue mission was rapidly planned. Now that the Jedburgh team had found him and was ready to evacuate him to safer environs, he was refusing to go. McDonald was outraged and bitter.

The watchtower suddenly erupted in a fiery explosion, killing the two P.O.W.'s manning the MG-42 as one of the armored cars turned its turret gun on it and fired a 50-millimeter shell, blasting the two men to kingdom come and destroying the machine gun. Then at Hengl's order, two half-tracks rumbled forward and began pushing the smoldering truck out of the way, swiftly upending it and tearing open part of the barbed wire fence. Another armored car turned its gun onto the gate itself and blasted it apart with two well-aimed shots, and shortly, there was a smoldering jagged hole where two wire and wood-framed gates once stood. And then from the rear of the column came the ominous sound of heavy metallic tracks. Two 50-ton Panther tanks rumbled forward, their twin machine guns spewing hot lead in every direction, their big 75-millimeter cannons blasting away knots of fleeing P.O.W.'s, scattering their limbs and innards to the four winds.

"Oh, Jesus!" McDonald moaned when he saw the two big German battle tanks rolling forward. "Our goose is cooked now."

"Yeah, I think you're right, Sergeant," Colonel McKavitt reluctantly agreed. "We can't fight those damn things."

"Time to retreat, eh, sir?" Corporal Edwards threw in.

"Time to retreat, Corporal."

But Colonel McKavitt didn't have to give that order. The lightly armed P.O.W.'s were already falling back, retreating into the facility, running away as fast as they could. The sudden appearance of the two tanks was enough to make most of the men flee, especially the Poles and Czechs. Some Russians lingered but not for long. A few of them were ex-tank crewmen, and they had seen the fearsome Panther tanks in action before and were not intimidated by them. But when they came smashing through the front gate, they too fled.

McKavitt and the three O.S.S. men ran from their covered position as the tanks rumbled forward. They were followed in by heavily armed SS-troops, each one equipped with a 7.92-millimeter StG-44 assault rifle, grenades, and long daggers. They even brought in a flamethrower. It looked hopeless for the P.O.W.'s. But then something miraculous happened. A reprieve was issued by the gods in the form of twenty tank-busting Thunderbolts. The thunderous P-47's fighter-bombers roared down from the clouds and hammered the two tanks, destroying them in short order with their triple-tubed rocket launchers. The 4.5-inch rocket projectiles practically blasted the turrets right off the tanks' chassis and left nothing but flaming hulks of steel. The P-47's eight .50-caliber machine guns also scattered the SS-troops in all directions with repeated strafing attacks, readily thwarting Hauptmann Hengl's assault and laying waste to a whole battalion of elite German soldiers. Colonel McKavitt and the three O.S.S. men stood by, watching in wide-eyed wonderment, seeing the Thunderbolts do their bloody work, wondering how they knew the Krauts were assaulting the facility whilst a ragged band of P.O.W.'s tried to defend it. McKavitt had his suspicions, and he had plenty of time to contemplate it aboard the C-40 transport plane, hours later, as he and six other O.S.S. men and four P.O.W's flew back to France, and to freedom. A certain Air Corps intelligence officer and a red-haired General came to mind. However, it was really Group Captain Hawker he had to thank for his miraculous escape.

JACK GUIDED the sleek, swept-winged jet through pervading overcast grinning like a gargoyle atop a church cloister, seeing the airspeed indicator registering an incredible 964 kph—599 mph! Herr Multhopp's Ta-183 really was the fastest plane in the world. And it truly was light on the controls; Jack couldn't resist putting it through its paces. He performed a few snap-rolls, corkscrews, a power-climbing Immelmann, and a couple of loops before he set the screaming little *Huckebein* on a direct course for Lechfeld Air Base, which was about 180 miles south of Kahla. It truly felt as if angels were pushing it, and he soon caught sight of the twin, turbo-jet-engine Me-262; it was cruising at 20,000 feet, just above the milky overcast. Jack eased the throttle to maximum power and felt the Ta-183 thunder forward, getting closer to the "slower" Me-262. When he got within a 100 yards from it, he saw it waggle its wings, the pilot evidently thinking it was Herr Multhopp at the controls of the Ta-183. Boy, was he in for a nasty surprise!

Jack noticed the little black button on top of the control column and wondered if the jet really was armed. He flipped the metal safety latch off and thumbed the trigger. But nothing happened.

"Dang-it all to hell!" he cursed. "I thought that Kraut mechanic said these guns were good to go?"

Then he realized he hadn't armed the four cannons yet. He toggled the arming switch on the instrument panel. And when he flicked the switch, the Revi 16B reflector gunsight began glowing with power and he felt something catch beneath the cockpit. Now the guns were ready! He lined the Me-262 up in the crosshairs of the glowing reticule, aiming for the jet's port engine, and thumbed the trigger again. And this time, the guns fired. A flaming volley of 30-millimeter cannon shells burst from the four gun ports, arching below the Me-262's engine—just missing. Jack had forgotten to "lead" the target, aiming a ahead of the jet to compensate for the distance. A rookie mistake. Well, Jack hadn't fired the guns of a fighter plane much less flown one in a long time. He was a rusty to put it plainly. Plus his right hand was hurting him. It was quite painful to grip the joystick and maneuver the jet around the sky.

Herr Kuppinger immediately saw this and put the jet into some evasive maneuvers. He realized that the man who had stormed onto the Walpersberg was now flying the Ta-183, and he was shooting at him! Kuppinger was an excellent pilot but he was no fighter pilot, and he knew it. He put the Me-262 through some masterful maneuvers, evading the much faster Ta-183. Neither plane was built for such aerobatics yet they zoomed around the sky like a lazy Sunday afternoon airshow, climbing, diving, stunting, stalling, looping, rolling, twisting and turning. It was quite the aerial display, a real aerobatic show, and only the gods of war and the angels could see it high above the overcast.

"Consarn-it!" Jack swore, trying to sight the Me-262 so he could shoot it down. "That fella is one crackerjack pilot, I tell ya what."

He certainly was. Herr Kuppinger was probably the most experienced man in Germany to ever fly the Me-262, more so than the best Luftwaffe pilot. But he was *not* a Luftwaffe pilot. He was, at best, a great test pilot. He'd never fired the guns of any fighter, propeller driven or jet-propelled. Even if the Me-262 had been armed, he wouldn't have known what to do. He was literally at the mercy of the devil. But Jack, on the other hand, knew exactly how to shoot down an enemy plane. He had done it twenty-seven times before.

He lost the Me-262 in the overcast a few times, loosing sight of it as both planes soared from 10,000 feet to 20,000 feet more than once. But after chasing it around for over half an hour, he finally got it properly sighted. He triggered a quick burst, hitting it in the left wing root, blasting the wing and engine completely off of it. The Me-262 quickly caught fire, and Herr Kuppinger bailed out, leaping into the cloudy void as the burning jet plummeted from 15,000 feet.

Jack watched it fall with his usual grim fascination as he had done so many times before fighting over the Pacific. He had just shot down his 28th enemy plane (an unofficial number in the annals of Air Corps confirmations) but 28 victories, nonetheless. He saw Herr Kuppinger drifting down in the parachute and wondered who he was, not knowing his name or anything else about him. He had flown admirably, handling the twin-engined jet like a seasoned veteran. Well, whoever he was, Jack thought, he was one heck of a pilot. One of the best he'd ever fought against. But before he could contemplate it further, bright yellow tracers suddenly flared past his cockpit canopy.

"Tarnation!" Somebody was shooting at him!

Jack jerked his chin over his right shoulder and saw no less than eight P-51 Mustangs bearing down on him, all six guns flaring on every one of them, forty-eight guns in all. Jack had been cruising at about 400 mph after shooting down the Me-262, so the Mustangs were able to catch up to him. He jammed the throttle forward and quickly accelerated to 500 mph, pulling away from the sleek American fighters. But not before catching a twenty round volley in the tailplane which fouled the elevator cables and shattered the right elevator. Jack was already having a time controlling the Ta-183, his hand hurting like hell, not just from his most recent injury, but from the one he'd suffered at the hands of the "Devil of Rabaul" Hiroyoshi Nishizawa. That wound had never healed properly, always causing him some serious discomfort, especially after prolonged use. It would get stiff and swollen, and cramp up, preventing him from fully closing his hand at times. And now as the once nimble Ta-183 jet flew like a heavy transport plane, pitching up and down, yawing uncontrollably, it was even harder to control. But it was still faster than the Mustangs.

After a few tense minutes, he was finally free of the Mustangs, easily outdistancing them, winging down below the clouds to 6,000 feet and escaping their fiery grasp. Jack was relieved. He didn't want to fight them; he didn't want shoot any of them down although it could've been done quite easily in the newfangled German jet. He was almost glad they had shot up his tailplane, preventing him from engaging them in aerial combat. Even so, the Ta-183 was badly damaged and probably unable to land safely, its elevators hardly functioning. Jack knew a landing would be a dicey undertaking if not downright fatal. He only had one option presently, bailing out not one of them. Now came the moment of his finest hour; now came the time for his final battle; now came the hour of his last hoorah. He was tired, wounded, war-weary, ready to fly down into perdition and claim his seat next to the devil.

Down below, he saw the Lech River, and knew he was near his final destination, Lechfeld Air Base. He followed it and came upon the air base. All along the tarmac and runway, Jack saw airplanes lined up in neat rows, most of them Me-262 jets by the looks of their slender two-engined silhouettes. Those jets were being armed and fitted with radios, he knew, and he decided right then and there he couldn't allow that. Those hated Messerschmitts had to be destroyed and not allowed to take flight—ever. They had to be taken out today, wiped out, obliterated, annihilated. And there was only one way to do it.

He eased the stick forward and forced the jet into a steep dive, his hand hurting like holy hell now, almost unable to grip the control column, the lamed jet fighting against his waning strength like a feral horse refusing to be tamed. Yet, the little *Huckebein* came down, down in a screaming power dive, down, easily surpassing 600 mph, down, reaching the speed of sound, down, breaking the sound barrier and going supersonic. As it zoomed low over the parked line of Me-262's, all four cannons erupted in a furious fusillade of gunfire, obliterating five jets in one fell swoop. Jack forced the Ta-183 upwards, crying out in pain as his hand finally gave out, pulling up into a half-loop, hanging in the sky barely a 1,000 feet above air base. Anti-aircraft was exploding all around him, trying to blow him out of the sky. But all the guns in Germany couldn't stop him now, and he plunged straight down in a spiraling death dive and crashed headlong into the remaining German jets. "Adios, my sweet Aussie Rose," were his final words.

A magnificent explosion wafted up into the sky. Flames and smoke billowed high into the atmosphere. Eleven Me-262's went up in flames as well as a whole squadron of long-nosed Focke-Wulfs. A fuel bowser blew up too, adding to the destruction, along with four Arado "Blitz" bombers, the world's first jet bomber. One hangar burned furiously out of control as several minor explosions went off all around it. German mechanics and pilots alike as well as crews of

Luftwaffe firefighters, scurried around in frantic mobs trying to put out the hellish flames, but to no avail. The whole airbase seemed to be on fire that day.

Everywhere one looked there was smoke and fire. Dead and burning bodies lay strewn out all over the tarmac. Even the airplanes parked in the protective revetments burned out of control. It was a fiery inferno, a literal hell on earth. And amidst that flaming chaos lay a burning hulk of a jet plane, a once mighty prototype of little known design, yet affectionately known as the *Huckebein*—the Focke-Wulf Ta-183—the worlds fastest fighter plane. And still seated in the remnants of its burning cockpit, the blackened body of a once famous American air ace—John J. Knight—Jack to his few friends, James Castillo to a very few, and Captain Nicklaus Daemon to the men of the O.S.S. And just like the Devil himself, he had been called by so many names that no one knew who he really was or where he'd come from. But he was home now. He was in the one place where he always knew he'd end up. The very place where his spirit must have first sprung up and claimed the life of another. The only place where his poor, wretched soul could ever abide; a place of pain and misery; the world of the dead; the abode of Satan and the forces of evil; where sinners suffered eternal punishment. Hell was the only place where Jack Knight could've gone.

EPILOGUE

ROSE MCKAVITT cradled the little newborn in her arms as she stood amidst a crowd of gawking onlookers. The 4th of July parade was in full swing at that hour. Long rows of marching bands and soldiers alike tramped by decked out in fancy dress uniforms and other formal military livery. People of all walks of life lined the streets watching the troops march by along with other units and various high school bands. Everyone was in a lively mood. The war in Europe was finally over. Germany had finally been defeated and had surrendered unconditionally to the Allied armies of Great Britain, America, and France. Only Japan fought on now, and she was close to defeat. Rose's baby, a blue-eyed, dark-haired boy of one month was a rosy-cheeked child with a calm temperament. He rarely cried. So little that she worried there might be something wrong with him. But her doctor assured her he was fine. He was a bouncing baby boy with a strong heart and a healthy appetite.

He'd been born at exactly 6:00 A.M. on June 6th—one year and to the hour after the magnificent D-Day invasion, an auspicious date that would go down in history as the greatest seaborne assault ever, and the turning point of the war in Europe. Rose's legs had scarcely healed when he came into the world, not uttering one sound, not even grunting when the doctor spanked his shiny little heine at the moment of his birth. At nine-and-a-half pounds, he was a strapping baby boy, bigger than any born in Alexander's Military Hospital. Her husband David McKavitt had been there to witness it, the ecstatic father and a recently liberated prisoner. He had not known she was pregnant until he was at last united with her that cold and dreary day in January.

And now as Colonel David M. McKavitt prepared to take the stage and give a speech about the 4th of July, about America, and the war itself, he realized how fortunate he was. He had come so close to dying so many times that he began to think himself immortal. Well, not completely. But perhaps very lucky. Luckier than so many others who did not return at war's end. The O.S.S. General Staff had supplied him with full details about the raid on REIMAHG, and all the men who had participated in it, Captain Nicklaus Daemon (a.k.a. Jack Knight), the focus of his interest. Colonel McKavitt learned the whole story about the daring young man from West Texas, about his escape from Japan, how he came to join the O.S.S., and yes, how General Truscott hid his sudden return from the Air Corps General staff and the newspapers. It was quite a story, indeed, one he could hardly believe himself, but one that would soon be known to everyone. The unbelievable story of John J. Knight would shortly be the subject of a biographical war book co-written by David McKavitt and a certain award-winning Australian reporter. A release date had been set, and the publisher had already secured 100,000 advanced book sales using a brilliant marketing scheme. It was a guaranteed million-seller, so said the publisher.

"Well, now, Colonel," said General Warlick, a long fat corona clenched between his teeth. "Here you are again in New York, ready to address your adoring fans."

"But it's not about me this time, General. I'm here to honor another man. A man I once knew. A man so heroic and so honorable that his story must be told, told to the millions of war-weary Americans who will appreciate it... and embrace it."

General Warlick scoffed. "Oh, god, what a load of horseshit, Colonel. You're just doing it to promote your book, that's all."

"Hmm, that's what *he* would have said, sir."

"You're goddamn right he would have! Jack was man after my own heart. Wish I could have met him just once. He was hard-fighting, hard-living son-of-a-bitch. The likes of which we'll never see again. That's why I recommended him for the Medal of Honor, a posthumous afterthought, but one he should've gotten long ago."

"I agree," McKavitt said with a nod. "Jack was a real hero. Not just a war hero, but one with a heart of gold and the guts to keep on fighting until the bloody end."

"That, he was." General Warlick nodded and puffed some smoke. "He single-handedly destroyed that German air base, wiping out a whole squadron of Me-262 jets along with a shit-ton of other high-tech aircraft. That's why I recommended the M.O.H. Not because of his 'heart of gold' or his past exploits."

"Of course, General—"

"He personally destroyed nearly a hundred aircraft that day," the General raved on. "More than the entire 479th did during its campaign against the German jets. Shit! More so than the entire 65th Fighter Wing destroyed during the entire war."

"So you actually believe he sacrificed himself? Crashing that jet into the ground, destroying all those Me-262's?"

"I do." General Warlick stabbed his smoldering corona into the air. "Colonel Tom Henderson saw it all, McKavitt. Witnessed the entire fiery, heroic end of Captain Jack Knight."

"He did?"

"He certainly did. It was his flight of P-51's that chased him after he shot down that Me-262. They watched him do it, not knowing what to think about it. Then they attacked him when they saw the German crosses on the wings of that jet. Knight escaped but not before taking some hits. Henderson and his flight followed him all the way to Lechfeld Air Base in the hopes of catching him in a landing pattern or when he landed. They thought he was a Kraut pilot, believe it or not?"

"Even after he shot down the Me-262?"

"That's what Henderson said." General Warlick grunted. "Later on when the details of the raid on REIMAHG were declassified by the O.S.S., we learned that it was indeed John J. Knight flying that fucking fancy-assed Nazi jet the... the..." He trailed off, exhaling irritably. "Damn it! I can't remember the name of that thing."

"You mean the Focke-Wulf Ta-183, General Warlick?" Rose interjected, overhearing the conversation.

"Yes! That's it!" General Warlick smiled suspiciously. "How in the hell do you know about that, Rose?"

"I'm a reporter, remember? It's my job to know such things."

"Aha." The General chuckled, puffing some smoke. "Guess I should've remembered that as well. A fine couple you two make. A reporter and an author."

Rose winked, then asked: "So whatever happened to General Truscott, General Warlick? What became of him, hmm?"

"Oh, not much, really," Warlick explained. "He was summarily relieved of his command by General MacArthur and then sent stateside to the War Department. He has since been ordered by President Truman to set up a special... *central intelligence agency, of sorts?* One that will work hand-in hand-with the military, mainly dealing with classified intelligence and wartime espionage."

Rose frowned. "That figures."

"He's a survivor—General Truscott," McKavitt commented. "I'll give him that much. I knew he'd wind up on top, somehow."

"You bet your sweet-ass he did," General Warlick returned. "That man has a knack for surviving. He'll go far in Washington—"

"AND NOW, LADIES AND GENTLEMEN... THE MOMENT YOU'VE ALL BEEN WAITING FOR," the announcer's voice suddenly boomed over the P.A. system. *"PLEASE WELCOME MEDAL OF HONOR WINNER AND U. S. ARMY AIR CORPS FIGHTER ACE... COLONEL DAVID M. MCKAVITT!"*

"Well, that's my cue, General," said McKavitt. "Time to address these fine folks. Time to take the stage and tell Jack's story."

"Yes, it's time, son." General Warlick nodded, the corona firmly clenched between gleaming teeth. He clapped McKavitt on the shoulders, then joined the assembled crowd in their elated applause.

McKavitt turned to his lovely wife Rose, and kissed her passionately, then dashed up onto the stage and seized the microphone. The gathered throng of some five thousand-plus people clapped enthusiastically, cheering, calling his name. He waved a salute to the crowd, then stood there a moment beaming proudly, soaking up the raucous adulation.

General Warlick turned to Rose and gazed at her handsome little baby. "That's a fine boy you have there, Rose. A fine boy, indeed."

"Oh, thank you, General Warlick," Rose replied, smiling once again. "David and I are quite fond of him. He's the apple of his mother's eye."

"What did you name him? Seems I can't remember that either."

"John—John James Mack McKavitt—to be exact."

"Ah, yes, I remember now. That's a good name for him."

"It certainly is. But I just call him... Jack."

HANS MULTHOPP stood up and made his way down the center aisle of the Fw-200 Condor, feeling excited and tired at the same time. The flight from Zurich had been long and taxing, taking five days to reach its final destination, stopping in Vichy, Madrid, and Casablanca along the way before crossing over the mighty Atlantic Ocean. Secret refueling stops in the Canary Islands and Cape Verde gave him some brief moments to get out of the confining cabin and stretch his legs. Then he took off again and headed for South America, landing many hours later in Rio de Janeiro. From there he flew south further still, finally reaching his ultimate destination a few hours later. The Condor touched down in the balmy atmosphere.

And now, as Herr Multhopp exited the big four-engine plane and stepped down onto the dusty tarmac, briefcase in hand, sweat accumulating on his brow, he gave a great sigh of relief. He was home at last. Well, his new home, that is. As he traversed the tarmac to the small airport terminal, a familiar face greeted him. A face belonging to one of the most influential men in the world of German aviation. And standing beside him, one the most powerful men in South America.

"Ach-ja!" said the man in the straw fedora and gray linen suit, proffering a very tanned hand. "Hans! So good to see you again."

Multhopp shook the hand offered. "Kurt, it's good to see you."

"I hope your flight wasn't too exhausting?"

"As much as to be expected, I suppose."

All three men laughed jovially.

The man in the straw fedora was Kurt Tank, onetime chief aeronautical engineer of the Focke-Wulf aviation company. He turned to the man standing beside him, grinning largely.

"This is General Perón, Hans. Leader of this great country

"Welcome to Buenos Aires, Herr Multhopp," said the man in the military uniform. He clicked his heels and nodded succinctly, his German parlance as natural as ever. "I am General Juan Domingo Perón, your humble servant and President of Argentina."

General Perón and Herr Multhopp shook hands.

"Nice to meet you, General Perón. I'm very delighted to make your acquaintance, sir. And I'm glad to be here, finally."

"Si, señor I am so glad you could come," replied General Perón, reverting to his native tongue of Spanish. And from that moment on, all three men spoke in that fine old romance language of old Spain.

General Peron directed Herr Multhopp and Kurt Tank to a long black limousine, a very shiny Mercedes-Benz complete with gaily colored pennants and ornate coat of arms stenciled on the front doors. Two armed guards opened the car doors for the three men, and they got in. Soon, the limousine was driving away from the airport and heading to General Perón's presidential palace in downtown Buenos Aires.

"I'm eager to see your new designs, *Señor* Multhopp," said General Perón. "If it is everything *Señor* Tank says it is, then my air force will have the most modern fighter in the world."

"It's all that, and more, General," Tank interjected. "You'll not be disappointed, I assure you. My associate, here, has come up with a world beating design that no one will be able to match. No one!"

"¡Excelente! ¡Excelente!"

"Yes, General Perón," Herr Multhopp added. "I'll be the fastest and most heavily gunned jet fighter the world has ever seen. Your air force will be second to none with it, best in the world, I think."

"¡Maravilloso! ¡Fantástico!"

Many minutes later, the limousine reached the palace and General Perón and the two Germans were escorted to the grand dining room by a gaudily accoutered honor guard. A sumptuous luncheon had been prepared for them which included some delectable German dishes as well as some fine Spanish delicacies. As they entered the grand dining room a trio of finely uniformed Germans greeted Herr Multhopp, SS-men, to be more precise. The leader of the trio stepped forward and rendered the all too familiar stiff-armed salute.

"Heil Hitler!" bellowed the man in the Gruppenführer's uniform.

"Ach Gott." Herr Multhopp cringed. *"Nazis?"*

Other Novels by Deke D. Wagner

THE EAGLE AND THE ALBATROS
COUNTS AND COMMONERS
ONLY THE EAGLE DARES
THE DEVIL'S LIGHTNING
BLOOD OF THE EAGLE
MISSION TO MARETH
AGRI DECUMATES
SATURNINUS
AVE AURIGA!

HISTORICAL NOTE

THE DEVIL'S HONOR is a work of fiction tempered with a good measure of truth, and any errors, historical or intended, are entirely mine. This story is pure fiction, inspired by events in the distant past and by the many military/history books I have read over the years. The characters and many of the events are imaginary, but some are true and actually did exist. It is a historical fact that the Nazis had jet-powered aircraft and rocket fighters as well as 'guided' flying bombs (V-1) and 'intercontinental ballistic missiles' (V-2) towards the end of the war. The Focke-Wulf Ta-183 prototype jet fighter, however, was developed only to the extent of wind tunnel models when the war finally ended. The basic Ta-183 design was further developed in Argentina as the IAe-33 Pulqui II. The nickname "Huckebein" is a literary reference to a trouble-making raven called (*Hans Huckebein der Unglücksrabe*) an illustrated story from 1867 by Wilhelm Busch.

One of the more remarkable advancements made by the German military in World War II was the production of turbine-jet aircraft. The most famous of these was the Messerschmitt Me-262, developed in 1938 and deployed in mid-1944. A special production facility was started in 1944 for quicker assembly line manufacture. But due to the setup at the main Messerschmitt factories, fast assembly line production was not possible, and these manufacturing sites were highly vulnerable to Allied bombing attacks. So accordingly, a company called *Flugzeugwerke Reichsmarschall Hermann Göring* (REIMAHG for short) was formed—a subsidiary of the Gustloff Nazi industrial complex.

REIMAHG eventually became concerned only with the Me-262 *Schwalbe* (Swallow), and the main production facility was located in an old sand mine for porcelain production in the Walpersberg Hill near Kahla (south of Jena), code-named "Lachs" (Salmon). Laborers from the Buchenwald concentration camp and other locations were put to work excavating the tunnels under harsh conditions. These laborers included some 350 American soldiers who had been captured during the Battle of the Bulge and were sent to the P.O.W. camp Stalag IX-B. In February 1945 a group of American P.O.W.s identified as Jews, or considered troublemakers, or chosen because their names or faces seemed Jewish to the Nazis, or simply chosen at random, were forces to work at the Walpersberg site.

—Deke D. Wagner

APPENDIX

SPECIFICATIONS AND DATA
OF U.S. AND GERMAN AIRCRAFT
(1939-1945)

North American P-51D "Mustang"

Engines:	1,590 hp Packard V-1650 V-12 liquid-cooled
Wingspan:	37 ft.
Length:	32 ft. 2 in.
Weight:	7,125 lb. (empty)
Max Speed:	440 mph at 25,400 ft.
Max Ceiling:	41,900 ft.
Armament:	6 × .50-cal. machine guns
Range:	950 miles without external tanks
	2,080 with external drop tanks

The North American P-51 Mustang was arguably the best American fighter aircraft of World War II. As with many new machines, this did not appear likely at first. The British government approached North American in early 1940 and asked them to produce the P-40 under license for the RAF. But North American convinced the British it could produce a much better fighter than the P-40, which was no better than average. And 117 days later, the newly developed NA-73 took off powered by an Allison V-1710 engine. Named the "Mustang" by the RAF, it was significantly faster than the P-40, but the RAF was not satisfied. Nevertheless, the USSAC ordered it and the rest is history. Dubbed the P-51, and eventually installed with a Rolls-Royce Merlin engine built under license by Packard, and armed with six .50-caliber machine guns, it is quite impossible to exaggerate the P-51 Mustang's importance in the European Theater of Operations.

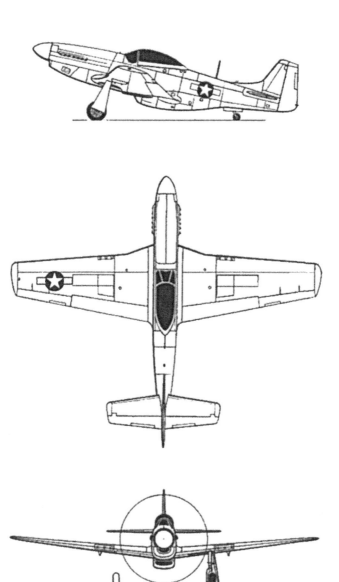

Republic P-47D "Thunderbolt"

Engines:	2,300 hp Pratt & Whitney 18-cylinder two-row radial
Wingspan:	40 ft. 9 in.
Length:	36 ft. 1 in.
Weight:	10, 700 lb. (empty)
Max Speed:	428 mph.
Max Ceiling:	43,000 ft.
Armament:	8 × .50-cal. machine guns
Range:	1,000 miles without external tanks
	1,900 with external drop tanks

The Republic P-47 Thunderbolt was the biggest and heaviest single-engine fighter plane of its day. American pilots nicknamed it the "Jug," short for "Juggernaut," a very appropriate name. From March 1943 to August 1945, Thunderbolts flew some 550,000 missions and destroyed about 7,000 enemy aircraft, 9,000 locomotives, and more than 86,000 trucks, and around 6,000 armored vehicles. In contrast, less than 1% were lost were lost during these missions! In its role as an escort fighter the P-47 was not as effective as the P-51 Mustang, so it was eventually relegated to fighter-bomber duties, and it was outstanding in this role. It was well-armed and a very robust fighter that could absorb lots of damage, which made it perfect for ground attack missions. Its Pratt & Whitney engine could withstand even the most severe hits.

APPENDIX

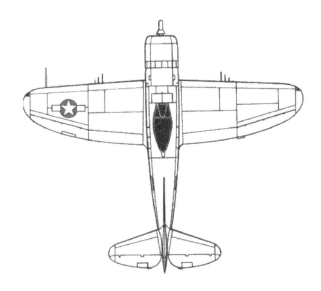

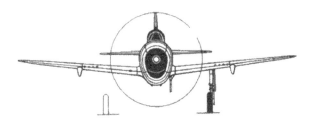

APPENDIX

Consolidated B-24J "Liberator"

Engines: 4 x 1,200 hp Pratt & Whitney Twin Wasp 14-cylinder two-row turbocharged radial engines

Wingspan: 110 ft.

Length: 67 ft. 2 in.

Weight: 36, 500 lb. (empty)

Max Speed: 290 mph.

Max Ceiling: 28,000 ft.

Armament: 10 × .50-cal. machine guns (in nose, upper, ventral "ball" and tail turrets, and beam positions.) Maximum bomb load of 12, 800 lb.

Range: 2,100 miles

The B-24 Liberator has always been overshadowed by the more famous B-17 Flying Fortress, although significantly more B-24's were actually produced (a total of 19,203 aircraft). The first production models were delivered to the RAF and used as long-range Atlantic patrols, where they attacked submarines and protected convoys. The B-17 had a reputation for sustaining more damage than the B-24, but according to 8th Air Force records, fewer were lost in combat over Germany. The standard model from 1944 onward, and the one manufactured in the greatest numbers was the B-24J, which had a maximum payload of 12, 800 lb. B-24's known as "Carpetbaggers" were used by the O.S.S.

APPENDIX

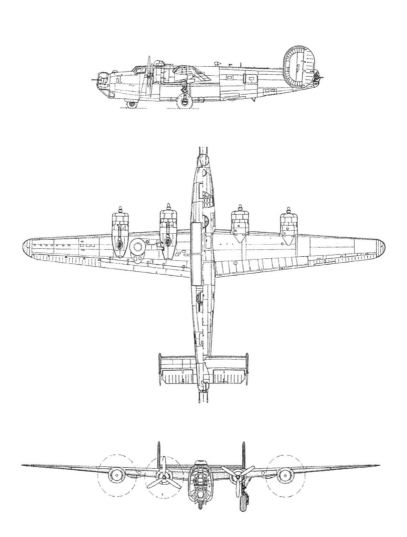

Boeing B-17G "Flying Fortress"

Engines:	4 x 1,200 hp Wright-Cyclone 9-cylinder turbocharged radial engines
Wingspan:	103 ft.
Length:	74 ft. 11 in.
Weight:	35, 800 lb. (empty)
Max Speed:	317 mph.
Max Ceiling:	28,000 ft.
Armament:	13 × .50-cal. machine guns (in nose, upper, ventral "ball" and tail turrets, and beam positions.) Maximum bomb load of 17, 600 lb.
Range:	2,000 miles

The B-17 Flying Fortress is one of the best-known American combat aircraft of WW II, second only to the P-51 Mustang. Along with the B-24, it carried out the majority of bombing attacks on occupied Europe with the 8th Air Force. The prototype made its first flight in 1935 and it was the first turbo-charged bomber in the world. From autumn 1943 onward, the G version was the most dominant model in the series, and 8,680 were produced. Initially, they suffered heavy losses at the hands of the Luftwaffe when deployed without fighter escort, but once long-ranged fighters like the P-51 began escorting them, losses went down exponentially. The B-17 could sustain heavy battle damage and keep flying, and for this reason, it was very popular with American bomber crews.

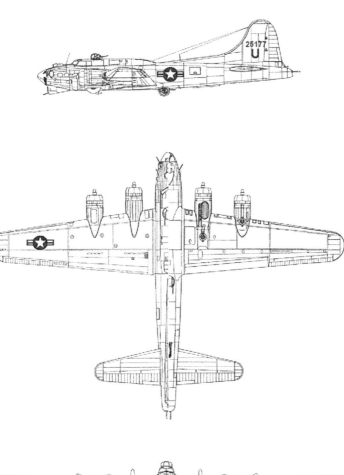

Douglas C-47A "Skytrain"

Engines:	2 x 1,200 hp Pratt & Whitney Twin Wasp 14-cylinder two-row turbocharged radial engines
Wingspan:	95 ft.
Length:	64 ft. 2 in.
Weight:	16, 970 lb. (empty)
Max Speed:	229 mph.
Max Ceiling:	23,200 ft.
Armament:	None (Transport aircraft)
Range:	1,500 miles

The Douglas C-47 Skytrain was a military version of the DC-3. The DC-3 made its maiden flight in 1935, and was a very innovative aircraft for its time, and it is still in service, to some extent, to this day. It was the Allies most prominent transport plane of WWII. It was used as a transport, a tug, an air ambulance, and a passenger aircraft, and was most notably used to transport paratroopers. It could carry 28-35 troopers. The RAF called it the "Dakota," and it was built under license by the Soviets, who used it extensively during the war as the Lisunov Li-2. Nakajima also built a few variants for Japan! The C-47 remained in service long after the war and was used extensively, for instance, during the 1948 Berlin Airlift.

APPENDIX

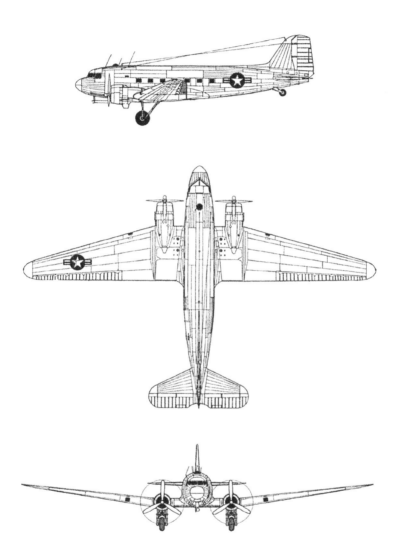

Messerschmitt Bf-109G "Gustav"

Engine:	1,475 hp Daimler-Benz DB 605E, inverted V-12
Wingspan:	32 ft. 6 in.
Length:	29 ft. 7 in.
Weight:	5,952 lb empty
Max Speed:	385 mph
Max Ceiling:	37, 895 ft
Armament:	1 × 20 mm cannon in propeller hub, or
	1 × 30 mm cannon in propeller hub
	2 × 13 mm machine guns in top decking
Range:	373 miles (621 miles with 300 liter drop tank)

The Messerschmitt Bf-109 was manufactured in greater numbers than any other military aircraft during WWII (approx. 35,000) and was the standard fighter for the Luftwaffe throughout the war. The first prototype made its maiden flight on May 28, 1935, powered by a Rolls-Royce engine. The first production model, the Bf-109 B-1, delivered in early 1937, fought in the Spanish Civil War with the "Condor Legion," and was easily the best fighter plane in that war. The version that was manufactured in the greatest numbers was the Model G, which was put into service in the late-summer of 1942. The Bf-109 was deployed variously as an interceptor, an escort, a fighter-bomber, and a reconnaissance aircraft. Many of the top Luftwaffe aces flew the Bf-109, most notably, Erich Hartmann, who scored 352 kills!

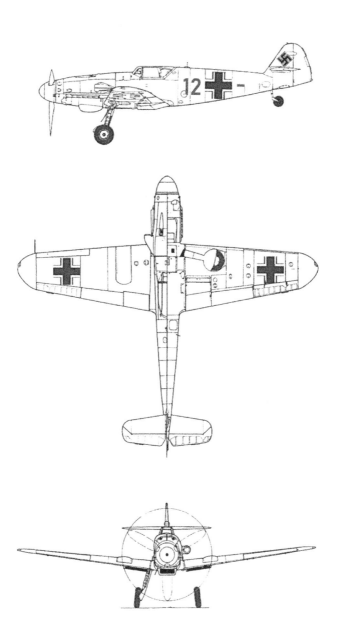

Focke Wulf Fw-190A-8

Engine:	1,700 hp BMW 801 18-cylinder two-row radial
Wingspan:	34 ft. 5 in.
Length:	29 ft.
Weight:	7,055 lb empty
Max Speed:	408 mph
Max Ceiling:	37, 400 ft
Armament:	2 × 20 mm cannon in wing roots
	2 × 20 mm cannon in outer wings
	2 × 13 mm machine guns in top decking
Range:	560 miles

During World War II, this trim little fighter was the best and most versatile piston-engine German fighter. It was deployed as a fighter, fighter-bomber, ground attack aircraft, a reconnaissance aircraft, a torpedo bomber, and for flight instruction. The prototype first flew on July 1, 1939, but there were problems with the BMW 801 radial engine. This delayed the Fw-190's development, and it was not deployed until the summer of 1941. However, as soon as it was deployed, British pilots soon found it to be faster and more maneuverable than their Spitfire V. It had superior firepower but was less maneuverable than its counterpart, the Bf-109, and could not climb as fast or as high. The Fw-190A-8 was introduced in late 1943, and had 25 gallon more internal fuel, and there were many sub-types of this model.

APPENDIX

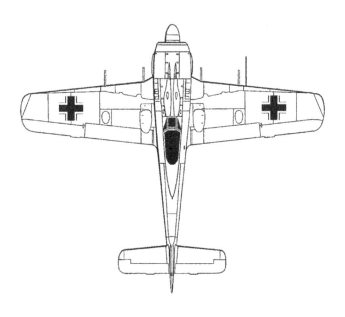

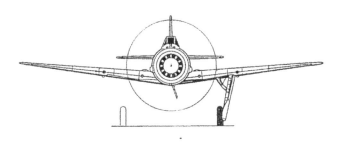

Messerschmitt Me-262A "Schwalbe"

Engine: 2 x 1,980 lb thrust Junkers Jumo axial turbojets
Wingspan: 40 ft. 11 in.
Length: 34 ft. 9.5 in.
Weight: 8,820 lb empty
Max Speed: 540 mph
Max Ceiling: 37, 565 ft
Armament: 4 × 30 mm MK 108 cannon in nose
Range: 650 miles

The Me-262 (Swallow) was the world's first jet-powered combat aircraft to be put into mass production. Its development began in 1938 when Messer-schmitt was contracted by the German Air Ministry to develop jet-powered fighter aircraft. But to due the slow development of the BMW jet engine, it did not make its maiden flight until July 18, 1942, and it was not put into service until July 1944. Some 1,433 Me-262's were produced during the war, but there were never more than 250 in service at any given time. Many were lost in accidents, and many more simply could not be flown due to lack of fuel or trained pilots. Although they could attain exceptionally high speeds, many were shot down; they were especially vulnerable when landing. Thus, Bf-109 and Fw-190 squadrons were often assigned protective CAP to defend Me-262 airbases.

APPENDIX

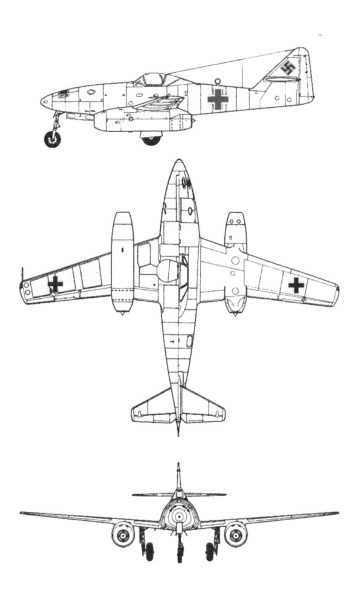

APPENDIX

Focke Wulf Ta-183A "Huckebein"

Engine:	1 × Heinkel HeS-011 turbojet (2,700 lbf)
Wingspan:	32 ft 9.75 in.
Length:	30 ft 10.25 in.
Weight:	6,240 lb (empty)
Max Speed:	593 mph (projected)
Max Ceiling:	45,935 ft.
Armament:	4 × 30 mm MK 108 cannon in nose
	4 × Ruhrstahl X-4 wire-guided AAM's
Range:	650-700 miles (approx.)

The Focke Wulf Ta-183 "Huckebein" was a jet-powered fighter plane intended to be the successor to the Messerschmitt Me-262, and other fighters in Luftwaffe service during World War II. It was developed only to the extent of wind tunnel models when the war finally ended. Development of the Ta-183 started as early as 1942. Hans Multhopp assembled a team to design a new fighter, based on his understanding that previous Focke Wulf design studies for jet fighters had no chance of reaching fruition because none had the potential for transonic speeds. The first production models would be powered by the Heinkel HeS-011 turbojet. The Ta-183A had a short fuselage with a bifurcated air intake passing under the cockpit and proceeding to the rear where the single turbojet engine was located. The pilot sat in a pressurized cockpit; a bubble canopy provided excellent vision. The primary armament of the aircraft comprised of four 30 mm MK 108 cannons arranged around the air intake; it was also designed to carry four Ruhrstahl X-4 wire-guided air-to-air missiles.

APPENDIX

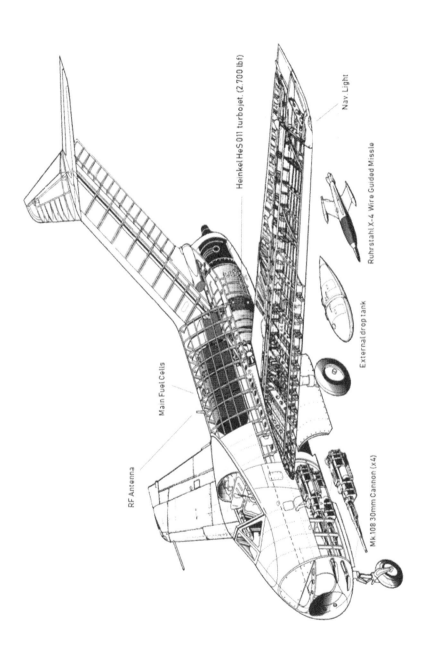

Heinkel HeS 011 turbojet. (2,700 lbf)

Nav Light

Ruhrstahl X-4 Wire Guided Missile

External drop tank

Main Fuel Cells

RF Antenna

Mk.108 30mm Cannon (x4)

GLOSSARY

AA, Ack-Ack, Flak: enemy anti-aircraft fire.

ace: Any pilot who shot down 5 enemy aircraft in flight.

Ach! (German) an informal interjection or mild expletive.

Achtung! Attention!

altimeter: An instrument graduated and calibrated to indicate the   height above sea level.

Ami: (Ah-mee) slang for an American.

ammo: Ammunition.

angels: An aircraft's reported altitude in thousands of feet. For   example: "Angels 6" is 6,000 feet. "Angels 1-5" is 15,000 feet.

Auf Wiedersehen: Goodbye.

babies: Code word for disposable droptanks used to increase range.

bandit: An enemy aircraft.

BAR: Brown Automatic Rifle; a light .30-caliber machine gun.

Bf-109: the Messerschmitt fighter plane.

BG: Bomb Group

Bingo: low fuel state.

bird: Any aircraft in general. Also "ship" or "crate" or "kite."

Bitte shön: you're welcome.

Bitte: please.

blackout: When pulling too many G's, blood leaves the brain, sight is lost and the pilot becomes unconscious.

Blitzkrieg: (lightning war) The highly mobile form of warfare developed by Germany between 1939 and 1941.

bogey: First sighting of an unidentified aircraft in flight.

box: The "bomber box." A tightnlayered, formation that allowed overlapping defensive machine gun coverage.

brass hats: Slang for High Command.

buster: To fly at maximum cruising speed.

buzz: To fly low over the ground; showing off by buzzing the tower or base headquarters.

CAP: Combat Air Patrol

chandelle : Reversal of course by a sharp climbing turn.

check six: Look behind to make sure the "6 o'clock" position is clear.

claim: Petition for credit for a victory over an enemy aircraft.

GLOSSARY

Condor Legion: a volunteer air group of Luftwaffe personnel fighting for General Franco during the Spanish Civil War (1936-39).

Dakota: British name for the Douglas C-47 Skytrain.

damaged: As claimed in air combat; an enemy aircraft claimed as partially destroyed but subject to repair.

Danke: thank you.

dead-stick: A dead stick landing is when the engine has lost power and the aircraft is gliding.

deck: the ground, the cloud level, or the deck of an aircraft carrier.

deflection Shot: the angle of a shot in gunnery measured between the line of sight to the target and the line of sight to the aiming point.

ditch: to force land an airplane in the water.

dogfight: Close combat between two or more aircraft.

Dulag Luft: Interrogation and processing camp for Allied airman recently captured in German-occupied Europe.

Dummkopf! Blockhead!

E-Boat: *(Schnellboot)* A fast German torpedo boat.

Eagle Squadrons: Three fighter squadrons composed of American volunteer pilots during the Battle of Britain.

element: basic combat unit of two fighter aircraft; leader & wingman.

external store: fuel tank, bomb, or rocket attached to a plane's wings.

feather: To place a propeller in an edge-on position to the direction of flight to cut down on the wind resistance (with engine stopped.)

FG: Fighter Group; code named "Foxtrot George" in this novel.

finger-Four: a four-plane fighter formation resembling four fingers.

Flak: another term for anti-aircraft; to give someone hell; to badger or harass. German acronym for *Flieger-abwehr-Kanone.*

flamer: an airplane shot down in flames.

flight: Four plane formation comprsing of two elements.

Fort: Nickname for Boeing B-17 bomber; Flying Fortress.

FS: Fighter Squadron.

Fw-190: the Focke Wulf fighter plane.

Geschwader: a Luftwaffe combat wing. The largest mobile (usually 108 aircraft) homogeneous flying unit.

GLOSSARY

Grease gun: Nickname for the U.S. Army .45-caliber M3 machine pistol.

ground loop: Loss of lateral control of an aircraft on the ground resulting in the aircraft making a sudden turn or change of direction.

hanger queen: An aircraft that spent more time being repaired than flying operational sorties.

Hauptmann: German Army Captain

Hauptsturmführer: SS-Captain

hedge-hopping: Sometimes called "contour chasing." Very low-flying over the ground, rising up over trees, houses, hills, etc.

Hellcat: the F6F U.S. Navy carrier fighter plane.

Herr: Mister or Sir.

hit the silk: Bail out of an aircraft with a parachute, even though most parachutes were made out of nylon after 1942.

Immelmann: combat maneuver; essentially a half-loop and roll. Named after famed WWI German ace Max Immelmann.

IP: Initial point; the point where the bomb run begins.

Ja: (yah) yes.

jarhead: slang for a U.S. Marine.

Jawohl: yes, indeed.

Jedburgh Team: O.S.S. special ops team; usually 3 or 4 men.

Jink / Jinking: To jerk an aircraft about in evasive action.

Joes: A slang term for airmen or soldiers; derived from "G.I. Joe."

KIA: Killed in action.

kill: A victory in aerial combat; destroying an enemy aircraft in flight. Does not necessarily refer to the death of the enemy pilot.

kite: slang for an airplane.

Komet: the Me-163 rocket fighter.

Kübelwagen: German all-purpose vehicle similar to a jeep.

Lazarett: a German field hospital.

lead: (rhymes with heed) the action of aiming ahead of a target.

Little Friends: bomber crew slang for friendly fighters.

Luger: Model 08 semi-automactic 9 mm pistol.

Mae West: Life jacket. Named after the buxom Hollywood actress.

Mayday: International radio signal of distress.

GLOSSARY

MG-42: German 7.92 mm machine gun with extremely high rate of fire.

MIA: Missing in action.

milk Run: A mission that experienced no action; a routine flight.

MP-40: German 9-mm machine pistol; sometimes called "Schmeisser."

MP: Military Police

NCO: acronym for non-commissioned officer.

Nip: derogatory term for a Japanese soldier or airman.

Nippon: Another name for Japan.

Nishizawa: Japanese ace "The Devil of Rabaul"; scored 86 kills.

nose over: When an airplane moving on the ground tips over onto its nose, damaging its propeller and possibly other parts of the engine.

O.S.S.: Office of Strategic Services; became the CIA after the war.

O'clock: The position of another aircraft sighted in the air was called out by its clock position from the observers point of view; 12 o'clock high being straight ahead and above; 6 o'clock directly behind.

Opel-Blitz: standard German utility truck.

Operation Bodenplatte (Baseplate) Major Luftwaffe aerial operation launched January 1, 1945; massive fighter attack on U.S. airfields.

OVERLORD: Allied code name for the D-Day invasion.

overshoot: In air combat, to fly over or past the enemy aircraft when following through with an attack.

P.O.W.: prisoner of war

pancake: When an aircraft made a landing by dropping hard from a low altitude, usually with the wheels up on land or water.

Panzer: German word for armored tank.

perch: position of tactical advantage prior to initiating an attack on an enemy plane; typically high and above.

POW: Prisoner of war .

probable: An instant in which a hostile aircraft is probably destroyed; it isn't known whether it actually crashed, but is considered badly damaged enough to make its crash very likely.

PTO: Pacific Theater of Operations.

Quatsch! Nonsense; baloney; bullshit; etc.

R & R: Rest and relaxation; leave or furlough.

GLOSSARY

R/T: Radio telephone or radio transmitter.

red line: A mark on the air-speed indicator showing safe maximum speed of an aircraft; or to fly very fast "red-lining" the engine.

reef back: to pull back on the yoke or control stick when flying.

Reich: (empire) Hitler's Germany was the Third Reich.

REIMAHG: Nazi aviation company founded by Hermann Goering. (*Flugzeugwerke Reichsmarschall Hermann Göring*)

Rhubarb: A wild dogfight. Taken from the old baseball term for a bench-clearing brawl or free-for-all.

RLM: (*Reichsluftfahrtministerium)*Reichs Air Minitry; Goering's head-quarters; it controlled all aspects of German aviation.

Roger: Radio jargon meaning: understood, message received.

Rottenfürhrer: SS-Corporal.

RTB: Return to base; head for home.

S-2: Squadron Intelligence Officer.

S.P.: Navy Shore Patrol; similar to Army M.P. (Military Police).

Saipan: The largest island in the Northern Marianas; U.S. forces captured the island from the Japanese in July 1944.

salvo: Release all bombs, drop tanks or fire all rockets at once.

Schwarm: a German four-plane fighter formation; finger-four.

Schwarmführer: flight leader.

Schwein! German derogatory term meaning: swine, pig or hog.

StG-44: 7.92 mm automatic assault rifle.

side-slip: quick maneuver used to lose altitude without gaining speed.

skipper: Slang for C.O. (Commanding Officer).

Skytrain: Douglas C-47 Cargo/Transport Aircraft

slip-turn: flat turn performed solely with the rudder, using no ailerons.

sortie: a mission flown by one aircraft.

spin: A plane's vertical descent while spiraling; out of control fall.

splash: Typically, shooting down a hostile aircraft over water.

split-s: an escape maneuver; a half-roll followed by a dive; results in a reversal of direction and the loss of much altitude.

SS: (Schutzstaffel) Special police force in Nazi Germany founded as a personal bodyguard for Hitler. The SS ran the concentration camps.

GLOSSARY

Stalag Luft: a Luftwaffe P.O.W. camp during WWII.

stick: Airborne jargon for a unit of paratroopers

Sturmbannführer: SS-Major

Tail-end-Charlie: The last airplane in a formation; typically a rookie's slot. His job was to warn other pilots of incoming rear attacks.

taxi: To "drive" airplane from point to point on the ground.

throttle-jockey: slang for a pilot.

Totenkopf: Death's head; symbol of the SS

tracer: A bullet containing a pyrotechnic mixture to make the flight of the projectile visible.

turbojet: A jet engine in which a fan driven by a turbine provides extra air to the burner, and thus, gives extra thrust.

Uncle: code name for Group Commander.

undershoot: to land short of the runway.

USAAC: United States Army Air Corps.

V-1: small jet-propelled winged missile that carried a warhead.

V-2: German guided missile (rocket) with a 2-ton warhead.

vic: a "V" formation of three airplanes.

WAC: A member of the Women's Auxiliary Corps.

Walther: semi-automatic 9-mm pistol Model P38.

washed-out: Failure to make the grade in a flying school.

Wilco: Radio telephone jargon, means: "Will comply."

wingover: an aerial roll-out followed by a high speed dive.

Yomi: the Japanese version of Hell and the underworld.

Zero: name for the Mitsubishi A6M2 Japanese fighter.

ABOUT THE AUTHOR

 **DEKE D. WAGNER** was born in Mississippi and raised in the Georgia. The son of an American Air Force sergeant and a German mother from Hesse-Darmstadt, Deke grew up having a keen interest in aviation and his German heritage. At the tender age of ten-years-old he read Baron von Richthofen's autobiography, *Der Rote Kampfflieger* (The Red Air Fighter), and has ever since been enthralled with tales of air aces and air combat. After high school and a stint in the U.S. Army and Reserves, Deke attended art school but made little progress. He spent the next two decades pursuing a semi-professional musical career as a singer/songwriter before attempting his first novel "The Eagle and the Albatros." Deke also enjoys singing, playing guitar, and recording music. He currently resides in Augusta, Georgia.

Made in the USA
Coppell, TX
27 April 2022

77134074R00204